REA

DO NOT REMOVE
CARDS FROM POCKET

TRIBAL SECRETS

BOOKS BY EUGENE IZZI

EUGENE IZZI

TRIBAL SECRETS

BANTAM BOOKS
NEW YORK TORONTO LONDON SYDNEY AUCKLAND

This is a work of fiction. Names, characters, places, and incidents are either the product of the author's imagination or are used fictitiously. Any resemblance to actual persons, living or dead, events, or locales is entirely coincidental.

TRIBAL SECRETS
A Bantam Book/October 1992

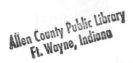
Library of Congress Cataloging-in-Publication Data

Izzi, Eugene.
Tribal secrets / Eugene Izzi.
p.   cm.
ISBN 0-553-07361-3
I. Title.
PS3559.Z9T75   1992
813'.54—dc20   92-3000
CIP

Published simultaneously in the United States and Canada

Bantam Books are published by Bantam Books, a division of Bantam Doubleday Dell Publishing Group, Inc. Its trademark, consisting of the words "Bantam Books" and the portrayal of a rooster, is Registered in U.S. Patent and Trademark Office and in other countries. Marca Registrada. Bantam Books, 666 Fifth Avenue, New York, New York 10103.

PRINTED IN THE UNITED STATES OF AMERICA

BVG   0   9   8   7   6   5   4   3   2   1

THIS BOOK IS DEDICATED TO
MICHAEL MCNAMARA, WHO SHARES SOME OF
MY OWN TRIBAL SECRETS.

TRIBAL
SECRETS

E dna Rose hadn't slept all night. It was Monday now, early morning, but she wasn't tired, even though she'd only had about three hours sleep each night during the past week. She'd been too keyed up to be able to rest. Her honey, her life, her entire reason for living would be starring in his own TV show, *Street Babe*, on Sunday night, and all she could think about was watching it, how he'd look, what he'd say. Would he send her any signals during the program? Any inside joke that only the two of them would know about? She'd bet that he would.

Edna had never met him in person—yet she truly believed she'd felt his touch, his hands on and in her body—even though she'd been writing to him for a couple of years. She would send the letters to the PO Box number that she'd gotten by calling a reporter who'd once written about him and she'd wait for weeks afterward, awaiting the response that never came. Before Babe, when she'd write to a soap opera star who never returned her passionate love letters, she would become enraged, would sometimes even stop watching the show the actor was on. She would write him another letter, threatening his life, the lives of his wife and children, too, and take a bus all the way into Chicago to mail it so the FBI People couldn't trace it back to her. But she'd write to Babe and he'd never write back, and she never got mad at him, ever.

It was all right with her.

She'd cry sometimes, thinking that he was stuck in that loveless marriage and was such a man of honor that he wouldn't tempt himself by meeting her until he somehow managed to get out of it.

That day, she knew, would come, and then her sadness and loneliness would end. Until then, she had her memories, her half-remembered nights of lovemaking with him which nobody could convince her hadn't truly occurred.

Edna knew he loved her, believed that even years ago, when she'd first spotted him in a local car dealer's pickup truck commercial, the man whose name she didn't know standing there with his shirt opened to the waist, leaning against the truck bed and extolling its virtues. She'd been stricken dumb by his looks, by the strength he propelled into her living room. In the commercial he was wearing blue jeans and the open shirt was the type that lumberjacks wore. His hair had been long and he'd had a handkerchief on his head that he'd used for a headband, another one, a red one, hanging from his back pocket. He'd been wearing cowboy boots.

The image was on the screen but the words came right into her heart, her mind. He'd say: "I love this truck," pat its side and step up into the seat, start it and put it in gear then look soulfully into the camera. "And I'll betcha you're gonna love it, too." He'd winked at her and had driven off and Edna had known what he'd meant.

It was a signal, a secret sign between them: *You're gonna love it, too!* Her man knew things about her, and she'd bet that nobody else in the entire world knew what he meant by that, since her father was no longer living.

The first thing she'd done back then was to run to her cabinet, unlock it, and take out the photo albums, sit down in her recliner and lower the lights and look at the pictures inside.

They were of Edna's only son, who'd died about a week before that first commercial had aired. She'd been numbed by that death, though she'd been prepared for it. The muscular dystrophy had taken its toll, her little baby had wasted away down to nothing. From a normal, happy baby to a toddler who walked on his tiptoes to a teenager who'd been unable to move, confined to his bed for the last months of his life, his mind healthy, his body consumed by his disease. When he'd still been able to move around, the Jerry Lewis People had come every day and taken him to school and it hadn't cost Edna anything. She'd ask them if there was a cure for this thing her baby had and when they told her that they were working on it she'd asked them why her baby had to go to school if it was a sure thing that he was going to die.

"We're *all* going to die." The woman who picked him up and drove him home in the special van was a smartass, and it was an answer Edna had half expected. "Why did *you* go to school, Mrs. Rose, when you're someday going to die?" She'd been slender and pretty and had long red hair that Edna wanted to pull out by its roots, but she hadn't. The Jerry Lewis People picked up all the medical bills and took her baby away for six hours every day and she didn't want that to ever come to an end, it was the only time she could pretty much be alone, with her secret thoughts and desires. She could push Mama's wheelchair into her bedroom and lock her door and the old woman wouldn't dare open her mouth, that's how scared she'd been of Edna. Edna could lock Mama up then do whatever she wanted to herself, thinking of her soap opera lovers, and even though the guilt was tremendous, the pleasure far out-weighed that guilt. She loved her son, adored him, but she needed those six hours every schoolday, or she knew in her heart that she'd go mad.

Which had almost happened when Arthur had left her. Not that he'd ever lived with her, even though he spent the night every so often. She was the daughter of a Baptist preacher who'd preached a lot more than religion, and since she hit thirteen they'd said Edna was a little slow, everyone said that, and her father knew it and knew the reason why, and he'd overinsured himself so that she'd have enough money to last her after he was gone. She and her mother lived together in the house after her father's death and her mama would sometimes enrage Edna by telling her that the money her father had left them was the only good thing the man had ever done for either of them in their entire lives. Edna would look at her crippled mother and the old woman would bite off her words. Mama knew full well how much Daddy had loved his little girl. As well as she knew what happened to her when her behavior angered Edna.

Arthur must have somehow found out about that money, al-though at first she'd thought that he loved her for what she was.

The same way she loved him.

He looked like Daddy, walked like him, even. Was big and tall and muscular and had dark hair and the blackest eyes. Edna could

turn the lights down and believe that Daddy was still alive, that he
was there with her, and as long as Arthur didn't open his mouth
when they were doing it Edna could even get a good and relaxing
come.

He would appear at the big white house they lived in when his
afternoon shift at the Ford plant over in Hegewisch was over, Arthur
clean and dressed up, wearing a suit and showing proper manners,
and they'd watch TV and she'd make him popcorn and she'd push
Mama's wheelchair into her bedroom but would unplug the old
woman's radio so Mama would have to hear the couch springs
squeaking when they started to go at it, and it hadn't taken Edna
long to realize that she was madly in love with Arthur. For reasons
many and varied.

On the weekends he would chase away the neighborhood children who would gather outside the house in the evenings and call
her and her mama names, sometimes even walking up the front
steps and pressing the doorbell that hadn't worked in twenty years.
Edna would sneak out the back door and try to catch them, would
chase them away with a broom and they'd laugh, escape to a safe
distance and shout at her: "Crazy ladies, crazy ladies!" and even the
people in the run-down Calumet City neighborhood, some of whom
had worshipped at her father's church, would stand watching on
their front porches and laugh.

But Arthur never laughed at them, would speak to her in a low,
intimate voice, tell her that someday he'd get out of that dead-end
job and then they could be married. He'd fix up the big white house
and they'd give Mama a whole tribe of grandchildren and everything would be just fine. He'd say that and she'd believe him and for
a year she even stopped writing her letters to the male stars of the
soap operas she'd taken to watching to pass her afternoons, she and
Mama sitting in front of that set, Mama drooling onto her house-
dress as Edna sat enraptured, absently popping her Fannie May's
into her mouth, not tending to Mama in her awe at the beauty of the
miniature men before her.

In her braver moments Mama would sometimes try to scold
her, would tell Edna that she knew what Edna and Arthur were
doing at night, that it was wrong, and that God would punish them
for giving in to their base and animal wantings. Edna loved those

times. She could just stare at Mama and shut her up and that made her feel so powerful, so strong. But she never came right out and told her Mama that there had been another man in her life once before, one who'd told her that what he was giving her would be her salvation before the eyes of the Lord. "You're gonna love it, too," the man had said, long ago, on that very first night.

Mama would sometimes even tell her that without that dirty thing between her legs no man would have anything to do with her, that women like Edna just weren't meant to ever have a man to love them. "Look in the mirror, girl," Mama would say, and Edna would sometimes obey.

Would see a plain woman, appearing outwardly normal, although ugly, Edna being heavily acned and fat. Baby fat, Edna always thought it was. Rolls of it around her belly and her pimpled thighs, which she'd cover with knee-length homemade dresses. Her flesh was too white, her teeth badly stained and crooked. Yet Arthur loved her. He told her so, when his hands were roaming while she was trying to watch the television.

She'd sometimes tell her mother, "*Daddy* sure did love me," smiling coyly, and she'd see the jealousy in her Mama's eyes. Daddy always did love Edna more.

But she'd turned up pregnant and then Arthur had left her alone and he wouldn't respond to her attempts to reach him at his home.

Which had accelerated the downhill tumble that had begun before she'd ever reached her teens.

It wasn't the first time she'd wound up that way. It had happened once before, many years ago, and when Daddy learned of her condition he'd gone berserk, had taken her somewhere and some people had done things to her and it was right after that that people began to whisper that Edna Rose was just not right in her mind and her parents had been forced to take her out of school.

The disgrace she'd felt then could never be repeated. She would have this child and raise it well.

She called Arthur's boss at the Ford plant, though, and told him what Arthur had done, and instead of firing Arthur the man had told her that it sounded like a personal problem, why didn't she talk it over with her priest? She'd never spoken to Arthur again after that, and she'd burned the few pieces of clothing that he'd left around her house. There was one other sign of his presence however, that Edna decided to keep.

There was a small gun he'd left there one night for her protection, after some of the local kids had gone a little overboard with their terror campaign. Arthur had left it just in case any of the neighborhood kids decided to break in and hurt her or her Mama, and she'd thought about taking it and shooting Arthur with it, but she hadn't; it would have been against God's law, and of one thing she was certain: She would never anger Him again. Every time she did He made her slower and fatter and dumber and she wasn't going to get any worse than she was, not if she could help it. And besides, if they put her in jail, who would tend to Mama?

So her baby had been born and she'd been alone and she'd done her best to raise him and tend to Mama at the same time. And Mama had been right, God had punished her for doing dirty before marriage by marking the child with a killer disease.

That night after viewing the truck commercial she had thought about her baby—her poor, dead baby—while sitting in her chair looking at the pictures. He'd had dark hair, black eyes, was so skinny and so sweet and tender . . .

If he'd grown up he would have looked exactly like the man in that commercial.

Edna had never gotten a driver's license and so didn't ask the Bank People for the money to go out and buy one of those trucks, which she would have liked to have done. Instead she bought one of those other new things, that VCR, and she taped hours and hours of programming, running the machine even when she slept, turning it on Record and letting it run through to the end of the tape because she could never figure the darn thing out. Then one day she had it, right there on the tape, her lover man captured forever on the screen.

It hadn't taken long before he was doing another one, and a third, and the time came when she could count on seeing him on television almost every night, even without the VCR, her honey doing another truck commercial and then a spaghetti commercial and then, finally, she'd see him in TV shows about Chicago, the big ugly city two towns to the north, and she'd been in heaven, able to watch him in small parts, angry because she knew that he was supposed to have his own show, was good enough to be the star instead of a supporting player.

She wrote him a letter, then another, then another yet, falling further in love with him every time she saw him on the screen. The letters, which had begun in simple, fan mail style, had grown more personal, intimate and filled with her secret desires, filled with her aching need for him. They'd be scribbled in her childish handwriting, with many misspelled words which she apologized for, explaining that she'd been forced to drop out of school when she had been very young. She'd take these letters to her child's grave and would burn them on his mound, talking to her child about his real father, the man who'd truly given him life. Arthur was completely forgotten. She wouldn't have recognized him had she passed him on the street; the only reminder of him was the tiny pistol which she kept in a drawer by her nightstand. In Edna's mind, the pistol, like her trust accounts and certain other legacies, had been left to her by her father.

She lived her days tending to her mama and her nights were filled with two kinds of dreams: sweet ones of the nameless handsome man who'd come into her life to love her; and terrible, horrible nightmares. When she was having one of the good ones Edna would awaken with her hands between her thighs and in the netherworld before waking she could imagine him in there, inside her, and she'd writhe on the bed, rubbing herself, her eyes closed and her tongue darting in and out of her mouth, into the mouth of the Television Man she could feel atop her, his hands on her breasts, squeezing them as he knelt above her and bent to kiss her in passion.

Then there were the other dreams, of Daddy coming into her room and doing what he did, taking his pleasure and making her love it, too. On those nights she would awaken screaming and would continue to do so until her voice was completely gone and Mama was all upset and crazy, lying in her bed in the next room and peeing on herself. Edna would exhaust herself and then feel ashamed. Why had she been so afraid? Hadn't Daddy been the first and only man who had really and truly loved her?

Every month Edna would imagine that her curse would not

come, that she would be pregnant with her and the TV man's second child, and every month when it arrived she would be filled with depression, determined to make love to him even more often so they could finally have their second son, to replace the child God had taken.

But that was not to be.

There were times when she knew better, knew that her dead child's name was really Arthur and she'd only made it up, his being called Babe, after reading about Babe Hill in a newspaper clipping. There were times when she'd go to the cemetery and see the stone-cut *Arthur Rose* on the headstone crossed out, the name *Babe* written in spray paint above. Times when she knew that she really wasn't making love to this Babe Hill from television, was only doing what Mama in her old-fashioned ways would call diddling dirty with herself.

But there were other times, too, when it all seemed so real. . . .

Reading about him in the local papers was her greatest passion, she would punish Mama when the old woman would bemoan Edna's silly expenditures, but Edna couldn't help herself, every time she saw something in the paper or a magazine she would have to have ten copies, one framed, the others for reading. She would send him the letters now that she had his address and his name, and he wouldn't respond, and she loved him further and deeper once she figured out the reason why.

The TV show *Street Babe* would be his crowning glory, and the weeks leading up to it had greatly added to her collection, all the many thousands of words written about him were now framed, on the wall of what had once been her mother's bedroom but which was now Babe's Room, waiting for the night of airing, for the show to begin, for her lover to show the entire world who and what he really was.

And maybe even to tell the world that he was leaving his wife to marry Edna Rose.

Now, early Monday morning, Edna sat in her dead mother's wheelchair and rewound the tape, back to the beginning. She stifled a yawn, then cocked her head, half-smiling, pretending that she was listening to something.

"Mama, I *told* you not to talk while the program's on!" Then: "I don't care if it *is* a commercial, damnit!" Now that Mama was dead and buried, she could speak any way she damn well pleased, any time she wanted. She would curse for no reason, just for the satisfaction of being able to do it. Would just be watching television and the words would come out: "Shit-piss-fuck-damn," and she'd smile. Although she never swore when there was company in the house, when the Church People were there, nor would she allow it around her. Edna rocked back and forth in the wheelchair, and when the tape was rewound she began to play it again, listened for the fourth time to the haunting music, paused the machine when STARRING BABE HILL appeared on the screen and looked at it for a while.

The walls of the room were covered with framed newsprint, some of them yellowed and old, others brand new, from Sunday's papers. The Arts sections of both Chicago papers had done huge writeups of the new show, and there had been in-depth interviews with her Babe, and she knew more about him than she ever had before, knew the general area in which he lived, even where he jogged and what time of night he went to do his running. Where he had grown up and how much he hated the area. *People* magazine had done a big story, too, and there were pictures of Babe with his arm around his wife but Edna could see the pain in his eyes, the suffering. The woman had to be a witch, keeping him captive with a spell. She'd read the stories while the commercial breaks ran, not wanting to Fast Forward the machine because it might make the tape wear out more quickly. She would read over and over again about the man she loved, read between the lines, too, about how lonely he was. She could relate to that.

Since Mama's death she'd barely gone out the door, except to walk to the Fannie May's once a week and stock up on her sweets, which she'd eat in front of the TV set, staring at the screen, her hand unconsciously stuffing her mouth with fudge, hour after hour. If it wasn't for the Church People she would never even have any regular food in the house. The Bank People would send her a check every month and she'd give it to that nice Mrs. McLain who was what they called her Guardian. Mrs. McLain would pay all her bills and bring her all the receipts and canceled checks and give Edna a hundred dollars a week for spending money, of which Edna saved half, had it hidden in a large canning jar in the basement. The other half, she spent on her goodies, on her treats. Mrs. McLain would tell her what a great man her father had been, and Edna would listen politely, although she'd be seething inside. What did this woman know of Daddy's greatness, of his capacity to love? But she kept her mouth shut. She knew what would happen if she ever told anyone, had learned after the doctors had done things to her when she was twelve. If she ever told, she'd burn in hell forever, and everyone knew how long forever was.

On the bed was a large white stuffed fuzzy bear that she would hold in her arms and hug, which she'd kiss with passion during the long nights that seemed to stretch on forever. The bear's legs and midsection were dark, stained, its mouth was matted, sticky and straight from her dried saliva. It sat on the patchwork quilt that Mama had made years and years ago, awaiting her need, and it was all she needed for the moment, but that wouldn't last for long.

Now that Mama was gone, she could concentrate more fully on her Babe. Maybe find him and throw herself at him, shamelessly. He had to know who she was, how much she loved him. Her letters were filled with her love for him, her desire. She blushed, thinking about them. She knew that he enjoyed reading them, and she imagined that when he did the dirty things with the wife he didn't love that he was really thinking of her, of Edna, in his arms, instead of that woman who had him trapped.

Edna knew what she'd have to do. She'd watch the magnificent show *Street Babe* for the fifth time, get a good night's sleep, then somehow find her way to Park Forest and to the high school where he ran every night. She would open herself up to him right from the beginning, tell him about her money and that it was all his if he wanted it. Tell him that their child had died and she wanted—no, *needed*—another from him. Tell him that she wanted him inside of her, that she would be his slave, his servant for life, would do anything he wanted her to do forever and ever in return for his love. Tell him these things and see how he took them.

On this early Monday morning Edna Rose was thirty-six years old and looked fifteen years older. She never looked at herself when she passed the faded mirrors in the filthy old white house, never tried to catch a glimpse of herself in the glass as she passed by the windows at night when the lights were on. She bathed only when the smell got too bad for her to take, and her teeth were rotten and twisted, green in spots from lack of proper care. There were pimples these days all over her face, most prominently on her forehead. Her hair was long and black and streaked with gray, and it hung in thick mats, down to her shoulders. When Mama had died and they'd given her the competency test she had cleaned up for them, knowing that they wanted to put her away, and at their physical tests she had weighed in at 248, and that had been months ago. As long as she was alone and no one would ever see her she didn't care what she looked like, but for what she had to do she would have to look her best.

In a couple of hours, as soon as the stores opened, she would take some of the bills out of the basement and she would go to the drugstore on Pulaski Road and she would buy pretty-smelling soap, fragrant hair shampoo. Some deodorant and some mouthwash. Frilly underwear and new socks and she would be needing a new dress and some comfortable shoes, maybe even expensive ones, like Michael Jordan advertised on TV. It would show Babe that she was current and—what was the word? Hip. She giggled at that. Edna Rose, hip.

Yet she could be. She knew that. She could be anything Babe Hill wanted her to be. An oak or a willow, a wild boar or a submissive hound. Whatever that man wanted in life, she would be, and she would spend all day Monday getting herself ready, making herself pretty. Then on Tuesday she would go and present herself to him, to her love master.

For insurance, just in case she was completely wrong and he didn't understand her love and wasn't willing to return it, she'd take the little pistol that was now sitting on Mama's bedstand, all shiny and sparkly.

Edna hit the Play button and let the tape roll, swooning as Babe Hill came onto the screen. During the love scene, even though she was jealous as all get-out, her hand wandered down toward her groin in spite of herself, as if acting on its own, and suddenly she wasn't jealous anymore, suddenly he was there with her, loving her and comforting her and it was like it had been, long ago, when they'd first started dating and were beginning to fall in love.

The Venezuelan's name had about forty letters in it but that didn't matter to Johnny because he always called him Goom. Not only this one, but the five others he had working for him, too. Johnny used nicknames so he could keep track of them, assigned a name to each and made sure they identified themselves over the phone in that way, so he could keep each one separate from the other. In person, he never had a problem, could call them Goom—short for *goombah*—but over the phone they all sounded the same to him, he couldn't tell one of these monkeys from the other.

The names were colorful, stamped in his mind. This one was called Moca. Besides him, there were Ginger, Brownie, Oak, Nestle, and Decaf working for Johnny. None of them was especially big, none was built like movie action stars, with bulging muscles that looked pretty but weren't good for much of anything else. There wasn't one of them you would give a second look to if you were a cop driving by or even walking a beat like in the old days. Every one of them was older, looked like he came out of the mills, working the big 16-incher, cutting pieces off of red hot steel poles with huge hydraulic scissors, the kind of work that put a permanent bend into your back and made you old before you were ready.

No cop would ever take a look at them and think: *gang*—even though the Chicago streets these days were filled with Latino gangbangers who killed over insults, real or perceived. These were older men, working men, who didn't overdress and who didn't drive flashy cars.

The one thing they had in common, which made them useful to

Johnny, was that in their homeland they had taken their machetes and shown their worth by taking another man's life. Once you did that, Johnny figured, you'd proved your manhood.

Another thing that he liked about them was that they were very grateful, didn't make plans behind your back on you, didn't have ambitions to take over and run the show themselves. They knew enough English to collect the bets out here on the Southeast Side, could count well enough to pay off when the suckers won. He'd give them three hundred a week, more, as a bonus on a real good week, and they never complained, treated him like a god even though they had weird senses of humor and sometimes liked to tease him.

This one here, Moca, sitting at the counter of the coffee shop with him, tearing into a cheeseburger, would call him up and tell Johnny that he was Ginger, tell Johnny that he'd lost the day's money and what was he to do? Then he'd laugh, tell Johnny that he was only kidding.

He was a big kidder, was Moca. Would grin and those two gold teeth in front would shine. You'd never suspect that he was a man who would stick his knife into your heart and twist it, watch curiously as the light went out in your eyes, his only concern being how slowly he could make you die, how much he could make you suffer.

It was better than the Italians, that's for sure. Those guys would forget their honor, where they came from and who got them there, the second they got pinched. They'd do a crime, get caught, look forty years in the face and go into the Witness Protection Program, begin singing for their supper. These guys, they'd never do that. They were like Johnny had been when he was younger, when he'd scored more than one sentence for a friend, doing a favor for somebody's somebody. Besides, there wasn't a prison in America that wasn't infinitely better than the homes they'd spent their lives in back in their motherland.

They loved America, did Johnny's gooms.

The only problem he had ever had with them was teaching them to lose one custom. Back home, when they wanted to kill a man, they would send him letters, stating their intentions. He'd had to teach them that here in America, the element of surprise was your greatest friend, and it was not dishonorable to kill a man without warning him beforehand. He rarely had any of them kill anyone, though, preferred to do the contracts alone when they were offered, because then he could keep all the money. But when the job was too big, when he needed help, he'd call on one of them, and the last thing he needed was a paper trail leading back to them, and to him. He had them break a few heads, bust a few kneecaps on slow payers or total deadbeats, but usually it was nothing worse than that.

Johnny looked at Moca now, feeling relaxed, in control of the situation.

"We have a good day?" he asked.

Moca spoke around a mouthful of beef, ketchup running down his chin. "A *very* good day, Goom," he said. He looked around the diner furtively, his eyebrows raised, to make sure there was nobody paying them any inordinate amount of attention, then he turned back to Johnny and he said, "And I brought that other money, for that piece of business that you and I were discussing."

"You didn't say anything to the others?"

Moca hurriedly shook his head. "They are my brothers, but you are my father. You say no tell, I no tell." Johnny liked that. Moca was maybe forty, but looked around Johnny's age, sixty-one. Johnny had a son older than this spic. To Moca, though, what he'd said had been high praise, a massive sign of respect, and Johnny believed that their secret was safe.

Moca wiped his mouth with his napkin, stared down at it, dropped it onto his plate. "I like the cheeseburger, I can never get enough of them." Then said, "What I do not see, Goom, what you must tell me, is why are you risking this once again? There is so much time for you in this country after a second drug conviction . . ." He slurped his fountain Coke through the straw.

"It's worth the risk. You just got to make sure you don't get caught." He said it as a teacher would to a pupil, always directing these guys, showing them in his friendly, reasonable way about getting ahead in the criminal underground of this country.

"You should let me meet the man all alone," Moca said. "If I get arrested, I will be deported. I will be back next week with a suntan and the clap."

"They don't deport you until you serve your time, and besides, we take the same risk, we share the same profit."

"There will be plenty of that, yes."

Johnny lowered his voice. "Ten grand apiece, Goom, invested, we make a hundred grand in two days when I turn it over."

"It is not right I make the same money in profit as you. You have the connection here to sell it, I do not."

"But you're taking the risk with me, and besides, you are my son."

That made Moca smile. "Could I have the check please?" The bored waitress didn't respond to the unusual courtesy, and slapped the stub down, slid it toward Moca, who looked at it, removed two huge wads of folded twenties, tens, and fives, stripped off a bill and dropped it on the check. He slipped the rubber band back on with a snap, making sure that the waitress saw the wad that he was carrying. "You keep that change, missy," Moca said to the wide-eyed waitress, and smiled his gold-tooth smile.

It was the way everyone was, Johnny knew. Even the most humble of men liked to show off now and then.

They left the diner and walked on broken concrete to the parking lot, in the fading day's light. The streetlights had already come on, and even though it was getting dark it was still warm enough so that they were comfortable in their shirtsleeves. Johnny was dressed in a long-sleeve dark blue shirt with pants that matched. Moca had on a short-sleeve white shirt, and you could see his undershirt clearly through the thin material. There was gang graffiti on the wall next to Johnny's shoulder, but it was too early for the punks to be out, they waited for full dark, which was a good thing. Johnny didn't want to waste time hurting some young jerk who might want to make a move on them, having seen Moca's roll when he'd pulled it out in the diner.

In the car, in Johnny's ten-year-old battered brown Chrysler, Moca handed both bundles over to Johnny. "The smaller one is the street bets for today. The gambling slips are inside. The other bundle is my life savings, for the yi yo."

Johnny put both bundles in his pants pocket, never taking his eyes off the road. Both of them were wearing their seat belts, both of them sat up straight and looked out the window, at the street before them. The radio was not turned on. The windows were rolled up tight.

Johnny drove slowly through the darkness, smoking, sticking to the speed limit. He had protection from the boys he worked for as far as the booking action went, but for this other stuff, he was on his own and if he took a pinch he'd never see daylight again.

Moca cracked his window to let out the smoke. "You call me your son, and that remind me. How you like that TV show last night? You never say, in the bar last night. You just stare at the screen."

"He's a chip off the old block, that kid of mine," Johnny said. "Good-looking boy."

"T'anks."

Johnny pulled the car into the black pit of a vacant lot in Indiana Harbor, Indiana, in the shadow of the once mighty Inland Steel plant. There were no working streetlights in this part of the Harbor, the only light coming from the burning waste outlet fires a couple of miles away at the Standard Oil plant. There was a chemical stink in the air. Faintly, they could hear sounds from the mill, ghost sounds that steadily pounded the night.

"I no see another car," Moca said. He didn't seem in any way nervous, which meant that he trusted Johnny, and Johnny was glad. He'd chosen the right man for this job. He shut the car off and flicked his lights on once, twice, then took the keys out of the ignition and got out of the car.

"Come on," he said. "Keep your eyes open, watch the street."

Johnny felt his way down the length of the car and fumbled the key into the trunk, opened it, and grabbed what was inside.

The soft glow from the trunk light lit up the blackness around him with the intensity of a headlight high-beam, gleaming off the long-barrel .22 pistol in Johnny's now gloved right hand.

"See anything?" he asked Moca, and Moca, with his back turned to Johnny, shrugged his shoulders, shook his head. He sucked his teeth, getting some cheeseburger out from around the gold.

"There is no one here. I do not like this, Johnny, I have a bad feeling all of a sudden."

"I'll take care of that for you," Johnny Hilliard said, and lifted the pistol, pointed it at the back of Moca's head and fired three times, following him to the ground, then stood over him and emptied the weapon into the front of Moca's head.

He dropped the weapon onto Moca's chest, slammed the trunk and hurried around to the front of the car, got in and pulled out of there, didn't turn on his lights until he was a block away.

It bothered him, killing Moca, killing one of the gooms, but what the hell was he supposed to do? He needed the money, and Moca always was the dumbest of the six Venezuelans. Calling him up on the phone and fucking with him.

At least he'd done it quick, and the guy hadn't suffered. If Landini, Johnny's crew chief, had found out that Johnny had been booking some of the bigger bets himself, he wouldn't have been so kind to Johnny, not by a longshot.

It was the price you paid in this life, Johnny thought, and put Moca out of his mind. He was thirsty, and the night's work would be forgotten a lot faster once he had a little Scotch under his belt.

He drove carefully, his seat belt on, his hands steady on the wheel, his fingers not shaking when he lit a smoke. He still had it, he thought, and that thought made Johnny smile.

3

I t was funny sometimes, the way life did you.

Babe Hill was thinking this, waiting his turn to speak, seated at the dais in the crowded junior high school auditorium, half-bored while the principal of the school listed Babe's many accomplishments, his dozens of acting jobs in TV commercials, his many bit parts in the movies, listing them all one by one and climaxing with the capper, last night's showing of his own tailor-made two-hour pilot, *Street Babe*. The school principal was taking all day to recite Babe's body of work. The thought of that made him smile.

He had one now, a body of work. One he could be proud of because he did it his own way and had never sold out.

He'd mention that to these curious kids, but wouldn't tell them the main reason he was proud of what he'd done, wouldn't tell them about the B&Es, the headbusting he'd done when he'd been a kid, the wild life he'd led and the terrible price it had cost him. He hadn't even told Kelly about most of it; the shame was too strong for him even to discuss it.

When he thought about how close he'd come, what might have happened to him if it hadn't been for her, if he hadn't lain eyes on little baby Mike, he would shiver, because there was no happy ending to that story.

A very small part of that story they could get from the massive publicity last night's show had generated. He had all the stories about him and the show: from *TV Guide*, from both Chicago papers, from two of the local magazines and from *Time* and *Newsweek*, all that print about him sitting on a desk in a converted bedroom in his new house, what he used for an office.

He had them, but he hadn't read them. Not one word of them. He didn't want to start believing it, let what they wrote go to his head.

He'd told the reporters very little about his upbringing, even though they were curious, knew about the manslaughter conviction and wanted to learn more, how he managed to beat prison time, why he was convicted and wound up with the sentence commuted to time served. The reporters always wanted to delve into what made him tick, but he managed to evade them, much to the annoyance of his publicist, but it wasn't her life, it was his, and he'd tell the world what he thought they should know and nothing more.

He even took them to Hegewisch, to the neighborhood where he'd grown up, shown them the streets he'd been raised on and let them draw their own conclusions about the area. He'd read the articles in the morning, now that the show was over and had been a hit, just to see what they'd thought of it, how they portrayed that part of Chicago to their readers.

He looked over the crowd in the auditorium, at the teenage girls elbowing their mothers and whispering in each other's ears, their eyes twinkling, and he couldn't help but be pleased.

Here he was, in his late thirties, successful—at least he thought he was, the international jury was still out on that one—being honored in front of his family before a standing-room-only crowd of teenagers who'd brought their parents, who'd come on their own time to hear him speak.

And to think that nearly twenty years ago he'd been in a cage, locked up like an animal. Was life funny, or what?

His wife Kelly was right there next to him, as usual these past thirteen years or so, and now she reached over and took his hand, squeezed it a little and hung onto it, put them both in her lap. "Nervous?" she whispered.

"So nervous I'm about to fall asleep."

Kelly laughed softly. "The man *can* talk."

The kids knew it, too, were squirming around in their seats, speaking to each other, not even trying to be polite while their leader droned on.

They were not what Babe had expected, this well-dressed group that had shown up on a warm early May evening. They were cleaner, somehow, than he remembered himself being as a teenager. Maybe more innocent, if that were possible in the dying years of the 20th century.

Babe's son Mike was in the front row, and every time he'd catch his father's eye he'd roll his own eyes up into his head, one of his new thirteen-year-old traits, showing exasperation without mouthing off. He'd duck his head down from time to time, his hand held up to his ear, fingers curled around the weather radio he carried with him everywhere, Mike's goal in life to be a meteorologist. There were times when Babe had to look away from the sight, shut his eyes and clear his throat to keep from breaking down. When he was thirteen, he'd carried an ice pick.

Sometimes he didn't know how to act as a father, seeing as he himself hadn't had much of one for a role model. Beatings were out of the question, though, as they'd never done much for Babe but fuel his rage, get him to daydreaming about violent acts of revenge. Mike would mouth off to Kelly and for a second Babe would see red, would have to calm himself down before he opened his mouth and straightened the kid out. Let him know that Kelly was his *wife*, buddy, and would be long after Mike moved out of the house. And nobody showed his family disrespect, did Mike understand that? Mike would tell him that he did.

These days, since Mike had hit puberty, were pretty rough sometimes. The boy had somehow figured out that Babe's parental authority was a topic of debate, of discussion, and after his initial shock Babe began to think that this was a pretty good thing.

How could it not be? He himself had never mouthed off to the old man, hadn't dared, had kept everything in, seething, and look how he'd turned out.

He'd curse himself when he caught himself thinking like that, did it now, shook his head a little and made himself remember that he'd turned out pretty damned good, all things considered. The first three-quarters of his life had been really screwed up, but these past ten years or so, things had been just fine.

This past summer they'd moved into a nice tri-level house less than a mile from the school, where both of their sons had their own bedrooms for a change. He drove a Lincoln Town Car, and Kelly had a new Taurus, both cars with phones in them. A far cry from the hundred-dollar wonders he'd driven for most of his adult life. The house had a fireplace and last winter they'd spent Christmas Eve in front of it, Babe, Kelly, ten-year-old Collin and Mike, the four of them singing Christmas carols, and Babe had to excuse himself a couple times, had walked into the downstairs bathroom and sat down on the toilet and held his head in his hands, taking deep breaths.

If anyone had told him how good it could be, he'd have changed his way of life a hell of a lot sooner than he had.

"And now, without further ado—" The principal looked toward him and held out his hand and Babe smiled at him, the smile that had launched an acting career that now looked to be about ready to go over the top. Babe stood when he heard his name and, to thunderous applause, to stomping feet, stepped to the microphone.

There were things he wanted to say, and that was why he was here. Two points, really, that he wanted to drive home to these nice suburban kids who were still young and impressionable enough to maybe get something out of what he told them.

He knew how to play it, too. After all, he was an actor. He'd stand there tall and straight, his black hair combed back, away from his high forehead. He'd rivet them with his black eyes, make eye contact with anyone he could as often as possible, let them know that he was speaking individually to them, one on one. He'd sip from his water glass at the appropriate moment, slap the lectern when the time was right, say what he had to, and during the question-and-answer period one of these kids would ask him if he'd ever met Tom Selleck.

Which was all right. Others, the ones he was here to reach, would understand, would take what he said home with them, and that was what it was all about.

Babe waited for the clapping to subside, and when it finally did he began to speak.

"The first thing I want to say to you is something very dear to my heart. There are those of you in here tonight who have parents who beat you up or call you bad names, who try and tell you that it's your fault. Well, that's just"—Babe smiled—"bullshit, if you'll pardon the expression." It had its desired effect, Babe had gotten his point across and broken the ice, gotten their attention with one simple word. Mike rolled his eyes and there were assorted giggles, plenty of snickering and elbowing. In the quiet, he heard the word repeated by laughing young male voices.

"Child abuse is *never* the child's fault." Babe lifted his hand for emphasis. "No matter what the abuser tells you." He nodded at them, smiled, then said, "Now, you want to hear about acting?" and they roared.

"Let me tell you the way I see it, and some of the mistakes I made along the way, the first of which was dropping out of school. *Big* mistake. Second mistake, I got involved with alcohol early on, and when I drank I got mean. I wasn't much older than most of you the first time I got arrested, and it wasn't the last." Babe lowered his voice, about to tell secrets to a couple of hundred kids. They were silent, in awe at the sight of the man they'd seen on TV screens since the time they were old enough to be mesmerized by the talking boxes in their living rooms.

"When I was a kid, I would watch my father come home drunk and beat my mother, I'd see the damage he'd do to her, with his fists, with his feet. I'd try to stop him and he'd turn on me, do a number on me like you wouldn't believe. These things happened to me and I swore to God that when I grew up I'd never drink and I'd never raise my hand to another human being.

"And when I was twenty years old I went to jail and spent nine months awaiting trial for getting drunk and beating a man to death in a bar fight. A human being lost his life that night and tonight I can't even tell you what the argument was about. So you go figure it out, does booze advance your career, does it help your life?

"Even after I got out of jail and into acting, the drinking stayed with me. I'd done a number of commercials and I could go down to Rush Street and girls would recognize me, would want to take me home, and there I was, twenty-five years old and not showing up for work, getting a bad name in the industry already. The phone stopped ringing, then it got cut off. By the time I was twenty-six I was a has-been, sleeping on the floor of a barber shop on the far

Frank, that he liked it rough in the sack, but only when the woman was dishing it out.

"That ain't funny, Frank."

"Seems to be working for you, Anthony. Ma's so broke up, what are you doing in a ginmill, drinking and giving me a hard time?"

"I ain't giving you no—" The blonde came out of the bathroom and was twitching her way toward him, walking with a lot more hip movement than she had when she'd gone in.

"Hi," she said, smiling. She looked vulnerable and shy. The way they all did until you got them to their apartments and they turned into wildcats, tore the clothes off your back and used words that pissed him off when he heard his mother use them.

Anthony said, "You are how?" Mixing up his words again, God, did he hate when he did that. "I mean, how you are—how *are* you?!"

She laughed. Not making fun of him though, seeming amused. The record stopped and Anthony was grateful for the silence, for not having forty sounds pounding into his head at one time. He could think more clearly, this way. "Buy you a drink?" he said, and it all came out the right way, and he smiled.

"I'll be waiting at the bar."

"Anthony?" Frank sounded angry, but Anthony waited a second, watched the girl sashay away from him because he knew she'd turn and make sure he was watching, right—*now*—the girl coyly looking over her shoulder at him, eyes lowered, peeking up. Anthony turned his back on her, and smiled into the phone.

"I'm gonna hang up," Frank warned.

"Don't do that."

"Anthony, you're transposing your words again, you know what happens when you get like that."

"One fucking time, you talk to Ma after she talked to some doctor, and you're all gonna tell me what all my problems are every time I talk to you."

"He was *your* doctor, and he was a shrink. It's mental, Anthony. You won't take your medication and you drink and you get goofy."

Again, the tinkling, derisive laughter from the background. He was sure he'd heard it this time.

"You calling me goofy?"

South Side, in the toilet in the back room. Sound like fun? Well guess again, it wasn't."

"But you're so successful now!" She was a pretty little girl, like a budding rose, sort of awkward and shy, putting her hand to her mouth as soon as she realized she'd spoken aloud, blushing. Babe smiled warmly, to put her at her ease.

"That's now, honey, this is over a decade in time and a million casting calls later, after I gave it up, the booze, the wild life. See, sweetie, that's for losers. People will try and tell you that it's glamorous, that it's what everyone's doing. But the quickest road to hell is through a bottle or with drugs, and that road is paved with self-delusion and rationalization. It's everyone else's fault, you tell yourself. You tell yourself that you're just unlucky, that things will break for you again, but sooner or later, if you're really lucky, you wise up, you find out that it's really your own actions that stuck you in the mud.

"For me, the moment of truth came when I was sitting in the barber chair at three in the morning, looking longingly at the razor blades on the counter. I figured I'd just get drunk enough where it wouldn't hurt too much." Smile. "Good thing I didn't do it, huh? Look what I'd have missed."

Babe paused while the kids politely laughed, shot a look over at Kelly, whose eyes were shining. His strength, that's what she was. She was smiling encouragingly, aware of the reason he'd come, knowing that he'd already said the things that were important to him and now he could lighten up, answer some questions and tell a few inside stories.

"So if you want to be successful as an actor, or at *any*thing in life, stay in school, learn your trade, stay away from drugs and alcohol, work like hell at it and then pray that you get lucky.

"I've been in four television pilots in four years, and in two different series. One lasted seven weeks, the other only three. You know what? I've *still* made more money from that fifteen weeks total work than your average family makes in five years. Not to mention all the years when I played the guy in the background, or the bartender, or the Man with Gun in Alley.

"The rewards are tremendous, if you stick with it, if you believe in yourself and don't let anybody convince you that you can't.

"And do it your way, folks.

"Everyone goes out to LA or New York and waits tables, they go to the cattle calls and sit for hours only to be told that their breasts aren't big enough, or their butts are *too* big.

"I stayed here in Chicago, working local theater, doing commercials, hundreds of them, along with the bit parts in almost every movie that was shot in town, and now, they're coming to me, these big shots out on the coast who judge their worth by the amount of gold they wear. Don't you think that makes me feel good? Makes me happy?

"See, the only way to do anything is your *own* way, within the law, within your limitations. Otherwise, it's not worth doing. Now, are there any questions?"

There sure were. Hands shot up throughout the room, all those kids sitting on the bleachers wanting to ask him about TV and movies, about the stars he knew. Some of the adults' hands were raised, too, but they could wait, and if he had time after the kids were through, he might call on them. He was here to speak to the kids, as a gesture of respect to his son. The parents, he figured, could get their own lives.

"You there, yes?"

"Mr. Hill, we watched the Sunday Night Movie of *Street Babe* Sunday night, last night?" The boy was tall, skinny, with acne. But he wasn't shy, spoke right up, speaking to Babe like an equal. Good self-esteem, Babe loved to see that in a kid.

"Did you like it?"

"You looked, on television, a lot *taller* . . ."

4

"**W**hat? You gotta speak up, I can't hear you!" Anthony Hilliard was speaking into the phone at the Placebo Lounge, a pay phone with no booth around it that was right out in the open near the toilets of the sports bar, The Clash screaming out loudly from a high-velocity jukebox that wasn't five yards from where he was standing, speaking to his brother, Frank. Or trying to.

He held a beer bottle in one hand and a Salem Light in the other, the phone stuck between his shoulder and his ear, Anthony trying to bounce out of the way of the people coming in and out of the bathroom every two seconds, it seemed like.

"I said I'm getting laid, what's the matter, you deaf?" Frank said.

"Ma's all broke up about that TV show last night." Anthony had to shout to make himself heard, and a blond chick heading into the ladies' room turned to eye him over her shoulder, giving him the once-over. He smiled at her.

He had the Hilliard good looks, was tall with a full head of hair, blue eyes instead of black, like his brothers all had, wore his hair long, combed out like Mel Gibson, and he knew he was a little skinny but there was no helping that. The girl disappeared into the bathroom and he took a sip of his beer, waited for an answer from his brother.

"Tell her to buy a bottle of bourbon, it always ends her anguish." Anthony couldn't be sure, but he thought he heard a woman laugh in the background, and he could picture what she looked like, what she might be wearing. There

"What if I am? You gonna come over here and whip my ass?"

"You think I can't?" Another song came onto the damn jukebox, even louder than the last one. He didn't know the name of the group, but it was some punk thing, which he usually liked but which now was a pain in the ass, as he was trying to speak on the phone and not transpose his fucking words so that Frank wouldn't think he was nuts.

"Anthony, look, go on home, pour Ma a drink, relax and get some sleep. How come neither one of you can ever call me unless you're three sheets to the wind?"

"Cause you're never home, that's why!"

"Good comeback, Anthony," Frank said, and hung up on him.

God, how he hated it when somebody did that. Ignored him, treated him like he was some dumb kid because he was the youngest in the family. He was twenty-six, a full-grown man. Someday maybe they'd start believing that he wasn't a child anymore.

He walked into the bathroom, and was grateful to find himself alone. Anthony stared into the mirror, liking what he saw—the hint of danger in the set of his jaw, the attitude he tried so hard to show—gazed into his own blue eyes and tried a seductive smile.

"So what's your name," he said, and none of the words were scrambled. He gave it another shot. "So what's *your* name, mine's Anthony." Piece of cake.

He had delicate features, there was no way around that. A lower lip that was so full it looked like he'd had collagen injections. Anthony knew women who'd kill for a lip like that.

These days, since the other jobs hadn't panned out, he was an actor/model and a thief on the side. His father had paid for a full portfolio of shots, Anthony posed in all kinds of positions, staring at the camera, sometimes trying to act horny, other times looking vulnerable and helpless, which he could do real well. It used to keep the old lady from beating on him when she was drunk, the way she used to beat on the other kids. But the modeling and acting wasn't panning out too well, and Anthony had taken to street muggings, driving his car to Jew Hill and attacking whomever he could find wandering the streets after dark. It was risky, but the money was good and he scored a lot of nice leather coats in the wintertime, which he could sell for a decent profit. He said it one more time, "Hi, I'm Anthony, what's *your* name," and smiled, guilelessly. He winked at himself once, feeling his oats, feeling the beers, too, and left the toilet, to hunt the blonde.

He swaggered down the short hallway, annoyed because everybody in the family knew that Frank snorted more coke than an entire NBA team, and the rotten skullsucker was giving him a hard time because he'd had a few beers to calm his nerves.

The beer always made him feel normal, like he imagined that everyone else always felt. Made him feel tough and strong, like his father. When he was drinking, even after only a couple, he'd fall into his old man's speech patterns, talking like his father, walking like his father, using his father's hand gestures and wasn't his father a stone killer? Didn't everybody fear him? You bet your ass they did, and they feared Anthony, too, he bet.

Or would, soon, as soon as Anthony made his mark.

Which he wouldn't be doing on some square job, working like a stiff for peanuts.

Was it his fault that he couldn't hold a job, that they made him nervous? His fault that the bosses all the time picked on him, gave him a hard time because he sometimes made mistakes when he talked? Well, he had scored good this week, three muggings and he'd sold two dogs he'd stolen back to their owners for a hundred apiece, and the dough was in his pocket, burning a hole through his pants.

The dogs were the fun part, because it was always a tossup with him, what he'd do with them. If they were friendly, licked his hand and treated him right, he'd lock them in the car and call the number that was on their tag, tell whoever answered that he'd "found" their pet, and how much was it worth to them to have it back in one piece, no questions asked? But if the dog snapped or bit at him, or if the owner gave him any shit when he called, then he did other things to the little barker, things that brought him pleasure when he was doing them but which filled him with guilt after he was done, usually the next morning when he woke up, hung over, piecing his actions together and wanting to puke when he remembered the vicious acts he'd performed.

But there was no guilt tonight, no shame inside him. He felt good and a little high. He'd have a few beers and if he didn't get lucky with the blonde, he just might go on over to Frank's and see how tough the guy was when he wasn't safe in his bed—probably tied to it—talking tough into a telephone. For some time now Anthony had felt that it was time to graduate from pets to people, see how much of a thrill there was in taking a person's life instead of a dog's or a cat's. Anthony wanted that experience, the way he knew his father had had it. He believed that it would make him a man.

The Placebo was packed, half the people watching the playoff games on the four wide-screen TVs, the other half dancing wildly on the hardwood floor that had been spray-painted with white lines and circles to look like a basketball court.

In the middle of the joint was a boxing ring, and the big spenders got to sit there, escorted right in by the waitresses, shown to tables that had reserved signs set down on the tablecloths. Anthony had never been allowed in there, though he'd tried to get through. One of the four bouncers would always stop him before he got past the first of the seven steps.

The big spenders could dance on the roof, too, from June 1st until the end of September, the roof was opened every year with a big ceremony that showed who was who for that season, which left the others, those who weren't picked to receive the blue ID roof passes, jealous and hurt. There was a ladder leading up there, one in here and one outside, both of them made of wrought iron, twisting, around and around, leading up, with handrails so that even if you were blitzed and fell you couldn't get hurt, couldn't sue anybody because the place had gone out of its way to ensure your safety. In the summer, when the roof was open to the big shots, the Placebo would hire an extra bouncer just to stand at the top of the outside ladder, to make sure that nobody got through who wasn't hip, who wasn't happening and cool.

The bouncers in this place didn't take a lot of shit from people. Already, in the two hours he'd been here, Anthony'd seen them throw out maybe six people, all of them young, none of them dressed well or with broads. He'd never seen a bouncer throw someone out who'd been sitting inside the ring, no matter how rowdy one of those yuppies got, and they could get pretty rowdy, thinking they were back in college and screaming, pulling off their shirts and pounding on their chests and sometimes even pouring beer on one another, rubbing it into each other's hair and laughing like hyenas on acid.

He wondered how it felt to sit up there, with the lesser humans dancing all around you, below you, like servants there for your pleasure.

He spotted the blonde at the bar, listening to some hairy-chested guy who had a heavy gold medallion hanging down from a chain into the middle of his chest, his shirt open about five buttons to show off his belly, which looked fat to Anthony. The guy had to be about forty, old enough to be the girl's father. He was about twenty years behind the times when it came to fashion. It wouldn't be a big challenge for Anthony, unless the guy was loaded with money.

Anthony fell in love with her as he walked toward her, with her long slender legs that the tight jeans couldn't hide the shape of, with her large breasts, with the way she held her head down and looked up at you, almost frightened as she sipped her drink through the straw, making her cheeks suck inward, erotically.

"Remember me?" Anthony said, and the girl looked at him, seemed happy to see him. He might be rescuing her from this boring old man with the gold chain and the money on the bar. She didn't look like someone who'd be impressed with money.

"Hi," she said, demurely, and looked embarrassed, stuck with two men there and too timid to tell the other one to go screw off.

The hairy ape said, "You need something, bud?"

Anthony took up a stance right in front of him, his beer bottle held low in one hand, by the neck, Anthony ready to use it if he had to. He dropped his cigarette to the ground, feeling the anger well up inside him, all the hatred of his lifetime compacted into this one second, focused on this one person. He stared at the ape, tried to make him feel it, to make him aware of the danger he was in but the idiot, he just gave Anthony a boozy, amused stare.

"I need you to get away from my date," Anthony said.

The girl looked shocked but caught herself, smiled enigmatically, and didn't say anything. The hairy ape grinned widely.

"You bring this woman here, did you?"

Was he making fun of Anthony?

"You ing-mak fun of me?" Shit! He was doing it with the syllables now, making an ass out of himself in front of the girl. He should have taken his medication, should have taken at least one pill before he'd left the house, but the doctor had told him that drinking while on the medication could send him into a psychotic state, so he hadn't.

"What'd you say?" The ape looked puzzled, then thought he'd figured Anthony out. "You a retard?" He turned to the girl, to Anthony's girl, grinning. "You come here with a *retard*? Well, you're leaving with a man."

The familiar buzzing was in his ears, the tunnel-hearing he'd get when an episode was about to commence. Anthony would not be able to hear anything, even if you were shouting in his ear, all he'd be able to hear was the high-pitched hum that filled his head until the thing passed, until he hurt someone or someone hurt him. It would calm him down, this sound, relax him, and sometimes a voice would speak to him, tell him what to do next.

It now told him that he'd win this one.

The ape was about Anthony's height but had to have him by fifty pounds, his shoulders were wide and meaty. He looked like one of the construction workers on the sites at one of the several jobs his father had gotten for him, the jobs he would always quit or get fired from.

Anthony was smiling broadly, going along with the joke until the buzzing told him what to do, until the voice seeped through the noise and into his consciousness. The jukebox might well not even be playing now, though he could see bodies gyrating around on the dance floor. He could see mouths open, talking and laughing, shouting, but not one sound penetrated through to him. The ape was saying something to him, smiling, and Anthony knew that it was bad news, that he was putting Anthony down, trying to impress the girl.

Before the man finished his sentence Anthony swung with the bottle and hit him, hard, on the side of his head, dropped the ape and the bottle at the same time and stepped smartly past him, lowered his ass onto the barstool next to the girl, the music beginning to penetrate, the laughter getting through to him now as the buzzing receded. Anthony stared straight ahead, at the multicolored stained mirror behind the back bar, hearing some shuffling behind him, some frightened voices speaking low.

He looked at the girl, who wasn't smiling now, who was staring at him in terror. Anthony knew just from looking at her that she wasn't for him, that she'd drop the dime if he stuck around. Knew, too, that he'd have to scare her, quick, and get the hell out while she was still in shock.

"You didn't see nothing," Anthony told her, "or I swear to

Christ I'll come back for you." He swung off the stool and almost
tripped over the guy, made a big thing out of discovering him, of
looking around in a bewildered fashion.

"What the hell is this? The guy have a stroke or something?"
The bouncers were there now, looking down at the man, worried.

"Anthony, you have anything to do with this, goddamnit!"

"Me?" Anthony told the bouncer. "Hell no. What *I* could have
with this to do?"

"You're trouble, and I don't care *who* your old man is."

Anthony stepped over the fallen ape, wishing he had the beer
he'd spilled, was heading for the exits when he turned around,
caught the girl's eye and lifted his finger, pointed it at her and used
his thumb like a gun hammer to shoot her, once. She turned away
from him, quickly, and faced the back bar.

Without thinking too much about any repercussions, Anthony
walked out of the Placebo Lounge, angry and frustrated, filled with
hate at the man for making him hit him and taking away his chance
with the girl, hating the girl because as soon as Anthony had hit the
guy she'd turned on him. Hadn't she known that Anthony had done
it for her? That bitch.

He sat in his mother's year-old light gray Chevy in the full
parking lot. He owned a fifteen-year-old Ford and had to beg his
mother to let him drive her car. She'd tell him, "You've got your own
car! You polish it twice a week! Why the hell you want to fuck up
mine?" and he'd become incensed at the way she talked.

Anthony was growing angrier by the second, breathing heavily
and glad that there was no one around, because he knew his tongue
would be twisted, that he'd never be able to speak a full sentence
right now. He stared up at the rooftop, at the class barrier through
which he'd never pass, and he got even madder, filled with hatred
toward those who dared to look down on him because he didn't
have a job, didn't drive one of these fancy sleek cars like the ones
right out there, parked all around him. Shit, he was driving his
mother's car because he was ashamed of the piece of crap that was in
his own name.

He let the anger flow through him, heard the tunnel wind
begin to blow, and when he got fully mad he began to hear the
buzzing sound, and the voice inside it told him exactly what to do.

At eleven that evening Babe parked his car at the edge of the Rich East running track in Park Forest, set the alarm and balanced the keys on the front tire, out of sight. He was in his shorts now, with his white sneakers on his feet, wearing only a dago T-shirt on top. It was still warm, although it felt like that could change at any minute; there was a faint smell of coolness in the air. His junior weatherman had told him it might get cold again before summer really came on.

He finished a cigarette while he stretched, crushed it beneath his toe, and began to run around the quarter-mile track, his mind wandering, the way it always did when he ran. He didn't wear a Walkman even though he could have used the distraction. The track was surrounded by a four-foot fence, and on three sides, there was a nine-foot fence a few yards beyond that. Still, if he listened to music, someone could sneak up on him and he would not know it until he felt that person's fist connect with his body. There was only an outside chance that that would ever happen, but it was not a chance he was willing to take.

He was a family man but one who enjoyed his solitude, a man who would sometimes make up excuses to take long rides alone, just to think, to be by himself to try and sort things out. The running now was a must, as he had to keep himself in shape. The camera was cruel, put weight on you, but he enjoyed running for its own pleasure, for the time alone, away from everyone.

He was a product of his experiences, of what he was, and there were times when it was confusing, how to act and when. Someone would say something to him that caused him fear and he'd want to strike out, to hurt them, to make them leave him alone. He hadn't done that in many years, but the thoughts never went away, the violent fantasies were always there and sometimes they would terrify him. When they came, when he was angry, he knew that he had to get off by himself until the anger worked itself out.

Kelly would tell him that his ideal mate was a mute and servile nineteenth-century Japanese woman who could cook, and he didn't argue with her, let her have her fun at his expense, although they were both aware that he was very much self-contained, that he didn't need a lot of social contact.

Kelly, though, Jesus Christ, he needed her, that was for sure. And Mike and Collin, too. Suddenly, though, because of that love, he had things to lose, and that made him uncomfortable. Life had taught him that whenever you had something to lose, there would be those looking to take it from you, any way they could. From money to dreams, nothing was sacred and nothing secure.

Babe ran, thinking about what he'd said to the kids in the auditorium earlier that night, thinking more about what he *should* have said.

He wanted to tell them about guilt, how it affected you. He knew men who didn't believe in the word, guys who killed coldly and went about their business. People like that were mutants, beyond hope, but there were a lot of crooks out there who were on the edge, on the fence. Who still had feelings no matter how hard they tried to bury them.

The bar brawl he'd been in when he was twenty had cost another young man his life, and it was true that Babe could not now remember what had started the argument.

What he could remember, however, was how he felt when he knew that he'd murdered someone. He saw it as murder, no matter what the courts called it. Manslaughter was a pretty word, but it was just a legal term. The guy he'd killed would be just as dead, no matter what Babe had been charged with.

He'd lie awake in his dorm at night in the County Jail, overcome with guilt. The emotion so strong that it even overwhelmed the terror he experienced in the jail's environment.

South Side, in the toilet in the back room. Sound like fun? Well guess again, it wasn't."

"But you're so successful now!" She was a pretty little girl, like a budding rose, sort of awkward and shy, putting her hand to her mouth as soon as she realized she'd spoken aloud, blushing. Babe smiled warmly, to put her at her ease.

"That's now, honey, this is over a decade in time and a million casting calls later, after I gave it up, the booze, the wild life. See, sweetie, that's for losers. People will try and tell you that it's glamorous, that it's what everyone's doing. But the quickest road to hell is through a bottle or with drugs, and that road is paved with self-delusion and rationalization. It's everyone else's fault, you tell yourself. You tell yourself that you're just unlucky, that things will break for you again, but sooner or later, if you're really lucky, you wise up, you find out that it's really your own actions that stuck you in the mud.

"For me, the moment of truth came when I was sitting in the barber chair at three in the morning, looking longingly at the razor blades on the counter. I figured I'd just get drunk enough where it wouldn't hurt too much." Smile. "Good thing I didn't do it, huh? Look what I'd have missed."

Babe paused while the kids politely laughed, shot a look over at Kelly, whose eyes were shining. His strength, that's what she was. She was smiling encouragingly, aware of the reason he'd come, knowing that he'd already said the things that were important to him and now he could lighten up, answer some questions and tell a few inside stories.

"So if you want to be successful as an actor, or at *any*thing in life, stay in school, learn your trade, stay away from drugs and alcohol, work like hell at it and then pray that you get lucky.

"I've been in four television pilots in four years, and in two different series. One lasted seven weeks, the other only three. You know what? I've *still* made more money from that fifteen weeks total work than your average family makes in five years. Not to mention all the years when I played the guy in the background, or the bartender, or the Man with Gun in Alley.

"The rewards are tremendous, if you stick with it, if you believe in yourself and don't let anybody convince you that you can't.

"And do it your way, folks.

"Everyone goes out to LA or New York and waits tables, they go to the cattle calls and sit for hours only to be told that their breasts aren't big enough, or their butts are *too* big.

"I stayed here in Chicago, working local theater, doing commercials, hundreds of them, along with the bit parts in almost every movie that was shot in town, and now, they're coming to me, these big shots out on the coast who judge their worth by the amount of gold they wear. Don't you think that makes me feel good? Makes me happy?

"See, the only way to do anything is your *own* way, within the law, within your limitations. Otherwise, it's not worth doing. Now, are there any questions?"

There sure were. Hands shot up throughout the room, all those kids sitting on the bleachers wanting to ask him about TV and movies, about the stars he knew. Some of the adults' hands were raised, too, but they could wait, and if he had time after the kids were through, he might call on them. He was here to speak to the kids, as a gesture of respect to his son. The parents, he figured, could get their own lives.

"You there, yes?"

"Mr. Hill, we watched the Sunday Night Movie of *Street Babe* Sunday night, last night?" The boy was tall, skinny, with acne. But he wasn't shy, spoke right up, speaking to Babe like an equal. Good self-esteem, Babe loved to see that in a kid.

"Did you like it?"

"You looked, on television, a lot *taller* . . ."

What? You gotta speak up, I can't hear you!" Anthony Hilliard was speaking into the phone at the Placebo Lounge, a pay phone with no booth around it that was right out in the open near the toilets of the sports bar, The Clash screaming out loudly from a high-velocity jukebox that wasn't five yards from where he was standing, speaking to his brother, Frank. Or trying to.

He held a beer bottle in one hand and a Salem Light in the other, the phone stuck between his shoulder and his ear, Anthony trying to bounce out of the way of the people coming in and out of the bathroom every two seconds, it seemed like.

"I said I'm getting laid, what's the matter, you deaf?" Frank said.

"Ma's all broke up about that TV show last night." Anthony had to shout to make himself heard, and a blond chick heading into the ladies' room turned to eye him over her shoulder, giving him a good once-over. He smiled at her.

He had the Hilliard good looks, was tall with a full head of black hair, blue eyes instead of black, like his brothers all had. He wore his hair long, combed out like Mel Gibson, and he knew he was a little skinny but there was no helping that. The girl disappeared into the bathroom and he took a sip of his beer, waited for a response from his brother.

"Tell her to buy a bottle of bourbon, it always erases all her anguish." Anthony couldn't be sure, but he thought he heard a woman laugh in the background, and he could imagine what she looked like, what she might be wearing. There were rumors about

Frank, that he liked it rough in the sack, but only when the woman was dishing it out.

"That ain't funny, Frank."

"Seems to be working for you, Anthony. Ma's so broke up, what are you doing in a ginmill, drinking and giving me a hard time?"

"I ain't giving you no—" The blonde came out of the bathroom and was twitching her way toward him, walking with a lot more hip movement than she had when she'd gone in.

"Hi," she said, smiling. She looked vulnerable and shy. The way they all did until you got them to their apartments and they turned into wildcats, tore the clothes off your back and used words that pissed him off when he heard his mother use them.

Anthony said, "You are how?" Mixing up his words again, God, did he hate when he did that. "I mean, how you are—how *are* you?!"

She laughed. Not making fun of him though, seeming amused. The record stopped and Anthony was grateful for the silence, for not having forty sounds pounding into his head at one time. He could think more clearly, this way. "Buy you a drink?" he said, and it all came out the right way, and he smiled.

"I'll be waiting at the bar."

"Anthony?" Frank sounded angry, but Anthony waited a second, watched the girl sashay away from him because he knew she'd turn and make sure he was watching, right—*now*—the girl coyly looking over her shoulder at him, eyes lowered, peeking up. Anthony turned his back on her, and smiled into the phone.

"I'm gonna hang up," Frank warned.

"Don't do that."

"Anthony, you're transposing your words again, you know what happens when you get like that."

"One fucking time, you talk to Ma after she talked to some doctor, and you're all gonna tell me what all my problems are every time I talk to you."

"He was *your* doctor, and he was a shrink. It's mental, Anthony. You won't take your medication and you drink and you get goofy." Again, the tinkling, derisive laughter from the background. He was sure he'd heard it this time.

"You calling me goofy?"

"What if I am? You gonna come over here and whip my ass?"

"You think I can't?" Another song came onto the damn jukebox, even louder than the last one. He didn't know the name of the group, but it was some punk thing, which he usually liked but which now was a pain in the ass, as he was trying to speak on the phone and not transpose his fucking words so that Frank wouldn't think he was nuts.

"Anthony, look, go on home, pour Ma a drink, relax and get some sleep. How come neither one of you can ever call me unless you're three sheets to the wind?"

"Cause you're never home, that's why!"

"Good comeback, Anthony," Frank said, and hung up on him.

God, how he hated it when somebody did that. Ignored him, treated him like he was some dumb kid because he was the youngest in the family. He was twenty-six, a full-grown man. Someday maybe they'd start believing that he wasn't a child anymore.

He walked into the bathroom, and was grateful to find himself alone. Anthony stared into the mirror, liking what he saw—the hint of danger in the set of his jaw, the attitude he tried so hard to show—gazed into his own blue eyes and tried a seductive smile.

"So what's your name," he said, and none of the words were scrambled. He gave it another shot. "So what's *your* name, mine's Anthony." Piece of cake.

He had delicate features, there was no way around that. A lower lip that was so full it looked like he'd had collagen injections. Anthony knew women who'd kill for a lip like that.

These days, since the other jobs hadn't panned out, he was an actor/model and a thief on the side. His father had paid for a full portfolio of shots, Anthony posed in all kinds of positions, staring at the camera, sometimes trying to act horny, other times looking vulnerable and helpless, which he could do real well. It used to keep the old lady from beating on him when she was drunk, the way she used to beat on the other kids. But the modeling and acting wasn't panning out too well, and Anthony had taken to street muggings, driving his car to Jew Hill and attacking whomever he could find wandering the streets after dark. It was risky, but the money was good and he scored a lot of nice leather coats in the wintertime, which he could sell for a decent profit. He said it one more time, "Hi, I'm Anthony, what's *your* name," and smiled, guilelessly. He winked at himself once, feeling his oats, feeling the beers, too, and left the toilet, to hunt the blonde.

He swaggered down the short hallway, annoyed because everybody in the family knew that Frank snorted more coke than an entire NBA team, and the rotten skullsucker was giving him a hard time because he'd had a few beers to calm his nerves.

The beer always made him feel normal, like he imagined that everyone else always felt. Made him feel tough and strong, like his father. When he was drinking, even after only a couple, he'd fall into his old man's speech patterns, talking like his father, walking like his father, using his father's hand gestures and wasn't his father a stone killer? Didn't everybody fear him? You bet your ass they did, and they feared Anthony, too, he bet.

Or would, soon, as soon as Anthony made his mark.

Which he wouldn't be doing on some square job, working like a stiff for peanuts.

Was it his fault that he couldn't hold a job, that they made him nervous? His fault that the bosses all the time picked on him, gave him a hard time because he sometimes made mistakes when he talked? Well, he had scored good this week, three muggings and he'd sold two dogs he'd stolen back to their owners for a hundred apiece, and the dough was in his pocket, burning a hole through his pants.

The dogs were the fun part, because it was always a tossup with him, what he'd do with them. If they were friendly, licked his hand and treated him right, he'd lock them in the car and call the number that was on their tag, tell whoever answered that he'd "found" their pet, and how much was it worth to them to have it back in one piece, no questions asked? But if the dog snapped or bit at him, or if the owner gave him any shit when he called, then he did other things to the little barker, things that brought him pleasure when he was doing them but which filled him with guilt after he was done, usually the next morning when he woke up, hung over, piecing his actions together and wanting to puke when he remembered the vicious acts he'd performed.

But there was no guilt tonight, no shame inside him. He felt good and a little high. He'd have a few beers and if he didn't get lucky with the blonde, he just might go on over to Frank's and see how tough the guy was when he wasn't safe in his bed—probably tied to it—talking tough into a telephone. For some time now Anthony had felt that it was time to graduate from pets to people, see how much of a thrill there was in taking a person's life instead of a dog's or a cat's. Anthony wanted that experience, the way he knew his father had had it. He believed that it would make him a man.

The Placebo was packed, half the people watching the playoff games on the four wide-screen TVs, the other half dancing wildly on the hardwood floor that had been spray-painted with white lines and circles to look like a basketball court.

In the middle of the joint was a boxing ring, and the big spenders got to sit there, escorted right in by the waitresses, shown to tables that had reserved signs set down on the tablecloths. Anthony had never been allowed in there, though he'd tried to get through. One of the four bouncers would always stop him before he got past the first of the seven steps.

The big spenders could dance on the roof, too, from June 1st until the end of September, the roof was opened every year with a big ceremony that showed who was who for that season, which left the others, those who weren't picked to receive the blue ID roof passes, jealous and hurt. There was a ladder leading up there, one in here and one outside, both of them made of wrought iron, twisting, around and around, leading up, with handrails so that even if you were blitzed and fell you couldn't get hurt, couldn't sue anybody because the place had gone out of its way to ensure your safety. In the summer, when the roof was open to the big shots, the Placebo would hire an extra bouncer just to stand at the top of the outside ladder, to make sure that nobody got through who wasn't hip, who wasn't happening and cool.

The bouncers in this place didn't take a lot of shit from people. Already, in the two hours he'd been here, Anthony'd seen them throw out maybe six people, all of them young, none of them dressed well or with broads. He'd never seen a bouncer throw someone out who'd been sitting inside the ring, no matter how rowdy one of those yuppies got, and they could get pretty rowdy, thinking they were back in college and screaming, pulling off their shirts and pounding on their chests and sometimes even pouring beer on one another, rubbing it into each other's hair and laughing like hyenas on acid.

He wondered how it felt to sit up there, with the lesser humans dancing all around you, below you, like servants there for your pleasure.

He spotted the blonde at the bar, listening to some hairy-chested guy who had a heavy gold medallion hanging down from a chain into the middle of his chest, his shirt open about five buttons to show off his belly, which looked fat to Anthony. The guy had to be about forty, old enough to be the girl's father. He was about twenty years behind the times when it came to fashion. It wouldn't be a big challenge for Anthony, unless the guy was loaded with money.

Anthony fell in love with her as he walked toward her, with her long slender legs that the tight jeans couldn't hide the shape of, with her large breasts, with the way she held her head down and looked up at you, almost frightened as she sipped her drink through the straw, making her cheeks suck inward, erotically.

"Remember me?" Anthony said, and the girl looked at him, seemed happy to see him. He might be rescuing her from this boring old man with the gold chain and the money on the bar. She didn't look like someone who'd be impressed with money.

"Hi," she said, demurely, and looked embarrassed, stuck with two men there and too timid to tell the other one to go screw off.

The hairy ape said, "You need something, bud?"

Anthony took up a stance right in front of him, his beer bottle held low in one hand, by the neck, Anthony ready to use it if he had to. He dropped his cigarette to the ground, feeling the anger well up inside him, all the hatred of his lifetime compacted into this one second, focused on this one person. He stared at the ape, tried to make him feel it, to make him aware of the danger he was in but the idiot, he just gave Anthony a boozy, amused stare.

"I need you to get away from my date," Anthony said.

The girl looked shocked but caught herself, smiled enig-matically, and didn't say anything. The hairy ape grinned widely.

"You bring this woman here, did you?"

Was he making fun of Anthony?

"You ing-mak fun of me?" Shit! He was doing it with the syllables now, making an ass out of himself in front of the girl. He should have taken his medication, should have taken at least one pill before he'd left the house, but the doctor had told him that drinking while on the medication could send him into a psychotic state, so he hadn't.

"What'd you say?" The ape looked puzzled, then thought he'd figured Anthony out. "You a retard?" He turned to the girl, to Anthony's girl, grinning. "You come here with a *retard*? Well, you're leaving with a man."

The familiar buzzing was in his ears, the tunnel-hearing he'd get when an episode was about to commence. Anthony would not be able to hear anything, even if you were shouting in his ear, all he'd be able to hear was the high-pitched hum that filled his head until the thing passed, until he hurt someone or someone hurt him. It would calm him down, this sound, relax him, and sometimes a voice would speak to him, tell him what to do next.

It now told him that he'd win this one.

The ape was about Anthony's height but had to have him by fifty pounds, his shoulders were wide and meaty. He looked like one of the construction workers on the sites at one of the several jobs his father had gotten for him, the jobs he would always quit or get fired from.

Anthony was smiling broadly, going along with the joke until the buzzing told him what to do, until the voice seeped through the noise and into his consciousness. The jukebox might well not even be playing now, though he could see bodies gyrating around on the dance floor. He could see mouths open, talking and laughing, shouting, but not one sound penetrated through to him. The ape was saying something to him, smiling, and Anthony knew that it was bad news, that he was putting Anthony down, trying to impress the girl.

Before the man finished his sentence Anthony swung with the bottle and hit him, hard, on the side of his head, dropped the ape and the bottle at the same time and stepped smartly past him, lowered his ass onto the barstool next to the girl, the music beginning to penetrate, the laughter getting through to him now as the buzzing receded. Anthony stared straight ahead, at the multicolored stained mirror behind the back bar, hearing some shuffling behind him, some frightened voices speaking low.

He looked at the girl, who wasn't smiling now, who was staring at him in terror. Anthony knew just from looking at her that she wasn't for him, that she'd drop the dime if he stuck around. Knew, too, that he'd have to scare her, quick, and get the hell out while she was still in shock.

"You didn't see nothing," Anthony told her, "or I swear to

Christ I'll come back for you." He swung off the stool and almost tripped over the guy, made a big thing out of discovering him, of looking around in a bewildered fashion.

"What the hell is this? The guy have a stroke or something?" The bouncers were there now, looking down at the man, worried.

"Anthony, you have anything to do with this, goddamnit!"

"Me?" Anthony told the bouncer. "Hell no. What *I* could have with this to do?"

"You're trouble, and I don't care *who* your old man is."

Anthony stepped over the fallen ape, wishing he had the beer he'd spilled, was heading for the exits when he turned around, caught the girl's eye and lifted his finger, pointed it at her and used his thumb like a gun hammer to shoot her, once. She turned away from him, quickly, and faced the back bar.

Without thinking too much about any repercussions, Anthony walked out of the Placebo Lounge, angry and frustrated, filled with hate at the man for making him hit him and taking away his chance with the girl, hating the girl because as soon as Anthony had hit the guy she'd turned on him. Hadn't she known that Anthony had done it for her? That bitch.

He sat in his mother's year-old light gray Chevy in the full parking lot. He owned a fifteen-year-old Ford and had to beg his mother to let him drive her car. She'd tell him, "You've got your own car! You polish it twice a week! Why the hell you want to fuck up mine?" and he'd become incensed at the way she talked.

Anthony was growing angrier by the second, breathing heavily and glad that there was no one around, because he knew his tongue would be twisted, that he'd never be able to speak a full sentence right now. He stared up at the rooftop, at the class barrier through which he'd never pass, and he got even madder, filled with hatred toward those who dared to look down on him because he didn't have a job, didn't drive one of these fancy sleek cars like the ones right out there, parked all around him. Shit, he was driving his *mother's* car because he was ashamed of the piece of crap that was in his own name.

He let the anger flow through him, heard the tunnel wind begin to blow, and when he got fully mad he began to hear the buzzing sound, and the voice inside it told him exactly what to do.

At eleven that evening Babe parked his car at the edge of the Rich East running track in Park Forest, set the alarm and balanced the keys on the front tire, out of sight. He was in his shorts now, with his white sneakers on his feet, wearing only a dago T-shirt on top. It was still warm, although it felt like that could change at any minute; there was a faint smell of coolness in the air. His junior weatherman had told him it might get cold again before summer really came on.

He finished a cigarette while he stretched, crushed it beneath his toe, and began to run around the quarter-mile track, his mind wandering, the way it always did when he ran. He didn't wear a Walkman even though he could have used the distraction. The track was surrounded by a four-foot fence, and on three sides, there was a nine-foot fence a few yards beyond that. Still, if he listened to music, someone could sneak up on him and he would not know it until he felt that person's fist connect with his body. There was only an outside chance that that would ever happen, but it was not a chance he was willing to take.

He was a family man but one who enjoyed his solitude, a man who would sometimes make up excuses to take long rides alone, just to think, to be by himself to try and sort things out. The running now was a must, as he had to keep himself in shape. The camera was cruel, put weight on you, but he enjoyed running for its own pleasure, for the time alone, away from everyone.

He was a product of his experiences, of what he was, and there were times when it was confusing, how to act and when. Someone would say something to him that caused him fear and he'd want to strike out, to hurt them, to make them leave him alone. He hadn't done that in many years, but the thoughts never went away, the violent fantasies were always there and sometimes they would terrify him. When they came, when he was angry, he knew that he had to get off by himself until the anger worked itself out.

Kelly would tell him that his ideal mate was a mute and servile nineteenth-century Japanese woman who could cook, and he didn't argue with her, let her have her fun at his expense, although they were both aware that he was very much self-contained, that he didn't need a lot of social contact.

Kelly, though, Jesus Christ, he needed her, that was for sure. And Mike and Collin, too. Suddenly, though, because of that love, he had things to lose, and that made him uncomfortable. Life had taught him that whenever you had something to lose, there would be those looking to take it from you, any way they could. From money to dreams, nothing was sacred and nothing secure.

Babe ran, thinking about what he'd said to the kids in the auditorium earlier that night, thinking more about what he *should* have said.

He wanted to tell them about guilt, how it affected you. He knew men who didn't believe in the word, guys who killed coldly and went about their business. People like that were mutants, beyond hope, but there were a lot of crooks out there who were on the edge, on the fence. Who still had feelings no matter how hard they tried to bury them.

The bar brawl he'd been in when he was twenty had cost another young man his life, and it was true that Babe could not now remember what had started the argument.

What he could remember, however, was how he felt when he knew that he'd murdered someone. He saw it as murder, no matter what the courts called it. Manslaughter was a pretty word, but it was just a legal term. The guy he'd killed would be just as dead, no matter what Babe had been charged with.

He'd lie awake in his dorm at night in the County Jail, overcome with guilt. The emotion so strong that it even overwhelmed the terror he experienced in the jail's environment.

It was where he'd learned to act, had become a professional at his craft, because if the animals around him even got a hint of his fear, of his guilt, they would swarm around and eat him alive.

He'd slept on a mattress on the floor, surrounded by a couple of dozen other guys who always wanted what you had, no matter what that happened to be. You were a virgin? They'd want that, because if you were white and young you could make a lot of money for them if they could intimidate you into being a whore for their gang. You had family on the outside? They'd want them to mule in drugs or cash money, street clothes they could bribe a doctor to say they needed to wear for their mental health. Dignity and respect? You could let those go when you passed through the gates. In the first place, the guards made sure you had none of those things left, made it clear right away that you were nothing more than a number, an anonymous face among the thousands. Your individuality was stripped from you the second you got off the bus, and the jumpsuits and soft tennis shoes they made you wear enforced that concept without their ever having to say a word. If you had any left after indoctrination, any form of expression that was uniquely your own, it would be your downfall, set you apart from the other detainees and make you an object of derision. You had to play it tough, walk hard and never back down, and Babe had never been any good at that without first having a few drinks under his belt to give him courage.

He had lain on the floor of that filthy jail, swiping at the roaches, listening to the rats scurry across the floor, overcome with guilt because he'd killed a man and wasn't that against a commandment, wasn't that an unforgivable sin? That's what he'd been taught.

The day after Halloween had been the worst, his first All Souls' Day after the other man had died. That was the day when the spirits roamed the earth, seeking vengeance or salvation. He'd convinced himself that the man he'd killed would come for him, would seek him out and take his life, and he'd stayed up throughout the night, jumping at every sound, facing ten years in the pen and knowing that he couldn't hack it, that he didn't have what it took to make it in the joint for an entire decade without hanging himself from the first steam pipe he saw.

Nine months to the day after he'd entered the jail he'd walked into a courtroom, and had walked out a free man. His father had pulled the necessary strings. Although the old man hadn't had the clout to beat the case, he'd been able to get Babe sentenced to time served, the rest of the sentence suspended. Babe had left, free in the eyes of the law and man, uncertain as to how God would look at him.

The guilt had stayed with him, had never left. Years ago, he'd thought about the death all the time, about the killing. Would only be able to accept what he'd done when he'd been drunk. At those times, he could feel like a man, brag about what he'd done and people would leave him alone.

When he was sober, it was another story.

He'd wandered into a couple of AA meetings but all they ever wanted to talk about was God and honesty, and Babe was certain, convinced in his mind, that God had abandoned him. As for honesty, forget about it. Who was he supposed to be honest with? To whom was he supposed to tell his secrets? What if the person he chose got drunk, blabbed about him in bars, or worse, went to the cops? He often wondered how he'd survived, how he had gotten through those years.

He'd been living a middle-class existence for some time now, and the death had occurred almost twenty years ago. But it still came back to haunt him, in his dreams mostly but sometimes when he was awake, and at the oddest times. He'd come to terms with it, had learned to live with it without having to drink.

But he still didn't know how God felt about him.

There were so many things he could have said to those kids, if he could have only found the words. He worked every day with people who'd been trained properly, and not all of them were fools, looking down on him for his lack of education. They would use all the right words, all the words they'd learned at acting school, and it would seem foreign to him, somehow phony. What was motivation? Method? Someone was shooting at you, you looked scared or you were a goof, it was as simple as that. You ducked, you shot back if you had a piece, stuck your ass down somewhere safe and tried to get him before he got you. Did you need to dwell on your grandmother's death to dredge up such emotions? You kissed a girl for the first time, you got a little breathless when you broke away. It was the way it had been for him with all the girls he'd ever kissed, and if it worked that way in real life, wouldn't it look good on film?

It was the way he operated, how he played the scene, but it went deeper than that.

In January he'd done an interview with a woman from *TV Guide* and she'd been kind, had tried to draw him out of himself, get into his psyche. He'd been filming the pilot for this show and it had already been slotted, had been set for viewing on broadcast television, but nobody knew then how well it would be received, so the interview had run in February, well before *Street Babe* began to garner widespread attention, and now that interview was a classic, was quoted everywhere, and that made Babe happy, as she was one of the few journalists who'd gone out of her way to be nice to him, didn't look at him as a hunk of meat who was there to be made fun of.

She'd asked him what he tried to show on the screen, and it had come to him, popped right into his mind without prompting. "When I'm walking down the street," he'd told her, "no matter where I'm at, where the scene's set, I want to give you the impression just by looking at me that I know where the crap games are in that neighborhood, where the best spaghetti restaurant is located. I want you to know I'm capable, that I fit in, that I'm hip to all that I see and I know where all the bodies are buried."

She'd printed it, just like that without making fun of him, had gone on in detail about how he'd beaten the odds, about his devotion to his family. She'd written about his humility, how he seemed almost apologetic about his lack of formal training. She'd seen, too, that he'd learned what he had on the streets, and didn't mention his manslaughter conviction, which he'd appreciated.

Babe pounded on, moving at a slow jog. He usually did three twelve-minute miles every night, even when he was working, five if he felt strong. He could probably tighten that speed up some if he quit smoking, but hell, he'd given up everything else and at least he didn't throw up when he finished anymore, the way he used to when he'd first started jogging. Now at the end of the run he only gasped, waiting for the knives in his lungs to be withdrawn.

The things he did for his art.

On his fifth turn around the track he spotted headlights, saw the squad car making its rounds, flashing its spotlight into windows, into the school's recessed doors, making sure there were no vandals writing smut on the walls, keeping Park Forest safe and secure. The cop was probably bored out of his mind; this was a relatively peaceful town.

On the close turn he saw who was driving the squad car, and Babe smiled and shook his head. It was a man he had no biological relation to, but who was, nevertheless, his brother.

Anthony bought the six-pack and the five-gallon can of gas at the same place, filled Ma's car up with unleaded as long as he was there, knowing she'd be pissed if he didn't. Ma got pissed off real easy these days, and seeing as she'd already had one son go bad on her, forget all about what she'd done for him, he felt that it was the least that he could do.

He drove back to the Placebo Lounge and parked around back, left the car running with the front end pointed out, heading out of the alley, and got the can out of the trunk, ran with it toward the fire door which by law, he knew, would have to be open, so he'd have to be careful not to run into some young couple heading into the alley for some blow or to smoke a joint.

It would be a piece of cake.

He began to climb the ladder to the roof, hauling the can up with him, held awkwardly in one hand while he muscled his way to the top. He reached the roof and climbed over the little safety gate, walked lightly on his toes to the far edge of the roof. He set the can down for a second, Anthony breathing hard, his arm tired. He never knew that five gallons of gas could weigh so much. He caught his breath and went to work.

He leaned down and grabbed the can, squeezed the lever that popped the lid and dragged the can backward with him, spilling gas all over the roof, the liquid spreading out as it hit the tile dance floor. The roof was covered with dead leaves, dirt and debris that had accumulated over the winter, and the gas made little rivulets around them, was absorbed by them, which was cool. The leaves would make good kindling.

Anthony was smiling by the time he finished the job, smiling and sweating, the stink of gas all around him, filling the air. He left the can on the roof—good luck to the cops trying to get prints from *that*—and stepped over the gate, clambered down the circular staircase, his hip bumping the railing at every curve, then stood at the foot of the building, reaching for his lighter.

A Zippo was guaranteed to work in any amount of wind.

He snapped it open and took a second to pull out the wick as far as it would reach, then flipped the wheel, pulled his head back as the four-inch lick of flame attacked the night. Anthony stepped back, reached far behind him and let go with all his might, using a lot more strength than he'd need to get the thing to the roof of a two-story building, and he bounced back on his heels after he threw, wanting to see the show.

He was unprepared for the enormity of the explosion.

Anthony had been expecting a small *poof* and then maybe the sight of flames slowly growing as they were fueled by the warm night air. Instead, there was a blinding flash and the flames leaped into the air along with a tremendous *whoosh* that tore through the night.

Anthony was running, was in his car and turning out onto Western Avenue before the first screams howled out of the night-club and into the darkness, and was a block away before the roof collapsed, trapping four young swingers who'd been caught on the stairs of the boxing ring, trying to escape.

Sergeant Tim Raglan fast-walked alongside Babe as Babe ran his heart out, the goof, dressed in his summer uniform but carrying about thirty pounds of stuff on his body, the gun, flashlight, mace, portable radio crackling static and the sound of a dispatcher's voice, Tim laden down but gliding along effortlessly and speaking in a normal tone as Babe huffed and puffed, shooting hateful glances at his best friend.

"Surprised to see you out here, Babe, after the *Trib* told the whole world that you're out here every night, running."

"Haven't read it yet, any of that stuff. Besides, you see any crowds gathering around?"

"Saw *Street Babe*, Babe," Tim said.

"Yeah? You and half the country, from what I hear." Babe didn't tell him that he himself hadn't been able to watch the show, even though Kelly had.

Tim speeded up, got in front of him. Did he think this was funny? Walking faster than Babe was running, now turning around and walking backward, speaking to Babe with just a hint of a smile on his face.

Babe glowered at him, but didn't say anything. It would only encourage Tim to play the fool more convincingly, spur him on to greater outrages.

"I got to tell you, Babe, you were great. It was like looking at a total stranger on the screen. And the story line, it was better than *Twin Peaks* used to be."

"I get my way," Babe said, "and this show will make *Twin Peaks* look like *Rebecca of Sunnybrook Farm*." He grunted. "Should make Edna Rose real happy."

"Hear from her again?" Tim's tone was guarded, casual, but Babe could see past it, to the cop interest there. Tim didn't take a lot of things casually.

" 'I cannot wait for until we be together at last, my dayling, as God intendeded.' "

"Want me to turn the letter over to the Cal City cops?"

"Let's just let it go, Tim. I've been hearing from her for a few years now, and if she was gonna do anything stupid she would have done it by now."

"How'd it go at the school?" Typical cop, changing gears on you in the middle of a conversation.

Babe said, "The place was jam-packed. Last year, I drew maybe twenty kids. Tonight, their parents were with them, all wanting autographs and wanting to pose with me for pictures, all wanting to know if I signed for the regular season."

"Want to meet The Next Big Thing."

"Would you for Christ's sake at least pre*tend* I'm not that easy to lap?"

"Quit smoking. It'll cut your time in half." Tim's shoulder radio squawked; he had a call. Babe watched him, his friend speaking into the little radio, putting his mouth right onto the thing. Tim disconnected and nodded. "I got a call."

"I take the vitamins, Tim, the smoker-packs and the beta carotene, the C."

"Oh, please, Babe, don't give me that bullshit." Tim hated to hear that stuff. His mother had died of lung cancer and his mission in life was to get Babe to give up the weeds, which Babe acknowledged and was grateful for, but sometimes, the man could get out of hand, take things overboard.

Like now, Tim turning and walking fast, heading out for his call, really moving in his leather street shoes, fading rapidly from sight as he power-walked away from Babe, arms swinging. . . .

Babe yelled at his back, "Back on midnights, are you? Congratulations, you son of a bitch!" Tim hated midnights, passionately, but didn't rise to the bait.

Tim said, "Only thirty-nine to go, Babe, and I'm off tomorrow and the next night," his voice receding as he pulled further and further away from his friend, long legs striding, muscular arms pumping.

Babe said, "You prick," at Tim's back, but not loud enough for the man to hear him; his first night back on midnights, you never knew how Tim would take to sarcasm.

Tim, who had a sixth-degree black belt in karate but who never mentioned it to anybody, who played it down when the topic came up in conversation. He wasn't the type who felt the need to impress people with his accomplishments; if anything, he sometimes went too far to gloss them over and play them down.

The same way Babe did. They had a lot more in common than their desire to work out together, than their agreeable personalities.

Tim didn't head out on the call right away. He watched Babe for a minute, smiled as his pal slogged around the track, slowly, Babe speeding it up when he hit the turn where Tim was standing, ignoring him, acting as if he wasn't working harder to impress him.

"You ever get done, give me a call from the car phone, I'll have a cup of coffee at 7-Eleven and watch you gasp down your Gatorade, celebrate the end of your run with a damn cigarette."

Babe waved his hand at him, nodded his head. He was on his last few laps and was saving his wind. As he passed, Tim shouted at his back, "You gonna do the series, or what?"

"They're talking about it," barely audible, Babe hurting for wind now. Tim walked away and got back in his squad car, the night supervisor and in charge of an eleven-person shift, pretty busy but he'd never be too busy for Babe.

"Talking about it." Tim shook his head as he put the squad in gear and continued his rounds around the high school. He wasn't smiling. He knew that if Babe said they were talking about it, that what they were really talking about was the way to screw Babe around all over again, and that wasn't something that Tim was going to allow if he could help it.

6

abe was indeed the topic of conversation in the bar, at the Polo Lounge of the Beverly Hills Hotel, where the producer, the agent, and the moneyman behind *Street Babe* had gone to discuss the ungrateful son of a bitch after their regular Monday night dinner in the hotel dining room, meeting there because Matteos was closed on Mondays.

Jerome Spinell was catching most of the heat, seeing as he'd promised that he could deliver the kid, and now the bastard was backing out on his deal, on his *word*. As if that wasn't bad enough in itself, Jerome had been forced to sit through a dinner and was now in a bar with these two old farts when he had tickets to tonight's Lakers playoff game at the Great Western Forum. Which was just as well; he never got to sit where you could see shit, anyway.

Jerome sat in the deep green leather-covered chair, sheepishly, sipping a Scotch and shaking his head as the powerhouse right next to him, his partner Maury Ackerman, talked. Jerome listened, as did Milland Grand, the HAA agent who represented the entire *Street Babe* talent pool, except for Babe Hill, who didn't have an agent.

Which was Jerome's fault. The other two men were mad at him because of this, thought that if Jerome was as good a friend with Babe Hill as he said he was then Babe would have signed with HAA. Which he hadn't done, and steadfastly refused to do. All because Babe lived in his own hometown and Jerome had tried to help him out, give him his break.

He looked at Maury, seventy years old and fat as a cow, with tits bulging out of the front of his Hawaiian shirt, his hair combed back in finger curls, dyed black except around the ears, where he let the gray show, like he was fooling somebody. Nobody ever said anything, though. Jerome had once seen Milton Berle come over to Maury's table to say hello, and Maury hadn't even stood up to shake Berle's hand. Now *that* was power.

Maury had one of his Cuban cigars fired up and was filling the air around the table with putrid smoke. Jerome fired up one of his own cigarettes, a Lark, Jerome trying to cut down now after twenty-five years of smoking Camels. Going to a gym for a steam every day, walking on the treadmill he'd had installed in his Valley house. He called it working out but it wasn't doing a lot of good, he was losing the battle of the bulge, himself.

Jerome was angry. Resentful and hurt. How could you be in trouble when the pilot you'd put together—produced and acted in—had been watched by one of the largest audiences in television history? Jerome didn't get it, why they were blaming him. He was of the opinion that they should be praising him for the brilliant concept, for coming up with the idea of *Street Babe*. He and Maury were the executive producers of the show, he'd busted his ass to get it going, to get it on the air, and it had been a huge numbers success, and twenty-four hours after its initial airing he was sitting here, half-drunk, getting chewed out, his veal scallopini going sour in his stomach while the Lakers were playing basketball. He'd bet that Jack Nicholson never had to put up with this kind of bullshit.

" 'Scuse me," Jerome said, and rose from the table. "I'll be right back." Maury grabbed his wrist and held him there, squeezed until Jerome sat down.

"You ain't fooling nobody with your weak kidney story anymore, Jerome, so just stay where you are. I swear to Christ, if I find out you're back on that cocaine, I'll blow off the entire thing, the series, everything. You'll be through in LA."

"*What* cocaine!" Jerome looked over at Milland Grand, but was getting no sympathy there. Grand was staring at him blankly. Man looked like a skinny lizard old retard of a human, which served him well with producers and all the other production executives. By the time they realized how tough he was, how smart, it was usually too late for them, Milland would have them by the balls.

"I don't know where you got this cocaine bullshit from," Jerome was trying for outrage and charm at the same time, showing his respect for Maury but letting him know that he wasn't some sissy about to back down and roll over, show his ass to everyone because the great Maury Ackerman had spoken. "I don't mess around with that bullshit."

"Since when?"

"Hey!" Jerome had ignored Maury, was now shouting at the passing waiter. "Where's the fucking drinks I ordered?"

The waiter looked over his drink tray, his eyes wide. "You never ordered—"

"The fuck I didn't! Get another round over here, right now, Hector." The waiter scurried off, his head down. His name tag read Alfredo. Other people in the crowded bar were staring at him now, silently chastising his rude, low-class behavior. Well, he had a show aired last night that would be in the top five, easy, would probably top the Nielsen's for the week, maybe be number one, from the numbers he was getting in. He didn't have to take any shit from anyone, let alone some little fag spic waiter. Jerome turned back to the table, where Maury and Milland were patiently waiting for him to calm down. Neither man said anything about Jerome's insulting of the waiter, because neither man cared about it. There was no profit in defending help.

"So," Jerome said, "where was I?"

"*You* weren't anywhere," Maury said. "*Me, I* was telling Milland that this cocksucker, this Hill, still ain't signed with nobody for nothing." Maury sat back and puffed a cloud of smoke Jerome's way. "Now, why is that, Jerome?"

Jerome was flustered, at a loss for words. His charm and good looks and mob connections had gotten him parts in four different TV series, two of which had lasted more than the three years that was needed for a syndication deal. One of them was shown on SuperStation 8 every night of the week, showing a young, studly Jerome to the world, the second lead in a hospital series. The second was shown on TBS twice a week, Jerome the fourth lead in a detective series set in Detroit. His main job on that show was to look at the star in a tough manner, while the actor playing the detective sergeant would give him orders, then say, sternly, "You got it, Michael," scurrying out of camera range, a man in a hurry. His face was syndicated in ninety-one countries, and this fat Jew piece of shit was talking down to him?

Jerome felt the urge to punch Maury out, to pull an Eddie Murphy and kick some ass, but he didn't for two reasons, the first being that right now he needed these guys, especially Ackerman. The town wasn't lining up offering work to a forty-eight-year-old, balding TV actor who was rumored to have a drinking and drug problem. Who were they to talk about his morality? The stories he could tell, shit, would some day, too, as soon as this old slob Milland got him a book deal . . .

The second reason being that he wasn't rich enough to have private bodyguards with him to pull him out of the violent jams he started, like Eddie Murphy was. But maybe he would be soon.

Jerome said, "I talked to this kid, I told him, 'Look, Babe, are we doing it for you or not? Did we go back on our word one time? Didn't we put an entire show around your ass, even use your name for the title? Aren't we brothers?' He says to me, 'Brothers? We ain't even *cousins*, Jerome.' What're you gonna do? I'm busting my ass trying to make this kid a star and he's fighting me every inch of the way."

Milland Grand said, "He's not easy, this Hill. I sat him down, spoke to him about it not a month ago. You know why he didn't sign with me? He says he doesn't like the way I talk to waitresses. I told him he could make three million this year if he plays his cards right, signs with HAA, and he tells me that sounds good, but by July he'll have a million and a half in his pocket and we'll have him running out for cigarettes and coffee, the way we treat people."

"The way we treat people? The way we fucking *treat* people? Who does this bastard think he *is*?" Maury was almost shouting, drawing more stares than Jerome's outburst with the waiter, which made Jerome feel good. The heat was off him and back where it belonged. He had to make sure he kept it there.

He leaned into the table, put his elbows on it and shook his head, speaking in a malevolent whisper directly into Maury's chest.

"Maury, I swear to Christ, he's a psycho. We're out there on location, he's meeting with the *writer*, Maury, every night. Not watching the dailies, not discussing anything with me or the other actors or the director, he's talking to the goddamn *writer*!"

"Who's this guy think he is, De Niro?"

"Maury, it's typical. We gave him his break, we signed him for the pilot. He fired that *scudatz* agent he had when he found out the faggot was stealing from him, but rather than sign with Milland, here, he gets a lawyer. Has the lawyer call me, rather than picking up the phone and telling me himself. This bitch shyster—she gotta be a dyke—she says Babe won't do a series unless he gets certain guarantees, in writing, that'll—here's exactly how she said it— 'ensure the integrity of the series and his character.' "

"Integrity?" Maury said, and looked at Milland, who shrugged.

"Artists . . ." Said wistfully, Milland explaining all the world's problems away with a single word.

"Call him up, find out how much he wants."

"I spoke to the lawyer today." Milland shrugged again. "She says it's not a question of money."

"Then what's his problem, for Christ's sake?"

"Integrity."

"All right, that's it." Maury smashed his cigar out in the ashtray, looked up angrily at the waiter, Alfredo, who was setting their new drinks down, removing their old glasses, "I ain't done with that, asshole," Maury said to him, and the waiter quickly placed the glass back down on the table, then withdrew.

"Tell you what you do. Milland, you represent the cream of the crop out here, every serious actor in the business, right?"

"Most of them."

"Get somebody else to play Street Babe in the series. I don't care who, as long as it's somebody we can control."

Milland disgustedly shook his head and waved his hand dismissively. "I wish it was that simple. The entire thing was created around Hill, we even used his nickname in the pilot, named the series after him. His Q rating went through the roof after last night. The network won't buy a show without him, Maury, he *is* Street Babe."

"So where are we now, what do we do, just blow it off?"

"If we can get him to agree to any terms, I can make a deal tomorrow for twenty-two episodes. You'll make, approximately, seven million dollars as exec producers and because you own the show, counting syndication fees. Fuck the three years for syndication, this show's already a cult hit, it'll go to USA or Lifetime right now for real money. And if it's a hit we can get a share of the ad money out of the network for the next season. The third season, you can double that."

"And it got to be with this Hill cocksucker?"

"Maury, there's no other way."

"All right then." Maury drained the glass in front of him and shouted for a waiter to get over there and take the useless thing away, the table was too crowded, for Christ's sake, then turned to Jerome Spinell.

"He's your responsibility, Jerome. You brought him in, you signed him for the pilot. You worked with him for three weeks, you told us you had him in your palm. Now you get him to agree to the series, I don't care how."

It was back on him all of a sudden. Jerome said, "Maury, I been trying to call him all day. He doesn't even want to listen to the Nielsens we brought in. I spoke to him for five minutes this morning and when I tried to call back later he's got his *machine* turned on, like I'm supposed to leave messages for him so he can not return them. The guy thinks he's Robert Redford all of a sudden." He turned to Milland, trying not to beg but the pleading was in his voice, in his body language.

"Milland, listen to me, can you get a guaranteed seven hours without Hill? I can do it, I can be Street Babe, the role will put me back on top."

"Jerome," Milland said, "you never been higher than the middle in your entire career."

"Hey . . ."

"That wasn't an insult, only the truth." Milland lowered his voice, about to impart more truth Jerome's way, diplomatic enough to know that he couldn't do it in front of the entire world.

He said, "You're getting old, and your face is too tight from all the plastic surgery. You're twenty pounds too heavy, and you got problems with the booze, the coke. Your wig even looks cheap these days. Why can't you go to William Shatner's guy, why you got to wear things look like dead animals on your head? You think people haven't noticed your deterioration? This is a small town, everyone knows everything about everybody. I go to the network and ask for seven weeks with you as the lead, they'll laugh me out of the office. No-body's laughed at me in forty years in this business, and I'm not going to let it start now. *Street Babe* or no *Street Babe*, you have to under-stand, Jerome, you play a tavern owner on that show. It's not much of a stretch for you or anyone else; we could drag a guy out of central casting for that part. The show's Hill's, and we need him on our side.

"Here's the deal, Jerome, like it or not.

"That kid Hill is hot. The phones at the network been ringing off the hook all day, women wanting to know his address, his phone number, if he got a fan club. When the mail comes in he'll know about it, that he's a star in the womb, about to be born. You brought him into this deal, and now you've got to get him to sign for the series before he finds out how good he is. If you can't, well, Jerome, all I can say is, you'd better be looking around for another agent, because I wouldn't be able to forgive a client of mine who cost me seven figures in commissions because he couldn't deliver what he said he'd deliver."

"That goes double for me," Maury said. "I let you be a partner in this deal because some serious people told me you needed a break. I put up two mill for the production company and put your name on the fucking thing. I let you come in and work with me, and now your bullshit is gonna cost me millions? Jerome, you get this kid signed, for the twenty-two hours, minimum, or I swear to Christ, before I'm done with you you'll be wearing a little maroon waist-coat, serving drinks in this fucking joint, listening to hotshot TV actors call you names."

"Maury, Milland, what can I do?" Jerome couldn't help him-self. He was begging now, pleading for his career, maybe even his life, knowing who Maury was connected to. "The guy ain't answer-ing his *phone*, Maury."

Maury signaled for the check, stared hard at Jerome, not dig-ging into his pocket for any money, either. "You ever hear of planes, Jerome?" Maury rose from the table, and so did Milland. "You better get your ass on one, right now, tonight, before this punk finds out he's popular. You can get the check, first." Together, the two Hollywood powerhouses walked away from him, and Jerome stared after them, his mouth open, until he noticed the waiter standing there beside him, check extended.

"Fuck *you* want, Juan? *I* didn't call for the goddamn check."

"But Mr. Ackerman, he—"

"Ah, gimme the goddamn thing." Jerome looked at the bill, reached into his pocket, slammed two twenties down on top of the check as if the cash didn't matter to him.

"Keep the change," Jerome said, and Alfredo was grateful.

"*Thank* you, sir," he said.

"Hey, Ramone," Jerome said, turning on the charm now that there wasn't anyone there to impress with the tough guy pose, emotionally insecure to the point where he wanted everyone to be his friend, "you hear how the Lakers made out this evening, or what?"

The Lakers were losing. Winning the game, but not covering the eleven-point spread.

Johnny Hilliard was staring intently at the nineteen-inch screen hanging in the corner of the nearly dead East Side bar, shaking his head from time to time. He'd finish his drink during every commercial and time out then order another one, let it sit there with the ice melting in the twelve-year-old Scotch whiskey while he watched his money go down the tubes.

"Lakers called a twenty-second time out, Johnny, you want another one?" The bartender. There was a time in his life when bartenders called him Mr. Hilliard, but that time was past; nobody called him Mr. anymore. A lot of other things, they called him, but never Mr. anymore.

"Fill it up and have one yourself," Johnny said.

He had a poker face. No one would ever be able to tell what he was thinking by looking at him, what was on his mind or how many problems he had. His ex-wife Margie used to eat it up, watching him in court, Johnny sitting at the defense table in expensive suits and staring at the jury or at the witnesses testifying against him. She'd bring him a restaurant lunch, to his detention cage in the back of the federal courts building, and tell him he looked inscrutable, smiling at him, the woman loving to play Virginia Hill to his Bugsy Siegel. The only problem was, every time he'd go to jail she'd wind up banging one of his buddies. Talk about problems? He'd had four kids with that woman, and wasn't sure that he was the father of two of them. Babe, though, of him there could be no doubt. Looking at that boy was like looking at a photograph of himself when he was younger.

Johnny sat there, watching the bartender pour his drink, not letting the bartender or the other three men in the bar see into him, know by his expression that he had troubles.

Tonight, he had a load of them.

The Bulls had lost the night before, the Lakers were losing tonight, and the goddamn San Antonio Spurs had already won, and he'd booked the action on all three games for a bunch of guys who'd bet serious money and expected to get paid on Wednesday, the same day and the same way that they paid up when they lost.

Seven grand down in two days. He'd scored ten off Moca, but he owed that to Parker, who'd already bitched to Landini because he hadn't been paid *last* fucking Wednesday. He wasn't feeling so inscrutable right now.

"No way the Lakers can pull this one out, Johnny."

"Seven seconds left and winning by three? I don't think they can cover the spread, no, I don't."

"You have them?"

"No."

"Oh," the bartender said, and hurried down the bar. Which was a good thing, it showed he still knew how to respect a man with a reputation like Johnny's, knew that he was still dangerous. A lion who'd been declawed but who still had teeth.

His problem was, he'd start getting ahead, then he'd wind up in a jackpot, score some time and wind up at square one when he got out. Usually a year or two here or there for interstate gambling, once a state rap for burglary, which he'd never do again, hell, the state joints were concentration camps, for niggers, not for serious men like himself.

He'd been arrested six times for murder and he'd done them all and plenty more, favors for the big boys who knew how to pull strings and who helped him down the road, and he was proud of the fact that he'd never been convicted for any of them.

When Johnny Hilliard killed them, they stayed dead, and dead men can't come back to haunt you, to sit in an oak chair and point the finger at you in a court of law.

The last time he'd been busted, though, it had broken his goddamn back.

He'd been moving a few kilos of heroin as a favor for a very heavily connected guy he knew, thirty-three keys with a grand apiece in it for him on payment. What nobody knew was that the buyer who'd set it all up had been working for the government, and even Johnny, with his years of experience with the government and its various police agencies, hadn't been good enough to smell him out. Fifteen years they'd given him, the maximum for a first-time drug pinch, and due to violent behavior on the inside he'd had to serve twelve, had been out two and now he was sixty-one years old and broke, getting further into the hole every time some nigger put his hands on a basketball, shit, killing his friends to try and make things right.

The worst part was that it didn't have to be this way, should not be this way at all. He had a kid who was rich and famous, a movie star who'd been in a TV show just last night, and everyone knew what kind of money those guys made, the head actor in the Sunday Night Movie of the Week. Had to get a million dollars for a shot like that. And if they turned it into a series, he'd make ten million.

The bartender had come over to grab the remote and change the channel, put on an old movie that Johnny could remember seeing at the theater when it was new. Now it looked dated, black and white, Clark Gable a joke as an actor. Next to Johnny's kid, Gable couldn't act his way out of a paper bag. So you'd think he'd help his father? Bullshit, he would. All over some stupid problems from a couple years back, from some harsh words spoken when Johnny was drunk on prison hootch.

They'd shot that movie right down the road in Hegewisch, and had he even been allowed on the set? He'd tried to get on, to see his kid, and the security guards wouldn't even let him near the trailers. He'd written messages but they'd never been answered. All this from a kid who might still be doing time if it hadn't been for Johnny pushing his weight around, getting a conviction carried for him. He'd turned a ten-year sentence into what had amounted to probation, and how did the kid pay him back? Just look at how.

"You see *Street Babe* last night?" he asked the bartender, and the guy looked at him funny.

"Watched it right here, with you and your little brown friends, Johnny."

"That's right." Johnny nodded, shook his head. He'd been

drinking a lot lately. Smoking too much, too. Eating like a pig and not taking care of himself, his gut was so far out there he looked like a pregnant woman. Still had more hair than this bartender, though, and he had to be thirty years older than the punk.

"You see the stuff he got from me, that he used in that movie? Holds the cigarette the same way, walks like me."

"Looks like you, too, Johnny, except that he's younger and bigger."

"Like hell, I'm better looking. Besides, Marciano won the title at one-eighty-five. In my day, they weren't growing them as big as they do now."

The bartender laughed, accepted another drink when Johnny offered it to him. Poured one for the both of them and took Johnny's money before he came back to drink it.

"*Salud,*" the kid said, and Johnny said, "*Jendann.*" They drank, Johnny enjoying, as always, the slow warmth that spread through him from the gut glowing outward, into his fingers, tingling his scalp. God, he liked to drink.

"You're sure proud of that kid of yours, aren't you, Johnny."

"Shit, why shouldn't I be," Johnny said. "He's a chip off the old block, ain't he? Loves his old man, too, you better believe we're close." He finished his drink in one long pull, then grabbed his change off the bar, swung off the stool and pointed his thumb at his drink. He'd have one more then head home, which was just across the street, above a meat store. First, though, he had to make a phone call.

As he walked to the back of the ginmill he didn't notice the puzzled look the bartender gave him, didn't hear him when the bartender leaned over toward one of the rummies in the joint and said, "Kid loves him? You ever see Babe Hill in here? Besides, he loved his old man so much, why the fuck he change his name?" The bartender chuckled and poured the old guy a shot of red wine, knocked on the bar twice and said, "That's with me," doing it not because he was a nice guy but because he had a few drinks under his belt and had just shot off his mouth about a guy who was supposed to at one time have been one bad motherfucker. Buying this shithead a drink would guarantee his silence; the bartender wasn't a gambling man, but he believed in hedging his bets.

Edna looked at herself in the mirror, turning left, then right, her lower lip between her teeth, studying herself with what she hoped was objectivity. How had she let herself go this far?

The dress she'd bought was flowery and billowed, yards of loose fabric that was supposed to cover sins. She'd seen heavy women wearing that type of dress and it had made them look regal and proud. On her, though, the fabric just sort of hung, flatly. It bulged at her hips and belly, and even though she'd bought a pushup bra there was no hiding the fact that her stomach had a lot more inches around than her chest did. Even with the new pushup bra she had bought, her breasts sagged. She'd turn sideways and check out her backside then close her eyes and shake her head, disgusted at the way her butt hung down. She'd bet that naked it looked all pimply and saggy, pitted. Well, she'd just have to make love to Babe with the lights off for the first few months, until she could whip herself back into shape.

She had no doubt that she could do that, lose the weight and firm up her body. Now that she had a reason for doing so. And besides, she'd bet that Babe wouldn't even notice that she outweighed him. Her love for him was so great, so overwhelming, that it would consume them both in its passion. And even if he did notice, even if he was a little hesitant about her weight, her blemishes, he'd soon forget all about it when he learned what she was willing to do for him.

The little shit at the dress shop, Bobby, he'd noticed the extra weight, though. Had made fun of her, smiling at the other workers when he thought she wasn't looking. "Going somewhere, Edna, got a hot date?" he'd asked, and Edna knew he was trying to make her into a joke, but she had other things to do and could not afford to get into trouble by causing a scene in the store. She'd said, "That's for me to know and for you to find out." Zinged him good with that one. He'd even had to leave the room. Bobby had run into the back room and she hadn't seen *him* again. The little idiot. If he only knew what she would do for her man, for a man who could win her love, he'd come begging for it, sniffing around like a dog that had its nose open. He'd be at her house every day if that little boy had even the slightest inkling of what she'd do for her man.

Which was anything. Anything in the whole, entire world that he wanted her to do.

With her Daddy it had at first been a matter of need, he'd told her that, would come into her room at night back then when she was little and tell her straight out that his poor wife was crippled, but God never slammed a door in your face without opening a window. That He'd blessed Reverend Rose with a daughter who could fulfill his earthly needs even as He'd taken all the joy out of the marriage. His hands would begin to trace Edna's belly, her backside, and she'd whimper and he'd shush her, tell Edna that everything was going to be all right, that she was just going to love it.

But he would always get done and then start crying, call her names and pull at his hair and slap himself in the face, cursing what he'd done.

It had been her fault, she'd made him unhappy. So Edna had gone out of her way to make sure that her Daddy was never unhappy with her again, and it got to the point where he wasn't. Where the crying stopped and Daddy would lie there later, holding her, and tell her that their love was special, that it was their family secret and nobody could ever find out about it. He would go back into his own room at daybreak and she'd hear him sometimes fighting with Mama and she'd smile. Mama knew who he loved most, and it wasn't her.

Later, with Arthur, Edna had improved on the techniques Daddy had liked so much, had made Arthur scream with desire and lust and she'd look up at him, Edna down there between his legs, and she'd smile, and bite him a little and he'd loved it. All Arthur had ever had to do was to tell her that he'd always wanted to try something and that would be it, Edna would be all ears, would eagerly submit to any of his demands, no matter what it was or how it made her feel later, after he'd gone home.

With Babe it would be the same thing. She'd *make* him love her, one way or another.

Edna applied lipstick, and decided that it made her look a little better, but not much.

uld see vapor clouds rising from their mouths and noses. Tim
anked God that it wasn't hot yet, a situation like this could get out
f hand in the summertime.

Tim put his hat on and stuck his baton into his belt, got out of
he car with authority and walked through the crowd of black faces.
At the edge of the crowd was an overweight black woman, being
restrained by a couple of men, but they couldn't stop her mouth.
She was cursing the officers, screaming shrilly, as if she were at a
funeral down home in Mississippi. A satanic funeral, though, where
profanity was offered up instead of prayers. She stopped screaming
long enough to spit at Tim as he passed them, and he looked at her
briefly but kept walking toward the TAC team.

"What's up?"

The first cop's name was Dugan, and he turned to Tim, scared.

"Got this guy cold, crack in his stockings."

"What's with the crowd?"

Mallory responded, talking over his shoulder as he shackled
the suspect's hands.

"Guy got tough with us and we had to drag him out of the
apartment. His old lady's over there, the one with the big mouth. I
don't think we've got trouble, though, Tim. Nobody else is doing
anything. They're just watching, man. I hope."

Tim turned and looked again, at the woman now calling him
names.

"You ain't nothing but a *pussy!*" She lisped the word, it came
out *puthy*. The woman turned to the struggling men holding her,
pulling one fat arm free. "Let go of me, you rotten cocksuckers!"
Tim turned to the TAC guys, and he spoke in a whisper, quickly.

"Get him out of here."

The woman had freed herself now, was stalking toward the car,
her hands balled into fists.

"Let my man go, he ain't done nothin'!" Playing for the crowd.
Tim hoped they were smarter than she was.

"You'll have to step back, ma'am, your husband's under arrest."

"They done *planted* that shit on him, I seen them do it when he
wouldn't bow and scrapes for they *asses!*" She was in Tim's face now,
spraying spit on his uniform blouse. Her huge breasts rubbed
against Tim's belly. "You *pigs* do us this way all the time!"

She'd taken a shower then a tub bath, then g[...]   c[...]
when she came home she took another bath, a hot [...]   th[...]
she'd made by pouring some of the shampoo und[...]   o[...]
water. She'd cleaned herself inside and out, and afte[...]
even sprayed some strawberry-smelling stuff she'd [...]
drugstore up inside her. She'd put on deodorant and[...]
had gotten dressed, and even with all the time and [...]
spent she knew that she still looked terrible.

It was hard for her to not cry, and she made hers[...]
straight face, only allowed herself a few whimpers and sni[...]
herself that if she cried she would destroy the makeup [...]
taken so long to apply. Edna turned away from the mirror an[...]
began to undress. Tonight was only a dress rehearsal. To[...]
night would be showtime.

Edna undressed and carefully hung her new clothin[...]
hangers. She went into the bathroom and ran another tub, [...]
believing that hot water would melt the pounds off her body. [...]
had she let herself get so fat, become so ugly?

In the tub, naked, her eyes closed so she wouldn't have to s[...]
the rolls of fat spreading under the water, Edna began to cry. Softl[...]
at first, the tears rolling down her cheeks silently, but then she let
them flow as the waves of self-pity rolled over her. She sobbed and
screamed and slapped at the water with her fists and after a time she
began to get tired and believed that she could sleep.

The call for a supervisor came from the department's two TAC cops
who'd taken a call that a drug deal was going down over at the co-
ops. A section of the village was all row apartments, duplexes that
were rented out or cooperatively owned or condos, built right after
the war as affordable housing for the returning soldiers. As the
soldiers grew older and moved into the homes that were built in
the village, the poorer people escaping the city swarmed into the
apartments. A fourth of the calls that came into the department
concerned some problems in the buildings these days.

Tim pulled to the curb and right away knew there was a problem. A crowd had gathered around the TAC guys, who had a suspect
laid over the hood of the unmarked car. The crowd was mostly in
night clothing, with light jackets thrown over their shoulders. He

She was trying to work up the crowd, but it didn't seem to be working. No one else was shouting at them, in fact, they seemed bemused.

Thank God for small blessings.

The TAC guys had the suspect almost to the car door, were opening it for him when he turned and screamed to his woman.

"They's gonna hurt me, baby, they gonna kick my ass in the station!" Dugan pushed him into the back seat hard and Tim winced as the crowd gasped, then he turned quickly to the woman, who screeched at the sight of the brutality.

There was only one way to defuse this now, and that was to take direct control of the situation.

Tim grasped her arm firmly above the elbow and began to walk her away from the scene.

"Come along now, ma'am, you can come with me if you want. I'll take you to the station and you can sit in the room with him while he's being processed, make sure that your husband's safe. Nobody's gonna touch him, I give you my word on that." Tim spoke softly but firmly, and he heard the TAC car start up behind him. The crowd was murmuring now, loud voices gaining courage.

"Let *go* of me, motherfucker!" The woman pulled her arm free and slapped Tim with the back of her hand. Chest heaving, face defiant, she put her hands on her hips. "You wife-beating, grubby, pussy motherfucker, you don't *never* touch me, you got that, white boy?"

"That's it, you're under arrest."

"What for?" The woman was backing away now, no longer tough but scared.

"Obstructing justice and assaulting an officer. The second one's a felony." Tim grabbed her and she began to fight.

"Get the camera, somebody get the camera!"

Tim pushed her against his squad car and leaned into her, his front to her back, as he grabbed the cuffs from his belt.

"I'm hittin' the lottery here, motherfucker, gonna make a million dollars off your white ass now!" Tim pushed into her harder, grabbed her right arm and pulled it behind her, snapped the cuff around her wrist.

"He trying to fuck my asshole! They's *witnesses* to this!"

From an upstairs window came a drunken shout. "I got a camcorder on your ass, motherfucker."

Tim didn't look up. He snapped the cuff on her other wrist and stepped away from the woman, who never stopped shouting, cursing Tim's dead mother, accusing him of having sex with her. Calmly, Tim opened the back door of the squad and as he tried to put her in the back seat she kicked at him, aiming at his groin, blessedly missing. Her shoe hit his knee and Tim buckled a bit but pushed her into the back seat and slammed the door before reaching down to rub it.

Behind him, there was a loud burst of collective derisive laughter.

His job in life was to serve and protect them, these same people who laughed at his suffering. And he'd do it, too, and be grateful that they weren't now attacking, coming to protect the oppressed sister.

Tim got behind the wheel and pulled out of there before the crowd changed its mind, the woman now giggling behind him, unafraid. She'd been this route before. Tim hoped that she had a long enough record that even a Cook County judge would send her away for a time.

"You made me a rich bitch tonight, motherfucker, it's all on film."

"We've never lost a lawsuit yet."

"You lose this one, honky, I got me some *wit*nesses."

"And you're going to the county for a few days. I've got witnesses that you attacked me."

"I can't wait till you try to fingerprint me, you pussy. I won't miss your dick next time."

"You'll have an hour or so to cool down, lady. I'll sit you in a cell and let you think about it for a while."

"Scared, motherfucker?"

"Having coffee with a movie star. Maybe grab a donut, too, you know what lazy bastards all us white cops are."

Babe met Tim in the parking lot of the 7-Eleven, Tim already sipping coffee and leaning on his squad car, somber. As Babe approached Tim handed him a quart of Gatorade, looked at his tight-muscled sweating body and nodded his head, once.

"Looking good. You're down what, ten pounds since Christmas?" Tim seemed distracted, angry about something.

"*Street Babe* went into preproduction in November, I was one-ninety-one. The morning the shoot began, in January, before I had coffee, I was one-seventy-eight. I'm floating right around there, give or take three pounds."

"Is that right?" Tim wrinkled his nose as Babe reached into the open window of his Lincoln and pulled a pack of cigarettes from the visor.

"So what happened with the series, you hear anything?"

"I called you but your phone was unplugged."

"I was trying to sleep. Between school and starting midnights, I'm dragging ass."

Babe lit a cigarette and took in a deep drag. "I didn't do this," —he lifted the cigarette—"didn't eat like I do, I wouldn't have to work out like an animal. Then again, as long as I can run I can figure there isn't a tumor on my lung."

"Guy was a runner? World class. He's losing weight, can't figure what's wrong. Wins a marathon on September first and by the end of the month finds out he got four spots on his lungs. By Thanksgiving, *ba-boom.*"

"You're a lot of help." Just to show Tim he wasn't scared, Babe took in another deep drag, blowing the smoke away from him, though. There was no sense in looking for trouble, and besides, something was eating at Tim; Babe could tell by the way he was looking at him.

Tim said, "My father's gonna die before the week's out, Babe. Lung cancer, the same as my Ma. Both of them were heavy smokers, smoked less than you, though."

Babe thought of two or three things to say in response. From what he knew of the man who'd fathered Tim, the man's passing would not be much of a loss for society. But he kept his mouth shut, rather than be ignorant.

It was one thing they usually never were to each other, ignorant, or cruel. They would tease each other and kid around when they worked out together, which they did like clockwork, but never when anyone else was in the room, or when somebody was close

enough to hear it, even if that person was Kelly. Their friendship was built on mutual respect and the fact that they'd both
survived childhoods that were far from idyllic, and they worked
with each other like men, treated each other as such, and neither
stepped over any lines with the other because they'd never even
tested them, never gone far enough to find out where the line was
drawn.

Tim would say something to Babe, calling him a name or
something, and then would apologize right away, and Babe found
himself doing the same thing, picking up Tim's respect and throwing it right back at him.

The money thing was never a problem, either, like it had been
with a lot of Babe's friends from before. Tim had been his friend
when he had lived in the co-op apartments, had been his friend
when he had moved into his first house, putting up four people in
four rooms, the kids in one tiny bedroom, and hadn't *that* been a
load of laughs.

Tim had been his friend through all that, and was his friend
now that he lived in the big house on the hill, the jewel of the town.
Had even helped them move in. A guy with a full-time job who
worked security part-time at the school, who took college courses
every semester to better himself, finding the time to help a guy rent
a van and move his family into their new home.

It wasn't the sort of thing that Babe would take for granted.

Babe believed that a lot of other guys, they'd sit in the bars
now, in the gym even, when Tim and Babe weren't around, talking
about what a prick Babe had turned into. They'd figured that out
right away after they'd learned that the bank was closed, that the
money Babe made went into funds for the kids' educations, into
retirement plans for himself and Kelly. There weren't any parties at
the big house, ever.

Now Babe said, "I'm sorry, man," and Tim waved it off.

"Eighteen years, I wasn't worth calling. Now the doctor calls
my chief, the old man wants to see me before he dies."

"Don't you let him off the hook," Babe said. "Don't you go
weak on me just because he's croaking. He wanted forgiveness he
should have looked for it thirty years ago."

Tim stared off at the traffic on Sauk Trail, nodding his head.

"I haven't decided whether I'm going to go see him," Tim said, then, gratefully, he changed the subject.

"You hearing from those creeps in Hollywood?"

Babe said, "Spinelloid called me this morning, wants me to do the series. Forty grand a week, ten weeks, guaranteed."

Tim whistled. "No kidding."

"I think I'm gonna pass."

"I never should have told you who his brother was, Babe, honest to God, I should have kept my mouth shut." Tim's anger was real, he was blaming himself.

"It's not just that," Babe said. He took a swig of his juice, shook some sweat from his forehead. It was nearing midnight and there was a chill in the air.

"This guy's a loser, a loudmouth and a drunk. I finally introduced him to my wife after we were done filming. I wouldn't go to the wrap party but I did go to a party for the crew that Universal had, and I took Kelly. Jerome wanders in, like he's doing everyone a big favor by showing up, he swaggers in, drunk on his ass, carrying publicity photos of himself, Tim. He goes around to each table, signing them, making a big thing out of his generosity, telling them all how much he loves them and how if the show gets picked up they got jobs for life, and he comes to my table and I introduce him to Kelly." Babe lit another cigarette from the butt of his last and Tim shook his head.

"This making you nervous, talking about it?"

"Stress, man." Babe laughed, derisively. "I used to live in the barber shop, now *that* was stress. Success isn't supposed to be stressful.

"Anyway, he calls Kelly 'honey' and 'doll,' signs a picture for her and asks for the kids' names and you know Kelly, she wouldn't embarrass me for anything, she gives him the names and he writes on the picture, 'To my adopted sons, love, Jerome.' Tim, he never even *met* my kids."

"What'd Kelly do?"

"She looked at it and kind of froze up, then picked it up and held my lighter to it, let it burn right there on the table."

"And Spinelloid?"

"He didn't do shit. By that time I'm half out of my chair, waiting for him to say something. All he did was stand there looking hurt. He said, 'What's the matter, honey?'

"Now is this a guy I want to work with every day, twelve, fourteen hours a day? Do publicity with and take pictures?" Babe smiled. "Besides, his brother's in the mob, you told me that."

"Babe . . ."

"I would have found out anyway. Those slobs were all over the set, every day, trying to get their mugs in front of the camera. I'd see them and walk away, and Spinelloid would call me over, introduce me, and some of them would go on and on about how they knew the old man in the old days, want to know how he was doing, if he was still in the joint. I'd tell them I didn't know, I wasn't in touch with him. If they wanted to talk to him, they should call his parole officer, find out how to reach him."

"Then you're an arrogant slob again, disrespectful, for not kissing their asses."

"Tim, I'm so used to people telling me how I should think, how I should act, that that kind of stuff doesn't even bother me anymore."

"You sure it doesn't?" Tim said. "Or are you just telling *me* that . . ."

Babe got into his car, lit another cigarette. A well-built young woman, rushing the season in tight shorts, passed between Babe's Lincoln and the squad car, looking into the car curiously, breaking into a smile as she walked on. She turned, walking backward, putting her hands to her face. Staring at a TV star. Babe waited until she entered the store before he spoke to Tim.

"I'm sorry about your father, Tim."

"Me, too," Tim said, then added, "Sorry it didn't happen twenty years ago."

"Make it thirty. You'd'a been safe then."

"See you, Street Babe," Tim Raglan said.

You sure it doesn't? Tim had asked him, and Babe hadn't known what to say. He wouldn't lie to Tim, that was out of the question. They were too close for that, although with other people Babe had been known to sometimes stretch the truth to get out of doing something he didn't want to do. To Jerome Spinell, he found himself lying more than he told the truth, getting out of dinners, keeping the ignorant little man away from his home, from Kelly and the kids.

But not with Tim, he couldn't lie to him, and expected the same honesty from him in return.

So, did it bother him?

He wasn't sure, but thinking about it sure was starting to get to him.

Like he was doing now, lying in a bathtub filled with hot water up to his neck, a book in his hand but he wasn't grasping a word he was reading, he was thinking about whether the way people thought about him bothered him.

Soon, he felt sure, a lot of people would want him, would want to be his friend. Would invite him to places he didn't want to go to spend time with people he didn't want to be with. Some of them would understand when he refused, accept his refusal the way it would be given, respectfully, regretfully. Others, he knew, wouldn't be so kind.

He'd be arrogant, as far as they were concerned, and they'd want to know who in the hell he thought he was.

It had already happened, to a certain extent. As soon as he'd started getting some major exposure acting groups had begun writing to him, wanting him to come speak at their meetings, to come watch them criticize plays or to have dinner with them. Some of the letters were transparent attempts at self-promotion, while others were so poignant that they made him wince inside, touched by their sentiment.

He refused them all, though, with equal respect, and had gotten some interesting feedback in return, had been called everything from a swell-headed bastard to an egotistical, pompous ass, just because he didn't want to go and feel like an ape in a cage on display for a bunch of people who spent their time meeting with other actors instead of out there doing it, out there acting, acting anywhere, for any fee, any time someone wanted them to perform.

Which was the way Babe had done it.

Worse though, were the letters from Edna Rose. He didn't tell his wife about them, would read them then rip them up and leave them in the post office garbage can.

Except for one letter and one picture, which was in a safe in his office, hidden under insurance forms and his will and the mortgage papers.

These days the letters were getting worse—the poor sick woman was obsessing on him. The one in his safe was beyond description, made him sick to look at it. He would take it out when he was feeling safe, when his present was overwhelming his past, and he would look at the picture of the twisted child in the wheelchair, and the fat, terribly ugly woman squatting next to it, grinning into the camera lens. The envelope was drenched in cheap perfume. The letter said, "Our angle now in heaven with God," and it was signed, "Love and kisses, ur Edna."

The letters had been simple at first, just nearly illegible scribblings telling him how good-looking he was, how much she appreciated seeing him on TV. *"You're really one hot Babe!"* she'd written. But they'd soon become darker, even frightening.

She would write to him, telling him that she'd been out to their child's grave that afternoon, that some mean old kids had scribbled dirty words on the headstone with marker and how she'd spent the afternoon washing them off. Would tell him that their child may have died young and she could understand Babe's leaving, his grief.

But they were still young, and they could have more children, couldn't they?

Now she wanted to have sex with him, would describe in vivid details the things that she wanted to do. Fantasies run rampant, but there was a ring of authenticity in the letters, as if the woman truly believed they had performed such acts before.

Tim would tell him to turn the letters over to the law, but Babe never would. Tim would tell him about the maniacs who were stalking stars and sometimes killing them, tell him about Rebecca Schaeffer and other stars who'd been murdered or maimed by rabid fans and star-struck fantasy lovers, and Babe would listen, but could never take the letters to the postal authorities.

She was just a sick, sad woman who'd had a child die on her. Wouldn't that put anyone over the edge?

Babe shivered as he got out of the tub and dried himself while the water ran down the drain, thinking of the woman. He brushed his teeth, then cleaned the tub. Kelly didn't play that tub-cleaning business, and wouldn't let him hire a maid. He put on his pajamas and walked out of the bathroom, into the large bedroom that was bigger than the living room of most of the places they'd lived in in their marriage, and there was Kelly, sitting up on the king-sized bed naked, holding a paperback book in her hands and smiling at him.

His wife. There were stretch marks now on her breasts and they sagged a little bit, and the flesh of her thighs and upper arms was soft. The marks were on her belly, too. It wasn't the body he'd first held in lust almost fourteen years ago. To him, it was improved. He could look at it forever, his face in repose, check it out in a scientific manner and come away impressed. Those marks showed her womanhood, what she'd done for love. He couldn't imagine having sex with another woman, even though he got more than his share of opportunities these days. It would kill him to hurt her in even a little way, and to cheat on her would destroy her.

"Hey, Mr. Movie Star," she said. "Got a few minutes for a hot, horny fan?" Babe laughed in shock, began to unbutton his pajamas as he walked over and made sure that the bedroom door was locked.

"Well, I'm kind of busy right now, but I'll fit you in," he said. "Next time, though, make an appointment with my secretary, would you?" He got into the bed beside her and pulled her to him close, made sure that he had her arms pinned so she couldn't hit him. "We big TV stars don't have time to do this at the spur of the moment with every doll that comes along."

She liked to watch him sleep, especially after they'd made love and he was relaxed and feeling safe.

That wasn't his usual state of mind.

Babe had guns hidden around the house that he'd thought she didn't know about, high up on shelves in the closet and the kitchen, with locks through the trigger guards so the kids couldn't fire them if they found them, but still there, deadly and ugly. She'd asked him about them and he'd looked sheepish, told her that they were there for emergencies, that he was in the public eye and you never knew when some deranged fan would look you up.

They weren't there for fans, and Kelly knew it. The house, the cars, and all the bills were owned by her and were in her maiden name, not even a fan with access to the tax rolls could find out where he lived.

He just didn't want to tell her the entire truth about it, and it was one of the things about him that she understood, that he was ashamed and a little frightened of who and what he'd been, of his past and the people who'd been a part of it.

Kelly hated guns, couldn't really understand his wanting them around, but then again, she didn't have maniacs for a father and brothers the way Babe did.

Would he shoot them if they showed up at the door? Kelly hoped she'd never find out.

Now she watched him, Babe sleeping, now grinding his teeth.

What did he dream about, why did he have nightmares all the time whenever he was under pressure? He wouldn't tell her, would hardly discuss his dreams at all. She knew about his record, and that he was mean when he drank, that he'd been a burglar when he was younger and that most of the people he'd hung out with while growing up were either dead or in prison. He'd tell her whatever she wanted to know about his life, but grudgingly, and whenever he discussed his upbringing he'd have nightmares for a couple of days in a row. She'd learned quickly and early that if it wasn't important, she was better off not asking.

Until they'd moved into this beautiful new house, then he'd opened up, staring nearly hypnotized into the fire on winter nights, Kelly beside him, holding his hand. Babe would sit in awe, talking in a faraway voice, amazed that such good fortune had come his way, and he'd talk. The fire worked on him like a Valium, and he'd sometimes get philosophical, would ruminate about his past, about how he was raised, how lucky he'd been the last few years. She'd ask about his life and he'd tell her things that she never ever wanted to know, and some thing that she wasn't really sure that she believed. Could parents be that cruel to a child? They had to be; Babe did not know how to lie to her.

She'd ask him about his parents, if he ever planned to see them again, and he'd get cold, mean looking, and say, "No," shortly, and then he would tell her why. He would be staring into the fire and the things he told her seemed casual and unrehearsed, but she suspected that he told them to her so that she would pick up on it and remember it, just in case any of them ever came around, looking to be family.

She'd liked her mother-in-law, in an odd way, once you got past Margie's alcoholic posing she wasn't too bad a person. Not sweet, but sad, in a way. Babe's mother lived in a state of self-pity, in self-delusion, would rewrite history at all the family gatherings they had once attended, until she'd gone overboard in front of the children and Babe had cut off contact with her. Kelly hadn't known about the other side of her, the side Babe had been subjected to while growing up. Not until those nights in front of the fire. After learning those things, finding out about the woman, Kelly never wanted to see her again, either.

Her father-in-law, Johnny, Kelly had only met once. She'd spoken to him several times in the first years of their marriage, when Johnny had called from the federal penitentiary, collect. And they'd gone up to see him once at the MCC when he was passing through Chicago on his way to another prison.

The waiting room had been nearly empty and there had been a huge black guy sitting in a chair in the corner, his female visitor on her knees in front of him, her head bobbing. Two other black inmates had been sitting directly in front of them, covering them. Johnny had ignored it, as had Babe, and her father-in-law had been charming, a true gentleman to her, but Kelly had never gone back, even though Johnny had been there for two weeks, and Babe hadn't asked her why.

When Johnny had called Babe a faggot for wanting to be an actor, Babe had hung up on him, had refused his calls from that day forward, which Babe seemed to be able to live with okay, although it infuriated two of his three brothers.

These days, there was only one that was civil to Babe, his older brother, John. John had been in AA for many years and he would talk to Babe about God and love, about understanding and compassion, and Babe would listen to it, would never get mad at his older brother. They'd talk on the phone sometimes for hours, the two of them like prisoner of war survivors, the enemy in their case being people with the same last name as themselves.

What about the other two, Babe's brother Frank, who was a year younger than Babe, and the baby of the family, Anthony? Babe never even mentioned their names around the house. Frank was a thief and a drunk who worked for his father, Kelly knew, and Anthony, who was much younger than Babe, she didn't know much about. She hadn't seen him in years, not since he'd been a teenager.

Babe kept track of them though, through John and others who knew them all. He paid attention to what they were doing, with whom and how often. He believed that the first rule of combat was to know your enemy, and over the years he had made it clear that his biological family was indeed his own worst enemy.

She wasn't sure if she agreed with that, thought that maybe Babe's worst enemy was himself, and would tell him that, watch his face fall and then he'd ask her, How could you say that? looking all upset. He'd tell her that she just didn't know, that things were different for him and that she shouldn't judge his behavior by someone else's white bread rules. Kelly never replied.

He had emotional walls up that were nearly insurmountable, that the average person could not climb. He would test new people in his life, those who professed friendship, and if he decided that it was going to be a one-way street he would cut them off, cold. She guessed that if he could do it to the people who'd raised him, then being detached toward strangers should be a pretty easy thing for him to do.

There was a long ropy scar down the middle of his back that he wouldn't discuss, not even in front of the fireplace. "War wound," he'd tell her, though he'd never been to war. As far as she knew she was one of the few people who ever saw it. He wouldn't do an acting scene with his shirt off, even though he was well built and otherwise proud of his body, wouldn't even go out of the bedroom without a T-shirt on, covering that scar. Did Tim know about it? He had to, they took showers together at the gym. But how many others? Was he sensitive about taking showers there, did he wait until everyone else was out? It wasn't the only scar on his body, not by a longshot.

Kelly would often wonder, as she watched him sleeping, how many scars were in his mind. There had to be a lot, and he was as timid about showing those hidden scars to the world as he was about showing the physical ones.

He was a good father, although he didn't think that he was, Babe always down on himself and saying he was too mean, too hard on the boys.

Yet she'd watch him out in the yard playing football with their sons, the three of them laughing and having fun, Collin having no regard for his body and throwing himself all over the ground to make a catch, while Mike played with a level head, outthinking Collin when Babe threw the ball his way. He took them fishing and to the movies, took them out to eat and to baseball and football games and to the park when they lived in the smaller house and didn't have a yard to play in.

There was a basketball hoop up in the backyard of their new house, and twenty square feet of asphalt laid down around it. Babe told her that he'd spent over a thousand dollars so the kids wouldn't have to go to the park and shoot hoops in baskets that didn't have nets, but she thought differently. Kelly thought it was so they could have their friends over and he could keep his eye on them, know where they were all the time.

It was as if he was terrified of losing them.

She'd asked him once why he was so watchful, so frightened for them, and he'd told her that he was scared to death that God was going to take them away from him as punishment.

What could he have ever done in his life to think God would be so cruel to him, that he deserved that sort of punishment?

It was another of the things that she never asked, and wasn't sure that she wanted to know.

He played his emotional cards so close to the vest that few could ever really get to know him, as if he was frightened that someone would get close to him, learn all about him then use that knowledge to hurt him. But he had to trust her, didn't he? After all these years? He put everything in her name and never tried to hide any of their assets from her, didn't have any hidden nest egg that she was aware of. Would he ever completely trust anyone, did he fully trust her? He wasn't an easy man to live with, that was for sure. Always testing, never trusting.

He prided himself on being home most of the time, on shooting his work in Chicago instead of going out to the Coast, wanting to be with his family, hating to sleep in strange beds without his wife and kids around. But when he was working, it was the same as if he was gone, and since the hoopla about *Street Babe* had begun he'd been nearly impossible to live with. He was withdrawn, absorbed in his work, lived it, ate and slept it, paying no attention to them at all except to kiss them goodnight, and even then he seemed distracted, consumed by his role, by the part he was trying to get down and bring to life with all his conscious being. At those times, he could be a real pain in the ass, seeing as all he seemed to ever play in the early days was heavies, street toughs and thugs, junkies. When they'd lived in apartments or in the small house, it had been almost unbearable for them, and she'd have to make apologies to the kids, let them know that daddy was engrossed in his work, was finding a way to become his character, a way to bring that character to life.

And yet, and yet . . .

He was never mean or brutal or violent, and certainly never raised his voice to her. The kids, sometimes, he'd yell at them, yes, but when kids were thirteen and ten they had a habit of getting on your nerves, of looking for ways to push your buttons. He was open about his love, would hug and kiss her and the boys all the time, and always before he left the house or before they went to bed.

He moaned a little now, in his sleep, his eyes squeezed shut, his lips turned down, and she thought about how you could spend fourteen years of your life knowing someone and never really get to know them.

She'd watch him when he didn't know she was looking, while he was sitting in the yard looking around, or in his office, surrounded by the electronic equipment he loved but for the most part couldn't figure out, most of which he'd brought home from the *Street Babe* set. He'd sit there playing with a mini-video hookup or an actual FBI recording device, or with his infra-red night-vision binoculars, or just looking out the window, Babe almost in awe at what they now owned, and she would see his pain, see him vulnerable, but she knew him well enough to know that if she went to him, if she tried to ease that pain, that he would take it as an insult, as a personal intrusion.

He never cried. At least not in front of her. He'd sniffle sometimes at a sad movie but then he'd wipe his nose and go about his business, as if he'd never watched a single frame.

Was there anything wrong with that, though? With not crying? She did it sometimes, not often, but every now and again she'd just feel the urge and would let go, and he'd freak out, would not know how to deal with it. Babe would run all around, thinking she was holding something back from him, that she'd been hurt or insulted by someone and it would only make things worse, his insensitivity at those times would only make her cry harder in frustration. Crying seemed to be a concept he just couldn't figure out. Or maybe he'd cried too much in his lifetime, maybe there was only a set amount, a supply of tears that was given to you at birth and when you cried them out you were finished for this lifetime, and Babe had shed his allotment.

Anger though, you obviously didn't get a set amount of that, and if you did, Babe had gotten more than his share.

It was one of the things that made him so good on a stage, on a movie set, that smoldering anger, the way he could look at you . . . He called it his controlled rage.

She knew about that firsthand.

When they'd have one of their rare arguments she could see it rising in his face, he would turn all red, even though his voice never rose, would remain level and even. He would clam up, go icy cold on her, then head out into the garage and pound the punching bags, thudding punches into them, and she'd wonder if he fantasized that he was punching her, punishing her . . .

He hadn't watched his own TV movie last night, had been out there hitting the bags, and Kelly had had to turn the volume way up in order to hear it, and had videotaped it so she could watch it again later, when he wasn't around making noise and messing the mood of the movie all up for her.

She'd sat there, mesmerized by the power of his work, as her Babe showed his controlled rage to the entire nation—to the world.

He wasn't especially handsome, his nose had been broken a number of times and it was too big for his face—he would hang spoons from that nose and walk around the house, impressing the hell out of the kids and their friends—and his eyes weren't quite centered, but he knew his business, knew how to spray feelings and emotions at the camera without even appearing to notice the thing there in front of him. And when he smiled, hearts broke, that grin lit up a room when he cut it loose. That might be because, from looking at him, you didn't expect it to ever happen. You'd think that a punch would head your way before a smile ever would. He had a thick head of hair that he didn't pay a lot of attention to, combed it straight back and by the end of the day it would be down on his forehead. When it began to get into his eyes, he'd go and get it cut at the same barber shop where he'd once slept. When he wasn't working he wouldn't bother to shave, would only cut off the whiskers when the itch began to get to him.

But you wouldn't know these things from watching *Street Babe*. All you'd see was his easy, casual love affair with the camera, his rapport with the thing, and you'd never guess that there were seventy-five people milling around out of sight, making the show work.

She'd watched that show, trying to concentrate but distracted by the slow, heavy punches he was throwing at his water bag, then he'd stop for a minute and then there'd be the steady *rat-a-ta-tat* of the speed bag. She'd watched it and sat knowing that he now belonged to the world, that her husband's image would be masturbated over that night by frustrated women everywhere who knew that he was a safe target. Some of them might even obsess on him, make him a target for their love. As that one woman had, for a couple of years now, what was her name? Edna Rose, a woman who was always sending letters to his PO Box, love letters that he wouldn't let Kelly see because he said that they were too sad and he didn't feel comfortable showing them to anyone. Whenever he got one, though, he'd become surly, more quiet than he usually was, and for hours and sometimes days it would be difficult to communicate with him. He would be off somewhere in his own mind, maybe thinking about the Rose woman. Maybe thinking of her naked, remembering some pictures she'd sent him . . .

Kelly would have to keep that sort of thinking out of her mind. It was his mail, not hers, and she either trusted him or she didn't.

He was sensitive about his fans, to a certain extent. Although he would never answer fan mail anymore, didn't want to begin correspondence with everybody who got in touch with him, he respected the rights, the privacy of those who wrote to him, even the people who sent the hate mail or the filthy pictures of themselves. Some of the photos were from women, others were from men, who just assumed that he was gay because he was an actor.

Well, she had to prepare herself for it now, because even if he wouldn't read the papers or answer his phone about last night's show, *she* wasn't burying her head in the sand. She knew that the mail and the pictures he'd received so far had been just the tip of the iceberg, that the avalanche would now begin, because of *Street Babe* there would be thousands of women in love with her husband and she'd have to learn to accept that fact.

She wondered how those women would feel if they really knew him, saw him sleep one time. If they knew—as she did, although he didn't tell her—that he hadn't watched his greatest moment on film last night because he was afraid, maybe even terrified that he was about to break out of the pack and become something he wasn't at all certain he wanted to be. If they knew how he was wracked with guilt. Sometimes she saw him as an emotional rag doll that had been torn apart and then somehow sewn back together, with pieces missing, parts that didn't fit.

That was the way he really and truly was; a man who was completely different, trying to fit into society, to be a part of it for once.

He was settled down now. It would be a good night, unlike some recently, when he woke up three or four times, gasping, reaching out and calling for something in the dark.

Her mother would tell her that he was a time bomb about to explode, tell her that he needed help and if he didn't get it he was liable to hurt someone. She would thank her mother, but she thought that if it hadn't happened yet that it wouldn't.

Babe seeing a shrink? The idea was laughable. If he wouldn't discuss his pain, his sorrow, with her, he certainly wouldn't with a stranger, with someone he'd have to pay in order to get them to listen.

Who knew the answers? All she knew for sure was that she loved him, and if he didn't want to talk a whole lot about his parents, about his childhood, then that was all right with her.

They'd come a long way, the two of them, further than most people had ever expected them to get. And there was a long way to go, too. Their future appeared to be golden.

She trusted him, that was for certain, with her love, and with her life. He was a good husband, a good provider, and a wonderful father. If there were things that he didn't want to share with her, well, that was his business as well as his right, and she had no business complaining, even if it did hurt her.

Kelly whispered, "I love you," and Babe seemed to hear her, smiled briefly in his sleep, on and off, tense brow momentarily relaxing. Kelly had to get up at seven, had to get the kids off to school then get cleaned up and be in class herself at nine. She should be sleeping by now, instead of lying here looking at a man she'd been married to forever.

But she wanted to look at him for a little while longer, wanted to burn his image into her mind, as if she now were keeping him safe by watching over him.

It made her feel good, thinking that. Possibly because he always tried so hard to bring safety and security to all of them all the time. Perhaps now, after midnight, in the dark house with his hidden guns lying dormant around the place, she could keep him safe, maybe even make him somehow feel it in his sleep.

Maybe he was on the way back to normal, if you could use such a word to describe him. He'd done well tonight at the school, had won the kids' hearts, and that was a far cry from the way he'd been these last few months. For once, tonight, he hadn't seemed withdrawn and remote. She'd talk to him about it soon, point out to him his reticence, his reclusiveness toward them. She could only hope that he'd understand, but you never knew with him. He took everything so personally, he had so much damn passion.

"I love you," Kelly said again, but this time he didn't respond. Babe just lay there, his mouth slightly open, breathing in and out rapidly, his chest heaving, and she saw that he was lightly sweating.

9

Tim worked the radio at the station house while the dispatcher ate her lunch, and it was slow, a Monday night in a town where they rolled up the sidewalks at ten.

They had their share of the action, as any town did. Theirs was totally integrated, twenty thousand people living and working together in a community that only had two taverns and only one of which was making money. The integration was a good thing from a community standpoint, and it might make points in Springfield when it came time to ask for State funds, but from a policeman's point of view it was sometimes a pain in the ass, especially seeing as how every time you arrested a black person, even if you caught them in the commission of the crime, they would scream that you were only doing it because they were black. Tribalism was big business these days, guys like Louis Farrakhan and Al Sharpton were raking it in with that genocide bullshit.

And some of these kids, they were pretty amazing. They'd wear their black Chicago White Sox baseball caps sideways with the price tags tilted to one side, depending on what "gang" they were pretending to represent. Out here, they were pseudo-gangsters, and not much more, although every so often one of the cops would grab some toughass who had carried a pistol to school. Tim would pinch them and treat them with detached respect, even when they were calling him names or telling him how their gang was going to even the score. Sometimes, though, he'd work with those he thought to be salvageable. With the hardasses, well, he'd get them alone sometimes when he had the time to try and reason with them, and when it was just the two of them in a room, the attitudes changed considerably. And even though he knew he wasn't doing a lot of good with some of them, he still felt that he owed it to them, to tell them what awaited them in the state penitentiary. Which was where they would find out just how tough they really were.

Even with the worst of the bunch, there was always something to learn, if only the new street lingo. For instance, when a bunch of them were getting together to go out and fight in another neighborhood, they called their excursions sorties, a word they'd learned during the last war. They pronounced it so-*tays*. There was always something to learn, even though sometimes Tim wanted to perform a so-*tay* upside their skulls to see if he could knock a little sense into them.

There were drugs in town these days, too, as there were everywhere in the country, which was driving the burglary rate through the roof. Brutality and child abuse were in every part of town, that part of human nature could never be swept out of society, even if drugs were. There were three or four rapes every month and usually a murder a couple of times a year.

In his twelve years on the force he'd seen it all, and the other officers had learned to give him his distance.

Tim never socialized with other cops. He didn't go to the cop parties or to the bars after work, didn't even go to the yearly picnics or swimming night at the AquaCenter. He was self-contained, in control of his emotions at all times. People thought he was distant or cold, but he knew that they were wrong. He just didn't believe in the touchy-feely nonsense, believed that you showed your feelings through your actions toward someone, not through spoken words or false, hearty hugs.

Babe understood that, although he probably didn't agree with Tim's point of view. Babe would always be hanging on his kids, and Mike didn't like it anymore, Tim could tell. Babe would drape his arm around that kid and Mike would gently pull away, not wanting to hurt his father's feelings, but getting his distance, all the same. As for Collin, he was a piece of work. Tough and smart, attached to his old man. Collin would kiss his dad before he walked out of the room to use the bathroom, for God's sake.

It was Babe's way and that was fine with Tim, although he could never figure it out. They'd been raised in much the same manner; violently, and that violence had taught Tim to keep it all inside, to never let anyone know what you were thinking, how you felt about things. Babe would tell him that his feeling would change when he had kids, but Tim wasn't so sure. First, he had to find a woman who could love him, and that had turned out to be harder than he'd thought.

He'd get something going with a girl and the time would always come when she'd confront him, want to know where the relationship was headed. Headed? Wherever it went, he would tell her. He didn't fool around on the women he dated, didn't play one against the other and he never, ever told a lie. He knew how to cook and he never asked anyone to do his laundry or clean his house. He earned his paycheck and wasn't cheap on a date, would take his girlfriends wherever they wanted to go and would even get out on a dance floor with them if that's what they wanted to do. Wasn't that enough for now? Did marriage and love have to be discussed?

You never touch me unless you want to fuck. He'd heard that more than once. What did they want him to do? Pat their heads when he walked by? He showed them how he felt about them, through his respect and admiration. Always complimented them on the way they looked and he could buy flowers with the best of them.

But never the little sentimental cards, those were out.

The relationship would end and Tim would sit in his easy chair, thinking about it, wondering if he was supposed to feel bad.

He never did.

There was a time when he was new on the force when he would feel bad due to his inability to feel bad, when he'd feel guilt because he was able to look with dispassion at the worst of crimes and realize later how little they had affected him. He never made fun of the dead, didn't involve himself in the dark humor that a lot of cops got into in order to hide their revulsion at what they were witnessing.

But he didn't share that revulsion, either. He wasn't hiding anything, putting on any act. He just disassociated himself from it. The bodies were just that, dead meat with no connection to him, even if at times he got a little mad at the killer.

A recent murder–suicide had been a case in point. They'd

been called to the scene by neighbors of the fighting couple, and it was far from an unusual occurrence between them, only the resolution was this time different. Both parties were known to them, the woman with the seven kids and the man who'd come into their lives, married the mother and then proceeded to rape the eldest daughter and threaten her into silence, the girl who soon found herself carrying her stepfather's child at the age of thirteen. The woman had learned of it and had thrown him out and the war had begun, the weekly battles, usually on Saturday night when the fool would get drunk and get it into his head that his wife would take him back if he showed up on her doorstep.

What had been in his mind? Tim wondered. Did he actually believe that if he got stinking drunk and presented himself to the woman that she'd take a whiff of his whiskey breath, his B.O., and forgive him, throw herself at him and rip his clothes off in her haste to reconcile? She hadn't gone anywhere near that far, that was all Tim was sure of. What she'd do was, she'd call the police, then refuse to sign a complaint, using the cops as an escort service. Tim had tried to tell her that an order of protection might scare her husband off, and when he'd finally killed her, Tim remembered his words to her, remembered too how she'd laughed it off, knowing how much good an order of protection was worth once the party on whom it was served walked out of the sight of the judge.

Three weeks ago her husband had shown up again and hadn't bothered with any sweettalk. He'd kicked in the front door and stormed through the house, shooting at everything that moved, wounding four of the children before he cornered the mother in the kitchen and shot her down like a dog, then turned the gun on himself.

The man was still alive when Tim had arrived on the scene, he'd been big and black and was now also red, blood-covered from the ugly hole in his chest. The broken little bodies had been lying everywhere, and blood was splattered all over the rugs, the walls and the furniture. Officers were crying while the paramedics choked back their own tears and rendered aid to the little victims. The family dog had been found licking the blood away from its master's face, trying to bring her awake.

Tim had looked at this, had taken it all in and had walked over and kicked the gun away from the killer's hand, then had leaned down and made sure that the man was alert, that he could hear him. When he was sure that he wouldn't be wasting his words, he told him, "You're gonna burn in hell for this, you know that, don't you?" mildly, sincerely, and had watched the panic fill the man's eyes, watched his lips moving wordlessly. Tim had smiled at him.

"Oh, no, you're dying, there's no way around that." A paramedic had been watching them, leaning over the man and applying a large bandage to the sucking chest wound. The paramedic was black, was wearing a belt buckle that spelled out JESUS in large brass letters.

"And God won't forgive this, you have to understand that."

The paramedic said, "Hey," and Tim had looked at him calmly, had said, "Thou shalt not kill, that's a commandment, isn't it?"

It had been the closest he'd come to showing emotion in his twelve years on the force, except for the time last year when he'd slapped the junkie, but that lying bastard had it coming.

While Tim waited for a call to come in he pushed his chair over to the computer and typed in some names, beginning with John Hilliard, Sr., then sent it off to the FBI computer and ran down the list, checking out all of Babe's brothers, even John, the one Babe got along with. He did this once every few months, to see if any of them had any new arrests, had been in any trouble. He understood Babe's unease, his fear of the emotional vampires to whom he was related.

Tim had a few of them in his own personal background, one of whom was right now dying in South Chicago Hospital. And how did he feel about that?

Tim was ambivalent, holding it all inside. He understood what Babe had tried to tell him, though. If Tim's father had loved him, he would have sought forgiveness before now.

But would that be what he was looking for? Maybe not. Knowing his father, the man might just want to see him one more time, tell him what an asshole he was before he checked out forever. What would Tim be able to do then? Kick a dying old man's ass for him? He'd done that once before, when his father had still been strong and violent, right after Tim got his first black belt degree. And the two of them hadn't spoken since.

The dispatcher came back into the communications room and Tim gave up her chair, told her that he had correspondence coming back from Washington and he'd appreciate it if she gave him a call when it printed out, and she said that she would, no problem. Few people ever gave Tim a hard time on this department, he was one of the rare cops everyone seemed to respect.

Except for the prisoners, who respected no one.

"I'm taking a lunch break, now," he told the dispatcher, and she nodded her head, smiling to herself, knowing how Tim spent his lunch breaks when there were prisoners in the cells, and on his side because of her knowledge.

He had a full day at the college tomorrow and then would be meeting Babe and maybe a couple of the others for a workout before he would get a chance to get home and sleep, which he knew from experience he would have a hard time doing. Midnights always kicked his ass, threw him off his schedule and if he could average four hours sleep a night he was doing about normal for his two-month shift. He might get even less sleep now. After almost twenty years, he might have to go and pretend that he cared about a man who'd terrified him until he was seventeen.

Should he go to the funeral? He'd never considered the fact of his father's dying before. Huge and strong and mean and drunken, his father was the sort of man who outlived everyone he knew. He had to get his mind off this; Tim had to stay in the here and now. Think about something else, like how much he hated midnights.

The only good thing about it was that it wasn't particularly busy on midnights, except on the weekends, and he could study the prisoners, have little chats with them, alone without witnesses. He would be doing his master's dissertation on these interviews, and upon the conclusions that he'd drawn from them. He had quite a few interviews already typed and filed away, but there was a lot more research to be done, one prisoner at a time.

Tim got his tape recorder out of his locker, and a picture file, locked his weapon inside and left the locker room, made a right turn and walked down toward the four prisoner's cells, looking in on the

sleeping woman, then unlocking the cage that held the walking
dead man.

The prisoner's name was Corporal Vance and he was tall, thin, black,
older and bald, with a face that had seen everything twice and was
shocked by nothing at all. He wasn't a man Tim would want to play
poker or any other game with. He'd seen faces like that before, eyes
that dead. Not often, but often enough to frighten him.

Corporal and his girlfriend, who was high-spirited and who was
now sleeping off her high in the next cell, had been arrested for
stealing carts full of liquor from Dominick's, charged first with theft
and later with assault when they'd attacked the security guard
who'd tried to bring them back into the store. It was a good scam,
one with little risk of incarceration. They'd swear before the judge
that they'd simply forgotten to pay for the alcohol, and even if he
didn't believe them, the prisons were already fifty percent over-
crowded in Illinois, would that overcrowding be eased by locking up
shoplifters? There were too many serious criminals out there, too
many brutal murderers, for shoplifting ever to become a crime that
did anything but put a black mark on your credit rating.

Corporal looked up at Tim from where he was sitting, his back
against the stone wall of the cell, his feet up and crossed at the
knees, Indian style. This wasn't his first arrest, and wouldn't be his
last, if he didn't die from an overdose, first.

Corporal had taken off his shirt and Tim saw that he was
wearing a filthy gold tank top over his scrawny chest. Saw too the
long prominent vein that reached from both shoulders down
through his thin biceps, extending all the way into the man's wrists.
At the elbow break, there were dozens of tiny needle pricks, discolored, some of them suppurating.

Corporal's hands were enlarged, pus-filled, his fingernails dis-
appearing into rolls of distended flesh.

Still, there were hundred-and-fifty-dollar sneakers on his feet,
basketball shoes which were now without laces.

The woman in the next cell was Corporal's exact opposite,
overweight and mouthy, with darting eyes that tried to see everything at once. His man here, he didn't seem to care one way or the
other what was going on around him. Tim got the feeling that you

could put him in a totally black room and he would wait until the door closed then would sit down, cross his legs, and wait for either death or a lawyer to come and let him out, and not care much either way which entity paid him the first visit.

Tim said, "Corporal, how you doing?" and the man grunted.

"Ain't making no statement, so you might as well just walk you ass back on out the door."

"This"—Tim held up the recorder—"isn't for a statement." Tim stood with his back against the far wall, straight, without bending his legs or even crossing them casually at the ankle. He was not here to make friends with this prisoner, he was here to study him, and did not want to give him the impression, through body language or any other way, that he was trying to become his confidant.

Corporal was looking at him curiously now, half-smiling. He said, "You tape that loud-mouth-ed bitch was in here screaming half the night? You'd'a put her in a cell with my old lady, my woman'd done the state's job for you. She'd'a kilt that bitch in maybe two seconds."

"She got bonded out. We had her in a cell by herself."

"You could'a put her in here with me, now, it would'a been a different story. I'd'a shut her up quick. That yelling gets on my nerves. Like you are now, talking shit and trying to trick me into making a statement."

"I'm not here to get a statement." Tim hit the Record button, then looked at Corporal. "There's nothing you say to me in this room that can be used against you in court or anywhere else. I'm a scientist, a police scientist, and I'm sort of taking a survey."

Corporal did not seem interested. Still, he said, "What kind of survey?" and smiled languidly. "You wanna know the brand of cigarette I smoke? It called: reefer. Specialty brand made up for me exclusive."

"I don't care about that, or your laundry detergent, or if you wear ladies' underwear or hate your mother. I just want to ask you a few questions, show you a few pictures and see what you think of them."

"You got any pictures of nekkid bitches? That bitch in the next cell, even with her clothes off, you can't see no pussy what for all the fat hanging off her belly. Tell you what, you show me the dirty pictures and I let you record me whilst I jerk off at it." Corporal grinned. "Got any pictures of Tammy Faye Bakker? *They* a bitch do something for me." He spoke in a friendly, slow manner, probably not even aware anymore that everything he said and did in the presence of a white man was a con, an act for the Man. He was so used to doing it that it came naturally to him, an act he slipped into as naturally as Babe slipped into one of his TV roles.

There was a faded blue jailhouse tattoo on Corporal's left forearm, three letters done up in a swirling style, a tattoo that had taken a lot of time and trouble to apply. The letters B. P. N., done up large, with curlicues and flourishes. It was a good starting point, and it would take the man's mind off running his game.

"What's that stand for?" Tim said.

Corporal looked down on it, then slowly back up at Tim. "Black P. Stone Nation, Sarge, that what it stand for. I an *Ancient*." This last said proudly, Corporal emphasizing the final word, as if it were mystical.

"One of the originals?"

"Back from the early sixties."

"You started young."

"Movement made us all old before our times."

This was good stuff, a classic example of self-delusion, this fifty-year-old junkie bragging and believing that the vicious street gang he'd belonged to had relevance, any sort of social merit.

"You fought for your people, then?"

"You ain't trickin' old Corporal now, is you, Sarge? Gonna wipe that part off the tape where you saids you cain't uses it 'gainst me?"

"I give you my word, Corporal, this is just between us."

Corporal sat up and Tim set his distance, but didn't move an outward inch. If Corporal tried anything, he could drop the recorder and file and then drop him before the man came fully off the cot.

"You got any idea how much trust I got in the white man's word?"

"My fault you're a junkie, then?"

"Huh. You and every other motherfucker spent the past fifty years keeping me down."

"Just you, Corporal? What about your people, what about their three hundred years of oppression?"

"Thems too."

"You've got one hundred and seven arrests, Corporal. Were they all white cops just giving you a hard time?"

Corporal ignored this.

"I want you to look at some pictures." Tim slid the first photo out of the batch in the file, held it so Corporal could see it up close, moving in with it and holding it in front of the man's face, down low so Tim could see his reaction.

It was a picture of two hundred Jewish kids being prepared for execution by the Nazis, the children staring at the camera, their expressions making it more than obvious that they were trying to please, as if believing that if they could somehow show they were harmless they might be spared. A nun was standing in the middle of them, smiling, her smile taking on the appearance of a death rictus. Except for the nun, who was in her black robes, they were all wearing striped prisoner's uniforms, with large black Js on their chests. The door to the gas chamber was open in the background.

"Do you know what this is, Corporal?" Tim watched the man's eyes carefully, for any sign of movement in them, for any sign of emotion.

"Bunch of kids and a nun, shit." He wasn't particularly interested, but he wasn't taking his eyes off the picture, either.

"This photo was taken ten minutes before they all stripped, and were marched into that room in the back. That's a gas chamber, Corporal, and fifteen minutes after this photo was snapped, all those kids were dead."

"No shit?" Corporal looked hard at the photo now, as if trying to shift it into the future. "You got any of them nekkid? After they stripped?"

"Does that thought turn you on, Corporal? Would you like to see a picture of crying children without their clothes?"

"Fuck the kids," Corporal said, "but I'd take me a shot at the nun, man, she look pretty good to me."

"You wonder at all what a Catholic nun is doing in a picture of a Jewish prison camp?"

"Who give a fuck, man?" Corporal took his eyes off the picture, sat back, bored. "She white, ain't she? Far as I concerned, Hitler should'a finished the job he started."

"And the kids, that doesn't bother you that they died?"

"They white and they Jews, Sarge, it all the same to me."

"Okay."

Tim slid the picture back into the file, removed the second one.

This was a picture of black men, women and children, taken on the West Side right after the area was burned to the ground, showing the victims of the race riot that had occurred the night that Martin Luther King was killed.

There were dozens of people in the picture, all of them walking around dazed, the burned-out buildings behind them still spewing smoke. Their expressions were almost all the same, equal parts of terror and confusion. Some of them held their hands to their mouths while others cried openly, the children hanging on to the legs of their mothers for protection, to keep them safe from the insanity surrounding them.

"What do you think of this one?"

Corporal barely glanced at it. "What's this, the homeless? Fucks 'em, let 'em go find they own hustle."

"Not your problem, either? Your own brothers and sisters?"

Corporal grunted a laugh.

"My brother got his ass killed in the Nam, and my sisters all hoo-res, like they mama was. *Them* there ain't family to me." He lay down on the cot and put his arm across his eyes.

"Go on now, get on out my house, I tired."

"You know you'll be going for an AIDS test in the morning?"

"Won't be the first time. I could save you all the trouble, I been positive since last Feb'rary."

"Let me ask you a question, Corporal."

"I tired of your questions, man."

"Just a couple, then I'll get out of your hair."

Corporal cursed, shifted on the cot, struggled to a sitting position.

Tim studied him. Corporal wouldn't admit it, might not even know it, but the picture of the black people had gotten to him. He kept his face rigid, but you could never hide the eyes—unless you lay down and put your forearm across them.

Which meant he wasn't hopeless, wasn't a psychopath, that he could still feel for others, no matter how shallowly.

"Corporal, before the movement, before you joined the nation, what was it like for you at home? Your mother was a prostitute, you've told me that, what did your father do?"

"Never had no daddy."

"How about uncles, how about any male in your life."

"Mens? There were mens in my life, that for sure." Corporal's face lost its hipster cool, and for a moment Tim saw some anguish there, some torment, before the mask slipped back on. "Don't want to talk about none of that, motherfucker."

"Now watch your mouth, Corporal. I'm the motherfucker has to get your breakfast in the morning."

Corporal looked at him, slyly.

"You wants to ax me questions? I need more than food right now, you dig what I'm saying."

"Can't get you any drugs, Corporal, but I might be able to slip you a couple of Unisom to help you relax."

"No brutality, I call you a motherfucker again you ain't gonna lay my head open with that stick?"

"I've only hit one prisoner in twelve years, and he lied to me, told me he wasn't carrying anything. I reached into his sock and got stuck with his needle, stood up and knocked him out for playing games with my life."

"Five Unisom, I talk to you for five minutes."

"Five Unisom, and you talk for fifteen, and you got a deal, Corporal," Tim said.

10

John had told him not to call him anymore when he was drunk, and had hung up on him. That little punk. Who the hell did he think he was, hanging up the phone on his own father.

Johnny thought about what would have happened if he'd ever done that to his father, when the man had been alive, what would have happened if he'd ever hung up a phone on him or shown him any disrespect. His father would have killed him, that's what his father would have done.

He'd spoiled the little bastards. They all cried and moaned about how tough he'd been on them, but the fact was, he should have kicked their asses a lot more often than he had, maybe that would have knocked some sense into their heads, gotten their goddamn respect.

He slid another quarter into the slot and dialed another number, waited until his ex-wife's sleepy voice came over the phone, then fought the urge to hang up. Sometimes she was friendly, and sometimes she was a bitch, depending on her mood, on how many drinks she'd had before bed. He paid half her bills, because the last kid still lived there, and you'd think that would carry some weight with her, but it didn't, she was still, mostly, a bitch.

But she'd been *his* bitch for nearly all of her adult life, since she'd been seventeen years old, and that had to count for something, had to somehow bind them together. Except for her and the kid, for Anthony, there was no one left.

He said, "It's me," and she asked him, wearily, what the hell he wanted at this time of night.

"I got to talk to you, to you and Anthony, about this goddamn Street Babe thing."

"Don't even talk to me about it, don't even mention his name. He's dead to me."

"He hates us, you know that, don't you. After all I've done for him."

"He hates me because I introduced him to *you*, that's why he hates me."

"He despises me more, though. He hates me more than he hates you."

"Bullshit," she said, and hung up.

"Shit," Johnny Hilliard said.

He fumbled around in his pocket and got out some more change, dropped the quarter in the slot and dialed again.

"Damnit to hell, Johnny, leave me alone!"

"You're awake now anyway, Margie, what's wrong with me coming over?"

"Cause I got to work in the morning, that's what."

"How can you face them people, how can you go in there and be a working stiff when you know they're laughing at you behind your back, because your kid won't talk to you?"

"I should have aborted him."

"Well it's too late for that." He gave it one more shot. "Lemme come over, I don't want to go back home, you know all that's on TV right now, don't you, every newscast? Pictures of our kid, Margie, of our Babe, everyone on the news going gaga over how a street kid made good."

"He's spreading lies to them, telling them that he had a rotten childhood." Margie sighed. "Anthony's been crying for two days now, ever since he saw the fucking movie."

He hated it when she spoke like a truck driver, used the F word like a man. But he didn't say anything because he could sense that she was about to give in.

"He should have called me, Anthony should have."

"He's been trying to beep you since last night." Johnny looked down at the beeper attached to his belt, feeling a twinge of discomfort because he hadn't returned the kid's calls and there was no way that he could lie his way out of having gotten them. Or was there?

He had the thing turned off now, because he knew the bastards who had won all his money tonight would be trying to reach him, to rub it in, and to place bets on tomorrow night's games.

He said, "I had it turned off all day, I been busy. He should have called me at the apartment." He said it hopefully, knowing that if she'd drunk enough before bed that it might go over her head, that she might forget that his beeper was his business. She might not, though, even drunk. Marge was as sharp as any detective or DEA agent he'd ever met, the way she smelled bullshit.

"He tried there, too. You have your phone turned off again?"

"Only when I sleep. Jesus Christ, Marge, you know I'm busting my ass to keep my head above water!"

"Johnny, come on over, I think Anthony's sleeping, but I'll wake him up, it'll be good for him to see you."

"I ain't sleeping," Anthony's voice came over an extension, the kid slurring his words. Johnny did not blame him. How could anybody live with that woman he'd been married to and *not* drink?

Margie said, "You were listening in? Listening in on my telephone conversation?" Acting all pissed off. Probably nervous because she talked to her boyfriends on the phone in her bedroom, thinking she was safe. And if Anthony heard them talking to her and told his father, Johnny might cut off her money.

Anthony began to argue with her over the phone and Johnny said, "I'll be there in twenty minutes," and hung up on them, wondering if he should go over there now, now that the two of them were fighting. Nobody could piss him off like she could, especially when the both of them had been drinking. Not even the guys he'd killed could make him as mad as Marge could, not one of the twenty-three of them had ever been done in passion. No, she could get to him, all right, and she had the scars to prove it.

He walked to the bar and even as drunk as he was he could notice that the bartender and one of the rummies stopped talking real fast, which meant that they'd been talking about him.

Johnny swaggered to the bar, staring hard at them, giving them the patented Hilliard inscrutable stare with a little spin on it, just to keep them on their toes. He grabbed his bills from the bar and frowned.

"You got something to say, you motherfuckers?" He liked the

way it sounded, tough, young. Took it even further. "I'll blow your
fuckin' heads off your shoulders, you fuck around with me."

The bartender was ashen-faced and the rummy stuck his head
down into his glass, eyes right down there in the beer foam. The
hand holding the glass was trembling.

"You want a piece of me, huh?" Johnny turned the glare onto
the entire room, swung his arm around in an arc, raising his voice
and including them all in the conversation. "Any of you? I'll kill all of
ya, and all of your fucking families, you fuck with me!" He waited a
couple of seconds, in the silence, the TV the only sound in the place,
Clark Gable calling some woman baby and her liking it, not like it
would be these days.

Johnny said, "Yeah, that's what I thought." Then turned his
glare solely on the bartender. "I come in here every goddamn
night, buy rounds for everybody, and as soon as I turn my back you
gotta run your mouth on me, you piece of shit?" He slammed his
money into his pocket. "See if I ever come back in this shithouse
again. Gimme one for the road, punk, in a glass." The bartender
was terrified now, quickly poured the drink freehand, twisted the
bottle away only when the ice was about to spill over the top of the
glass. He put the drink down on the bar and stepped back, stood
against the back bar, looking at Johnny, trying to see if Johnny was
carrying.

Johnny didn't even think about paying for the drink, just
picked it up and walked to the door, feeling better than he had in
weeks, in control of the situation, with people cowering in terror at
the sight of him, the same way they had in the old days.

He'd picked his shot carefully, knew full well that the only one
who might dare talk back or otherwise give him trouble would be
the bartender, but the thought of having his head blown off had
stopped him from trying anything physical. Which was one of the
reasons that he always wore his shirt outside his pants when the
weather was too nice to wear a coat. It made people think, gave
them fear, especially those who knew that you were a killer.

He knew how to work the magic, that was for sure, and if any of
them had tried anything, he'd have come back in tomorrow night
with the two kids who still loved him, who still respected him and
did what they were told, bring the gooms with him, too, and the

eight of them would bust this place up so bad it would have to be condemned by the city.

He turned at the door and gave them all one more glare, pleased when they all hurriedly looked away. "Cowards," Johnny spat, with scorn, then slammed out, feeling ten feet tall.

He'd said twenty minutes but she'd bet that he'd be an hour.

He had to worry, these days, about things like DUI arrests, the sort of thing that would have made him laugh forty years ago, even twenty years ago. She couldn't say ten years ago because even though he might still have had it in him, he'd been in jail ten years ago, losing whatever manhood he had left, so she couldn't be sure either way.

Margie Hilliard sat at her dinette table in the superbly furnished three-bedroom apartment she shared with her son. She prided herself on her taste, on her class, and nobody had to know that everything she owned had been bought on credit, that she had no net worth, that even the fur coat she wore in the winter months had been bought with a credit card, that she was making payments on a dead coyote.

Anthony, freshly bathed, hair still wet, was sitting over on the couch, watching a tape of *Street Babe* on the VCR his father had given them, Fast Forwarding through the commercials, punishing himself. He was drinking a beer, and there were tears in his eyes. A cigarette hung from his mouth, the ash long.

"Don't you get any ashes on my furniture," she warned him, and he didn't reply.

She was smoking herself, and there was a Manhattan in a rock glass in front of her, Marge drinking, sitting there waiting for the man who had caused her all her problems in life, or, to be fair, most of them.

She could remember a time when a Chicago policeman had pulled Johnny over for speeding and had made them follow him to the station when he learned that Johnny's license was expired. Johnny had stood on the steps of the precinct house and had called him a motherfucker, right to his face, over and over again, telling him he'd have his goddamn job, and the cop hadn't said one word back, had just stood there afraid.

It was the way Johnny used to be, the strength he once pro-jected.

She'd seen even judges appear apprehensive when Johnny stood before them. He'd sneer at them, lean on the railing, do anything to show his contempt short of cursing, because then the judge would have no choice but to do something rash, hold him in contempt of court or send him away because the insult would be on the record for any reformer US attorney to read and wonder about.

Back then, in the fifties and sixties, Johnny had rein over half the judges in the city, had them in his pocket because he did favors for people who owned those black-robed crooks lock, stock and barrel.

It didn't take a stretch of her imagination to think back, to the days when Johnny was hard as a rock, tough as nails, and was feared throughout the entire South Side.

It had been his idea to bring Bolita, the numbers racket, into the mob's fold, his idea to wipe out the black hoodlums who ran the game and collected all the profit. He'd gone to the mob with it, had talked them into it, shown them how much money there was in nickels, dimes, and quarters, and they'd been impressed.

But did he get a piece of it? Guess again. The dagos made all the money and threw him bones, screwed him over, like usual. Even if she had to admit that they'd gotten Johnny off the hook a dozen times when he'd been pinched, they still owed him.

What none of them, including her husband, seemed to under-stand, was, all of the times they'd gotten him off the hook, it had been because of things he'd been arrested for doing at their request! How could Johnny be so stupid, act so dumb as to think he owed these people, these guinea bums?

They'd been good to her, he'd tell her. Sure. He'd been inside for selling dope for them, for doing them another favor, and she'd picked up 250 a week from them because Johnny was doing time and keeping his mouth shut, even though he was getting old and a government deal must have looked good to him.

What she wanted to know was, if she got the 250, how much was Johnny getting altogether? She'd bet it was a thousand. It was just like him, not to think of anyone but himself.

Margie took a sip of her Manhattan, a drag off the cigarette.

She was fifty-eight years old and she'd had her first kid when she was seventeen, and Mother's Day was next week, and did any of the three adults she raised plan on taking her out to dinner, on honoring her in any way?

She sighed, loudly, and shook her head.

Not one of them. She'd be surprised if any of them even called. John would, yes, he'd feel guilty enough about the way he treated her the rest of the year to give her a ring on Mother's Day. Babe, though, the one who had all the money and forgot who'd raised him, who'd *sacrificed* for him her entire life, he wouldn't even go near a phone, the thought of calling his mother would be the furthest thing from his mind.

She knew why, too. It was because of that bitch he'd married, Kelly. The whore. One roll in the hay, and he forgot all about his mother, what she'd done for him, how she'd worked her fingers to the bone her entire life to make sure he never needed anything.

"Child abuse." She spat the words out. It was what Babe had accused her of the last time they'd spoken, right before he asked her to leave his house, right before she'd thrown her drink in his face and before she told that bitch, Kelly, exactly what she'd thought of her. Marge had sure shown *her*, and right in front of those little brats she'd given birth to, one of which, at least, was nothing more than a bastard.

"Say something, Ma?" Anthony said, distracted, watching his big brother on the screen, the brother he'd once idolized.

"No, hon," she said, wearily. There was no use burdening Anthony any more than he already was, her fragile child carrying the load of knowing that his older brother hated him, hated them all, hated the people he should love the most in the world. . . .

Hadn't she honored her family? She most certainly had, and she still did, even the ones who'd been true child abusers. That term turned her stomach, made her sick. Didn't The Holy Bible say "Spare the rod, spoil the child"? You're damn right, it did.

Her mother had never spared any rods, not once in Margie's life. Had beaten her damn near every day until Margie had had enough, had married the first good-looking prospect to come along, the wildman, Johnny Hilliard. It was only years later that Marge had understood that what her mother had done had truly been for

Marge's own good. If only she'd figured that out before she'd married Johnny.

She wound up divorcing him enough times, too. Four times, to be exact. Dumping his ass every single time he was convicted of something and would go away for more than a year or two. That long a wait she could handle, but anything over, say, two years, and he was history. After all, she'd still been young, she still had her life to live, and most of it was ahead of her.

He'd write her all those loving letters, tell her how he'd change when he got out, that this time he meant it, and she'd take him back, marry him again and before you knew it, he was once more doing the same thing he'd sworn hundreds of times that he'd never do again.

He'd start beating her. Get a few drinks in him and go wild at any incitement. John and Babe and Frank would watch, in terror, John and Babe sometimes attacking their father and getting their own asses kicked for their loyalty.

Well, she wasn't any young girl anymore, impressed by tough-guy hustlers. If Johnny ever laid his hands on her again, there was a 9-mm pistol in her nightstand that she knew how to use, and she wouldn't hesitate, she'd take that thing out and blow a hole in his head that was bigger than his pecker.

How'd that glass get empty all of a sudden? Marge got up and poured herself another one, listing a little to her right. Was she having a stroke? Was blood seeping into her brain, the way it had with her mother? It wouldn't surprise her if it was, what with the pressure she was under, had been under for her entire life. She sobbed a little, looking around her, at all the things that she'd had to buy herself, that no man had given her.

The 250 a week when Johnny had been locked up was nothing, a pittance, less than what he actually owed her for raising four of his children all by herself while he lived at the government's expense in some jail somewhere. The money he gave her now, half the bills he covered, the extra money he'd slip her when he had it, was the same thing, to her way of thinking. What she had coming. The tens of thousands that she'd borrowed from her father and her brother before they'd died on her was not a matter of charity, she'd been intending to pay it all back, it wasn't her fault that they were both dead now. And the fifteen thousand she'd inherited from her brother upon his death, how could anyone say that that money wasn't what she had coming, as Babe had?

Oh, she remembered *that* night, all right, without any problem. Margie never forgot any hurt that she'd suffered in her fifty-eight years, never forgot one single ounce of pain that life had inflicted upon her. Especially not the pain her little rotten children caused her.

What was it Babe had said, exactly? She'd been trying to tell him that she was a feminist, was really one of the pioneers of the movement, living alone and raising her kids without help from any man, and he'd looked at her as if she was crazy, right in her own damn house, and had asked her what she called the money that her brother had left her, if not help from a man, what the money was that she'd taken from her various married boyfriends over the years, if not handouts from men, and he'd gotten her so flustered that she'd slapped him across the face and rather than hit her, he'd taken it out on Anthony when her youngest, her baby, had come to her defense. Babe had beaten poor Anthony so badly that the child hadn't been able to come out of his bedroom for three days, his self-image had been so brutally damaged.

She'd gone to a lawyer, tried to sue that son of a bitch but the lawyer had asked her for five thousand up front before he'd file suit, and when she'd asked didn't they work on a one-third basis anymore he'd told her, "Not unless we got a chance at winning the case."

Johnny had been locked up for his dope dealing at that time, or else he might have killed Babe, for insulting her, for abusing Anthony. As usual, whenever she needed that good-for-nothing loser, he was away somewhere, doing time. Well, so what? Nothing she had had come from him, or from any of his friends. Or from Babe, who all of a sudden had disappeared from her life, now that he didn't need her anymore. Now that he had that whore to take care of him.

She'd seen another lawyer just a couple of months ago, when the *Chicago This Month* magazine article about her kid had come out and he'd made the statement, publicly, that: "The only statement I'm willing to make about my childhood is that I thank God that it's over" for all the city to read. Everyone at work had laughed at her, she knew that, not that she expected any of those assholes to be her friends. She didn't have any friends and she damn sure didn't want any this late in life.

Still, she couldn't get over it. How dare he insult her like that? She'd called the editor of that damn rag and had given him hell, had sent him copies of the letters she'd kept from when Babe had been seventeen years old and in the Marine Corps, in boot camp, and writing little whining letters to her every night, begging her to help him get out, telling her how he realized what a mistake it had been, his running away from home, his thinking she was mean. He'd sure needed her then and hadn't she gone to bat for him? Hadn't she done everything she could to get him a hardship discharge? Even though it hadn't worked out and he'd had to do his three years, she'd still done everything she could to try and help him.

The editor had sent back the letters, through the magazine's lawyer, who'd written some legal doubletalk about Babe's right to privacy, how his private letters to people were privileged and sacred communications and could not be published without his permission until after he was dead.

She should have let Johnny do what he really wanted with them, shouldn't have made him lighten up on them all the time. How many whippings had he given her when she'd stopped him from kicking those kids' heads in? More than a couple, that's for sure. If she'd let him tear them apart, maybe they'd appreciate her today, instead of ignoring her, treating her like dirt, blaming her for all their problems.

It had been three and a half years since she'd seen Babe last, since the scene in his house. She'd brought over her own booze, as always, since Mr. Holier-Than-Thou wouldn't have it in his house, and she'd had a couple of drinks, right before Christmastime, and she'd asked him straight out why he'd changed his phone number and hadn't called to give it to her.

"Because you're a drunk, Ma," he'd told her. "A drunk and a child abuser."

A drunk and a child abuser. Speaking to his own mother!

"How *dare* you!"

"And I can't deal with it anymore." Babe staring at her hard, that whore Kelly standing right behind his chair, her hand on his shoulder, not saying anything but egging him on all the same. The kids were there, too, looking out their bedroom door, watching everything, nosy little shits.

She'd thrown her drink in his face and that had been it, she'd gotten through that self-righteous act of his right away. From the way he'd looked at her before he'd yelled for her to get out, she'd thought for a second that he was going to hit her and that had been a little exciting, that moment, Marge sitting there smirking and wondering.

He'd see her next in her coffin, if he had the nerve to show up at the funeral. She wouldn't have anything more to do with him in this life, and she'd bet that God wouldn't forgive him, either. Wasn't the third Commandment Honor Thy Mother and Thy Father? Well, Babe sure fell short on both counts there.

The doorbell chimed and she started, put her hand to her heart and lowered her head.

"What's with the dramatics, Ma?" Anthony said. The beer must have been getting to him, to talk to her that way. "It's only the doorbell." He paused the VCR and got up, swaggered over to the door and opened it without looking out.

Thank God it was only Johnny. With all the niggers that were moving into the neighborhood, Anthony should have known better than to have opened the door without asking who it was. He was just like his father had once been, wasn't he? Ballsy and tough and he didn't give a fuck about anything, never took any shit from anybody. The fruit didn't fall far from the tree, did it?

Except for that one time, that time when Babe had slapped him all around their apartment without half-trying, like he enjoyed humiliating his younger brother.

She wondered if Anthony ever thought about that, if it affected him, mentally, that beating he'd taken for coming to her defense.

Then knew what she would have to do to make everything right. She'd been thinking about it for a long time, since Babe had thrown her out of his house.

Johnny had come in cautiously, eyeing her, seeing her sitting there in her bathrobe with the top half of her breasts exposed and she knew that he disapproved, and she enjoyed his disapproval. It was her goddamn house and she'd dress anyway she pleased, and if he thought her dressing like this turned her kid on then he was a filthy pervert and she didn't want him in the house, anyway.

He took her glass without saying anything and poured them both another drink, while Anthony went back to the couch and started the tape back up, with tears in his eyes now that his father was there, an audience he could milk for sympathy. Oh, she'd raised some wily ones, and it was all her ex-husband's fault. If he'd been there for them, given them guidance and fatherly direction rather than sitting in prison cells most of their lives . . . But how much could one woman do on her own? Alone and receiving no help from anyone, ever?

She knew Johnny still wanted her, but he'd given her a dose of the clap once, years ago, and she hadn't had anything to do with him since, not that way, at least. His money, though, she'd spend that. Didn't she have it coming?

It wasn't that she was prudish, it was more the fact that today, the clap was the least of your worries in that department, there was stuff out there that killed you slow, and she wanted no part of it.

She let her robe fall open a bit more, provocatively. She looked good for her age, and people were always telling her that she looked like Ava Gardner did after she'd divorced Sinatra. She knew that they really meant the way that Gardner had looked when Ava was living in England, past her prime, heavy and old. Still, it wasn't too much of an insult. Ava had still been a raver.

Her hair got dyed every other week, Marge doing it herself over the bathroom sink, putting up with Anthony bitching about the way it stunk up the house. Her makeup was always properly applied. Her legs had veins showing all over them now, but you couldn't see them past the robe. She shrugged her shoulders, gave Johnny a sorrowful look as he placed the drink down in front of her then sat down across from her, looking pretty sad himself. Babe, at least, had good reason for hating his father.

She waited until Anthony was searching through a commercial and there was silence in the apartment before saying, loudly, "I'm going to shoot him through the heart, then turn the gun on myself," with conviction, and didn't *that* get their immediate attention.

Anthony quit playing with the VCR and looked over at her, in shock, while Johnny stared at her for what seemed like an eternity, his mouth open, seeing her glassy eyes, the cocky expression she would set her mouth in when she was drinking. He said, "Jesus Christ, Marge, are you fucking nuts, or what?" and she demanded, right there, that he get the *fuck* out of her house before she killed him.

Then, with Johnny cursing his way out of the door and with Anthony comforting her, Margie broke down in wracking, heart-wrenching sobs.

Morning was never a lot of fun for Babe. As a child it was the worst time of day, opening his eyes and hearing bellowing from downstairs, the battle already engaged by one or more of his brothers.

Later, it had been a time of sheer dread, because the DIs would come banging in the barracks door with a garbage can in one hand and a baseball bat in the other, banging the bats inside the can and bellowing as loud as their sadistic mouths could roar. By the time that boot camp ended, the troops would roll out of their bunks at the first sound of the DI's hand turning the knob. After that there had been jail, and you never slept inside. Bad things could happen to you if you slept too soundly.

In the years after the county, when he was drunk every night, he would spend a good hour in bed each morning, lying there trying to figure out how badly he was damaged, running his fingers over his face, his chest, down his legs. It would shock him, back in those days, to finally drag himself out of bed and to look in the mirror and discover that he looked just the same as he always had. He always felt so ugly when he had a bad hangover.

Now he only had to suffer through a cigarette hangover, hacking and coughing his way through the first fifteen minutes of his day, which was always fun.

Tim was right, he should give them up before they killed him. But not today, he'd wait a while longer, until the heat was off.

The white noise machine was drumming out the sounds of a rainfall, loudly, soothingly. Babe reached out a hand and turned it up slightly, so the morning noises of the house wouldn't disturb Kelly. She could use an extra hour's sleep, with the schedule she kept.

Babe forced himself quietly out of the bed and threw on a robe, covering his mouth with his hand and trying to hold the coughs inside, wanting to take care of the kids for Kelly as a sort of half-ass apology for the way he'd been acting the past few days. He'd feed them, get them off to the bus, then wake her up so she could get ready for school herself. While she showered he'd read the papers in his office, drink his coffee and smoke himself awake. It wasn't a big sacrifice. As a matter of fact, he had some serious making up to do toward Kelly and the kids. The last week or so, since the craziness had started over *Street Babe*, he'd been acting like an idiot, and he knew it.

He padded down the hall in his bare feet, shaking his head to clear it, stumbled down the steps and got into the kitchen and put the coffee on, sat down at the table and shook out the first cigarette of the day and lit up.

Mike came out of his second-floor bedroom, dressed and ready to go. "Gonna be seventy-four today, seasonably warm, with a forty percent chance of rain towards evening."

"You want me to make some pancakes?" Babe spoke and saw the smile fade from his son's face.

"Uh, no thanks. I already had some cereal."

"You don't like my cooking, is that what you're saying?"

"You make good spaghetti, Dad." Mike the diplomat walked back into his bedroom. Before he closed the door he called out, "You made the front page of the paper, by the way." Then the door closed.

Paper? What was the kid talking about? His eyes weren't ready to even focus yet, and here his kid was telling him he was on the front page of the paper. Why would there be a review of *Street Babe* two days after the show aired? It was probably something about the show's numbers, they would want to brag about their hometown boy being in a top-rated Movie of the Week. He'd go downstairs to his office—where Mike put the paper on top of his desk for him every morning—and read it, as soon as he was more alert, as soon as the coffee was ready.

The toilet flushed and Collin came down the hall and into the kitchen. "Hi, Dad." He raised a hand in greeting and let it drop quickly. More like him than Mike was, temperamentally, Collin not being much in the morning.

"You want me to make you some pancakes?"

"Are you serious?" Collin's tone made it clear that he was hoping his dad was kidding. "No, uh-uh." Smartass, too. Which Mike wasn't.

How can two kids, from the same family, raised in the same environment, be so different so early?

Collin was digging around in the silverware drawer, looking for his lucky spoon.

"What're you going to eat?"

"Cocoa Puffs." He was wearing Teenage Mutant Ninja Turtle pajamas, which he loved, but he'd have been devastated if anyone told his friends about them. It was one of the things Mike used to keep him in line. Muffled electronic sounds came suddenly from the direction of Mike's bedroom, and Babe stood, listened in, said, "I don't believe this," then said to Collin, "Cocoa Puffs? Try the Cheerios, they're better for you, or the Rice Chex." He walked down the hall and knocked once on Mike's door before entering.

To find his son sprawled in front of the TV set, fingers working a Nintendo keypad.

"Forget about it, Mike, you don't play that thing in the morning before school."

"I do every day, Mom said I could." Mike was angry, staring at him with resentment.

"Well I say you can't."

"I'm on the Honor Roll, you know." Mike was snotty, but he was shutting down the machine.

"You want to stay on it, you study, you don't play video games during the school week."

"I do it every day," Mike said, having to get the last word in, and Babe figured he'd better leave the room. He wasn't alert yet, was still on autopilot, and he might say or do something that he'd be sorry for later.

He said, "Not today, broham," and pulled the door shut behind him, getting the last word in himself.

Back in the kitchen, Collin was eating Cocoa Puffs, the bowl full. Babe could see a sprinkle of sugar on top of the stuff.

"They weren't sweet enough without sugar? And what'd I say about Cheerios?"

"You told me to *try* them, Dad, I already tried them and I like Cocoa Puffs better."

Babe looked at the coffee machine, saw that the glass pot was full. He bit his tongue. As he was pouring his coffee he heard a door open and close and he was about to tell Mike to for Christ's sake be quiet, his mother was still sleeping, when Kelly came marching down the stairs, into the room, sleepy-eyed, and looked at him, puzzled.

"What are you doing up?" She seemed genuinely surprised, and for once in his life Babe managed to think up a good comeback before he had three cups of coffee inside him.

He said, "Finding out that I couldn't make it in this life without you," and she said, "Aw," and smiled.

Then said, "Take your coffee downstairs, honey, you don't want to be around here in the morning."

"I hear you," Babe said, then did as he was told, walked down the stairs with his coffee in his right hand, smelling it, wanting it something terrible, proud of himself because he'd kept his mouth shut, hadn't said a word to her about letting Mike play that stupid Nintendo game before school.

The front page had a headline story with a picture about a fire that had destroyed a local lounge and killed some people, and under it was a large color picture of angry faces shouting, under which was the caption: STREET BABE TV SHOW DRAWS PROTEST!

Babe sat down in his leather chair and shook his head, shut his eyes tight then opened them, but the words were still the same.

What protest? He opened the paper and found out that dozens of Hegewisch residents had picketed at the local affiliate of the network that had aired the show, opposed to the way their town had been portrayed.

"He's a liar, is all he is," one woman was quoted as saying. Another had told the reporter, "He's got junkies and hookers hanging around in a tavern, and we just simply don't have that in Hegewisch." Yet a third took a more personal tack.

"You read the article in your paper about him Sunday? Talking about the drugs and the boozing he did growing up? About the vile slum he made our neighborhood out to be? Who does he think he is, saying he knows over twenty dead guys from Hegewisch?! That piece-of-trash show he's in ought to be banned from the air!"

Babe read on, about their coalition, about how they saw the show as a plot, a conspiracy Babe had entered into with the city, which was planning to put a third airport in their community. He read the article, then read it again, then threw it down and said, "Jesus Christ," then picked it up again and began to read it all over again.

It was only after two smokes and several readings of the article that Babe noticed that there was a fax for him hanging out of the back of his machine. Babe ripped it off, his cigarette hanging between his lips, and read the first page. The cover letter was from a reporter he knew at the *Tribune* who told him that the following two pages had been sent in by an "artist" who wondered if the paper could run the picture. He'd replied over the phone, telling the woman that to work in the cartoon department of the *Tribune* you had to have two things: talent and wit, and she had none of the first and only half of the second.

Babe rolled the paper down, looked at the cartoon.

It was crudely drawn, a third-grader's work, showing him with a smoke in his mouth and with a too long, pointy nose. He was pointing his finger into a window, shouting, in a cartoon bubble, "Sex, violence, death!" Inside the window, you could see a television blaring.

The next page was her letter to the reporter.

"This is my rendition of Babe Hill, the liar. Although I've never lived in Hegewisch, I have friends who have, and who tell me that none of what he said is true. If you'd like to buy this you can reach me at . . ."

Babe crumpled the fax, sat down at his desk and ironed it out with his hand and read it again.

"You little slut," he whispered.

By the time he finished reading it again Collin was walking down the stairs. He could always tell which of his family members were heading into the basement by the way their feet tread upon the stairway, and now that sound was soft, hurried, Collin half-running down the steps. Babe could picture him leaping down the last two to land lightly on his feet, throwing a karate punch at imaginary foes on his way to his father's office.

The ashtray already had four butts in it, the first large mug of coffee was long gone. Collin knocked on the door to the office and Babe turned on the smoke-eater, and told him to come on in while he fought to compose himself, to hide his resentment at the foolishness he'd read this morning.

The boy was dressed now, his hair wet from combing, the brown hair brushed to the side, tight. Collin didn't have a lot of interest in his appearance yet, the way Mike did. Babe knew that this would change when he discovered girls.

"What's up, broham?"

Collin was sheepish, ashamed of something, and Babe had to force himself to be patient. The boy was coming to him with something, and he had to act mature, couldn't jump on it or he might scare the kid off. He waited, his eyebrows raised, half-smiling.

"Dad? Remember when you told me you wanted to know about it when I got into trouble at school?" Babe nodded, waited.

"Well, I got into a little yesterday." Collin looked down, and Babe wondered if he was going to cry.

It sure broke his heart, seeing his child troubled. Made him proud, too, that he had decided to tell his dad what had happened.

"What'd you do?"

"It wasn't my fault, I—"

"Collin." They'd had this discussion before. Babe's insistence that the children take responsibility for their actions was not a new topic in the household. He said the name in a warning manner, looked sternly at his son.

"Well," Collin said, "Mrs. Feathergill said we could talk, but I was talking too loud to Fushay and she made me stand out in the hall until the next class."

"How loud?"

"Real loud. Am I in trouble?"

"You'll never get in trouble with me for telling the truth. But why didn't you tell me yesterday?"

"Cause you had to talk at Mike's school and I didn't want you upset."

"You sure that's it, or because Mom told you to tell me just now."

"A little of both, Dad, really."

"You know how grown-up that is, not wanting to hurt someone? That's the way a big boy acts."

"Am I in trouble?"

"Keep it down at school, Collin. There's only a few weeks left. Pass, move on to the fifth grade, and I'll be happy."

"Thanks, Dad!" Collin hugged him tight, around the neck, Babe leaning down to accept it, patting Collin's back. He kissed him on the cheek and turned him around, pushed him softly on the back.

"Now get on to school, I'll see you this afternoon."

"It's weird, Dad, having you up when I go to school."

There were a lot of things that were weird for him, too, that he never talked about with the kids.

The way Collin would walk up to him, no matter what Babe was doing, what he was in the middle of, come right up to him and crawl up into his lap, snuggling there without hesitation. The child had no insecurities about Babe's love, not even the slightest doubt in his mind as to his acceptance by Babe or Kelly. That, to Babe, thinking back on his own childhood, was weird.

Or Mike, with his weather. Knowing at thirteen that it was a different thing and that some of the other boys wouldn't understand it. Some boys on the bus even called him a wimp once, and Babe had asked him how he'd felt about that and Mike had shrugged. "I know I'm not a wimp," he'd told Babe.

Secure in a personality already? At thirteen? If someone had called Babe a wimp when he was thirteen, he would have taken a brick to the guy's head. Hell, he might even think about doing that today, even. Look at the way he was reacting to a bunch of fools from Hegewisch who were looking for a little attention, a little notoriety at his expense.

Tim might be right, maybe it was indeed all in the way you

were raised. He had to give Kelly credit for that. He sure wasn't much of a father.

He felt a vague unease, a discomfort, some memory was trying to dislodge itself and come to the front of his mind. Babe looked at his phones, to have something to do, knowing that if he just let it, the idea would pop up on its own, and that if he forced it, it would never come.

There were two phone lines in this office. One was his private line, which maybe five people had the number to, the other was his business line, connected to a fax–answering machine, which every-one had. Yesterday the business phone had rung so many times that his forty-five-minute recording tape had run to its end, and before bed he had flipped it, without listening to any of the calls. No one had called since he'd done that, around eleven-thirty. The two calls that had come over his private line he had answered, personally. Babe looked at the machine for the business line, decided to listen to yesterday's messages, and to get another cup of coffee before making a game plan, before forming his response to these assholes who were calling him a liar.

What was niggling at him, causing him grief? Something Collin had said. This was not the pain you would suffer when someone called you a liar, hell, Babe had been called far worse by people who'd meant far more to him in his life. No, it was something about the hallway.

He looked at the front page of the paper again, at the people of Hegewisch, the home of his youth. The hallway . . . Hegewisch . . . The school hallway . . .

He made the connection as his private phone rang and he grabbed it, picked it up, and was pleased to hear his brother John's voice, John saying, "Babe, did you see the paper this morning?" barely getting it out before Babe jumped on it, asked him if he remembered the three of them standing in the hallway at St. Co-lumba School.

12

They had already started writing their letters.

Johnny was in his tiny apartment above the meat market, smelling the blood from downstairs. Always an early riser—you got used to that in prison—he was padding around the place in a ratty bathrobe that did little to hide his sins and excesses, that didn't even pretend to cover the belly. His legs and chest were covered with thick gray hairs. The scar that ran from his neck downward into his belly was clearly visible from the open neck of the robe. He sat slurping coffee and smoking Camels, reading the papers and worrying about his future.

No matter how much he drank, he'd be up and at it at seven, no later than eight, as you had to do a lot of hustling to cover the nut these days, as tight as money was.

And did he have a nut to crack now, or what?

He read the papers, loving the front-page story in the one paper, reading it over and over again, the people of Hegewisch giving the kid hell. He'd call Marge at work, later, tell her about it if she hadn't seen it, maybe it would cheer her up.

What the hell had gotten into *her* last night? He'd gone all the way over to her apartment in Homewood and she'd thrown him out after ten minutes, he remembered that much. Had he said something? That he could not remember. He'd more than likely simply responded to some stupid remark she'd made, and she'd told him to leave. If it wasn't for the kid, for Anthony, he wouldn't have anything to do with her.

They started downstairs early, cutting the dead animals up,

hanging the live geese upside down by their talons and slitting their throats. The blood would drain into a large vat that was positioned directly under his bedroom, and the smell would rise, not all that unpleasant, the freshness of the blood keeping it from being too bad.

It wasn't like he hadn't smelled fresh blood before.

The Letters to the Editor column had three letters in there about his son, and he wondered how they got in there so soon, it was only Tuesday. Then he got it.

They'd have gotten their Sunday papers Saturday morning, would have read all about Babe, read his interviews with reporters from both papers, his observations on his upbringing, on the way he remembered Hegewisch.

Try as he might, Johnny couldn't disagree with what Babe remembered. The area was a dump. If he didn't have business to transact there, he'd never even head over that way. The East Side was for him, the East Side and South Chicago. As far as Johnny could tell, people from the rest of the city thought that Hegewisch was a part of Indiana.

The first letter called Babe a no-good opportunist, who'd do anything to get a couple of people to watch his show. It was signed by a man who now lived in Belmont. The second letter called him a liar straight out, the writer a woman who lived in Villa Park and had happy, carefree memories of Hegewisch. She tore into Babe for his having said he had brutal memories of St. Columba School. The third wrote that he and his wife lived in Hegewisch to this day, and they never feared walking down the alleys, even at night.

Johnny grunted a laugh at that one. She probably would be safe in the alleys. From the way this guy sounded, she'd be carrying a purse full of two-dollar bills and be wearing kneepads.

Still, it was funny stuff, someone giving that punk his come-uppance, and he laughed for a second until the doorbell rang and the smile faded right from his face.

John had been in the eighth grade and Babe had been in the sixth, their brother Frank in fifth, when they'd been sent out into the hall.

That was tantamount to a death warrant, at St. Columba. If you were standing in the hallway, the principal would come by and slap the shit out of you and *then* ask you why you were out there.

In the second grade Sister Maria Francis had caught Babe laughing at some stupid thing when he wasn't supposed to be and she'd shoved him into the trash can, made him sit there and when some of his classmates had giggled, she'd pushed the can under her desk. "Trash should be dumped," she'd said, and he couldn't figure out for the life of him what the hell that was supposed to mean, but he was in no position to respond.

So he knew about the brutality they could lay on you, when they got it into their heads that you were a problem.

He didn't know it anywhere near as well as Frank did, though. Frank, he was always in trouble.

As he stood in the hall that early fall day Babe had sworn that if he got his ass kicked over some crap that Frank had pulled, well, Frank would be in big trouble.

The hall lights weren't on yet, and it was shadowy, scary out there. He whispered to John, "What'd we *do*?" and John shrugged, shivering. Back then John had worn horn-rimmed glasses and a lot of the boys in his class called him Four-eyes. Babe wasn't too popular, either, with his classmates. Frank always seemed to have a lot of friends coming around.

There were pictures of all the graduating classes since the school's inception on the wall above Babe's head, lined up in order, from 1951 until the year just past. To try and shake his fear, Babe moved away from the wall and studied them, the smiling students' faces, the stern nuns' countenances . . .

He heard the office door slam and the school principal, Sister Mary Julianna, came sauntering down the hall, staring at them hard over the tops of her glasses, robes swishing around her legs.

The woman, she walked like a man, like a tiger on the prowl, never slowing down. She'd stalk down the aisle going about thirty miles an hour and would reach her target, whack him on top of his head a few times then be back at the front of the classroom before you hardly even knew she'd moved.

She was walking that way now, a nun in a hurry, and Babe hoped that she'd start on him, because John was fragile, would break down when someone hit him. Please God, let her start with me, or better yet, on Frank. By the time she worked her way up to John, she might be out of steam.

But she didn't stop to hit any of them. What she did was, she stopped at the eighth-grade door and John actually flinched as she looked at him, nodded at him and said good morning, then she opened the door and flew inside. Within seconds, they could hear her voice raised in anger.

"Shit," John whispered, "if she's giving that to *them*, what's she gonna do to us?" and Frank laughed out loud while Babe stared at him, hard.

"Shut that up," Babe said.

"Screw you," Frank said.

"Wait until after school, Frank, we'll see who you cuss at." That shut him up.

But John had started crying. Was standing there shivering, sobbing, his chest heaving as he tried to hold the sobs in.

The doors to their classrooms were about three feet away from each other, and all Babe had to do was take two sideways steps toward his brother to reach him. The two of them stood there, John crying and trying to stop, Babe patting his shoulder, their backs to the wall. Babe reached down and took John's hand and squeezed it, and John squeezed back, hard enough to make Babe wince. His brother's hand was trembling.

"What'd we *do*?" John wanted to know, and Babe had no answer for him.

From two doors down, Frank said, "Pussies," and stood his ground, ready to take whatever any of those Brides of Christ had to dish out.

Babe and John ignored him, stood there holding hands. "It's all right, John," Babe said. "It's gonna be all right."

The principal swished out of the door and squinted at them in the dim hallway. "What are *you* blubbering about? Get into the little boys' room and wash your face, then you may enter your classroom."

The relief on John's face was evident. "Thank you, Sister," he mumbled.

"I don't appreciate the school routine being disrupted this way, gentlemen, I really don't."

Babe wanted to tell her that this wasn't doing a whole lot for him, either, but he kept his mouth shut. It was Frank who spoke up.

"Sorry, Sister Mary Julianna," Frank said, and she looked at him and harrumphed.

"Well, *somebody* in the Hilliard family should sure be sorry, right about now." Spoken cryptically, then she was gone, into Babe's classroom, and the shouting began again.

"What's going on?" John wondered, and Babe told him he didn't know, but that John ought to get his ass into the bathroom before she came out and found out that he hadn't followed orders. John left and Babe sidled back to his own door, relieved, it was dawning on him that whatever the problem was, it was being settled, and that settlement did not involve an asskicking for any of the Hilliard clan.

To Frank, he said, "Sorry Sister Mary Julianna," mockingly. "You little kissass." Before Frank could respond, the principal was back in the hall.

"You may enter your classroom now," the nun had said to Babe, and he'd thanked her, had hurried inside and had seen every eye in the place riveted on him.

Without speaking, he lowered his head and scurried back to his seat, knowing in his heart that somehow, some way, he had done something worthy of shame.

It didn't take long for them to find out what it was all about.

Their father had been arrested for murder the night before, and their mother didn't believe that it was in their best interest to know, had requested that the nuns speak to the rest of the class and warn them to keep the tragic news from her sons.

A silence which lasted until lunchtime, when nearly every child in the school couldn't wait to tell them what they'd learned.

Even in the sixth grade, Babe had been able to figure out that now everyone knew, even the kids whose parents wouldn't have told them, the kids whose parents had never even heard of the name Hilliard, those who hadn't even watched the news or read the papers that day.

But now they all knew, and by the next day, even the few kids who had been his friends were avoiding him, on orders of their loving Catholic parents.

Now he said to his brother, "Do you remember the three of us standing in the hallway?"

"Remember it, how could I forget? That asshole, Billy Tomscak, he couldn't wait to tell me all about it as soon as the nun went to the lavatory."

"That's what they used to do, John, you're right, they'd go to the lavatory. Could you imagine one of them saying, 'Well, class, I got to go take a piss now.' "

"From what I remember of a couple of them, you can bet they needed to stand at a urinal." Then he got serious, his voice low, sharing a frightful secret with his brother. "Pa called me last night, drunk."

"Is that right?" Babe kept his voice level, kept himself under control, but he was wide awake now, paying attention. He looked at his watch, as he always did when he spoke to John, because the time always flew by so fast. John would be at work now, and might not be able to talk long, but still, Babe got a kick out of knowing how long the conversations lasted. He lit a cigarette without thinking about it and said, "What'd *he* have to say?" Then held the phone to his ear and listened carefully.

13

Jerome Spinell was startled out of his king-sized bed at the Four Seasons Hotel by some serious ringing noises. Loud, intrusive, he at first thought it was the phone and he smashed at it, angry because he'd told the operator to hold all his calls, then grabbed the receiver and barked "What!" It took him a second to realize that he was hearing a dial tone. "God*damnit!*" Jerome was in his shorts, sitting on the side of the bed now, his back to it, his hands shaking from a combination of the drugs and booze he'd ingested the night before, and from the fear inside him.

What had that been? He had no idea. Maybe it was an angel come to get him, or, worse, a devil. When it happened again, he realized that it was the doorbell.

Jerome searched frantically for one of the hotel robes and, looking for it, was shocked at the sight of the woman on the other side of the bed. She was smiling up at him, her eyes puffy. Lying flat, her breasts flattened out like pancakes, and the fat at her hips spread out underneath her. Christ, what a dog. Where had he found *her*?

It was another sign of the times, of the hard times he'd fallen on. He found one of the robes in a bundle at his feet, mad at the girl now for being fat and ugly and in his bed, madder at himself for messing around with her. Ten years ago, when he'd been on top, it had been fine big-titted blondes only and if they weren't completely natural he'd throw them out, go back down to the bar and find her replacement in ten minutes time.

Now the idiot outside the door was pounding on it, sounded

like he was kicking it. Oh, someone was going to pay. Jerome closed the bedroom door on his way to the front door, smiling at her, "Someone's at the door, honey," the smile fading the second the door closed. Grateful that he'd been around big money long enough to have established the belief in always traveling first class or not to go at all. If he hadn't been in a suite, if he'd just been in a regular room, whoever was at the door would see this pig on the bed and would know the truth about how far down he'd gone.

He could get anything he wanted in a first-class hotel. Hadn't the night doorman sold him some cocaine late last night? When you were famous and important, you could get anything you wanted.

"Keep your shirt on, asshole," Jerome said, over the pounding, then, without looking through the peephole, he threw the door open, about to kill somebody, about to say something smart about how the hotel had better be on fire, then losing his cockiness the second he saw who was out there.

His brother Milo said, "I was getting ready to kick in the door, I thought maybe you'd died in here." Milo smiled at Jerome's appearance, stood towering over him, the eldest of the family and the biggest in more ways than one. "What did you just call me, after 'keep your shirt on'?"

"I didn't know it was you." Jerome stepped back and let Milo in, let in, too, the couple of big kids with him, weightlifting types with bad complexions. He closed the door behind them and looked nervously at the door to his bedroom.

"Jesus, Milo, you should have called."

"Been trying since seven, kid, and the operator told me you left a stop on your phone." One of the musclebound oafs was pulling the television from its cabinet, sliding it out on its castors, while the other was looking through the bar. He grabbed the orange juice, both of them, and flipped one to the other ugly zeke, then the two of them sat down on the large sofa. The guy who'd pulled out the TV hit the remote and the room was filled with the sound of people clapping at something someone on the Oprah Winfrey show had said.

Jerome's head was on fire, his nerves shot. He had his hands stuffed down into the pockets of his robe, and he was trying to deal with the resentment inside him, rapidly, madly welling. They'd come into his room and had just taken over. Still, they were Milo's boys . . .

Jerome walked up to them and shoved out his hand. "I'm Jerome Spinell," he said, and the uglier one, if that were possible, looked at him strangely.

"We met you on the set of *Street Babe*, don't you remember?"

His partner said, "You signed *pic*tures for us," the two of them whining, sounding hurt, like they were supposed to be important enough for him to remember.

The first one said, "You was s'posed to get us jobs as stunt men when the series started." He was eyeing Jerome skeptically, as if he was considering whether to get angry.

"Oh, yeah," Jerome said, "*that's* right, now I remember!" Then he smiled broadly. "I'm half-asleep here, fellas, come on, I wouldn't recognize my own mother, she walked in here."

The second guy said, "You recognized your brother, no problem."

Jerome realized that he was still standing there with his hand out. Quickly, he shoved it back into its pocket. He said, "Nobody ever forgets Milo, fellas, you don't know that by now?" A gentle rebuke, his face stern. Fuck these punks.

Milo said, "Sure, people forget about me, they do it all the time. Like you, coming to town and not giving me a ring."

"I was gonna call you right away, as soon as I woke up. I didn't get on a flight until midnight, Milo, come on, you think I wasn't gonna call you?"

"I don't know, the way the star of your show acted like I had the AIDS when I met him, I thought maybe he rubbed off on you, convinced you I was a guy you didn't have time for anymore." Milo smiled, and it was scary, seeing that face light up. Then it was gone, and Milo was just standing there, menacingly, and Jerome felt afraid. But that wasn't fair, it didn't have to mean that Milo was mad at him, because Milo probably looked menacing when he was sitting on the toilet.

Jerome tried his charm on him, God knows it hadn't worked with the two gorillas.

"Come on, what's eating you? I ain't seen you since January and you're not gonna even gimme a hug?"

"Hug?" Milo said, like he'd been waiting for it. "You hear that, Billy, Floyd, he wants a *hug*." The two men looked at Milo, then looked back at the television. Oprah was standing in the audience with a microphone, looking interested in some other shine broad who was shaking her finger at the guests, telling them that if teenage gang members can kill someone, then why the *hell* shouldn't they get the death penalty. This wasn't the muscles' problem, they got paid to back up and protect the boss, not to play straight men for him.

"You're out there twenty-five years, and who got you the jobs, made you all the money?"

"You did, Milo, I know that, when did I ever not acknowledge that?"

"Shut up when I'm talking."

Milo leaned against the television set and it rolled back into its cabinet and Milo caught himself, turned a little red because his slick move had been busted in front of everybody, then he leaned back slowly, until his butt was against the front of the cabinet, as if he'd planned it that way all along.

"You've made a couple million over the years, am I wrong? A bunch of shows, ringside at the Vegas fights, first-class hotels when you travel. You got a nice house, two cars, a pretty wife you're gonna wind up killing with some venereal disease and a couple of spoiled kids you ain't never around so you try to buy when you are." Milo spat in disgust, right on the shag carpet, and Jerome looked at the saliva in awe, the invasion on his rug. What was in the guy's ass, had he gone nuts?

But he didn't dare ask. He'd seen Milo like this before, but usually late at night, when he'd been drinking. When he was like this, there was no telling what he'd do.

"Maury Ackerman calls me up last night—unlike my baby brother, I spend the nights with my family—and he tells me you've lost control of the project, that the million five I put up with him to form the production company is about to drop down the tubes because you can't control your people." Jerome opened his mouth to plead his case but Milo raised his hand, cut him off without a sound.

"A million five, that's a lot of money, but I can live without it, *capeesh*? It'll hurt, but if it's gone, I can live with it."

Behind him, Oprah had jumped into jive spade talk, like she sometimes did when she was kidding around, and the audience was tittering at her comments, oblivious to the fact that Jerome was in deep shit. Milo looked at Jerome and nodded three times, solemnly. Still staring at Jerome, he reached into the inner pocket of the conservative blue suit he was wearing and pulled out a cigarette, stuck it into the corner of his mouth. Reached in again and brought out a thin gold lighter, lit the butt then stuck the lighter back, all the time staring at Jerome.

Jerome was aghast, knowing he was on the carpet, in deep trouble with the guy who'd given him everything and who could take it away just as easily as he'd provided it. His hands were shaking so bad now that he could feel it in his arms. He tightened his biceps but that didn't help, his entire body was shaking and they all could see it happening.

Milo said, "Maury told me about your fucking around, that you're beating your wife up these days." He took a deep drag on the cigarette. "Thirty-seven years I been married, I never laid a hand on my wife."

"You knew Bette, Milo, Jesus, she thinks she's a man."

"You tame her then, you do what you got to do, but you don't hit a broad, don't you know that? Look at you. You're getting fat as a pig, your wig's falling apart, you're shaking so bad for a drink you can't hold still." Milo patted his own flat gut. "I'm gonna be sixty years old in June, you see any fat on me? See me wearing a wig? See me ever get any plastic surgery?"

"I'm an actor, Milo, my appearance—"

"You're a two-bit punk I did a bunch of favors for, that's all you are, and don't you ever forget that. There're guys in this town I did the same for, and you want to know something? I walk into their restaurants, their bars, the joints *I* gave them the money to buy, and they're on their knees, rolling the red carpet down in front of me. They're no different than you, except they know their places in this world."

"When did I ever not respect you, when did I ever dishonor you?"

"You think snorting that shit through your nose doesn't dishonor us, wouldn't break our mother's heart if she learned of it?"

That fucking Maury, that son of a bitch! Who did he think he was, telling Milo that without any proof?

"Milo, that's bullshit, I ain't—"

Without warning Milo spun, raised his foot and kicked his heel through the screen, killing Oprah in mid-sentence. He turned back, breathing heavily, fighting to control himself. He dropped his cigarette onto the white carpet, ground it out with his shoe and shook his head, turned away from Jerome, and walked toward the window.

Billy and Floyd had stood up, were looking at their boss, waiting for orders. They'd obviously seen him like this before, too.

Milo stood at the window, his hands behind his back. "Clear day," he said. "What is this, the forty-fourth floor?"

"Forty-fifth," Billy said.

Calmly, Milo said, "Billy, Floyd, throw that lying piece of shit out this window."

Was he kidding or what? Jerome didn't think so, forgot about it altogether when the two apes began walking toward him, splitting up, going to either side to grab his arms and lifting him off the ground as if he weighed nothing.

He said, "Come on, guys, Jesus Christ," and they began walking him toward the window, where Milo was, staring at him, hard.

Jerome began to struggle, trying to pull his arms away but it was tough, they were squeezing his biceps and he had no balance. His feet were swinging, kicking at air, and he tried to aim the kicks, to hit Billy or Floyd but they knew their business, stepped away a little bit, holding him like a rag doll until he screamed aloud.

The two muscles lifted him high, grabbing his waist, and Milo said, "Right through the glass, fellas, make a lot of noise."

"Nooo!" Jerome shouted, and kicked, his foot connecting with Billy's belly and having no apparent effect. "Jesus God in heaven Milo, no!"

Milo stepped back to give the boys room and at the same moment the door to the bedroom opened and the woman from last night yelled "Ahh!" standing there with a pillow in front of her.

Jerome stopped struggling because the two maniacs had stopped lifting him, their attention was on the woman.

As was Milo's. He was looking at her, at the witness, weighing whether he should throw her out the window, too. Jerome knew that's what he had to be thinking, the way he was looking at her. One thing was certain, there could be no observers; if Jerome took a high dive, the woman took one, too.

There was a layer of fat hanging down from her belly, almost to her pubic area, which was in sight because she was holding the pillow up around her chest. She backed into the bedroom, slowly, her mouth working, terrified.

Milo stared at her, watched her as she retreated, as she turned and ran, her pitted backside jiggling, pudgy legs waddling, and he began to laugh.

Which broke the tension. Billy and Floyd didn't ease up on him, they were still holding him almost above their heads, Jerome now flat out on his back, four powerful hands at his shoulders and ass.

He made his move.

He threw his legs over his head, bringing them all the way up, his stomach muscles screaming from the unaccustomed exercise, and he arched his back as his legs passed over his head. He tumbled head first out of their hands, managed to twist in the air, landing hard on his right shoulder.

"Make sure she don't get on the phone," Milo said, and as he hadn't addressed either man specifically, they both headed into the bedroom, talking to each other in low, amused voices. They sounded disappointed.

Milo was still chuckling, amused. Jerome had by now worked his way up into a sitting position, was rubbing his sore shoulder, wondering if anything was broken or dislocated. There were tears in his eyes, and his lower lip was trembling.

Milo hunched down on his heels and looked Jerome in the eye, not giggling now, staring him in the face with disapproval, disappointment.

"That fat whore the best you can do?" Milo said, and Jerome didn't answer him, just looked at him, at his brother who had betrayed him.

"You gonna kill me?" Now he was begging, his voice breaking. He hated himself for it but there was no stopping it, he couldn't control it, and he let it come, let his terror roll to the surface.

"Maybe. You and that coozy, too, kiddo." He sighed. "You give me your word, you're through with the junk, with the cocaine."

"Milo, I swear to God—"

Milo slapped him, hard, across his right cheek. Jerome covered his face with both hands, rolled over onto his side, cowering away from him.

"You lie to me now, you go skydiving without the parachute."

"Milo, I'll never touch it again, I swear." Jerome rolled away from Milo, got to his feet and held his hands out, pushed them toward Milo in a watch-this gesture.

Jerome slowly backed into the bedroom, looked around, ignored the two goons who were standing on either side of the bed, watching the broad and smiling while she held the sheet up to her neck, like she had something a sane man might want in broad daylight without a fifth of booze in him. He found his suit coat, reached into the pocket and removed his vial, his two-gram stash, and walked, uncapping it, into the bathroom. Jerome poured the dope into the sink then turned the water on, watched it swirl down the drain, then threw the vial to the floor, smashing it to pieces. He turned to his brother, hopefully.

"That's it, I'm through with that shit, Milo, I swear to God, I'll never touch it again, it's just that out in LA it's used the way vino is out here, everybody does it."

"Everybody ain't my brother, ain't got a mother who worships him, neither. Who'd die if she found out her baby was on that garbage." He turned to his boys.

"Okay, men, go on out in the hall, wait for me. Floyd, as soon as the lady gets dressed, I want you to give her a ride home or wherever she wants to go. Then come back here and meet us in the restaurant. Billy, wait for me outside." He said to the woman, "You go on and get dressed, and my man'll take you home."

She was shaking her head, back and forth, her mouth moving but no words coming forth.

"That's a good girl, go ahead now." Milo looked at Jerome, who was standing in the doorway of the bathroom, his head hung down, knowing he'd beaten death and never wanting to face that again. It was the first time he'd ever really confronted his mortality.

"Come on out here with me, kid, while she gets her clothes on." Jerome followed him out of the room and Milo closed the door behind them.

They were alone now, just two men in the room together, in a six-hundred-dollar-a-night suite that had a broken television; a smashed cigarette butt and a hocker on the carpet. Milo said, "You ever use that shit again, and I'll let them boys loose on you, and I ain't kidding."

"You weren't really gonna let them do it, were you, Milo? I don't believe that, I can't believe my own brother was gonna have me murdered." There was wonder in his voice, awe.

"If that broad hadn't come in when she had, it'd be all over by now."

"Milo, no, come on, don't say that."

"We'll never know, will we, Jerome? All you can know for sure is that if I even think you're on that shit again, I'll kill you, because you been warned, it'll be the same thing as if you spit in my face in front of people, you wouldn't leave me no choice."

"I'll never touch it again, Milo, not here, not in LA."

"You better not." Milo smiled at him. "Look at it this way: Billy and Floyd? They're your own personal Betty Ford clinic, and a hell of a lot cheaper. They got connections into every pusher in this entire fucking town, and don't think we can't find out if you go out on the street and get some shit." Milo sneered at him. "Now go wipe the snot off your face and reglue your wig, meet me in the lobby restaurant. I want to talk to you about your golden boy. His old man been fucking me around, and I want to make sure there won't be a lot of heat when I have his ass cut into little pieces."

Kelly entered the room as Babe was hanging up the phone with a smile on his face, the way there usually was when he talked to his brother John. The ashtray was filled already, the room was heavy with smoke, even though the smoke-eater was on. Kelly walked to the window and opened it, stood and smelled the morning breeze. It would be a lovely day.

"Remember me telling you about that girl in grade school, the one whose mother raised hell about the yearbook?" Kelly had a vague memory, from long ago. Had he still been drinking when he'd told her about it? Lord knew it had taken him a couple of years to get totally free from alcohol.

"No," she said, and he shook his head, sure that he had told her.

"There was that teacher who was so nice to me, Mrs. Pomerance, remember I told you about her?" Kelly nodded. "I had her four years out of eight at St. Columba, it was like she was requesting transfers to different grades, following me around to keep an eye on me.

"Anyway, in the eighth grade, she wrote a little yearbook thing for us right before graduation, and mimeographed it, gave a copy of it to everyone in the class. She wrote up a forecast, a prophecy of the future, what we'd all be doing in twenty years."

"I remember now, and she had you down for the heavyweight champion of the world, and you were married to someone in the class."

"I knew I'd told you. Janice Howell, I was married to her and living in a mansion in Winnetka and we had three kids and were happy."

"Her mother did something, right?"

"Came into school the next day and tore into that teacher, ripped her up one side and down the other, told her that her daughter would never be married to a juvenile delinquent animal like me, ever, right in front of the whole class."

Did it bother him, remembering this? It must, but he wasn't showing it, in fact, he was smiling.

Kelly could picture him, thirteen years old, my God, Mike's age, sitting in a classroom and trying to act like it didn't bother him while some classmate's mother called him names in front of everybody.

"So to make her happy, Mrs. Pomerance had to collect every one of those damn yearbooks, I don't know what she did with them. The kicker was, the rest of the class blamed *me*, like it was *my* fault they had to give up the little shitty yearbooks."

"What'd you do?"

"What else? I went out after school and got bombed, talked shit about how I thought it was funny with some of the older high school guys."

"You were drinking even then?"

"Kelly, I started young."

"Babe?" Kelly waited while Babe lit another cigarette, drummed his fingers on the desktop. "Doesn't that bother you, talking about that?"

Babe's smile grew wider and he winked at her. "Used to, not

anymore. You know how John has a listed phone?" He paused for effect, smiled through the smoke at her. "Guess who called him first thing this morning?"

"Mrs. Pomerance?" Kelly was puzzled.

"Naw," Babe said. "Not Mrs. Pomerance." He raised his eyebrows, pleased with himself, and shook his head, grinning for all he was worth. "Janice Howell called him, good old Janice, and she wondered if John would give her my phone number, just so she could give me a ring, talk over all the good times we had in school, I guess."

"Talk about how happy your marriage is, more likely." Kelly gave him a level glare, keeping outwardly calm, although she felt a twinge of jealousy.

"You know what I hope?" Babe said. "I hope old Janice calls her mother up and gives her all kinds of hell for wrecking her chance at the big time."

"Does it matter, what she does, do you care?"

"Care, do I *care*? Honey, that's what this is all about, don't you realize that?"

Kelly looked at her watch to hide her shock. She said, "I've got to get to school."

"Did you happen to make another pot of coffee?"

"Do I look like Juan Valdez? Or a waitress? Or like Janice goddamn Howell? Get your own coffee, I'm not your goddamn servant."

"What'd I do?" Babe said, Kelly hearing him as she walked down the hall, on her way out the door to a college class which she knew that she'd be paying little attention to today.

What had he done? Babe wasn't sure, but it was typical for them, it always happened this way.

The day would be starting out good and he'd say something innocent and she'd get on her high horse, get all irate at him and then not talk to him for a couple of hours, no matter how much he bugged her.

She thought he could read her mind, that had to be it. Thought he knew what would piss her off and what wouldn't. What had he asked her, if she'd made some coffee, what was wrong with that?

How many times had he been in the kitchen and put water in her tea kettle, brought her a cup just because he thought she might want one? There was nothing macho about wondering if she'd made coffee, it was a two-way street in this family, all the way, wasn't it?

Well, part of the way, anyhow.

Was it something he'd said before? The story about Janice Howell? He told her because he thought she'd appreciate the irony of it, the girl who wouldn't even glance his way twenty-five years ago now trying to look him up.

What he hadn't told her was how it had killed him, sitting there pining away over that girl, Janice fragile and pale, with the veins showing clearly in her forehead, Babe feeling lightheaded and woozy when he'd first read the yearbook. He could remember blushing and hiding his head, wondering how Mrs. Pomerance had known that he loved Janice. Nor did he tell Kelly how he'd suffered when that girl's mother had walked into the classroom and had begun her tirade. He never told her things like that, because it embarrassed him, made him feel as if he were looking for sympathy, for her to look at him and say Poor baby or something.

There was another part of the conversation which he'd kept from her, that he'd learned from John. The things his father had said the night before.

How he was going to stick a hand grenade in Babe's ass and pull the pin. How he was going to suck Babe's eyeballs out of his head and bite them off. He had been about to say something more when John had hung up on him.

By tonight, John would be feeling guilty about that, it was the sort of man he was, too sensitive, too kind for his own good. He'd offer his veins to Dracula, if he thought the count needed a drink.

No, he'd keep the old man's ravings to himself, the same as he always did. The guy was getting old, he couldn't last much longer. At that age, in the shape he was in, what harm could he do Babe? Hell, what could he do at all besides make phone calls and shoot off his mouth when he was drunk? Impress Anthony by buying him things, giving him stolen VCRs and watches.

No, Babe thought he was in pretty good shape in that department, in no danger anymore from the old man. Although it might be a good idea to take the pistols down and clean them, check them out real good. Just because he hadn't done it in a while and might not get around to it for some time to come, what with the kids getting out of school soon.

But that was the only reason he'd be doing it, not because of his father, or out of fear. His father was a washed-up old has-been, and nothing more.

Babe turned the machine off on the business line, went to get his guns and his cleaning kit. He'd listen to yesterday's message tapes while he cleaned them, see who had called him besides Spinell. While he was upstairs, he'd put on another pot of coffee. He'd have to now, after what asking about coffee had cost him.

At the same time that Babe was sifting coffee into the filter, the man he saw as the washed-up old has-been who'd fathered him was stalking toward his apartment door, a .357 Magnum in his right hand. He still held the cigarette in the other, the smoke rising, making him squint. He walked lightly, feet sliding on the floor, moving diagonally away from the doorway in case whoever it was behind it decided to shoot through it.

There were maybe ten people alive who knew where Johnny lived, and none of them ever came calling. He'd meet people in the street, in bars, anyplace where he could conduct his business without bringing them here. He was ashamed of this place, of having to live here after the years he'd spent living in high style, in fancy apartment hotels and sometimes even in elegant homes which he'd buy under his wife's maiden name, the credit established by large amounts of money in accounts in her name.

Didn't he wish he had that money now.

But he didn't. What he had was someone knocking at his door at nine-fifteen in the morning.

He walked over and stood to the side of it, the pistol pointed up, held in both hands, next to his ear. The cigarette was smoldering on the tile floor. He would not go to prison again. He was too old to even think about it being a real possibility in his life.

But if they were coming for him, he'd take a couple of the bastards with him.

He took his left hand off the pistol and reached over, threw the lock off and grabbed the knob, twisted, turned, threw the door open and had the gun back in both hands, stepped into the doorway in a combat stance, ready to fire.

At his kid, for Christ's sake, at the dumbass kid of his, Anthony, standing there with a half-smile on his face until he saw the gun.

Johnny lowered it, shaking his head, held it at his side.

"What the hell do *you* want."

"I'm glad to see you, too, shit." Anthony said it with his hurt right out front, turned to leave and Johnny had to ask him not to because he knew that if he didn't the kid might go home and slash his goddamn wrists or something.

Anthony, who sometimes switched his syllables when he spoke in complete sentences, saying "therfa" instead of father, "eymon" instead of money. The kid who'd written Johnny letters every day, sometimes two a day, when Johnny had last been in the penitentiary. Anthony was the child whom Johnny had seen grow up by degrees, being taller, older, every time he saw him, having missed a year or two of his life.

This last time, had there ever been a change. Johnny had gone away and had left behind him a twelve-year-old kid, a pre-teenager who'd worshipped his father, who followed him around and tried to talk like Johnny and walk like Johnny, a kid who'd written to Johnny in all those letters about his teen years, about his heartbreak and the girls he'd lost, about the kind of cars he'd want to have when he got his license. Later, the letters would be whining appeals for sympathy, about how nobody understood him, about how he'd been fired from yet another menial job. He'd come home to find that the kid he'd had all that hope for was now a sullen, skinny loser with no balls, a twenty-four-year-old man who still thought of himself as a mixed-up kid.

When Johnny had been twenty-four, he'd already seen action in Korea, had done his first bit after deserting from the Army, and he'd already killed his first man. Anthony was still living with his mother, at twenty-six, didn't work, couldn't manage to hold down a job, and now seemed to have the family failing. He sure did like his beer.

They sat at the kitchen table, smoking, Anthony doing the talking.

"She's got this thing, Pa, when she drinks. Always gonna kill somebody, you, me, Babe mostly. It's his fault she's broke, that she don't own nothing."

"Can't blame him for not going to see her."

"She sees him, she'll shoot him, that's for sure."

"She ain't gonna kill nobody," Johnny said. "She just likes to hear herself talk. Like a truck driver."

"It's worse than that, Pa." Anthony got up and walked to the refrigerator, deep in thought, opened the box and looked around inside.

"No beer?"

"Anthony, it ain't even ten in the morning."

"I can't tell you what I got to tell you without a drink."

"Force yourself."

The room was smoky, the air thick and stale. The gun was on the table in front of him, cold and deadly. Anthony opened a window and came over to the table, would not meet his father's eyes.

"She's turning into a whore, Papa, guys from work are coming over with bottles and she gets drunk with them and then goes into her bedroom."

"Ah, Jesus, ah shit."

"The other night, there was *two* of them, guys looked younger than me. I come home, she introduces them to me, and you could see them, the way they were looking at me, like making fun of me, daring me to say something about them being there to screw my mother." Anthony's eyes filled with tears and he swiped at them angrily with his sleeves.

"I split, man, I ain't gonna sit still for that, watch it happen. I come home four hours later, she's layin' on the carpet in her bedroom, naked, passed out like she'd tried to make it to her bathroom and was too drunk to get there."

"What'd you do?"

"I covered her up and went and sat at the kitchen counter and cried."

"Ah, shit," Johnny said again. He knuckled his forehead, kneaded it hard, his eyes squeezed shut tight. "The booze got her, Anthony, and it's gonna get you, too, if you ain't careful."

"I want to kill them, Pa, I want to take a gun and blow them away, all of them."

"Don't talk like that, stop that kind of talk right now." Johnny rose to his feet, enraged. "A kid like you, you couldn't make it five minutes in the joint, killer jacket or not. Someone'd take a look at you and have you picked out as his old lady before you got out of R and I."

"Ain't nobody gonna fuck me, man," Anthony said, and Johnny looked at him.

At his soft, full lips, the lower one pouting. At the long eyelashes, the rosy cheeks. At the skinny arms and the sunken, hairless chest.

"You don't have no idea what it's like in there."

"I'd get by."

"Survive, maybe, sure. Most guys do."

"You think I ain't tough, that I can't handle myself?" Was he getting fierce with him, playing bad? Johnny couldn't believe his ears, his eyes. From Babe, he would expect this, but not from Anthony.

Margie had written to him in prison about the change in Anthony's behavior, about his gloominess, his depressions, his fits of temper, as if there was anything Johnny could do about that shit from the inside. Had told him what the doctors had said, that he was a borderline psychotic with schizophrenic tendencies, and that when he didn't take the medication that they prescribed he would lose it, break things and have tantrums. Which was fine for you to have when the only person around to see it was your mother. But if he pulled that act in the joint, around some *real* tough guys, they'd laugh, then knock him down and take their time, take their turns.

But he wouldn't tell Anthony this. The kid was at a point in his life where everything he did was to prove something to somebody, and Johnny could just see him, doing something stupid in order to go to prison, to prove to them all that he could handle it.

Which he couldn't do. No way on God's earth could this kid ever do time, not even in the county, not even in a federal penitentiary. Somebody, somewhere, would turn this kid out, maybe even hurt him bad. Hell, if he wasn't Johnny's own kid, Johnny himself might take a shot at him in a cell late at night, and Johnny needed young ass less than most.

Instead, he just looked at him, trying to be a father and not knowing where to begin.

Anthony, sulking, spoke in a dull whisper, as if afraid that the room was bugged, and the words he spoke turned Johnny's spine to ice.

"You think I couldn't do it, that I couldn't whack somebody out? Well let me tell you something. You hear about the fire at the Placebo Lounge, killed four motherfuckers last night? You read the papers yet? Well, take a look at the front page, if you can see past the picture of your goddamn *famous* son." He sat back and calmed himself, then jabbed his thumb into his chest. "It was me that lit the ing-fuck match."

Johnny looked at his baby, stunned to silence. Stared at him with his mouth open, disbelieving. Saw the kid as he really was for the first time, not looking at him as his son now, now he was seeing him as the type of man he'd come across before in his lifetime. Johnny was looking at a young psychopath, at a guy who'd do your ass in in a second as long as he felt secure that no one else was looking. He looked at him for what seemed to be eternity, thinking it over, at the problems it posed and the future profits that might be gained from such a discovery, and then, for the third time in ten minutes, Johnny Hilliard said, "Ah shit."

And his youngest son, his baby, said to him, "And I'll do it to her, too, if I gotta stay in that house one minute longer."

"Where you gonna stay, you ain't got a job, you ain't got any money."

"Well I thought I could stay here with you," Anthony said.

"Anthony?" Johnny spoke in a cracking voice, cleared it once and spit on the floor. "Anthony?" There, that was better. The last thing he could afford to do in this life, from this point on, was to show this kid any weakness, any faults that he could exploit. Anthony looked up at him, his secret out, his eyes shining, his mouth set in the same cocky pose his mother's would have when she was about to tell you to go fuck yourself.

"Yeah?"

Johnny said, "Forget about it, you can't stay here."

"Then she's dead, her and whoever she brings home tonight."

"That's not what I meant, I don't want you to go home, not tonight, not ever. We'll get you a place, probably worse than this, but it'll be your own."

"Can you help me out, Pa? Can you get me in with you?"

"Anthony," Johnny said, "I don't believe you'll be much out of demand, once some guys I know get to know you better."

"Can we go get a beer, now, Pa? This ain't been easy, telling you this."

"Let's go get that beer, son," Johnny said, and rose from the table, wrapping the robe tightly around his belly, belting it again. "I'll get dressed and we'll go and get you your beer." When he left the room, he made sure that he took the pistol with him.

16

"So this son of a bitch, out of loyalty, I throw him a bone, a living," Milo said, and Jerome was trying to pay attention, to make sure that Milo didn't get mad at him again, but it wasn't easy.

What did he care about this mobster bullshit? He wasn't one of them. He was an actor, for God's sake.

He'd come down to the seventh-floor lobby and taken a right past the concierge's desk, walked through the massive entranceway into the large dining room, spotted his brother sitting at a window table, with Billy, the two of them staring down at Michigan Avenue, at the people seventy feet below them. If the window was open, if it was officially summer, Jerome could see them spitting down on people, dropping butter patties on their heads as they passed below. There was a fire going in the fake thing in the corner that Jerome hated, one of those gas deals that didn't smell of burning wood, had a big rock cut into the shape of a log in the middle of it, painted brown so dumb or retarded people might be fooled into thinking that it was real. Back home Jerome had a real fireplace, one even bigger than this one. He had a wife back home, too, that he loved the most when he was in some kind of trouble, when there was no one else for him to turn to.

Milo said, "He gets out, he gets almost forty K, that he blows like he's young and got prospects, instead of taking it and retiring, like he should'a." What did Babe's father have to do with him? But Jerome couldn't tell Milo that he wasn't on speaking terms with Babe, that Babe was mad at him. Milo had put up almost half the money for the production company and Milo's partner, Maury, that stoolpigeon slob of a prick, had put up the rest. Jerome hadn't put up a dime and would be sharing in the profits, a full third, for putting it all together, for doing the work that the agent, Milland Grand, should have done. And now that dip, Grand, would be getting ten points from damn near everyone in the series who wasn't union wage, would take the electricians' dough if he could.

That damn Maury, telling Milo all his personal business. That fat old Jew-boy slob! Jerome knew a few things about *him*, too, about the young girls he had a penchant for, the teenyboppers who were the only ones who could get his ancient snake to dance. When he got back to LA, he'd be sure to drop a dime on Maury, make sure his old lady knew about his outside action. Hell, she probably already knew. She probably even watched.

"He comes to me, broke, crying. 'Milo, come on, I kept my trap shut, help me out here.' So I give him the handbook action in the far South Side, not the phone stuff, just the street shit. South Chicago, Hegewisch, East Side, they're all his. Gets ten percent off the top of all losses, nothing from the winnings, unless the winners throw him a bone, I don't know. He got runners out there working for him, but not our boys, not even white guys. South Americans, he got, some spics from Venezuela or some damn place. He's running his ass off, working like a dog, making a good buck and he got no complaints."

"So what's the problem, Milo? Guy asks for a job, you give him a job, he does the job, plain and simple." Jerome shrugged. "What would you want to cut him into little pieces for?"

He was feeling more comfortable now, still a little scared but in control. The restaurant was only about half full right now, but everyone knew who he was, were shooting furtive looks his way. Recognizing him from Sunday night's show. The waiter referred to him by his television name, had called him Mr. Papajohn, with delight.

"The problem," Billy said, "is that you ain't listening, that you're doing all the talking."

"Hey," Jerome said, "who the fuck you think you're talking to?"

Billy smiled. "Think seven stories up ain't high enough to hurt you, I throw you out the window now instead of upstairs, shorty?"

"That's *enough*," Milo hissed. He was staring at Billy with blazing eyes, and Jerome almost felt sorry for the kid. When Milo gave you The Glare, it was the second worst thing he might do to you. "That's my *brother* you're talking shit at, Billy."

Billy was right away contrite, aware that he'd overstepped his boundaries. "Hey, Milo, I'm sorry."

"You could be sorrier, you don't shut your trap." Milo looked around him, snapped his fingers at the waiter, stared at Billy until the waiter arrived.

"Yes, sir?" the waiter said.

Milo said, "Take this lug's food over there to the next table, give him anything he wants and put it on my bill."

"Yes, sir," the waiter said, without even raising an eyebrow, and did as he was told and Jerome watched him, watched Billy, too, who didn't have the guts to shoot dirty looks at Milo but who had no problem giving them to Jerome, blaming him for the humiliation. Jerome wanted to thank Milo for giving him one more man to be looking over his shoulder for in life.

"Where was I?"

"South American Venezuelans collecting gambling bets."

"Yeah, that's right." Milo sipped his coffee and looked thoughtful. The crumbs from the muffin he'd had for breakfast were on a delicate little bread plate at the side of the table, along with the three plates that had been Jerome's, which had once held buttermilk pancakes, eggs and sausages, and toast. Billy, he was still eating, his head sunk down in a plate, shoveling away and washing everything down with a Diet Coke. Even from a table away, Jerome could hear the guy grunting. "Now, you got to understand, the guy's been doing the job with them, no problem. He uses the spics and one of his kids, the perverted one likes to get spanked by broads. He ain't skimming too much, or he'd be in the lake right now, movie star son or no. But I find out today he's been booking some of the bigger bets himself."

"Okay if the bettor loses."

"Only if he pays up."

Jerome immediately began to appreciate the fact that Milo was talking to him like an equal now, it suddenly made him feel important. When Billy had been there, he'd felt embarrassed, foolish under the animal's cruel stare. But now it was almost fun, like doing a Showtime original movie about gangsters, Jerome feeling that he was one of them and yet able to turn it off when the director yelled Cut. This wasn't any more real than Oscar night, and he knew in his heart now that Milo had been running a game on him earlier, hadn't really been about to have him thrown out of his window.

When Jerome spoke now he played it as if it was a role, talking hard out of the side of his mouth, being a tough guy.

"You mean he owes money?"

"I got a call from his crew leader, Landini, been with me forever, who tells me one of the immigrants owed a guy money and didn't show up with it, the guy it was owed to called Johnny, and Johnny told him that he'd given it to the spic, that he'd straighten the guy out, he'd get him his money and bring him the spic's ears, all kind of shit like that, but see, Jerome, he didn't. So the winner called Landini. Johnny ain't answering his phone all of a sudden, ain't answering the winner's beeps, either. The winner calls Landini, Landini, he calls me before he brings it to Johnny on account of at one time Johnny was a real heavyweight, and some of my guys don't know how far to go with the guy."

"He got it in him, still?"

"I don't know." Milo looked preoccupied as he thought, like a college professor trying to think up the precise and proper phrase to describe a philosophical theorem to the class.

"Fucker can get whacked, don't matter how tough he is," was Milo's theorem. "Anyway, one of the spics winds up dead in a empty lot over in the Harbor, and I told Landini this morning when he called to wait, to see if the other guy gets paid, the guy the spic stiffed."

"So he ain't turning in money, is that right?"

"The money's right, Jerome, pay attention, will you?"

"But you just said it wasn't, that the guy was robbing you."

"Listen to me. Even if he pays the guy, he's still late, and that reflects on me, on my business. And if he don't pay the guy, and the guy knows that I'm the head man, and knows that I still want his business, that I ain't about to lose a steady customer, who you think got to pay the bill owed?"

"You."

"That's right."

"So what are you gonna do?"

"How tight are you with Johnny's kid, with Babe Hill?"

Without hesitation Jerome put his hand up and crossed two fingers and lied. "Like this. We're like brothers."

"That's a good thing, because I been thinking. I kill this Johnny, I'm in the hole for what he lost, and that's the end of it. But if you can convince his kid, who's making a pretty good buck, that his old man's gonna die if he don't cough up the dough, we not only get the dough, but we got a well to go to, a bottomless pit that's signed for the season. He can cover for the old man, say a few K every week, or we make it clear to him, his old man goes down the tubes, gets cut to pieces and dies real slow. He pays, the old man gets to live, playing around for peanuts out in Hegewisch, on the East Side, dies of natural causes and we hope he lasts another ten years." Milo grinned. "By then, we'll own Babe's soul."

"That's you, Milo," Jerome said, his heart sinking. "Always thinking." It was a good idea, a great one, if the kid loved his old man. This would solve all his problems. Get Babe to thinking that Jerome had saved his father's life, get Babe in his debt. Knock that chip off the punk's shoulder and get him grateful to Jerome, teach him some humility. Get him to make the series for maybe twenty grand a week and put the rest in his own pocket. There were, however, just a couple of small flies in the ointment: Babe wasn't returning his calls, and Jerome knew for a fact that the kid hated his old man.

There were other things here to consider. Maury could not have told Milo about their troubles with Babe, or Milo would not have asked how close Jerome was to him. Milo had to know that the kid was balking, he was, after all, one of the principals of the production company, but he didn't know about the bad blood, about the animosity between Babe and the rest of them out there in LA. Which told him that Maury was as scared of Milo as everyone else, was telling him as little as he had to in order to keep Milo in Chicago and off his back. It was good information to have, would come in handy when it was time to send some paybacks Maury's way.

Still, he couldn't let Milo down, couldn't let him know that things were out of control. Milo could say anything he wanted in front of his boys, but Jerome would bet all the future residuals from his two syndicated shows that the act this morning was more in anger at Babe Hill not signing for the series yet than it was about

Jerome's drug use. It was a sudden and rare insight for Jerome, to understand this, underscored by the fact that, for a mill and a half, Milo would cut their mother into small pieces, make her die real slow, right along with Babe's old man.

"So you'll talk to the boy?"

"I'm on my way out there this morning."

"Where's he live?"

Jerome panicked for a minute, having no idea, but he got it back right away, said, "I ain't sure, I got the address up in the room. How much does his old man owe you?"

"Let's start with, say, ten grand, see how the kid reacts to that. I'll send Billy with you."

"No, not one of those gorillas, a kid like this, like Babe, he got to be handled just right or he might blow up."

"More the reason to have some muscle with you."

"Believe me, Milo, it's a bad idea."

"Have it your way, but if he gives you a hard time, let me know. So now, when you gonna get over and see Mama? She knows you're in town, you know."

Jerome was saved from answering because Milo noticed Floyd enter the room and he smiled, pointed his chin at the big guy, amused. Floyd's arms were bulging the material of his short-sleeve shirt. He stood there looking around, ignoring the waiter who was standing there trying to look down his nose at a man who was six inches taller than he was. Floyd spotted them, began walking toward them, shooting quizzical looks at his partner, banished to another table.

He came over, stood before them, his face a blank slate, held up both of his hands, palms outward. "I interrupting something?"

"No," Milo said, leaning back to look up at him. "So you get the lady home all right?"

"Yeah," Floyd said, and snickered. "She offered me a piece of ass if I'd bust Jerome up for her, said he treated her like shit after we left the room."

"What'd you tell her?" Jerome said.

"Tole her I'd pick her up at seven, we could discuss it," Floyd said, and Milo laughed.

"I got to go," Jerome said.

The talk radio show host's name was Waldo Heltz, and he was the morning drive-time guy with the largest ratings in a very big town. When he called Babe on the business line during the ten o'clock news and commercial break, Babe had been happy to hear his voice, as he'd been half-expecting Spinell to be on the other end.

"Babe, Babe, it's a tough one, the way they're treating you."

"Who's that?"

"My lines have been ringing off the hook for the past two mornings, half the calls irate listeners wanting to bust your hump, the other half supporters, girls wanting to marry you."

Waldo was extremely fat, with a low, sexy voice and a way of sneaking up on you. He'd been in town forever, knew his way around that microphone. Babe had done the show a half a dozen times, some of the interviews conducted in the studio, others done over the phone, and they never went the same way twice. You had to watch your step around a guy like Waldo.

"It doesn't matter what they say about you, as long as they're talking."

"You sound like one of your flacks. Like that publicity broad for your production company, the one that used to work for the book publisher with the Catholic saint's name? She calls me up, wants to put some stiff actor from your show on the air, pushes me, tells me I *need* her. You ever hear the story about her, how she got from New York to LA?"

"How's that?"

"There was this writer, doing all right for himself, wrote about South Florida and was making millions. His agent sends his next manuscript out to this publisher, whom she worked for as an editor, just to see what they might offer, and she read it, called the writer up and told him, 'I think it might work, but lose the boat and have this McGee fellow live in a condo, and think about changing that silly name.'"

"No, that's just a story, right?"

"I swear to God it's true, she'd never *heard* of MacDonald, they don't teach you about him at Mills."

"Good Lord," Babe said.

"So it doesn't bother you?" Waldo wanted to know, switching gears, reminding Babe of Tim. "Doesn't hurt your feelings that your old neighbors see you as a traitor?"

"Come on, Waldo, how much does it matter? A bunch of people who don't have jobs, listening to radio shows at ten in the morning, talking about me, how could it hurt?"

"You know that, and *I* know that, but the sponsors, kiddo, they just eat it up, this kind of controversy. So how about an hour?"

"When?"

"Right now, after the news. You're there, in the safety of your house, the line's open, you say what you want. We put some of these unemployed and unwashed masses on the line and you tear into them."

"I'm not interested in stirring things up worse than they already are."

"Look, I already told the audience I'd be reaching out for you during the news. Don't you want to tell your side of the story? How's this sound? We do fifteen minutes, talking, you give your side of the thing. Then we open the line for forty-five, you can say any damn thing you want to them."

"Anything?"

"Well, within FCC regs."

"You on my side in this, Waldo?"

"Always, kid," Waldo said.

"Make it fifteen talking, fifteen open line, and you got a deal."

"I love you Babe, I really do."

So now he was waiting, sitting in his office with the ringer turned off on his other line, the door closed, the window open now because he knew he'd be chainsmoking throughout the conversation, Babe looking out the window at ground level, seeing green mown grass, absently twirling a clean and empty pistol around on his right index finger.

This was always the worst time of a radio interview, the waiting before going on, and he'd learned that you couldn't trust the interviewer unless he was aware that you knew where he lived and that you were capable of stopping by, showing your dissatisfaction at the way he'd treated you.

He'd had experience with them. He'd talk to them, take the calls from their listeners, be polite, and everything would seem to go okay, they'd thank him afterward and tell him it had been a pleasure, then his publicity people would call him, ask him what the hell had he said, ask him how had he alienated the host. Tell him that the producers had said he'd been evasive and that he went off on tangents, wouldn't answer straight questions with straight answers.

What was he supposed to do? He'd always been diplomatic with these people, was never rude or ignorant, even when he felt the urge to be. They'd ask him questions about the most personal aspects of his life and he was supposed to bare his soul to raise their ratings points a fraction? Like hell, he would.

Now the big leagues were calling, wanting him on their shows. On the tape he'd played back had been a call from the company's PR people, wanting him on *Good Morning America* and the *Today* show next week, to spend five minutes talking about the series he hadn't signed to do. Leno, too, his people had called, and Babe would like to meet the guy, see if he was as funny in person as he was in front of the camera.

Geraldo sure wasn't. Babe had been invited onto his show and had invoked the man's wrath by walking off in front of millions of viewers when he'd learned that the topic was "TV Hunks," and Geraldo personally called the production company to tell them that no one they hired would ever be on one of his shows again, ever. Babe had received supportive letters over that move once the media had reported it. Now, maybe it was time to take some heat, he didn't know.

But would soon find out, because he could hear the news winding down, a woman doing the weather then the traffic reports.

It was all beginning for him, the things he'd dreamed about. And hadn't he known all along that sometimes even the most pleasant of dreams could turn into nightmares?

But that sort of thinking was for later, right now the producer was in his ear, prepping him, talking into the phone in a self-important voice, then counting down the seconds until he heard Waldo's voice . . .

"And this is Waldo Heltz, welcoming all you wonderful listeners back for another hour of laughter, discussion, and the fine, forgotten art of conversation. And have I got a treat for you. With us from his home in Park Forest, Illinois, is the man you've all been talking about for the past two days, Mr. Street Babe himself, Babe Hill! Babe, thanks for being on the show."

"Good to be back on, Waldo."

"Always a pleasure to have you. Tell me, why did the producers name the show after you? I mean, that's never happened before, that I'm aware of, that a network has named an entire show after one of its stars."

It was the way Waldo was. In conversation away from the mike he rarely fractured his syntax, would always speak in educated tones, clearly, concisely. Once he was on the air, he would go off on you, speak in sentences you had a hard time figuring out, acting just a little bit dumb, as if that would endear him to his audience, make them his friends. It sure had worked since as far back as Babe could remember.

"The idea behind it, Waldo, was to build the show around me, make it mine. The writers and I worked hard together to personalize it, to make it entirely what we wanted it to be. I'm very proud of the way this show turned out."

Shit! He hated it when he said stuff like that. Hated it when he sounded phony. Hated doing live radio interviews altogether. Should he hang up? Not yet. He'd wait, see how the callers reacted.

"So it's entirely your show, is what you're saying?"

"Pretty much. The producers knew up front that I'd be starring in it, they designed it around me, let me do what I wanted."

"Isn't that rather unprecedented, that sort of thing in Hollywood? I mean, there are thousands of actors out there willing to sell their souls to get even a bit part in a Sunday Night Movie, and here they are, custom-building one around you."

"They wanted me right from the start, they came to me. One of the producers, Jerome Spinell, was born and raised in the city, and he had faith that I could pull this off. And besides, as far as the actors who'd sell their souls for a good part? I ain't one of them, Waldo. It's not an act I could pull off."

"What you *have* seemed to have pulled off, Babe, is the sort of controversy we haven't seen since the Nazis marched in Skokie. In these past few days, we've had callers lighting up the phone lines wanting to discuss the show. Most of it's been positive feedback, mind you, but there've been enough calls from people wanting to know why you're portraying Hegewisch in such an unfavorable light for it to get your attention."

What the hell had he just said? Babe couldn't figure it out. The man got on the air and spoke doubletalk at you.

"They obviously never read any of the articles about me. It's the same thing that happened when *Bonfire of the Vanities* was filmed in the South Bronx. People picketed the set, tried to disrupt the production, crying about how the movie was portraying the South Bronx as a hell hole. Waldo, you ever been to the South Bronx?"

"So what you're saying, then, Babe, is that Hegewisch is to Chicago what the South Bronx is to New York?"

Babe began to get flustered. Was Waldo deliberately misunderstanding him, or was he not expressing himself clearly? He spoke fast now, getting his words out before anyone in the audience could take his silence as agreement. "Waldo, that's not at all what I'm saying. What I'm saying is that people get provincial. They can't take any criticism—even perceived criticism—of their neighborhoods. Hegewisch isn't some hell hole, and it's certainly not the South Bronx. We shot it the way it was, the way I remember it. We used the South Shore Inn—a real tavern—for our interior bar shots, and we brought in tens of thousands of dollars for the community. If somebody has a problem with that then we'll shoot in Cal City, or build a damn set in LA, see how much attention the area gets once we're out of it."

"You never said Hegewisch was—and I quote from today's *Tribune* now—a 'brutal slum'?"

"Anyone who said I said that is a liar. Waldo, what I've been saying all along is, I made some stupid choices, me, nobody else. There were influences that guided me, but I take the rap for what I did back then." Should he open up now? He never had before, not to any interviewer. But maybe it was time. Even past time. He'd take a shot, tell them a few things and see how they took them.

"I got out of the car about ten minutes before Edward Cieleski got his head torn off in a wreck on the S curve; I walked by Little Park on the way to school the morning that Bob Ellis was found against the fence, dead. I was pals with Ronnie Valance and Larry Sobieski, who are both dead, Larry's brother Hitter was one of my few friends. They and maybe twenty other guys I knew personally didn't make it to thirty because of some stupid, unnatural death.

"I was arrested for burglary six times before I was twenty, Waldo. Once for inciting to riot and then later once for attempted murder. And you and everybody else knows that when that guy died I was arrested and convicted of manslaughter. A stupid bar fight that turned ugly wound up costing a man his life.

"Why am I telling you this? Believe me, I'm not bragging, not proud of what I was. I'm trying to make a point, which is that I'm certain that most of the people in Hegewisch are good, hard-working, God-fearing people. The day after a blizzard you can walk six blocks in a row in that town and not get your shoe leather wet because the sidewalks will be shoveled clean. The mills closed and did you hear anyone crying, see anyone marching, trying to get the government to support them? Uh-uh, they picked themselves up, dusted themselves off, and found other work.

"But Waldo, for anyone to say that there wasn't a subculture, an underclass of thieves, of drug users and pushers in that town in the seventies, well, that's garbage, because I was there, I was part of it. I'm ashamed to admit it, but I was. The people who deny that reality are sticking their heads in the sand, and the further you stick your head in that sand, the more of an opportunity you're giving to someone walking by with sodomy on his mind."

"Pretty strong language, Babe."

"Let the FCC sue me." He was into it now, feeling his dander rising. Feeling a little self-righteous, too, and that was always fun. He said, "These people who are attacking me made the right choices, were born into the right homes, had the proper upbringing and went on to college and good careers. I applaud them. But to say I didn't have my negative experiences is stupid. It's all in the way you lived, Waldo. What they're saying, is, they didn't live it, so it didn't happen. That's just plain dumb."

"Well, let's take a break and when we come back we'll go to the phone lines."

Babe heard the commercial, Waldo on tape hyping some car dealership, then heard Waldo's voice live, directly in his ear.

"Doin' great, Babo."

"Waldo, you said fifteen minutes of talk."

"It's been fifteen minutes."

"It's been less than five."

"No, your watch is off, and remember, there's nothing to be afraid of, these are unemployed idiots, aren't they? Here we go!"

"And we're back live with Babe Hill on the phone and your calls are lighting up my board like the mayor lights the Christmas tree in December. Hello, Melissa, you're on the air!"

"Waldo, am I on?" Her voice was soft, insecure. She sounded afraid.

"Yes indeedy," Waldo said.

"Mr. Hill? Babe? Are you there?"

"Yes, Melissa."

"I just *loved* your show, Babe, and I really need to know, are you married, Babe?"

Babe felt the anger rise inside him and fought it down, but damnit, people didn't pay attention. He'd just told these listeners more than he ever thought he'd ever tell anyone, and all this girl wanted to know was if he was married. He forced himself to speak calmly, tried to sound relaxed.

"You see, Melissa, that's exactly what I was talking about. You've obviously never read anything written about me, you're judging me strictly from a visual point of view, relating me to the character I play. I've told every reporter I've ever spoken to that I'm married, that I've been married almost a third of my life and that I'm gonna *stay* married—"

"You don't have to be so rude." She sounded about to cry.

"I didn't mean it, Melissa, it wasn't personal, but those Hegewisch people have me worked up . . ." The Hegewisch people, and Kelly, storming out of the house, and his father, threatening to stick hand grenades in his ass, and Waldo, with his phantom fifteen minutes . . .

"Hello, you're on the air!"

The next four callers were supporters, people who told him to keep up the good work and he had to bite his tongue, did they think that he was planning on doing some *bad* work?

He was polite, said the right things, and was under control when the first caller from Hegewisch came on the line.

Her name was Rita and she claimed she'd gone to school with him, remembered him in high school before he'd dropped out, then said that he had always been alone, that he always looked so sad and brooding and that he never smiled.

He told her, "Rita, I'm afraid I don't remember you," and she said that didn't surprise her, that he didn't seem to have any friends back then.

Had it been that bad, had he really been so isolated? He didn't remember it as being much fun, but he didn't recall always being alone, never smiling.

"Hello, you're on the air!"

"Yeah, my name's Jabbo." The man spoke with an insolence born of ignorance, and Babe could picture him, fat and sloppy, sitting in a bar somewhere with his belly hanging over his belt, having a beer and telling everybody how he'd told off the movie star.

"Jab*lon*ski. You remember me, Babe." Saying it as if they'd been partners, old friends. Every sentence ended with a down turn in his tone of voice, the exact opposite of a question, as if he knew everything, had all the answers and could see through everybody. Babe had met his kind before. Hell, he was re*lat*ed to people like this. The man hadn't said anything yet, and already, Babe couldn't stand him.

"I'm the mailman, but I knew you from Smiley's."

"Smiley's tavern."

"Right. Sox games and Bears football, that's us."

"Jabbo, I haven't had a drink in over ten years."

"But you used to come in there."

"Years ago."

"And you were a two-bit punk then, and you're a two-bit liar of a punk now." Babe was shocked for a second and Jabbo must have felt that he'd stunned him into silence, continued in a vein that made Babe's skin crawl.

"Know your old man, too, if you know what I'm talking about. Know how you got off for the murder without having to go to prison, like anyone else would have."

"Those are pretty strong words!" Waldo chimed it in, heating it up. Babe knew that he was egging the man on; you could hear the glee in Waldo's tone.

"I'd say stronger if we wasn't on the radio, if that two-bit punk was here with me."

Babe found his tongue. "It's easy to talk trash from the anonymity of your home, Jablonski." Babe said it dryly, giving the man a taste of his own medicine, making it clear that he was not impressed or intimidated. "Over the phone lines. Go sit in Smiley's, ace, tell them what a big man you are. We know better, though, don't we, *Jabbo*. Guys like you fold when the heat's on, every time. Unless you're drunk, then you might take a swing at someone with that liquid courage inside of you."

"You little punk, why don't you come down there sometime."

"Because I don't soil my hands shoveling garbage."

Waldo said, "Mr. Jablonski, hold on a minute," then said to Babe, "Babe, I believe I'm going to terminate this call."

Babe said, "Don't you dare, I want to talk to this guy!"

"I think not," Waldo said.

Babe ran to the upstairs entertainment center and flipped on the radio, had to turn it to AM then flip through the dial until he found Waldo's show. Waldo was talking to that Jablonski asshole, soothingly.

"—too often happens when a person from this town makes it big, or thinks he has."

"When he started talking mean to that little girl, I just had to tell him off. He never was nothing but a punk, Waldo, and believe me, I known him since he was about eighteen, sitting in the bars telling lies."

"Well that you did, Mr. Jablonski, and I thank you for it. What some people seem to forget is that it's you out there, you in your homes, who made them what they are. No matter how far any entertainer rises in life, he'll fall flat on his face the second he forgets that simple fact. Babe Hill seems to have forgotten it. Let's hope he remembers it before he winds up broke and alone. Now we have Stella calling.

"Hello, Stella, you're on the air!"

Stella said, "Waldo, I'm glad you cut that man off, but I wish he was still on all the same, I'd like to give him a piece of my mind, the way he was treating people! He's so ignorant, ain't it? I'm from Hegewisch for sixty-one years and I'm goll-darned proud of it!"

"He forgot one simple fact, madam," smooth-talking Waldo Heltz said, "this is a people place, and mine is a people show. When Babe Hill remembers that, and if he's willing to apologize to my listeners, then maybe I'll have him back on, but not before then."

"Well, *he* ain't nothing but a *dupah yosh*, but I love your show and I love you, Waldo!"

"And we love you too, madam," Waldo said, intimately.

18

The mountain bike was tearing around the curves at the forest preserve, even though the signs said you were only supposed to go eight miles per hour, tops, or else the radar rangers would ticket you, bar you from the trail. Babe didn't much care.

He pedaled hard, breathing heavily, his Walkman up around his ears, turned up loud, pumping his legs as he listened to the people rapping with that traitor, Waldo, calling Babe names and telling them how much they'd enjoyed it when Mr. Jabbo had given him hell.

"Son of a *bitch!*" Babe said, between gasps.

Every so often he'd pass walkers and joggers, drug dealers, too, who these days made it a habit of hanging out there, as there was a large pond in the middle of the preserve into which they could throw their product on the off chance that an officer of the law came by. Not to mention the fact that with a million trees, there were plenty of hiding places for them.

Their gang graffiti was everywhere, sprayed on the concrete, on the trees. A couple of years ago they'd dug up the body of a kid Babe had known, a druggie who couldn't get off the junk and found out just how tough he was when he tried to rip off his supplier. There was a tree next to the spot where he'd been buried, and someone had carved three sixes onto that tree, as if they were marking the spot.

Babe shivered every time he passed that spot, as if Chuckie's ghost was watching him. Tim had been one of the cops who'd dug up the corpse, had told Babe that it hadn't been pretty. It had been buried for a couple of years before the killer confessed after he'd been busted for something else.

Babe pedaled on, only using three of the bike's fifteen gears, trying to avoid the twinkling brown glass that was everywhere because of the broken beer bottles that the gangbangers smashed onto the pavement for kicks.

"Hello, you're on the air!"

"You were rude to that man, to Mr. Hill," an irate male caller was defending him, and Babe felt a moment's resentment. He didn't need anyone apologizing for him!

"I grew up in Hegewisch, too, and none of your callers seemed to mention that a Chicago police officer was beaten to death at Wolf Lake a couple of years ago, or that an off-duty cop shot and killed my pal Davey for no reason, then the city screwed his widow out of her settlement. Nobody seems to want to talk about the decapitated head that a rival gang threw through the window of the biker bar back in seventy-three—"

"Sir, hold on, let me stop you right there. Can you prove any of these allegations? These aren't the sort of things that my other callers have been talking about the past two mornings."

"They're a matter of record! Your last caller was saying that Babe's a liar for saying he lived in a rooming house that had winos and cockroaches in it, and I can tell you there were more than one like that! Those winos used to buy our beer for us! One of them, the Starlight Lounge, got torched in seventy-two, killed two guys were up there sleeping it off at six in the afternoon. That was on TV, Waldo."

"Well, *I* don't remember seeing that," Waldo said, and terminated the call.

Just before Babe passed people walking or jogging on the trail he would sometimes see them look up, appearing bored at his approach until they recognized him, and if there was more than one they would grab each other, point him out—Is that *him*?—shout things out to him as he raced away from them.

He didn't respond. None of them had ever looked up or shouted anything at him in the years that he'd been driving this route, six days a week when the weather permitted and he was in town. Where were they then? When he'd needed some encouragement?

And why was he torturing himself, listening to this stupid show? Waldo had set him up, had done him in on purpose, even though he had to admit that he had been at least partially to blame.

He could be a real asshole sometimes, and he knew it. He prided himself on being in control, on having his buttons hidden. Because he'd been in jail for killing a man in the heat of anger, he was more aware than most as to what could happen when you lost control.

So why had he blown it? Gone on about sodomy and insulted some stupid fat slob of a mailman? After a little thought he'd remembered Jabbo—remembered him being drunk all the time, sitting in Smiley's in his uniform, his undelivered mail in a brown leather saddlebag at his feet—but wouldn't give the bastard the satisfaction of telling him that he remembered him. Babe wanted all of them to think that he was above that stuff now, the sitting in the bars and watching sports and bad-mouthing the spouse and getting high, but the fact was, the further away from it he got, the more he seemed to miss it.

The idea seemed attractive to him at the moment: Head into Hegewisch and have a few drinks, see who wanted to say something to him face to face.

Now there was another woman on the line, speaking to Waldo in cut-short phrases, slapping her consonants hard as she told that wrinkled old Benedict Arnold son of a bitch that Babe Hill was nothing but a damned disgrace, pardon her French, and Waldo, eating it up, encouraged her.

Babe braked hard, nearly flew over the handlebars as he squeezed both hand brakes abruptly. He came to a swerving stop, sweating heavily, breathing through his mouth, the deviated septum that he'd never had fixed—a present from his father—not allowing him the luxury of normal breathing. He removed the Walkman and aimed it at the nearest tree, threw it as hard as he could and watched it smash against the bark, break into several pieces. One of which ricocheted back at him and he ducked, cursing.

"Fuck you, Waldo!" he shouted, then heard a sharp intake of breath and turned quickly, saw a grossly overweight woman waddling on the far side of the track, holding a large, antisocial mongrel on a leash, the dog nearly pulling her off her feet as it lurched toward Babe silently, salivating, teeth bared. The woman now leaning down and fingering the snap that would free the mutt for attack.

"I apologize," Babe said. "I didn't know anybody was there."

"Just drive your ass away, mister, and nobody will have a problem."

"I—"

But there was nothing more to say. Babe hit the pedals and zipped away, wanting nothing more than to make the next curve, get out of the woman's sight, although her voice followed him for a second as he hurried away.

"And don't be leaving your trash all over our forest preserve!"

Her words didn't bother him. They could have been worse. At least she hadn't recognized him, and for once in his career, he truly valued that.

At the next exit he turned off, wanting out of there before he went around again and had to face the woman a second time.

He knew one thing for sure; when he met with Tim that afternoon, he'd be in just the proper mood to spar a few hard rounds.

Last night's depression was gone. Edna had taken her time, had shampooed her hair again and again, applied the conditioner and had combed it out with one hand while she blow-dried it with her other. She'd taken her time putting on the makeup, too, applying it carefully to her cheeks, her eyes, her lips. She puffed them out, opened them and made a big wide O with her mouth, and knew that Babe could never resist that. No man could.

It was all they ever really wanted, and everyone knew that.

Mama had made sure that Edna knew it, back before Daddy died, when Edna still had to listen to her and act as if she was paying attention.

"That dirty thing we've got is all they want, and when you can't give it to them the way they want they go looking somewhere else." Mama would speak bitterly, giving Edna knowing looks, and Edna would feel her cheeks blaze. But inside, she felt happy, gleeful.

"You can't go giving it away to any man who comes around with his fly open, Edna." A twinge of sarcasm was in the woman's voice, and Edna was filled with a shameful joy. She knew! And there was nothing she could do about it.

It made her powerful, more powerful than her Mama, and that knowledge made Edna strong.

She'd spent so long living in terror, wondering what her Mama would do to her if she ever found out, and now she knew that Mama was aware of it all, that it wasn't a dream, that the family secrets she shared with her Daddy was real and Mama knew and *there wasn't a damn thing she could do about it!*

Edna didn't say anything except, "Yes, Mama," quietly. Softly enough so Mama would think she was feeling guilty, so Mama wouldn't know the joy Edna was experiencing in her heart.

Daddy was hers, and Mama was just another cripple in his flock.

He couldn't resist her, couldn't give up their secret love.

Until it killed him.

She rarely thought about that night, but she thought about it now, staring into the mirror, her makeup flaking around the pimples on her forehead.

Daddy atop her, his pajamas on the floor beside her bed, Edna's mouth buried into his neck so Mama wouldn't hear her squeals of pleasure. Daddy had come into her and had stiffened up the way he always did and Edna had opened her eyes because she loved to watch.

Daddy would generally get up on his knees once he got going real good, his hands on the bed next to her shoulders when they weren't squeezing her breasts, his arms locked, rigid, holding himself above her so he could watch her body jiggle. When he came his eyes would bulge and his face would contort, Daddy appearing in agony, as if it was painful, and then he'd pump harder and harder then stay completely still, rigid, and then he would slowly relax, begin to pump again, gently, lowering himself down onto her body for a time.

She'd watch him and she would feel the most overpowering sense of control, of might, knowing that she was in charge and that she was strong, in command of his body and his soul.

Only this night he never relaxed, Daddy stayed rigid and his face looked pained, as always, but suddenly it appeared terrified and his eyes nearly popped from their sockets and Edna began to push at him, screaming, screaming. . . .

She somehow managed to get him off her, Edna trembling, knowing Daddy was dead and hearing Mama screaming now from the next bedroom. She pushed him to the floor and he fell with a thud that sounded final.

Edna didn't know how she did it, but she got him dressed, his thing down there stiff and forming a tent in his pajama bottoms, but there wasn't anything she could do about that. She dressed herself and grabbed Daddy under the armpits and pulled, straining, until he was in the doorway and she had to stop and rest.

It took Edna an hour to get her Daddy into his own bedroom and she hadn't even looked over at Mama until Daddy was in the bed next to her. Mama was wailing like a crazy woman, her hands over her face, Mama scratching at the flesh of her face, digging furrows into her skin.

"Hush now!" Edna said, and slapped her, hard, with a trembling hand. "You just *hush* now!"

"You killed him!" Mama cried, and Edna slapped her again, harder still.

"He was in here with *you*. You two was doing it and he dropped over, you hear me, Mama?" The old woman did not reply. "You hear me, Mama!" Edna tried another tack.

"If you don't do as I say, I swear to God, I'll drown you in the bathtub, Mama." That had got her attention.

Edna had waited until her mother stopped wailing, and then had gone over to the telephone and had done what she'd had to do.

And they all said that she was stupid.

Well, she knew better.

Could a stupid woman have raised her son the way she had, and taken care of a crippled mother at the same time? Diminished mental capacity, the Medical People said she had. Said too that her baby's illness was genetic, probably came from being born to a retarded woman. Well, let them think what they wanted. They would, anyway, no matter what she said or did.

It worked to her advantage, too, their believing that. They thought that simple people were harmless, could not hurt anyone or anything.

Edna smiled into the mirror now. She could hurt people when she had to, that was for sure. Like Bobby at the dress store, that little shit. When she came back home with Babe she'd take care of him, maybe even the same way she'd taken care of Mama, who finally *had* said one word too many while Edna had been bathing her.

Yes, Bobby could die and violently and nobody would ever look in Edna's direction twice. She had her a dose of diminished mental capacity, didn't she? She was harmless, wasn't she?

Babe would think so. Would see that she was weak and help-less, that she needed him so badly. He would come home with her, no matter what she looked like. One sentence, one word, even, and he'd know. Realize that he'd been waiting for her his entire lifetime.

Edna tore her eyes away from her reflection and got her heavy coat, in case it got cold tonight. She had her pretty new white Reeboks on her feet. She got her Mama's black purse out of the closet and dusted it off, put her money and her little shiny gun in there. She had one stop to make, and then she would go to the bus station and find the schedule that would take her to Park Forest, to her Babe. To her secret lover.

Edna walked out of the house carrying the coat, her purse clutched tightly to her side. She checked the street warily, making sure that no one was looking at her, following her. She made sure that the door was locked and then began to waddle, quickly, toward the bus stop on the corner.

Jerome Spinell sat on the bed in his suite at the hotel, holding his head in his hands, trying to get things right in his mind. Why had he told Milo that lie, why had he said that he and Babe were like brothers?

Because if he hadn't, Milo might have pictured his mill and a half wearing wings, flying out a window, and then there would be the possibility that Jerome would follow, closely behind.

He rubbed his face, hard, determined and fighting for compo-sure. He reached out and picked up the phone.

"Hello, room service? This is Spinell, in forty-five-seventeen. Send up a pot of coffee, strong and hot. No, I don't want decaf, I want the real thing." He depressed the hook, let it up and punched out the Beverly Hills area code—213—then hit the numbers for the production offices of Spinell-Ackerman productions.

Jewel answered, the woman having the proper name, she was a gem all right, the only broad alive who could ask if she could help you while making it radically clear that she didn't think that she could.

"Spinell-Ackerman, might I help you," her voice going down about four octaves after the "might," descending in sequential degrees until by the time she was done even a strong man felt the urge to quietly hang up.

He said, "It's me, baby, I need an address."

"Mr. Spinell." She didn't appear to think much of him, ever. He suspected that she got all wet when she put a man down. There were two types of women in his world; those who lusted after him, and those who were homosexually inclined.

He put all the strength he had into his voice; there was no way she would ever see that she'd gotten to him. "Gimme the mailing address for Babe Hill, where we send the checks."

"PO Box 5484, Park Forest, Illinois, 60466."

That Jewel. Sometimes, she amazed him. That amazement was in his voice when he asked, "Didn't you even have to look it up?"

"Was there anything else, Mr. Spinell?"

Dyke bitch. He said, "Yeah, that ain't good enough. I don't care if you got the address and phone number of every employee we got there in your head, Jewel, what I need is a street address, somewhere I can find a living soul without having to get a federal court order."

"We send his checks there, his contracts, everything. He's never given us a street address." She didn't seem too upset by his outburst. She acted as if he'd asked her the time of day.

"All right." Jerome thought for a second. "Get me the number of that faggot agent he used to have, what was his name?"

"Mr. Hilliard's ex-agent? That would be Thiery Ploussard."

She rattled off the agent's number as quickly as she'd given him Babe's address, and he couldn't help himself, after he scribbled it on a scrap of paper he had to ask her, "That's all right there on a computer in front of you, right? You don't really remember all those fucking numbers, Jewel."

"Is that all, Mr. Spinell?"

"Goodbye, Jewel," Jerome said.

He'd have to find a way to write this trip off, it was getting expensive. The brown-skinned kid had brought up his coffee and for what they charged he could have ordered it direct-delivery from Juan Valdez himself. It was probably so expensive because they served it in a silver pot. Maybe they had a cow downstairs, for the fresh cream, and a couple of Cubans whacking off the cane sugar with machetes. Jerome had to tip the kid a five, because he didn't want to appear cheap, and now, after pouring down the first cup, he had to make another long-distance call, the price of which would be inflated by the hotel, for the convenience of calling from his room.

Which meant he'd be paying good money for the pleasure of talking to this Frog faggot, this Ploussard character. Jerome put it off, didn't want to make the call, remembering the man, how revolting he was.

A typical Hollywood agent, in Jerome's mind, queer and middle-aged, who'd be selling his ass on the street to rough trade if he hadn't learned how easy it was to market handsome flesh. Which afforded him the luxury of buying rather than selling.

Ploussard was a fifty-year-old guy who played racquetball on Monday nights with a bunch of other sissies and thought that kept him in shape. He'd wear purple shirts, have argyle sweaters slung over his shoulders, the sleeves tied around his neck. Always acting superior, urbane and sophisticated, better than everybody else because he'd been born and raised in France.

He and Jerome had hated each other at first glance, Jerome had almost socked him when Ploussard had eyed him, openly, right there in the restaurant with Maury and Milland watching, shit, the two of them laughing at Jerome's discomfort.

How could he approach the guy now? What could he say? They both knew damn well that it had been Jerome who had poisoned Babe against the agent; Jerome, who, right there in front of everybody, had pointed out the fact that Ploussard wasn't a packager, as he'd told Babe. Who'd told Babe right in front of the man that he'd been robbing Babe blind, double-dipping on him.

"That right?" Babe had said, not seeming too upset. He'd acted like he'd been half-expecting it.

Ploussard had tried to plead his case and Babe had interrupted him, politely but firmly, had kept saying his name, as a question— Thiery? Hey, Thiery?—until the sissy had shut up and looked at Babe, his eyebrows raised. "You're fired, Thiery. Now get away from the table, or your whole life is gonna change right here this afternoon."

That kind of balls, how could you not admire them? Babe staying in control like that but swiping right at the Frog's manhood. Everyone at the table had been relieved when Ploussard had stormed out of the restaurant, no one more than Milland Grand, who had smiled broadly, the dollar signs in his eyes until Babe had dropped his napkin on the table and had gotten up and left without even thanking Jerome for tipping him off about the way the Frog had been doing him dirty.

Would the man even take his call? There was only one way to find out. He dialed the number, lit a cigarette, and took deep breaths while the phone rang.

"Monsieur Ploussard's office," some other fag said, and Jerome told the dolly who he was, to put the man on. It wasn't easy, referring to Ploussard in that manner.

How long could they put you on hold before the dial tone came back on? Jerome had a feeling that he was going to find out. He waited, sipping coffee, his confidence somehow growing with each passing second.

He imagined the Frog scared, terrified at the prospect of speaking with him but knowing the consequences of refusing his call, the call of the producer of the hottest picture of the week, maybe even the month. Hell, maybe even the year. The damn thing might have beaten out *Roots*, for all Jerome knew.

He had a thought of how to put Ploussard in his place just as Ploussard picked up the phone and said "Might I help you," in a way that would have made Jewel proud.

"I thought you could, yeah, for a minute, but now I ain't so sure. See, I got to feeling bad about our last meeting, was looking for a bunch of guys for the regular cast of *Street Babe*, but I couldn't take them from an agent makes me wait longer than the pilot played over the air."

That got his attention.

"Mr. Spinell, I assure you, I got to your call as quickly as I could. Burt was on the other line."

"Burt, who?"

"An indiscretion, one should never mention one's clients' names to anyone not in the fold."

"So you ain't mad at me?"

"I've been hurt, not angry, Mr. Spinell. I lost more than a little money as I advanced James's career. Consistently and over a period of many years, I might add. And just when it appeared that he might reimburse my expenses, well, we both know what happened that cold, dark afternoon."

James?! Was Babe's real name *James*? He couldn't ask this guy, that was for sure, couldn't let him know that there were things about Babe about which he was unaware. "Is that right? The hundreds of thousands Babe made with the commercials, you took a loss on that? You ought to work for Paramount, the way you do your accounting."

"I really don't have the time to sit here and trade barbs with you, sir."

Barbs? Was he calling him Barbs? Like some broad?

"Did you wish to audition a few of my actors, or didn't you." Saying it act-ores. Try finding a thee-ay-tor in the swishy West Hollywood neighborhood his office was in.

"Thiery, this may be your lucky day. Play your cards right, I might put you together with Babe again, might drop the bug in his ear that you're all right."

"I doubt that you could." Then, he took a nibble at the hook. "Is there some problem with Ms. Richmand?"

"That lawyer? That lezbo? I can handle her. The question is, can she handle Babe, that's my question."

"And there's qualms as to that?" Oh, he was eating this up with a spoon. "My understanding is that she's more than capable."

"Thiery, Babe's gonna be making *millions*, not a million, not two million, many, many millions, and real soon."

"I'm aware of that." The coldness was back in Ploussard's voice, he was thinking about ten points of those millions that he'd never see.

Hurriedly, Jerome said, "Can you work with me and Maury, do as you're told if I get you Hill back in the fold?"

"Yes." Jesus, what an asswipe. Didn't even act like he was even considering a balk. Still, Jerome understood. For ten points of Babe's future, there weren't a lot of agents in Hollywood who wouldn't fall on their knees in front of the devil.

"Tell you what you do. Send four of the biggest, blackest, meanest looking guys you can find down to my offices. There's a woman sitting at the inner desk named Jewel. If they can convince *her* that they're Crips members, if they can scare the shit out of her, then they got the job, eight weeks guaranteed. And I'll be with Babe this afternoon, have a talk with him. He'll do what I tell him."

"James's in LA?"

"I'm in Chicago. I'm meeting him for lunch, we're gonna hang out the afternoon, then go to Ditka's for dinner."

"Those men will be there within the hour."

"Take your time, Thiery, I only want the best."

"I've got men that make Bubba Smith look small."

"Perfect."

"Will that be all, sir?"

"One more thing. I left my damn phone book at home and my wife's at acting classes. Give me Babe's address, would you? I want to send his wife some flowers."

"Kelly? I didn't know that she liked them."

"*All* broads like flowers, Thiery, Jesus."

"Just a second." Jerome could hear him flipping through a Rolodex and he smiled, held his pencil poised over the pad of paper the hotel had right there by every phone. When Ploussard came back on he carefully wrote down the address he gave him, then thanked him, got his word that the four gangsters would be there impressing Jewel before the end of the work day, then he hung up and laughed aloud, giggles that escalated into guffaws and hurt his gut. That dumb shit. Thirty years in the business and he didn't know when he was being snookered.

When he had himself under control he looked in the hotel

guide and found the extension he needed, dialed it and ordered a rental car delivered as soon as possible, telling the boy on the line that he'd be needing directions to Park Forest, Illinois, with the car, and the kid told him that it was absolutely no problem, sir.

It was the thing about traveling first class, they met all your needs.

Jerome hung up, nodding to himself, and got out of his clothes and into the shower. He'd wear a suit, take some roses with him to impress the kid's old lady. Maybe some candy, didn't Babe have kids? Yeah, he'd do that, impress the wife and kids then get Babe on the side, alone somewhere, maybe in a bar, let him know that his father's life was in danger and wasn't it time to bury the hatchet, put things back together with the old man before he was attending his father's funeral?

And if the kid showed any interest, if there was even the slightest flicker of concern in his eyes, Jerome would have him, would know how to play him, would be his best friend for life because he just happened to know a way that Babe could get his old man off the hook, for a small price, paid weekly.

He came out of the shower and walked over to the phone naked, called his production office again.

"Jewel," he said, acting all concerned. "Listen, I just talked to a guy out there, he told me the Crips were on the warpath in Beverly Hills, that they've broken into two office buildings and raped a couple of secretaries, you hear anything about that?"

She knew the type of people he knew, and that might be why she was always such a bitch around him. But he'd scored this time, because she sucked in her breath before speaking.

"Uh—no, sir, I haven't." Was there a quiver in her voice? God, he hoped so.

"Well, be on the lookout, would you? Shit, I wish I was there, I'd come over with my .44 and wait for those black bastards. You want me to send some people over there to stand guard?"

"No, that's quite all right, Mr. Spinell." She caught herself and came back on all professional again. "I'll make Mr. Ackerman aware of the situation as soon as he gets in."

Maury wasn't there? Outstanding.

"Watch yourself, Jewel," Jerome said, and Jewel told him that she shall.

He hung up, smiling, wishing that he could be there when the four jigs walked through the door.

Since coming back to the room, the day had gone well.

19

ohnny watched his son Frank stroll into the bar and he wondered what the hell his wife had raised, where she'd gone wrong.

Anthony, he was a write-off now, and that didn't particularly break Johnny's heart. He needed someone he could use, someone loyal to him who'd break any rule, do anything he was told, and he had the strongest inducement in the world to get Anthony to do his bidding; the kid loved him.

Frank now, that was a different story. He had to be handled differently, had to be treated in an entirely different manner. Love wouldn't work with Frank; he was motivated by money.

He was sharp, probably the smartest of the four kids, but he was as sick in the head in his own way as Anthony was, a total degenerate. Johnny knew some of the hookers Frank hung out with, and they'd tell him things, trying to get him mad, but he didn't bother losing his temper with hookers. Everyone knew that they were all lesbians and manhaters, and as long as they weren't spreading lies about Johnny himself, it didn't really matter. It was, in fact, good information to have. Johnny believed in working all the angles, and you never knew when information could be turned into ammunition.

The best way to deal with Frank was through the implied acceptance of his perversion. Johnny knew this the way the lion knows that a gazelle is downwind; instinctively, intuitively and without conscious or rational thought. Just as he knew that the worst thing he could ever do to Frank would have nothing to do with physical harm. Frank might physically fear Landini and he certainly feared Milo Spinell, but he'd face them both naked and unarmed and go on the attack before he could face the knowledge that his father was aware of his sexual depravities.

His oldest son, John, was a working stiff, a square punk who went into some office every day, then went home to a wife who owned him, who'd taken away his guts. He had three kids who ran all over him, pushed him around as bad as his wife did. Every time he talked to John, sometime in the course of the conversation the kid would tell Johnny that something Johnny said had made him feel bad, and he always wondered if the kid thought for even a second that Johnny gave a shit about his feelings.

Babe, now there was a tough case. The biggest of the crew, the toughest, strongest, physically and mentally. When they were kids and they'd make him spank them, John would whimper and cower, Frank would wail on top of his lungs, scream that he hated his father, but Babe, he could never make him cry after he was maybe six or seven. No, after that, no matter how hard he hit him, Babe would just take it.

He'd see Babe later when the kid thought nobody was looking, hugging his knees in the corner of his bedroom, his head down, rocking back and forth real fast, stopping whenever someone came into the room, but he wouldn't be crying, wouldn't be sobbing, even. Just rocking, back and forth, back and forth.

As for Anthony, he'd never been beaten, at least not by Johnny. He'd calmed down a lot by the time that one was born, and besides, Margie had told him that if he ever laid a hand on her baby that she'd kill him in his sleep, and he didn't put it past her, as nuts as she was.

Today Frank had bags under his eyes, the kid was not getting enough sleep. What a crew he had. Four kids, one a wimp, this one a degenerate, the baby certifiably insane and the other one, the only one who had made something of himself, wouldn't have anything to do with him, even after Johnny had saved his fucking life.

Frank was eyeing Anthony as he approached, Anthony, who was sitting next to Johnny in the cool darkness of the bar's back booth, staring into his beer bottle, lost in thought. Johnny had gotten the kid a cockroach-hotel room next to the cancer clinic steakhouse down the street, and the kid had looked at it as if it was a Lake Shore Drive penthouse. His happiness hadn't lasted long, though. Anthony was brooding now, probably feeling sorry for himself.

What was he thinking of? Was he getting the fears, the terrors? Johnny knew about them, got them the first few times he'd hit someone himself. The guilt and remorse would descend upon your ass and make you so ashamed of yourself that you even considered going to church and confessing your sins to a priest. They'd go away, though, after the heat died down, as soon as you were certain that the cops weren't looking for you.

After that, Johnny had discovered, if you did the job right, there was nothing really to fear. If you weren't related to the dead body, if you didn't have any link to him, the cops could never find you. They were almost as big a dummies as the guys were that you killed.

Frank slid into the booth, on Johnny's other side, and it was surprising how secure that simple maneuver could make Johnny feel. How safe. If he played his cards right, he could have them around him forever, or at least until they got pinched or messed up and got themselves killed.

This wasn't the way he'd planned it when he'd seen their crying, tiny faces in the hospital nursery, not what he'd thought of as he'd left the hospitals and gone out and gotten drunk, celebrating the fact that he had a male child, buying drinks for everyone and acting as if he'd done something important. But life had a way of throwing wild swings at you, and if there was one thing Johnny Hilliard was an expert at, it was rolling with the punches.

"What're *you* doing here," Frank said, and Anthony looked up, shrugged.

"I'm with you guys now," he said.

Johnny said, "Take him around today, show him the ropes, but especially make sure that he sees where Parker lives. He don't *meet* the guy, I don't want Parker even knowing Anthony's with us, but he has to see where the guy lives, all right?"

"Parker?" Frank looked at the beer in front of his kid brother, with disapproval. "You want me to introduce him to Parker? Shit, we still owe him money, don't we?"

Johnny took out a large folded roll of bills from his suit jacket pocket, so big there were several rubber bands wrapped around it to contain it, handed it over to Frank under the table. "Not anymore," he said.

"Get this from Landini? Christ, he'll shit he finds out we been doing this."

"I told him the beaners were screwing us up, robbing from us. We got nailed for another seven grand just last night."

"He gonna kill them?"

"He's gonna talk to Milo about it. Until then, it's business as usual, they can't find out anything. You two"—Johnny motioned to his sons—"are the only insiders, the only ones I trust. Let the beans make the collections, take their dough, but remember, from now on, it's all family.

"But when it comes to the killing, Frank," Johnny said, throwing his arm around Anthony's shoulders, "that's what we got Anthony here for. He'll handle it before Landini ever gets a chance for a sitdown with the boss." Frank just stared at his brother, his mouth wide open.

"Now don't give that to Parker until later in the day, you got me? Until maybe six, seven o'clock. We want him making a bet with you and watching the playoffs, at home. He can go to whatever bar he wants at half-time, but that first half, he got to be sitting at home."

"Take any bet he wants?"

"Any bet. And the rest of them, too, cause the gooms are gonna be out and you got to pick up the slack. If Landini wants their asses then we'll have to give them to him, within the week. We're off the hook for now, but you never know, if he calls one of them in, decides he can't trust us . . ." He let it hang on purpose, not wanting Frank to moan about the extra work, wanting him thinking about his own mortality, about what Landini was capable of doing. Frank could fear Landini, fear his ferocity and his power, a lot more than he could fear whatever physical beating Johnny had to offer.

As long as Johnny kept his mouth shut and played ignorant, it was the way it would be, and he'd been around long enough to know that you didn't always lose face when your enemy thought that you were weak or frightened. It was always a gas to see how it shocked the shit out of them when they found out just how tough you could be when you had no other choice.

Kelly had sat through class without retaining much of what the professor had said, but she'd be all right because she'd taped the entire lecture, had the microcassette player right there in her purse, next to her on the car seat as she headed for home.

The school parking lot was always a mess after a mid-morning class, the younger kids taking their lunch periods and racing around the lot as if they were still in high school. Well, most of them were barely past that age, were young and wild and didn't she know about that?

She'd been pretty wild herself, until she'd met Babe. Only then had she truly learned the meaning of the word for the first time.

She would sleep with older boys because she'd wanted them to love her, had dropped out of school and had run away from home when she was sixteen, tired of the rules, of someone telling her what to do all the time. Free and on her own, she'd seen herself as an adult, a grownup, and she'd taken to it naturally, wearing the heavy makeup, the short skirts, waiting tables and living with three other girls, all of them constantly taking speed so they could work double shifts and maintain their lifestyle, acting older than they were and believing the fantasy myths that they'd discuss when they were home and there weren't any men around.

He'd come swaggering into her life and she'd thought that he was the best-looking man she'd ever seen, this hunk from the city with his charming talk and his flashing smile. The fact that he was an actor who'd made money from it turned her on; the fact that he'd killed a man in a bar fight was a plus to her, nothing to fear. He couldn't hurt her, could he? He only fought other men. He seemed dangerous and alive, although he drank an awful lot. He was no threat to her. He loved her, she was sure.

Or so she'd thought. When she'd told him she was pregnant, that belief sure changed in a hurry.

"It's not mine," he'd told her. "I hardly know you." Her friends had comforted her, had talked nasty about him but hadn't offered a lot of advice to an eighteen-year-old girl who was starting to show, whose belly was beginning to swell with child.

She'd keep tabs on him, try calling him, reaching him at his place in the city and a couple of times even borrowing a car and driving past his mother's apartment, looking for his car, imagining that he'd see her, sitting in her borrowed car outside the apartment building, Babe suddenly realizing the mistake he'd made, sweeping her up into his arms and marrying her. They'd live happily ever after.

He'd hang up on her when she called him, and after a time, she stopped trying.

Her father was a plumber and he'd disowned her when she'd run away, but he'd changed his mind, softened up when he'd learned that his baby girl, the youngest of four daughters, was carrying his grandchild.

"He ain't no dago, is he?" her father had wanted to know. "That kid ain't got no dago blood in his veins, do he?" The man being from the South, trusting Italians less than he trusted the average Yankee, which wasn't a whole lot to begin with.

She'd assure him that the father wasn't Italian, was grateful when her parents took her back in, even though she knew that her mother resented the intrusion, was jealous that her father was lavishing attention upon her. But she never complained, didn't argue with her mother. She cooked all the meals and kept the house spotless, got herself on welfare so the State would pay for her prenatal care, her hospitalization.

There was a child inside of her, growing, and sometimes she could feel it kicking her. It was time to become a woman, to live up to her responsibilities.

Which did not please her mother, who wanted her to give the child up for adoption.

Bull*shit*, she would.

When the time came for Kelly to go to the hospital her father had dropped her off at the County Emergency Room on his way to work and her mother hadn't even gotten out of bed, and she'd delivered Mike in a charity ward all by herself, with no one in the Father's Room, poor but proudly waiting.

It was part of the deal she'd made, and she tried not to feel too sorry for herself.

The self-pity coursing right out of her when the nurse put that little bundle of love in her arms, smiling at her even though she was a welfare patient and didn't have a husband. That was pretty much the norm at the County Maternity Ward. Kelly had looked at Mike and thought: How could something this beautiful have caused her so much pain?

"He a pretty one," the nurse said, and Kelly had told her that he sure the hell was.

Pretty? He was gorgeous. He had white hair that curled already, a little scrunched-up face that was adorable even when he was crying. "I gave up speed for you, do you know that? Quit smoking, too." Her first words to him, telling him of her accomplishments, her idea of sacrifice, Kelly prepared to make many more on his behalf.

"God, I love you," was the second thing she said, and she held the baby closely to her and cried along with him.

She was at a stop light, and someone in a little red car had pulled up next to her, was honking at her, and Kelly shook herself, looked over there and recognized one of the boys from her class, waving for her to roll the window down. She did, puzzled.

The kid was about nineteen, gawky, but cocky, always making remarks in class, coming in late, sometimes not bothering to show up. She recognized him but did not know his name.

"You want to stop for some tacos, or something?"

Kelly said, "Are you serious?" then regretted it, seeing the hurt pass over the boy's face, briefly, there then gone. She said, "Not today, all right? My husband's expecting me." As nice a way as any to let him down, in case he hadn't noticed the two-carat flawless D diamond in the gold setting on her finger, Babe's twelfth wedding anniversary gift to her. Was that only last year? She hadn't ever taken the ring off her finger, although she preferred the old one, the cloudy cracked one he'd taken a loan out to purchase. She still had that first ring, in the corner of a drawer in her bedroom, and sometimes she'd take it out and look at it, think back to the hope that it had once represented; the joy.

The light finally changed and she waved brusquely to the boy in the red car, let him screech his tires and pull out in front of her, not about to challenge him to some silly race.

It was a nice feeling though, knowing that a kid that age could be attracted to her. Kelly smiled, remembering times when she'd felt far less attractive, what she'd done to elevate her self-esteem, and suddenly she wasn't smiling anymore.

Her father had bought her a dirty orange Mustang, several years old and in great disrepair, and had loaned her enough money so she could rent a tiny studio apartment not far from the family home, and she'd gone back to work, leaving baby Mike with the mother of one of her best friends, a woman who'd raised seven children herself and so knew how to handle them.

Sixteen-hour days, six days a week, on her feet and listening to bullshit from men who now thought she was open game, once the word was out that she had a kid and didn't have a man. She'd sometimes go out with one of them, forced out of the apartment by a girlfriend who would watch the baby, tell her that she was young and she was going to waste her life if she didn't get out and have some fun. But the dates never went well, the men always expected more than she was willing to give, and she took to staying home, to being alone with her child.

Until she heard about Babe.

It had started as gossip, her friend Mary telling her what she'd learned in a Rush Street bar, that Babe had fallen on hard times, that the booze had finally gotten to him and he was sleeping on the floor of some barber shop somewhere, all the time drunk, staggering around town during the day when the barber had customers who might be put off by the sight of him.

She had felt, at first, a cold moment's joy. He had it coming, didn't he? Didn't he deserve to suffer? The baby looked so much like him that it wasn't funny, every time she looked at her son she saw Babe, in miniature, with blond hair instead of black. He had dropped out of their lives, had hung up the telephone on her when she'd called.

But there had been something there, something she'd seen past the bluster and bravado. A sadness, certainly, deep and dark, which would break her heart when she'd see it on his face.

But something else had been there, too.

A strength.

She had the knowledge of what he was, but she couldn't explain it, could not articulate it, not then and not now; with a six-month-old child to support, she didn't have a lot of time to think about Babe, to analyze him.

One night, before the pregnancy, in her shared apartment, a drunken Babe had asked her, "Why are you with me, what the hell do you see in me?" and she'd been astounded. Didn't he look in the mirror? Didn't he wash that body in the shower? He had to know what he looked like, how well he was built. At that time she had thought that any girl would be happy to have him. There were enough in the restaurant chasing him around, that was for sure.

Something had come to her mind, though, and she'd spoken it before she could stop herself.

"I see what's really there," she'd told him, "as much as I see what you're trying to show me."

"What the fuck did you just say?" he'd said, and had gotten up to pour himself another drink.

There was something there; he could deny it as much as he wished, but there was no denying the fact that it wasn't just his physical appearance that attracted people to him, men as well as women.

He had a presence, some intangible inside him that made roomsful of people stop talking and pay attention when he entered the room. Something so powerful that there were times when people were tongue-tied around him, even when he was being funny or telling jokes. She'd see the guys he was with just staring at him oddly, as if trying to figure him out, and she'd get murderously jealous when other women would approach him, as they always did, drawn to him even when they were with other guys.

It was there, it was real, and there was no denying it. All that he really had to do to develop it fully was to get off the booze, get his life back in order.

He could do that, she was sure. If she could give up the speed, he could give up the booze. He at least deserved the chance, the father of her son deserved that chance.

She decided to give it to him, and if he was as big an asshole as he pretended to be, then she'd let him go, move on with her life. And if he wasn't? Well, she'd see . . .

She turned off onto the gravel that led to the driveway of her beautiful home with the private drive, the largest house in what was known as The Hill, the subdivision of ten homes being well above sea level, almost as if telling prospective buyers that if they took the plunge they could look down on the rest of the village.

This still gave her a thrill, almost a year after they'd moved in: driving through the trees, through the density, their thickness, Kelly feeling joy as the trees suddenly spread apart and there was their house, sitting a couple of hundred feet away from the point where you could first see it, where you gained sight of it, with the round driveway so you never had to put your car in reverse to leave.

She hit the button on her garage door opener as she negotiated the last curve, knowing that she'd see the house in a second or two, now thinking that she hoped she'd never take the place for granted, the way Babe did, calling it a pain in the ass to care for if she wouldn't let him hire a gardener, not understanding her point; that it was *theirs*, and only *they* could take care of it.

She'd talk to him about her anger, her feelings of jealousy, how it had begun the night before as she'd watched him sleep, as she'd become fully aware that the women who'd thrown themselves at him before were only the tip of the iceberg. Discuss it with him and apologize, if he'd allow it. He could be such a male about apologies, wave his hand at her and tell her to forget about it, he already had, when the two of them knew full well that he hadn't done any such thing.

She made the turn, and was startled to see the white Cadillac parked in front of her home, at the sight of a man standing there, backing away from the garage, edging toward the car like a thief . . .

She was about to hit the brake and call the cops from the car phone when something about him, maybe it was his stature, or his hair, made her stop. She recognized him, from somewhere, even from behind.

Jerome Spinell, that's who it was. And even from way back here she could tell through the open garage door that Babe's Lincoln was gone.

Spinell hadn't noticed her yet, seemed somehow afraid of the open garage door. His back was to her. Could she throw the car in reverse and back around the curve before he spotted her? She actively disliked this man, did not want to try and be polite to him, even for the sake of Babe's career. Yet Babe didn't care for the man, either.

Whose house was this, anyway?

Kelly stepped on the gas and drove toward her house, her face set in a firm, stern expression.

He noticed her and turned, broke into a wide grin as she passed him without even a wave, pulled the car into the garage, and got out to see him leaning into the open window of his vehicle, on his toes as he reached for something inside.

Spinell bumped his head on the door as he pulled it through the window, cursed, dropped whatever he was holding onto the front seat, then put both hands to the top of his head, patted it firmly, nodded, then reached in again, backed out holding a large long flower box in one hand and a heart-shaped red candy box in the other. The candy had a ribbon wrapped around it, a bow tied in the center.

"Hiya, honey," Spinell said, and she cringed.

"Jerome." Kelly looked around. "How'd you find this house?"

That took him aback. His smile wavered but he caught it, got it back and brightened it up some, going to win her over with his olive oil charm. She wished her father was right there, with his Remington .12 gauge pump. Between the man's smarmy smile and the fact that he was Italian, anything might happen, and they were isolated enough where no one would even hear the sound of the gunshot.

"Some house!" Jerome strolled toward her and she had to stop herself from taking an inadvertent step backward. He stopped when he was close enough to push the flower box toward her and she ignored the gesture, looked up at the trees, tried to focus on the birds singing . . .

"Yes, it is," she said.

"I went over to the other one, the house on Oswego? Was puttering around knocking on the door when the old lady next door came out and recognized me." He shrugged boyishly, acting as if being recognized on the street thousands of miles from home was no big thing. "She told me you'd moved, after I gave her an autograph. Gave me the address, too, directions over here. It's, what, a mile away from the other place? But a thousand miles up in class, baby. What do you got, five, six acres?"

"Three."

He stopped pushing the box her way and stood there looking where she was looking, up and around.

"Seems like more, must be the long driveway."

"Babe's not here."

"Yeah, I guessed that, rang the bell then went around back, see if maybe he was laying in the sun. When that damn door started opening I thought it was a part of the security system, that Rottweilers were going to come charging out at me, I didn't hear your car."

She looked at him and was pleased to see that the smile looked forced, that he was fighting to be polite. She knew this only meant that he wanted something from her, but still, it was an effort for him.

"Are those for me?" Kelly said, and took the flowers from him.

"Yeah, three dozen, paid a yard and a half for them, outta sight, the prices for roses downtown. And the candy, that's for the kids."

"How kind."

It was beginning to get awkward, Jerome standing there obviously expecting to be invited in, and Kelly not wanting this man in her house, trying to think of diplomatic ways to send him packing.

"If you're looking for Babe, I've got a pretty good idea where he is."

"Well, I've been trying to hunt Park Forest down for about two hours, I could sure use a Coke."

"They've got a machine, over at the gym," Kelly said, and smiled sweetly.

That bitch! That *bitch*! Jerome thought it but didn't say anything, just put the car in gear and fought the urge to floor it, run her down as she unlocked the door and walked in, without even looking back at him. She'd left the flowers and the candy outside the door.

Who the fuck did she think she was? Was arrogance a part of their family makeup?

He drove away without leaving any rubber, without spinning any gravel after he got off the asphalt. He wouldn't show her that she'd gotten him mad, wouldn't give her that satisfaction.

The gym, huh? He could go over to the gym and have an audience with her husband, is that how she saw it?

He'd pictured himself checking out the house, the broad giving him the tour, maybe even knocking off a piece before the old man got home; she wasn't bad-looking, though a little long in the tooth for his taste, if he was gonna be honest. Pictured Babe coming in to see him sitting in the kitchen with his wife, and the doubt would always be there, even if they hadn't done anything: Had Jerome put the moves on her, had anything happened? It would put the kid in his place.

It sure hadn't worked out that way. He'd bet that she had him castrated, that Babe gave in to her every whim. Hell, at *his* house, everybody knew who the boss was. Hadn't he pushed that bitch he was married to into the pool just last Sunday, at the *Street Babe* screening party he'd had? Shown two hundred and fifty people who was in charge of *his* house.

That's what this one needed, some lessons in humility, in who was in charge in this world. Proof that the world's leaders didn't have titties. He'd take it up with Babe, *after* he had the kid where he wanted him.

Hell, he never even got an opening where he could tell her that he knew about the rape job he'd heard his old celebrity-gazing buddy Waldo Heltz lay on Babe while he was driving on the expressway, trying to find this backwater town. He'd been incensed because the rental car didn't have a phone, he couldn't call in and tell the producer who he was, get right on the air. Babe didn't have the experience that Jerome did with interviews, didn't know how to turn them around and use them to his own advantage. Jerome could have won Waldo's heart and mind in about five minutes, could have made that interview a classic, if he'd had the chance.

But that was all right, he could call Heltzy tonight at home, set up his own interview for tomorrow. If things went right with Babe today, Jerome could do a little damage control tomorrow, make the people of Hogwash roll over and bare butt for Babe, by the time he got through singing their praises.

That would be an Oscar-winning performance, for sure. He'd hated the town, there was no place to eat, no real lounges, just taverns and saloons with workers in them, who'd give him the eye and ignore him. It sure wasn't LA. But seeing where Babe and his family lived, Jerome could see why Babe loved Hogwash, insisted on shooting the pilot there. There wasn't much of a difference between the two damn areas, although he had to admit, Park Forest had more trees and a lot more niggers, from what he'd seen.

Jerome made the turn the way the bitch had told him, but he was going the wrong way, was heading back toward the expressway. Cursing, he pulled into a driveway to make his turnaround, and slammed his hand on the steering wheel when he had to wait for a bunch of traffic to come by.

He should have called for a limo. If he had, he'd have been able to chew the driver out for being so stupid as to have made the wrong turn after Babe's wife had given him implicit instructions. But now, all he could do was wait.

Babe had thought that he'd been through with the Exercycle, but he was so frustrated, so angry over the phone interview, that he reset it, did another ten miles and he was sweating pretty good before Tim even got to the gym. He slowed down while Tim was in the locker room, because he knew that Tim would right away hop on the treadmill, right there next to the bike machine, and run his three miles alongside Babe. He wanted to save his strength for when Tim could be there to remark on it.

The first thing Tim said to him was, "Thirty-nine more, Babe, just thirty-nine more."

He looked like hell, his eyes heavy with dark bags under them. Babe wondered if he'd gotten any sleep. Tim set the machine, began walking on it for a total of five seconds before he pushed the Fast Accelerate button and kept hitting it until he was at six-minute miles, ten miles per hour, then Tim hit reset, began to run in earnest.

"Got an A on the psychology paper, on the interviews."

"With the kids?"

"Yeah. Put them in the room with the victims, one on one, let them see the people they'd hurt as humans instead of as honkies or niggers or just someone to get some dope money from. Eighty-three percent of the kids broke down, couldn't deal with it." Tim was running effortlessly, wasn't even sweating yet.

"I'm working on something else with them, if I can make the time. Want to put the more violent ones in a setting, maybe in the forest preserve, but just me and them, one at a time, with a baseball bat, some ground beef, and a skull."

"Where you get a skull?" The sweat was pouring off Babe now, and he was starting to gasp. He slowed it down some, noticed with a little perverse joy that Tim was starting to sweat a little, that he was breathing heavily. The joy left him when he realized that Tim hadn't slept in over twenty-four hours. He was bushed, and still in better shape than Babe was. Should he ask Tim about his father? Babe decided not to. If Tim wanted to discuss it, he'd bring it up. Babe hoped that he wouldn't. He might offend the best friend he had if he told him what he really thought.

Tim said, "You kidding me? I'm a cop. I can get all the skulls I need, discount."

"Then what?"

"These kids, their only perspective on violence comes from TV, from the movies. They see Stallone getting hit in the head with baseball bats, then kicked in the balls, then he gets up and kicks everybody's ass.

"I got a theory. I think if I fill the skull with beef, to represent the brain, then cover it with leather, for skin, then let them take a baseball to it, just for one whack—"

"Shit, it would explode the beef, drive skull bones into it."

"That's the point. I want to take the leather off and show them what they do to someone when they hit them in the head with a blunt object." Tim wiped his nose on his arm, took a deep breath and hacked, once.

"I want to personalize it for them, let them know that what they're doing isn't some cold, dispassionate act that has no consequence. I want to show them what they really do to someone, then let them meet the people they've mugged, see how it impacts on them."

"That's an undertaking, there."

"What else am I gonna spend my money on? I'm a veteran of Illinois, so I go to school free, and I don't have any kids, no wife. Anymore." Tim shrugged. There had been no bitterness in his voice. "I wish this damn thing went faster."

"You do that on purpose, to show me up?" Babe began to pedal harder, wondering where the other guys were. They didn't take it as personally as Babe and Tim did, had no vested interest in staying in shape.

"I do it to stay awake. Even at this pace, I'm liable to pass out, bust my skull on the damn handles."

"Have a heart attack maybe, and don't be waiting for me to give you any CPR."

"You don't know how?"

"I don't open-mouth kiss my wife, even, these days, with all the garbage in the air, infecting you."

"Watch those toilet seats, the shower stalls."

"Mosquitoes," Babe said, "they're carriers, too."

"Babe, I'm too damn tired to laugh."

A voice from behind him said, "He's just being nice. He'd laugh if you said something funny, Babe." This from Arlene, who was working the gym today. "Good thing you guys showed up, I was going nuts, staring at the walls."

"Making phone calls," Tim said, "at the members' expense."

Arlene was the assistant manager, thin and strong, with Chris Evert muscles. She ran the gym until the first of June then taught tennis lessons for the park district throughout the summer, when the gym was closed. She had a good sense of humor and backed Tim up whenever some clod would light up a cigarette in the place and he'd get an attitude.

"Good show the other night, Babe," she said now, "you gonna do the series?"

"Arlene, I just don't know."

She'd come from behind the counter to speak to them, and Babe knew that it was only because Tim had shown up; that she'd have never approached him if he'd been alone. Tim gave people strength just by his presence and the force of his personality. The phone rang and she bounced down the two stairs to the counter, picked it up but Babe couldn't hear her voice over the sound of the Exercycle's whirring, the noise of the treadmill.

"Babe?" Arlene hollered. "Hey, Babe, your wife's on the phone."

The gym was small, little more than a large house with an upstairs and a basement. The exercise room was cramped. There was a Universal machine with twelve stations, ruled by pulleys which Babe wasn't crazy about. He preferred free weights. There was the Exercycle next to the treadmill, which he rarely used unless there was too much snow on the ground to run the outdoor track. The locker rooms were downstairs and they had saunas, which Babe did use, enjoying the feel of the dry heat on his skin. The village maintained the place, hired the staff and charged a nominal fee for membership, and after the dinner hour the place was usually packed, but until then it was dead. Babe and Tim rarely had to wait for a machine.

It was the upstairs they cared about, anyway.

The village manager had let them strip the room, lay down plywood and canvas, cover the walls with gym mats. It was a bare room for which only the two of them had a key. They kept it clean and never entered wearing shoes, bitched when anyone would come up in there to watch them.

It was where they sparred.

As soon as Babe hung up the phone he went over and asked Tim if he'd mind cutting his run short, he could finish it later, there was someone coming to see him and he wanted that person to see him in action because maybe it would stop the guy from being too much of an asshole. Tim agreed without comment, and they carried their gym bags up the stairs, kicked off their gym shoes at the door, and stripped off their socks. Once inside they quickly wrapped their hands, reached into their bags and took out 16-ounce boxing gloves, with Velcro closures so they didn't have to fumble around and try to tie them with their teeth.

"No headgear today?" Tim said, and Babe just shook his head. Tim never wore it but Babe usually did. His face was his livelihood.

"You all right?"

Babe had been setting a three-minute timer against the wall when Tim asked the question, was bending down with one glove on and the other glove ready. He snapped the timer all the way over and shoved his hand into the glove, bounced toward Tim with his hands up, his elbows tucked into his side, partially crouching.

"I don't think so, Tim," Babe said, and attacked.

Tim wasn't used to this, to the relationship being a one-way street like it had all of a sudden become. He knew he was tired, it had been somewhere around thirty-one hours since he'd slept. Should he let it go or should he say something? Was it him, or was it Babe? Time would tell.

Babe danced around him, flicking jabs at Tim's face, most of which Tim deflected with his gloves, but a couple of them got in there, were stinging. He was tired, and he felt slow, was taking his time and waiting for his shot because although Babe had never had any formal training, he was very good, and if you made a mistake he would make you pay. Still, he didn't attack Babe. It would be easy for Tim to hurt the man, and Tim was very tired; he was afraid he might forget his degrees and just beat the shit out of Babe.

He sidestepped a straight right and caught Babe with a hook under the ribs that staggered him, made him drop his hands as his wind was forced out of him, and Tim shot a double jab at the exposed head, not fast, hard punches, just enough to get Babe's attention.

Tim's old karate classmates sometimes showed up at the gym, and when they did they'd work mostly with the focus mitts, pounding on them and getting a good aerobic workout but not much else; the mitts were good, but they didn't do a whole lot for your timing, for your defense, and they did absolutely nothing to help you absorb the shock of a punch.

When it was just the two of them, the mitts stayed in the bag and they went to work with the gloves.

Tim danced away from Babe, both breathing heavily, through

their mouths. Tim's nose had been broken more times than Babe's, and it was sometimes difficult for him to regulate his breathing once he got going hard.

What was wrong with the man today, what was bothering him? They'd sit in the sauna, the two of them alone after a workout, and they'd talk openly, tell each other things no one else would ever hear. This person he was sparring with bore no relation to the man he spoke to so openly downstairs. Babe had never acted like this.

Tim got nailed with a right hand and Babe stepped back, bouncing on the balls of his bare feet. Enough thinking. He would just react, kick the shit out of this guy and save the sentiment, the sensitivity, for the proper time.

The rules were that they used their hands and that Tim wasn't allowed to kick. When the other guys were there he'd ask one of them to hold the banana pad for him and Tim would work his legs, kicking them, the force of the kicks driving the man into the wall, which was why they'd put up the mats. But when they were sparring it was hands only, and even then, with Tim not able to use half the weapons in his arsenal, Babe was still no match for him. A fact that Tim never brought to Babe's attention. They weren't there to hurt each other, or to prove their manhood to themselves or anyone else.

It was the way they got out their aggression, the way they worked through their anger, their hatred.

What they were doing, they both knew, was beating their fathers' asses under controlled and regulated conditions.

Very controlled, as a matter of fact. Neither man would ever throw a power punch; if you couldn't pull it, you couldn't throw it. If one man was staggered the other man didn't step back and wait, he went to him and steadied him, made sure he was all right. They never threw more than three punches in a flurry and they didn't ever go below the belt. No elbows, no head butts, no stepping on toes. None of the rules they might use in a real ring applied for them when they fought, and neither man had ever been hurt.

Today it looked as if Babe was trying to bend those rules. He was jabbing hard, snapping them in there, moving forward and trying to cut off the ring, instead of dancing away as he usually did.

Tim moved in and tapped him twice—right left—on either

side of his jaw, the punches getting through and Babe got mad, moved in on Tim and Tim was afraid that there might for the first time in this room be some real bloodshed when the timer bell rang and they both dropped their hands.

"Hey, good round, Jesus Christ, you guys are pretty good!"

The voice came from the doorway and Tim looked over, gasping for air—how did the pros ever last twelve rounds with someone trying to kill them?—to see a jowly man with a crooked smile standing in the doorway, clapping theatrically.

He looked as phony as Babe said he was, wearing a pastel suit and a white shirt with a blue collar, a white tie. White shoes and belt. And who did he think he was kidding with that wig?

Babe had bent over and was breathing hard, his hands on his knees, sweat dripping from his face onto the canvas. He turned his head to the side, spotted the guy and looked back down at the floor, his face grim.

The guy strolled over to Tim—his white shoes digging into the canvas—and put out his hand, trying to shake with a man wearing 16-ounce boxing gloves. "Jerome Spinell," Spinelloid said, "how you doing, Tim old buddy?"

"Were you standing there long?" Babe asked him. He made a point of staring down at the man's shoes, then looking over at his and Tim's gym shoes, lying in the doorway, the socks scattered around them. Babe was standing tall now, but he was breathing heavily, his chest heaving, and he was sweating a river.

"From the time you said, 'I don't think so, Tim.' How you think I knew the guy's name? Saw the whole round. You guys, you're not bad."

Tim wanted to ask him if he thought he was better, wanted to challenge him, knowing up front that the guy would back down, but still, he wanted this prick to know it, too. But it was Babe's game, and he would make the rules.

"You don't seem surprised to see me." Babe was better now, breathing almost normally, his hands on his hips. His undershirt was covered with sweat and it clung to him, defined the oxygen-pumped muscles. He looked good. Lean, dangerous.

"Kelly called, said you were on your way over." Babe shrugged. "I expected someone from the network, from the production company, to come around."

"You should have called me after the show, Babe, let me know what you thought of it. A couple of minutes on the horn yesterday morning, pal, wasn't right, not after all I've done for you."

"After that beef, after the problems on the set, I didn't think it would be a good idea to be yakking on the phone like nothing was wrong between us."

"Babe, we got to talk." Jerome looked at Tim, pointedly. "Alone."

"Did I introduce Tim as my brother? Did he have the same name as me? That should tell you something, Jerome." Spinelloid looked puzzled.

"We got to talk." What was he doing, talking out of the side of his mouth like that?

"You want to talk to me? Call my lawyer." Babe had moved closer to him, was now in his chest, up close. "You don't come into this gym with your street shoes on, insulting Tim with your Hollywood demands."

The man, was he nuts or what? He was glaring at Babe, looking ready to swing. It was time Tim took control of the matter. He stepped between them, looking at Spinell, trying to tell him to back off without saying the words.

"He gets like this when our workout's interrupted." He turned to Babe. "I'll go back to the treadmill, Babe, you talk your business, all right?" He looked deep into his friend's eyes, didn't see much there except for maybe a little anger, as if Babe thought that Tim was siding with Spinell. Tim backed away slowly, the tension broken, Babe nodding at him and dropping his hands off his hips. By the time Tim got to the door, Babe had stripped off the gloves and had dropped them to the floor, was shaking his head, and Tim could tell that he was fighting to keep control.

He hoped to God that Babe would be able to maintain that control, because if he couldn't, there was liable to be one less Spinelloid in the world before the afternoon was over.

Tim went to the treadmill and turned it up fast, got up to speed and pounded on it for less than a minute before Arlene was there, watching him, a look of rapture on her face. "Jerome Spinell, in my gym," she said. "I used to watch him every week on *Michael*

Diamond, Private Eye." She giggled. "I actually got his autograph."

Tim looked at her.

"Tim?"

"Yeah."

"Would you watch the door for a minute? I want to run home real quick and get my camera, or nobody will believe me."

Spinell seemed to have figured it out. As soon as Tim left he walked over to the door and kicked off his shoes, stepped on the backs of them instead of bending down to untie them, leaning against the door with one hand out to support himself. He came back into the room, looking hurt.

"I didn't know about this, that you're running some Jap gym here, Babe. I'm sorry. My kid was in one, a karate joint, for two lessons. I walked in the door to check it out, there's my kid on his knees, bowing to some gook. 'That's it,' I said, 'you don't bow to no fucking zip.' " He paused, and when Babe didn't smile, continued.

"But on the rest of that shit, you were way out of line.

"I came a couple thousand miles to talk to you, Babe, to help you out with something. Was on a jet all night, didn't get hardly any sleep at all, and I spend hours driving out here today, trying to find this joint, and what happens? What do I get for trying to do you a favor? First, your old lady's so rude to me she could only make it worse by spitting on me, then I find you and you embarrass me in front of one of your friends."

Was he for real? Babe walked over to the corner and turned his back to it, slid down until he was sitting, hung his forearms off his knees. He wondered what Spinell wanted, what the hook was. This was the first funny thing that had happened to him all day, and he was beginning to enjoy it.

"Did I come take you out of a casting call and build an entire pilot around you, or didn't I? Did I give you total freedom on the set, script approval? Did I or did I not tell you that I was going to make you a star? I did everything I said I was going to do, and now you don't return my calls. How'd you think that makes me look with Maury, with Milland? Not to mention that I saved you thousands of dollars with that creep agent you had and you didn't even thank me, didn't show your appreciation by signing with Milland. How you think that makes me look with those guys, after we all busted our asses to make you a star? You forgetting where you came from?"

It was better than watching a movie, seeing Jerome work himself up. He was pacing now, slowing down only after his silk stockings slipped on the canvas and he had to do some fancy footwork to keep from going on his ass.

The funny thing was, he'd gotten scared when Kelly had told him that Jerome was on his way over. Of what, he did not know. But he'd been looking for something or someone to lash out at, and had started taking it out on Tim before this stiff showed up.

Now, he wasn't feeling afraid. Now, he was feeling almost amused.

And didn't that feel good? Watching this Emmy-winning performance relaxed him, made him forget about Hegewisch, about the Heltz show. He could feel the tension drain out of him, as surely as if he'd been sitting in the sauna after a three-hour workout.

It was due to the fact that this man had traveled all this way to see him. Babe understood this. It made him feel important, took away his insecurities. Watching Spinell squirm made him feel important.

Which made him as bad as Spinell, needing someone else's pain to take away his own.

Get off it! he scolded himself, dragged himself back and made himself pay attention to what Spinell was saying.

"Babe, I treated you like a brother, better than a brother. Like a son. I paid you two hundred and fifty grand for a job I could have got any other actor to do for half that price, and for something like *Street Babe*, any other male lead would have thrown in a blow job from his wife, every Thursday for the show's run. Why are you jerking me around, why are you biting the hand that fed you?" He paused and waited for an answer, but Babe didn't say anything, and Jerome became physically uncomfortable. He continued.

"You wanted to shoot in Chicago, *bang*, I had it shot on location. You wanted to shoot in that tavern you hang out in, *boom*, we shoot in the tavern. You wanted revisions in the script, *bing*, I fly in a writer. What more could you want from me than what I've given you?"

"Honesty, Jerome," Babe said. "That's all I ever wanted from you. You'd have given me that, I'd have been the most loyal friend you'd ever had in your entire life."

"When wasn't I honest, when did I ever lie to you!" He splayed his fingers across his chest, in anguish. His eyebrows were raised, his mouth open in shock. He reminded Babe of his mother.

"The whole thing was a scam, and I almost fell for it. From the beginning, you guys had designs on me, you came to me with these great ideas, what you were going to do for me. You think I never ran across guys like Milland and Ackerman before? I knew a lot of them, only they were wearing county jumpsuits instead of two-thousand-dollar Armanis."

Jerome snorted. "Maury never paid more than two hundred and fifty for a suit in his life."

"You know what I'm saying. Someone hands you a smoke in the joint, you know what they want in return? It's the same thing, Milland telling me I'd make two million if I signed with him. He'd have me opening supermarkets in Boise if there was a commission in it for him. And Maury, he's nothing but a bean counter, an accountant who curses at people who can't fight back, and he cheats on his wife."

"Watch it now, Maury's been good to you."

"And I've been good to him, and to you, and to Grand!" Babe got to his feet, quickly, in a fast, sudden move. But he didn't storm toward Jerome, he walked around the room, angry, ready to finally put his cards on the table with no agents, accountants, studio executives or lawyers listening in.

"I gave you guys the best performance of my life! Gave it all, and I knew when I was giving it that none of you would understand it, would appreciate what I was doing. I gave you moves not seen in the history of television, and all any of you could think about was getting me to sign on the dotted line, getting me to have dinner and take pictures with your friends from LA, getting me to shake hands with the scumbag mobsters who were always on the set.

"You know why that show got the ratings that it did? *Because* I fought for location shooting, *because* I asked for the writer on the set, *because* the ex-speakeasy tavern was there in half the shots. You think the audience isn't ready for some realism, to watch a show that isn't all car chases and tits? I made that show and none of you understood what the hell I was doing, none of you got what I was doing or why I did it!" He stopped when he realized he was shouting, saw that Spinell was lighting a cigarette. "You ever hear of gym etiquette?"

"What's that mean?"

"It means you don't smoke where someone's working their body."

"Let's go sit on the outside steps then."

Babe looked at him, at the TV actor in front of him, and for a moment he felt sorry for him. The guy was acting all sincere, and wasn't a good enough actor to pull it off.

"Forget the steps," Babe said. "The deal is, you want me on the series, I get a hundred and fifty a week, escalators shooting it to double if we keep the audience past six weeks. I get a full share of the production company, total script control, and I approve the director. You bring in the son of some mob punk who went through film school, and I walk."

"Is that all you want?" Jerome said, and Babe nodded.

"You think I came out here to try and talk you into the series? You think that's what this is all about? You talk about insults, all you've done since I've been here is insult me."

"Why did you come, Jerome?" Babe gave him that much, caved in one single inch, and, just like the camel, Jerome jumped at it, wanted to get his entire body into the tent. When he spoke his voice was low, conveying serious intent, and Babe had to lean forward to hear him.

"To tell you that your father's gonna get hit, Babe, and me and you are the only guys who can stop it from happening."

Babe knew that he was a good actor, knew that he had a power inside him to express himself on film that was rare, special and important.

But he wasn't good enough to handle this, to hear his father's name mentioned in this place, by this man, and not react.

He wasn't good enough to keep the blood from draining from his face, wasn't good enough to stop his legs from weakening, wasn't good enough to stop himself from leaning against the mat on the wall, from staring at Spinell with vacant eyes.

Jerome came over and put his hand on Babe's shoulder, squeezed it, then patted it encouragingly.

"It's all right," Jerome said, "I took care of it."

Babe straightened up, slapped the hand off his shoulder. "You *what!*"

"I took care of it." Jerome stepped back, startled.

"How?"

"He beat some serious people out of a lot money on the gambling, Babe. Over a hundred grand. I made a down payment, to the guys you never wanted to meet, who, if you had met them, would have forgiven the debt just because they were your friend. But you were too good to shake their hands, to talk to them or pose for pictures. So now when your old man screws up, they want his blood."

"If they kill him, it won't be my fault, Jerome. I didn't lose anything gambling."

"You ever hear of an accomplice to suicide? Someone who whispers *do it* in the ear of someone ready to put a pistol in their mouth? It's the same thing, and you can't get around it.

"I paid ten grand to those guys today, Babe, to keep your father alive, and I come here to warn you that somebody better pay the rest of that money, and quick, and you go nuts, treat me like I came here to shit on you, after all I done for you."

"I'll give you the ten grand."

"Forget about it." Jerome spoke derisively, turning his back and walking over to the door. He put the cigarette in his mouth as he bent down and slipped on his shoes, stepping on the backs of them, squeezing his heels down in there. He stood as tall as he could manage to, stared hard at Babe, with disgust.

"He's your *father*, Babe," Jerome said, then dropped the cigarette on the mat and stepped on it, crushed it under his heel. "And you just snuffed out his life as sure as I just snuffed out that smoke."

He stared at Babe for a couple of seconds, his expression one of repugnance.

"Your father." Whispered. Jerome said, "I'm at the Four Seasons if you decide to remember who gave you life," and walked out the door.

23

Why wasn't he tired? That's all Babe wanted to think about as he stood in the shower, soaping down. He was forcing his mind off of Jerome's visit, forcing himself not to think of it.

But it wasn't working. He knew why he wasn't tired. Even though he had gotten up early and had taken a brutal bike ride and had come over here and ridden again, then gone one hard round with Tim, then gone down to the Universal machine and worked his arms, he was still wide awake, bright-eyed, not even exhausted.

He was filled with adrenaline, is what it was. Jerome's visit had made him seriously consider calling his father for the first time in years.

He owed him that much. He didn't want that son of a bitch around his kids, didn't want him to know where he lived, but he could get his number from John, call him on the phone and tell him to get his ass out of town, right now.

How long would Jerome's ten grand last? How far would it protect his father? He hated him, wanted nothing to do with him, but he didn't want to see him killed. Death should come in your sleep, visit you and take you away softly, kiss the breath out of you without your ever knowing it. In the mob, they had a habit of beating you to show their displeasure, breaking all your bones and then burying you alive.

Did the man deserve better, though? Did he?

It was something to consider.

Babe sat in the sauna, alone. Tim had finished his run and had headed into the locker room without comment, had come out with his hair all wet and combed back, had walked to the door and on his way past the equipment had said, "See you," and Babe had said, "Yeah."

Babe regretted it now, his alienation of his closest friend, his brother. He appeared to have a habit of pushing away everyone who loved him.

Stop that!

He made himself stop thinking like that. His parents had not loved him, saw him as nothing more than property, something to take all their anger out upon. To them, he was a living, breathing punching bag, and nothing more.

Still, he could remember once, on his eleventh birthday, his father taking him to the racetrack, introducing him to the jockeys and letting him hold his tickets. Remembered the happiness on his father's face when his horse won, how he'd told Babe that he was his lucky charm.

His Ma, too, she was big on telling them that she loved them, and for years he associated the word *love* with pain, with suffering.

She'd beat him and come into the room later, drunk, tell him that she was sorry but that didn't take away the bruises. She'd kiss his forehead and tell him she loved him and he'd repeat the words back at her, but only so she wouldn't smack him around if he didn't, if he let his silence show her scorn.

He was good at learning from his mistakes.

Men don't cry.

Babe sat in the sauna, his head hanging, his knees wide apart, a towel wrapped around his waist and another around his shoulders, watching the puddle his dripping sweat was making on the cherry-wood floor, repeating his mantra, the one truth he'd taken with him from his childhood.

It's what his father had told him, and it had been his battle cry ever since, whenever he'd been suffering.

He'd bite his tongue until it bled, but he'd never let them see him cry. They'd hit him, chase him through the house and use their fists on him, their feet, whip him with coat hangers and shoes, and he'd clamp his mouth shut and take it, would hide later in the corner of his room, curled up with his back to the wall, hugging his knees, rocking back and forth and repeating it over and over. *Men don't cry.*

He sure felt like breaking the rule right now.

He'd come close a time or two.

When he'd first lain eyes on Mike, when Kelly had run him down at the barber shop and had shown up one night at the door, holding his son, man, had he wanted to cry.

He'd been sitting in the barber's swivel chair, staring into an unopened bottle, a hangover killing him, wanting that fifth of booze in him something fierce but punishing himself, making himself wait until he was ready to beg for it, to do anything to get it open and down his throat. The fifth had been sitting atop the barber counter, next to the razor blades, and Babe was trying not to drink it because he knew that if he did, tonight would be the night to go all the way, that the barber would have to find some other wino to come in and wash Babe's blood off the mirrors, the floors . . .

She'd tapped on the window lightly and it hadn't startled him, nothing scared him then because he'd had nothing left to lose, even his soul was already gone. He'd turned around slowly in the chair, pushing himself around with his feet, and their eyes had locked.

Then he'd noticed the kid, in her arms, stretching and yawning as she held him.

He'd gotten up and had unlocked the door, opened it, looked at her as he stepped back to let her in.

Wasn't she beautiful? Tall and elegant, with some character in her face that hadn't been there the last time he'd seen her. Her childishness seemed gone, replaced by what, by womanhood? She was staring at him and the baby was making noises, baby sounds. Kelly trying to challenge him with her eyes but he saw something else there, too, longing, love, desire for him.

He'd closed the door, let it swing shut behind her and he'd cleared his throat, but couldn't think of anything to say.

Instead, he acted.

He turned and walked to the counter, opened the bottle then looked up, caught her eye in the full-length mirror on the wall, watched her reaction as he stood tall, turned the fifth upside down and let it drain out into the sink.

The look on her face when he'd done that, man, had it made him want to cry.

But he hadn't, nor would he now, as he sat there in the sauna thinking that Mother's Day was Sunday and about how, even all these years later, since they'd been able to hurt him, he had to walk out of the room when a sentimental commercial came on the air, showing a loving mother and son. Father's Day was even worse for him.

Did he owe them anything? He'd made the offer.

Through John, his big brother. Made sure that John relayed to both his parents Babe's promise to pay their way through rehab, to get them the best counseling money could buy. He'd made sure that they'd known that he would do anything he could to help them, but until they sought that help, they were dead to him.

And now it looked as if the old man might be dead, for real.

Would that hurt him? How would he react?

He wouldn't go to the funeral, that's for sure. It would turn into a three-ring circus if he showed up. He could see Anthony, throwing himself at Babe, trying to kick his ass. The poor, sick kid who denied he had a problem and who could blame him, considering where he came from? He could picture Frank laughing at the sight, maybe throwing in with Anthony, out of some sense of family loyalty. He knew what John would do. The big lug would start crying. The old man's early brutal lesson had never sunk into John's head.

What would Ma's reaction be? No, he wouldn't even try to find out. He would speak to the funeral director, slip him a few bucks and go in there, see his father's body before visiting hours or maybe later. Stand far outside the crowd at the funeral, with a trench coat on, the collar pulled up around his face.

Babe had to laugh a little, bitterly.

He'd once loved them. They'd once been his entire world.

But love never died a natural death. It had to be tortured out of you, he knew. And the mutants who'd raised him had done their best to make sure that his love for them had not only died, but had been buried so deeply in him that resurrection was impossible.

Did he feel a stirring of it now, though, when one of them faced imminent danger? Was what he was feeling love for his father? He had to think it over. How did Tim feel, was he as confused as Babe? He'd have to ask him about it, if Tim ever spoke to him again. Think, Babe, figure out how you feel.

Sadness, that was there, for the wasted life his father had led. If Johnny hadn't been so brutal, so hateful a person, Babe might be feeling pity. But he wouldn't take it that far.

He'd changed his name so that his father's past would not haunt him, that the only weight he'd have to carry through life would be his own. But it went deeper than that, further down inside of him.

"Ah, shit." Babe said it with feeling, as the door slowly opened. Babe hurriedly made sure the towel around his shoulders was covering his scar, then dropped it when he saw who it was.

"Ah, shit, what?" Tim said.

He had a body on him, that's for sure. Tim never put on a towel to take a sauna, never wore a bathing suit in the whirlpool. He was natural about his nakedness, never seemed ashamed of it or embarrassed to show it off.

He had round, firm muscles, with a lot more tone to them than Babe's own, more bulk and size, definition. His muscles didn't ripple exactly, they just sort of stood out, were such a natural part of the man that you took the size of them for granted. You could look at a picture of Tim's face and be able to have a good idea in your mind of how he was built, what his body looked like. He took it as it came, never showing off, but never covering up, either.

One time some moron had brought his little daughter into the locker room, though, and Tim had gone through the roof, had told the man off and Babe had been afraid that Tim was going to hit the guy, especially when the guy told him he didn't know what he was talking about, that he had a dirty mind.

Tim was like that, always thinking about how what a kid saw would impact upon him. Maybe it was because he saw so many kids who'd had things impacted on them.

Now he sat next to Babe, not speaking, the two of them knowing that Tim had made a big move here, a major league move, for him. And that the ball was now in Babe's court.

Well, he had a few moves, too.

"I'm sorry, Tim," Babe said.

"Forget about it," Tim said, and Babe knew that it would be all right.

"What'd Spinelloid want?"

Babe grunted. He took a deep breath and let it out, slowly. "My father's gonna get hit."

"That's a good thing, Babe, it's the only way your kids will be safe."

"He might kill me, but he wouldn't hurt my kids."

"Babe, if there was a way to make a buck at it, a guy like your father would put your kids between slices of bread and eat them alive, and don't you forget it. Just because he's got the same blood in his veins doesn't make him family."

It was how Tim saw things, always clear and crisply, never beating around the bush to try and avoid hurting your feelings.

But he spoke the truth, and never said anything just to hear the sound of his own voice. If he didn't mean it, he didn't say it.

Still, Babe had to try. Tim would have to talk him into believing this.

"But he is my family!"

"Like your mother is? Family? How'd you get the scar, Babe?"

Just like that, Tim took the wind out of his sails.

How'd you get the scar, Babe?

His mother had given it to him, a little present to her son. Had shot him as he'd been diving for the gun, the two of them drunk, Ma pulling her favorite act, going to kill him and then herself because he'd said something that had hurt her feelings.

She'd come to the hospital, whining and crying, screaming, asking him over and over what had happened, who had shot her baby?

"Less than five percent of all abusers ever admit it," Tim said. "Even when they're sent to treatment. They resent the doctors, sit in the meetings with their noses in the air, proclaim their innocence even when they're caught in the act. And they keep trying to win back the kid's love, because kids are the most forgiving creatures on earth. They convince you they didn't hurt you, and even if they admit they did, then they tell you that it was your fault. Then they convince you that you should love them some more, give them another chance. Your old man, he wouldn't see it as you saving his life, he'd see it as the bank opening up. You ever feed a hungry cat? Bet you didn't only once, cause they keep coming back."

Babe said, "I'm not going to help him."

"You'd be a chump if you did. You know what it would do? It would sink his hook in you, and he'd reel you in, bleed you dry and when you were all used up, Babe, he'd cast you aside, gasping for air."

"I can't tell Kelly, either."

"She'd want you to help him."

"I never told her about most of it, she wouldn't understand."

"I do, though, Babe, I've *been* there, and I'm telling you like my brother, you can't help that man."

"I won't," Babe said.

"That's good," Tim said, then said, "Can you imagine how the press would treat it, when they found out your father died, was hit?"

"I'd hear it from everybody, from all angles, how he got me where I am, how his connections made me."

"His connections didn't do you a lot of good when you were sleeping on the floor of the barber shop. Maybe it would be a good thing, though, maybe the publicity would work the other way, get people on your side."

"I'd rather be dead than to get publicity that way. Tim, I'd honestly rather die than make the front pages because of something my father did, or any other way than through my talent."

"Babe, ah, shit, Babe, when are you going to get it through your head? You've already made it, man."

Edna kneeled before her son's grave, smiling at the tended plot of lawn. Spring was here and the sod had been mown a couple times, and she had spread the coat under her before she'd knelt so she wouldn't get grass stains on the new white tights that she wore under her dress.

Would Babe think she was a nurse, with the white gym shoes and the white panty hose? All the better. She wanted him to know that she was capable.

But she could think of Babe later, for the rest of her life, as a matter of fact. Right now, she had other things to do.

"Hon?" Edna spoke aloud, then waited, as if listening for a reply. She smiled, beatifically.

"I'm going to bring your daddy home, honey. He'll come see you tomorrow." Edna blushed, thinking of what they'd probably be doing tomorrow. But her son couldn't know about *that*. He was too young to learn of such things. "Or maybe the next." She folded her hands and squeezed them, bit her lower lip and lowered her head.

Edna Rose opened her eyes, reached out and gently stroked the headstone. When she spoke again her voice was barely a whisper, and her eyes were wet and shiny. "Bye."

Edna got slowly to her feet and folded her coat over her arm, stood looking down at her son's grave for a long, long time.

"Daddy's coming home, baby," she said, and turned and walked away.

Had he? Had he made it?

He thought about it driving home, was thinking about it as he pulled into the driveway then stopped, saw that the garage door was open and that there were bikes all over, blocking his way in.

"Shit," Babe said. "Goddamn kids."

He left the car hanging halfway out of the garage and got out, stormed through the garage and toward the sound of a bouncing basketball around back, walked through the door leading from the garage to the backyard and saw his kids, playing, the little guy driving hard to the basket and the big one blocking his way, his hands in the air, jumping up and down. There were two strange kids on the court, black teenagers Babe didn't know, all four kids absorbed in the game, three of them staring at the burning intensity on Collin's face.

"Go ahead, *shoot*," Mike said, taunting him. He was too tall and Collin had already stopped, so couldn't use his superior speed to dribble around him. Mike moved a little closer, crowding him, and Collin stepped back, threw the ball into Mike's face, hard.

"You little *shit*," Mike hollered, and grabbed Collin, threw him to the asphalt and Babe felt his anger begin to take over, was about to step out into the yard and was opening his mouth to yell when a hand grabbed his arm and Kelly said softly, "Leave them alone."

He backed into the garage, into the darkness, out of the children's sight. He could hear Mike and Collin tussling, hear the other two kids cheering them on. His children, his sons, were cursing each other like sailors.

"Leave them alone? They're killing each other."

Kelly stepped out of the doorway, said, "Hey," and Babe moved over, to see what happened.

Saw his kids look up shamefaced and immediately stop fighting, to stare at their mother in anguish.

"But he—" Mike began and she cut him off.

"Rico, Scott, you'd better go home now."

"Ma, come *on*." It was Collin, begging. "Please let them stay, it's only four, we got all night." There was a whine in his voice that Babe didn't care for, but it was better than the hate that had been there when he'd been cursing his brother.

"I won't have you out here cursing each other, fighting like animals."

"I'm sorry, Mom." Mike was always the first one to say that.

"Me, too."

"He started it—"

"I don't care who started it, it's not civilized. If you want to hit something your father's got a thousand dollars' worth of boxing equipment in the garage."

"Can Scott and Rico stay?"

"If there's one more fight, it's over for the rest of the week, no outside, no bikes, no basketball, nothing."

Then she was blocking his way as she walked back in, glaring at him, walking to the front of his car and angrily pulling the bikes out of the way.

"You can put your precious fucking car away, now," Kelly said, and walked through the access door into the house.

Here they went again. Babe felt his anger rising and fought it, took deep breaths and tried to relax, but it wasn't easy. He suddenly noticed that she'd been on this high horse for weeks, decided it was time that he knocked her off it. It hadn't been anything important until now, so he'd kept his mouth shut, gone through the motions because he was aware that it might have been him, the tension he was under from the show might have made him paranoid, overly touchy.

Now, though, he could see that it was Kelly, not him.

He'd thought she'd lightened up last night, initiating sex like that, being cute, but it appeared now that it had only been an aberration—she was suddenly starting to be cruel.

He caught up with her in the bedroom. Kelly stood by the bed, her back to him, hugging herself.

"What's your problem?" Said coldly, from the doorway. "You got a problem with me all of a sudden?"

"Problem?" Kelly whispered it, her back still to him. "Problem?" Said loudly now, Kelly turning, facing him angrily.

"You've given all of us a problem for the past goddamn month! We have to walk on eggs around you, and just now you were ready to hit those kids and don't you deny it."

"I wasn't going to hit anyone—"

"You think I can't tell from your face? Think you can hide it that well? Remember, Babe, I've seen it before, years ago, the way you'd look before you punched somebody."

He'd straightened up, took a step back from her verbal assault. Could she believe that about him, that he was going to hit his kids?

"I was drunk then, I'd never hit the kids." Shit, why was he defending himself?

"No, there're other ways to hurt them."

"What?"

"Mr. Sensitive,, Mr. TV Star. You know that little girl in the audience at school last night, the one you kept calling 'honey'? Mike's had a crush on her through the entire year, and guess what she spent the entire day talking about? About *you*, Street Babe. About how much she loved you! How do you think your son felt? How do you think that made him feel, big shot?"

She was glaring at him now, her arms at her side, hands balled into fists. "You better make up your mind about one thing, and goddamn quick, Babe. Do you want to be a TV star or don't you? Because I promise you one thing, your children aren't going to grow up terrified of raising their voices in their own house, or crying because you won't let them play Nintendo, for Christ's sake."

"They don't need discipline? They should be able to play fucking games before school, is that what you're saying?"

"You want to know what I'm saying? Pay attention, buddy. I'm saying that in the last month, since the country has caught Street Babe fever, you've turned into a selfish, self-important, self-absorbed asshole, that's what I'm saying!"

Babe wanted to hit her, felt the urge, strong and powerful, nearly overwhelming. He looked around the room, at the things he'd given her, the closet full of clothing, the king-sized bed. The jewelry box on her dresser. So that was the way it was going to be. Now that she had everything, she had no use for him anymore.

He was breathing heavily, as if he'd run a fast mile. He noticed that his own hands were fists, that he'd tightened the muscles in his arms.

In his mind's eye he could see his father, charging his mother, the two of them drunk and about to go toe-to-toe and Babe powerless to do anything to stop them. He pictured Mike and Collin cowering from him, in terror. The thought sobered him. With an effort, he forced his hands open. Stared at her, his mouth working.

Babe said, "I'm getting out of here," without conviction, and

Kelly told him not to bother coming back until he could respond to childish fistfights without acting like his goddamn father.

He puttered around in his office for a couple of minutes and then slammed out of the house and she watched him leave from the bedroom window, Babe carrying a small black tape recorder in his hand. Kelly held the drape back an inch, half of her wanting to call him back, respecting him because even though he was mad he backed out of the driveway slowly, his head darting around, making sure none of the kids were in the way. What was he doing with the recorder?

And what was it suddenly that made them so mean to each other? Last night, at the school, she'd worshipped him, felt her worship grow with every word he spoke, every kindness he'd shown toward the innocent and powerless. Today, she couldn't be in his presence without going on the attack.

But she'd seen him, known that he was about to go out there and spank the kids for the first time in their lives, at the very least scream his rage at them and terrify them. His face had made his intentions clear.

Should she have shown more compassion, more understanding? This was obviously a hard time for him, he was working so many things out in his head.

But he was so much easier to love these days when he wasn't around the house.

That thought hit her hard, and she watched the Lincoln fade away in the dying sunlight, wondering if it were true.

Was she jealous of him? Of his success, of the women who'd be wanting him now, of the people clamoring for his attention?

Kelly closed the drape and sat down on the bed, held her head in her hands. Then shook herself, got up and walked with purpose into the bathroom, splashed water on her face. There were children downstairs who were counting on her to be strong, who needed at least one parent to guide them. She and Babe had been so damned absorbed in their own problems that they hadn't paid a lot of attention to how this whole business was affecting the children. It was time one of them did.

She'd put him out of her mind for now. She'd said the things she'd needed to say, even if they hadn't been spoken in the proper tone of voice, in a mature manner, but how could she express herself maturely when she was dealing with a man to whom criticism of any sort was devastating? When he came back—and she knew he would come back—she would take him into his office and they could discuss this like adults. Until that time, there were a couple of young boys who needed to be told that, once again, their father wouldn't be joining them for dinner.

The beast resided within him, raging. Babe knew this and had long ago learned to live with it. There had been a time in his life when his worst fear had been that he would look in the mirror and see his father's image; that something would occur within him to change him into the man. He'd grown more secure in his personality since then, but the knowledge was always there, in the back of his mind: He'd come from a family that had scraped their genes off a cesspool, and he had to be always vigilant that he didn't fall into their behavioral patterns.

He'd fallen for it for a large part of his life, and he could see it now for what it was. All he'd been trying to do was win his father's love, his respect. In his insecurity he'd wanted to be like the man, he'd perceived his father as strong.

There had been a time in his life when he'd wanted nothing more than to be recognized as the spitting image of his father, but that time was long past. In fact, the last time he'd spoken to his brother Frank the kid had said to him, "You'll never be the man your father is," and Babe had said, "Thank God for that."

But he didn't feel the need to enumerate the reasons why he felt that way, had no desire to point out their father's shortcomings to his brother. They were obvious to all who saw them, right up front to all who knew him. The man lived his life by a rule of instant gratification, his own selfish needs and desires were all that truly counted.

And Babe was his son, carried that legacy.

When Kelly had taunted him about wanting to hit the kids, she'd been right. For a moment it had been in his mind: Get their goddamned respect, right now. Slap them around and show them what happened when they did not follow his orders.

He wouldn't have done it. He would have calmed down. He'd felt the urge before, and had never acted on it. Yet. Today, his biggest fear wasn't that he'd turn into his father. Today, his biggest fear was that someday he'd lose control, revert to what he truly was and wipe his family out in a psychotic rage.

It was a possibility. Years ago, when Anthony had started getting into trouble in school, going to jail and seeing the shrinks to get out of doing time, they'd told him that he had a mental illness, and that there was nothing to be ashamed of. That a lot of times it was genetic, that it had been part of his makeup before he'd even been born.

Babe came from those same genes.

Would it happen one day? Would other people die at his hand in a moment of uncontrollable rage?

He could talk to Tim about it and Tim would listen, intently. His eyes would be shining and you could just tell that he understood.

But he never said anything, never said that he himself ever felt the same urges, had the same violent desires.

Babe pulled the Lincoln into the parking lot at the 7-Eleven, went in and got a cup of coffee and a donut to tide him over, he would be missing dinner this evening. He stood on the sidewalk in front of the store, chewing the donut, the covered coffee cup resting on the flat lid of the garbage can next to him. He wouldn't eat in the car, didn't want crumbs in his vehicle.

He thought about what he would be doing in the next couple of hours, about the plan he'd formulated in his mind. For a moment he wanted to cast the plan aside, go home and try to live a normal existence with Kelly, maybe discuss their problems, but he couldn't see that happening right at the moment, the beast was still there, bubbling right under the surface, and Kelly had seen it coming, had called him on it before the monster had a chance to get loose.

Anger had always been his strongest emotion, fear running second by a nose. When he was younger he would fight at the drop of a hat and he knew even then that he was doing it out of fear, that he was afraid that the other people in the bar would see him as weak, as a sissy.

As dumb, stupid, clumsy and ugly.

The tapes never stopped playing.

So he would fight, charged by his rage, his terror driving him to what he believed at the time to be acts of great courage, the courageous acts being recognized as stupid the next morning, when he would lie in bed in the throes of a hangover, wondering how much of an ass he'd made of himself the night before, what it would cost him in terms of the things that money could not purchase.

Until the day that he'd awakened in a jail cell with the distinct impression that last night's fight had gone a bit too far.

It had been a badge of honor within his family, his killing a man. His father had gone to bat for him and pulled some strings, had made sure that Babe's charge had been reduced to involuntary manslaughter, when it could have been much worse. At first, the state had charged him with attempted murder, and after the man had died, first-degree murder. There were witnesses who'd testified that Babe had threatened the man's life seconds before the first blow was thrown, and he never could remember if he'd uttered them. A good defense lawyer had taken those words and twisted them around, had asked the judge how many times he himself had known people to threaten to kill others in a bar brawl or during a family disturbance, and it had worked, the judge had dismissed the original charge and along with it, it was understood, Babe's manslaughter sentence would be suspended to time served.

His old man probably still thought that Babe owed him for that.

He wiped his hands on a napkin and dropped it in the garbage can, picked up his coffee and got into the car, not opening the coffee until he reached the stop light on Route 30, directly before the expressway entrance that would take him into the city. He opened the coffee and lit a cigarette and held them on the wheel in one hand while he dialed information on his car phone with the other, speaking to the woman on the line as the light turned green and Babe turned off onto 57, North. He touched the keypad of his hands-free phone, taking down the number the recorded voice spoke to him, juggling the coffee and the cigarette and the steering wheel with his left hand while he hit Send then reached up to steady the wheel with his right.

"Shit!" The car was drifting, and Babe hurriedly steadied it.

The tape recorder on the seat next to him slid over to the passenger-side door and hit it, stayed put.

"Four Seasons Hotel, this is Bridgette, how may I be of service?"

"You can hook me up with Jerome Spinell's room," Babe said. He had his free hand on the wheel now, steadying the car, in control and pulling into the passing lane.

As the phone buzzed, Babe got the Lincoln going ten miles above the speed limit and set the cruise control, speeding down the road in light evening traffic. It was after seven; he'd beat the rush hour traffic when he went downtown.

Jerome said, "Hello?" and he sounded tentative, afraid.

"It's Babe Hill. I'll be there in an hour and a half. Meet me in the restaurant on the seventh floor, and bring the guy my father owes the money to. I'll wait five minutes, and if you don't show, you can kiss my ass for the money."

"Babe, *Babe*? Babe, I knew you'd—"

Babe cut him off and cleared the keypad, dialed in another number from memory, but didn't send it out yet.

He could feel it inside him, the beast raging, and it felt good. When he felt like this he could tell himself that he was a player, could rationalize away his true motives and feel that he was getting over on the straight world, on the working stiffs. It was a game he had played for years and now it brought him guilt.

Jesus, next thing you knew, he'd be in a Hegewisch tavern, looking to kick ass on a slob of a mailman named Jabbo. Still, he couldn't deny that at that moment he felt good for the first time in a while.

Would he ever be normal, ever be like everyone else? How he wished that he could. Just once, just for one day, feel the happiness others felt, the joy in his accomplishments. Without the ever-present need to do more, without the insecurity that dogged his every move.

And without the goddamn selfishness that seemed to be a part of his life all of a sudden.

He wasn't a good father and he knew that, wouldn't even argue the fact with Kelly when she'd try to convince him that he was. He'd try, God, how he'd try. Ball games and outings, trips to Wisconsin and Michigan alone with the boys last summer, the first time he could afford to enjoy such luxuries.

But no matter how he tried, there was always a niggling doubt about them in his mind. Would they grow up straight and strong? Was he setting a bad example for them? He would tell them straight out about his past when they asked, never lying to them, and he could see that Collin admired that, what he'd been. One of the reasons Babe had never taken his sons to the beach was because he did not want them seeing the scar on his back. He could not tell them about that. At least not yet. Would Collin try to emulate his father, as Babe had tried to emulate his own? Collin didn't have the upbringing that Babe had had, did not know how vicious you had to be to survive inside. Jail would end the boy's life.

What he wondered was if he was telling them these things to be honest, or if there was a sort of sick pride in it, Babe saying to his kids, Look at me, look at the tough guy I was.

The selfishness was always with him, even when he thought he was covering it up.

Take last night, at the school. He'd gone there for Mike, as he'd done last year around the same time, wanting to help his kid out with the teachers, with the principals, maybe score a few points with the children there who were being abused at home the way Babe had been as a child. And what had he done? Talked to the little girl Mike had a crush on, looked at the budding rose and called her honey, sweetie. He thought with true horror about how he'd have treated her if he'd come across her when he was in jail, when the beast still had total control. Not with courtesy and respect, that was for sure. She was thirteen and would have been open game.

Dear God, did a guy like him have any right to have children? And how far would the legacy get handed down? Would it affect Mike and Collin when they were adults? Would they be predisposed to smoking, drinking, fighting and stealing? Would they live their adult lives filled with mental confusion? No matter how much he tried to cover it up, what he showed the world, that was his usual psychic state. How much of it was genetic and how much was environment? And even if it was *all* environment, what kind of men would they become with Babe as their main role model in life?

There were tears in his eyes now as Babe thought about how badly Mike wanted that little girl to look at him the way she'd looked at Babe. How could he have not seen that? How could he have been so goddamn insensitive? He'd been watching the kid throughout the night, had an eye on him throughout the entire speech, making sure that Mike didn't make any silly moves that would embarrass him.

It was always like this. He'd do something wrong, or worse, not do something right, and then be filled with shame, with a sense of inadequacy. Maybe he should just keep going, keep the car on the road and not stop except to gas up and eat, run it to the end of the road and see where he wound up.

Babe hit the Send button on the telephone and tossed the empty coffee carton to the floor. He was lighting another cigarette when his brother John's voice said hello.

"John, it's me," Babe said. "I need you to do me a favor . . ."

Johnny Hilliard was sitting in his booth in the Tamburitza Tavern, jotting down numbers in his notebook and wondering how far he could take it before he got caught stealing the same ten grand over and over again.

Maybe another time, maybe just once more, and he would be home, or close enough to it that it wouldn't really matter.

There was forty grand that would have to be accounted for, and he had convinced Landini that the gooms had stolen it from him, had booked the money themselves instead of turning it in. Which meant that the gooms would have to go, which caused him sadness. They were loyal, and hard workers. Trusting to a fault. Which made them stupid.

And a good thing that stupidity was, too.

He'd talked to the remaining gooms that afternoon, had told them in coded sentences spoken over pay phones that Moca had been a warning from Landini, that he'd been caught with his hand in the till and what had happened to him had been his righteous due. They were dumb enough to fall for it, Johnny was certain of that, and he'd told them to take all the money that they could this week, to accept every bet that came their way because they had to cover the loss of Moca's absence, to convince Landini that they weren't themselves trying to be a little too greedy.

It was part of the deal, you were expected to steal. A little here and there to prove that there was larceny in your heart. Landini expected it from him, as Milo Spinell expected it from Landini and Johnny expected it from the gooms. Hell, he knew that even his son

Frank was dipping into the well a little; it was the cost of doing business, one of the perks of being a crook. You were expected to try and get over and the profits were so great that a little bit of cash missing here and there was never even missed.

But forty grand was a lot more than a little bit of cash, and Johnny had seen what happened to men who'd taken Landini for a tenth of that amount. He wouldn't let it happen to him.

The figures he was working on made him smile to himself. If Anthony played his cards right, did what he'd been told to do, then Johnny would only be down twenty. Which meant he'd only have to come up with ten. If he could convince Landini that the gooms were the culprits all along, the man would expect a loss of maybe ten grand, no problem. But then the gooms would have to die, and quickly, and where would that leave Johnny?

Shit, he'd worry about that when the time came. There were plenty of people out there who'd stand in line to work for him, he could pick and choose as he wished. Now that the mills were closed, it would be easy pickings.

He'd turned his beeper on over a half hour ago when he'd decided that things would work out okay, and since then had taken four calls, and this guy calling him now made it five. Johnny took out his beeper and stared at the digital readout, wondering about the number, who it could be. It wasn't a Hegewisch or an East Side or a South Chicago exchange, where most of his calls came from. This was an exchange he had never heard of before.

It didn't bother him too much, because most of his business was done over pay phones. He'd once become a target of a probe of political corruption because some ignorant son of a bitch of a judge had called him at his home, asked him where the monthly payoff was. The feds hadn't even been looking his way before that, but they sure had come hunting after the call, and Johnny had done three years in Atlanta behind a thirty-foot stone wall fighting off jigs and Cubans while the judicial thief had served a year in a Florida Army camp, playing tennis and golf.

So these days he said little over the phone that wasn't couched in deep code, decipherable only to those who were familiar with his jargon. He would tell someone to meet him at the usual place at three and that meant the meet was on for one, at the last place they'd met. It would make it impossible for the law to get there ahead of him, bug the place and catch Johnny again. He couldn't be doing any more time, he was just too damn old for that.

He would return calls and just say, "Yeah," and if the other party mentioned his name or he didn't recognize the voice Johnny would hang up and ignore his next beep. If the party on the other end knew him, his ways, and played the game the right way, spoke guardedly and with no names mentioned, they could do entire deals over the phone and appear to any listening ears to be discussing where they would be having their lunch the next day.

Johnny liked to believe that he learned from his mistakes.

Which made him cautious about returning this call. He'd been feeling secure in the knowledge that he wouldn't do any more time over a telephone conversation, and the unknown exchange bothered him, made him consider a federal setup.

Still, he was curious. And he could always hang up if he didn't like the sound of the caller's voice.

Johnny stuffed the notebook in his back pocket and walked to the back to make his call, signaling with his hand that he wanted another drink sent over to his booth. The punk bartender, Mikey, he was free-pouring one before Johnny even gave him the signal. Johnny kept his face blank but he felt warm inside. This guy, just like the gooms, had to have some fear sprayed at him from time to time in order to gain his respect and admiration.

Johnny dropped the quarter in the slot and squinted at the crystal digits, floating there on the top of his beeper, wishing he'd brought his reading glasses with him from the booth. His memory wasn't what it used to be. He finally got it and the phone on the other end rang once, twice, burring with an unusual tone, this wasn't Ma Bell he was reaching. When the line was picked up Johnny heard the sound of rushing wind and took it to be a line tap for a second, nearly hung up but instead said, "Yeah," and nearly dropped the phone when his son Babe's voice came over the wire.

"I'm ten minutes away from 130th Street. Give me an address where you'll be in twenty."

"What's wrong, are the kids all right?"

"Pa . . ."

"I—I'm at the Tamburitza Tavern, across the street from Mario's Meats, off 99th and Ewing, you know where that is?"

"I'll find it. Twenty minutes," Babe said, and the line went dead.

Oh, man.

Johnny hung up the phone with shaking fingers, taken out of his world and deposited down in another, one over which he had no power or control. In the straight world, in his son's world, one filled with success and happiness, with riches and fame and broads and nice cars that didn't have holes where a lock used to be. He'd been taken into that world, the world he'd rejected as a teenager, without warning, and that had never happened to him before, he'd always been able to pick and choose his ventures into it, prepare himself for what he'd find there.

He was left in that world by a kid whose voice held nothing but contempt for him, and he looked around himself and realized that wasn't a hard feeling for Babe to have.

Christ, a stinking hole of a tavern, where he was the king rat in a rotten cheese factory.

Johnny pushed his way into the men's room and staggered into a stall, secured the cheap hatch and sat down on the commode with his pants up.

He'd felt this way before, usually in some prison when he had plenty of time on his hands and he had to take a long hard look at the wasteland that his life was painted upon. Insight wasn't his greatest mental asset, was, in fact, his enemy. Denial and disavowal were the tools of his trade, rationalization and shortsightedness his strengths.

There had been one guy in the last prison he'd been in who had a hand-lettered poster on the wall which read LIFE IS WHAT HAPPENS TO YOU WHILE YOU'RE STRUGGLING TO SURVIVE, and Johnny thought that had been the smartest thing he'd ever read.

He held his head in his hands, fighting the onslaught of depression, ashamed for one of the few times in his sixty-plus year life. Afraid, too, of what his son would see.

A broken old man who cared about the hustle more than anything else, whose life had meaning only in the context of its own survival. He could talk to mob chiefs and South American killers and feel at home, one of them, but he had just spoken to his boy for the first time in years and look at him, how it had affected him. Shaking and near tears in a toilet in one of the few ginmills in town where he could be perceived as a big shot. The only people he respected were those from whom he could take a profit, and his treatment of others was based entirely on their ability to cause him physical harm.

Babe was above that, now, far above what his father had ever been or could ever hope to become, and it made Johnny feel as if he were meeting with the President, with someone so far beyond his own realm it would be like talking to a martian.

And this was his own child, his own flesh and blood.

The others were a disappointment; his oldest son was a pussy, a wimp who let women push him around. His son Frank was a good soldier but a pervert, liked to have pushy dykes strap on two-sided dildos and lay it to him. Anthony, he'd once had hope for but he could see now that the kid was a mental case, a schizophrenic, yeah, but a killer, too, without conscience. Johnny had gone to prisons for trying to give them a better life than he'd had and in his absence Marge had ruined the kids, made them weak. Babe was the only one who'd broken away from the pattern, who'd become a man. So why wasn't Johnny proud, why did he suddenly feel the same way he had when he'd been seventeen and on his way to the state joint for the first time? All weak in the knees and frightened.

Then he felt something come over him that he felt most comfortable with, the feeling that was with him through most of his waking hours.

Johnny began to feel hate, strong and hot.

The same hate he'd felt as a kid when his father had cured him of his fear of the dark by tying him to a pole in the basement and turning off the lights, leaving him there through the night. The same hate that he experienced when he stood in front of a judge who wasn't on the payroll, some rich fat slob who'd had nannies and servants to pamper his spoiled ass, who grew up with all the advantages and then felt the righteous indignation of the rich when he looked down at Johnny from his privileged heights. That hate was strong now, filling him, and he wiped his forehead hard with both hands and took a deep breath, stood up and nodded his head a few times, bounced on the balls of his feet, his lips tight and curving downward.

Fuck that kid. He'd given him life and if he had to he'd take it away from him. Who did he think he was, telling Johnny Hilliard what to do, what time to meet him?

Johnny stormed out of the toilet and swaggered to the bar, leaned on it and waited for the bartender to notice him and come hurrying over. In a soft, casual voice he told the guy that his son Babe was coming by for a drink, and if he got there before Johnny got back to give him what he wanted and have him wait in his booth, he'd be right back.

From his trip across the street, where he'd pick up one of his guns. The kid wanted to get pushy? Well, Johnny could push back.

He checked his watch, saw that it was seven-thirty and that it was dark outside. Where the hell were Anthony and Frank? He could sure use them right about now.

Anthony was walking up the stairs to Parker's two-flat while his lazy ass brother was sitting over in the South Shore Inn, having a beer while Anthony did all the work.

Anthony was terrified. There was a difference between performing a violent act during a drunken rage and walking into a man's house with a gun in your hand, committed to an act of murder.

He tried to will the voices to come to him, to give him direction, but the wind wouldn't even blow. Tonight, he was on his own. His hands were trembling and he was even thinking in disjointed images, transposing things in his mind. He hadn't dared try to speak for the last couple of hours.

This guy, he was a big one, too, heavy with a lot of fat on him, but Frank told him that when he was drunk he could mix it up pretty good, and he was usually always drunk.

His older sister lived upstairs, in an apartment Parker had renovated for her. He was single, was known to take a hooker now and again and keep her at the house for two or three days, wearing himself out until the next month rolled along. He had no visible means of support and always seemed to have a lot of money.

Was he a player? A mobster who'd have friends out looking for him the second the word of his death reached their ears? Shit, this wasn't as easy as Anthony thought it would be.

He hadn't even been able to have a real drink today, either. He'd taken a pill this morning, needing to level out when he'd learned that his actions of the previous night had gone beyond simply arson, beyond kids' games. He'd taken another pill this afternoon, and with the three beers in him he'd really felt it. He'd like to take another one right now, maybe two or three to stop his hands from shaking and his mind from racing.

He reached the top of the stairs and felt for the pistol grip in the waistband of his pants, under the shirt he'd pulled out to cover the thing. Frank had stepped inside to pay the man and had said that he'd pressed the button on the old-fashioned door lock that would leave it open to the outside knob. Anthony fervently wished that he hadn't, that the knob wouldn't turn. He could tell his father that the door had been locked and that he didn't want to draw attention to himself, kicking a door in with a gun in his hand right there on Carondolet Avenue.

He reached for the knob with a left hand that was jerking violently, his right on the pistol butt, and the thing turned in his hand and he quickly opened it, stepped through and silently closed it behind him.

He was in a vestibule, with a staircase to the upper floor in front of him, a closed door at the top that he could see from where he stood. To his left was a white wall with hooks hanging out of it, several coats, both men's and women's, hanging from them. A half dozen pairs of shoes were under the coats, side by side on the floor, next to a full umbrella rack. There was a doorway about midway down the wall, with ornate brown framing. From somewhere in that room came the sound of a basketball slapping hardwood; a crowd's cheer.

Anthony's heart was pounding, the gun now out and in his hand, weighing a ton. His forearm ached from holding it up; his fingers were cramping. Oh God, what had he gotten himself into?

But he couldn't back out now. To back out would lose him his little place, the tiny apartment the old man had set him up in. He'd have to move back home with his mother, see her boyfriends, face that humiliation all over again.

Worst of all he'd lose the respect of his father, would never again see the look he'd seen that morning, the look of admiration that had shone on his father's face. If he walked out of this house right now, that face would only show him scorn, as it always had until today.

Anthony walked through the door with the gun held in both hands, safety off and a round in the chamber, the gun jumping crazily up and down in time with his heartbeat.

"The where's money, suckercock!"

Parker threw his hands into the air, sitting there in a dirty undershirt that was now riding up his belly, the man instantly terrorized—which made Anthony feel more in control, a little bit powerful. There was a tension in his groin that he couldn't believe was happening at this time. Parker was scared to death, but that didn't stop his eyes from shooting quickly to the pile of money on the coffee table before they came back to Anthony. Anthony smiled.

He didn't trust himself to speak again. He walked over to the pile and took his right hand off the gun, scooped up the cash in small bundles with his left and stuffed them into his pants pockets, one at a time. Somewhere in the house he heard a door slam.

"Landini's gonna hear about this!" Parker spat out saliva as he spoke, scared shitless but still having to have the last word. Anthony spoiled it for him.

"Eventually," he said, proud that he'd gotten the five-syllable word out in one piece, no transposing, hell, he didn't even feel that nervous anymore. He leveled the gun at Parker's chest and the guy, he was fast for a fat man, tried to come out of the chair at him and Anthony shot him, once, right through the middle of his chest.

He stood there in amazement, watching the blood that had shot out of the man's back in a fine spray settle to the ground like dust. Should he shoot him again, see if he could raise another cloud like that? All red and yucky.

The scream pulled him out of his thoughts and he turned, saw the older woman charging him with an umbrella and he turned fully around, fired a shot that went into the wall and she nailed him one, hard, on the side of his head and he saw stars. Anthony dropped the gun and fell to his knees, seeing double, his hands grabbing frantically for the pistol. The umbrella hit him again and again and he jumped away from it, stood and charged the woman, grabbed her by her throat and pushed her against the wall, held her there while he choked her.

She got weak real fast, the woman did. Flailed at him with the umbrella for a minute then dropped it, tried to scratch at his face but he ducked her, leaned into her, pushed her into the wall, the woman not all that old, maybe a couple of years younger than Ma, built about the same, her breasts now against Anthony's chest, in there close. The tightness in his groin was now an ache, and Anthony leaned further in, rubbed himself against her. He could close his eyes and imagine that this woman was his mother, and he was one of the drunks from work. . . .

He let her go and she fell to the floor, gasping for breath, her hands around her throat, rubbing it. She was on her back, which saved him some trouble.

Anthony walked over and found the gun, walking bowlegged, his erection stiff in his tight jeans. He wasn't the least bit nervous anymore. He carried the gun over to the woman, who saw his legs and raised her head, staring at him, breathing heavily. He pointed the gun at her.

"Ma," Anthony said, "you shouldn't have never brought those guys home from work, Ma." Anthony said this and began to unbuckle his pants, never even noticing that he hadn't transposed a single word.

There were a couple of ways Babe could have gotten to the East
Side quicker, but he didn't take them. For him, the only way
to the East Side was down 130th Street to Baltimore, from
there to 133rd and then left down to Avenue O, then left again
all the way down past the S curve—with its big yellow sign: SLOW
DOWN 29 DIDN'T! six of the twenty-nine being people he'd
known—then up to 112th, where, in his mind, the East Side began.

He'd lived in Hegewisch on and off for most of his life, since his
childhood and on into his adult years. Had come back to it when
he'd been released from jail, lived in a rooming house that had a
communal bath, shared with three other men. The tub in that place
was always dirty, and Babe would scrub it, bathe, then scrub it again
after he was done. He always took a long hot tub bath when he'd
lived there, every night before going out. He'd had too many twice-
a-week showers penned up in a filthy stall with a dozen other guys
milling around, fighting to get to the shower heads before the hot
water was gone. He'd lie on his back in that big claw-footed tub and
dream that someday he'd have the things that were his today. Back
then he'd take his Ajax and sponge with him, back to his room. Place
it on the old wooden chest of drawers, next to his bottle of liquor.
That boardinghouse had been the last stop before the floor of the
barber shop, and when he'd lived there he'd been happy. His
previous place of residence had been a two-inch mattress on the
floor of a dormitory in the county, shared with a couple dozen guys
who were always looking to score with him.

Did memories flood back to him now or what? How long had it

been since he'd come back this way? He'd worked here on *Street Babe*, up the street at the South Shore Inn, where they'd filmed the interior bar scenes, and in a lot of other areas, showing the gritty reality that steamed up from the sidewalks in this part of town. But he'd been too busy then to remember a whole lot, to let the memories flow to him like this. Back then, he'd been trying to make himself a star.

He drove down 130th Street and past the rows of neat brick houses and past Mann Park, where he'd go as a kid and play blackjack for quarters, lag nickels and more often than not get into fistfights with the other young toughs. The bigger guys would charge them a buck and a half for a dollar six-pack and always brought them their beer, never ripped them off for two reasons: they'd have lost half their income if the word got out that they were cheats, and the younger kids like Babe had been known to defend themselves against bigger kids with baseball bats and bricks.

Which were about the most exotic weapons any of them ever used. He could remember the day that the son of a cop brought a pistol to the park, remembered the awe with which they'd passed it around. Babe had been known as an odd one, an outsider who everybody knew but nobody really hung around with, the kid with the father in what back then had been called The Syndicate, and he'd taken the pistol in his hands, held it lovingly and knowledge-ably, then passed it on without a word.

He knew what they were used for, had come close to them before. Someone had come to their apartment once and had taken a shot at his father through the glass front door, the bullet had ripped through the door and passed through two walls before embedding itself in a closet, in his parents' bedroom. His father had thrown himself to the ground and shouted for the kids to get down but the shooter, he'd split right away, after taking that first shot, and Babe heard his father telling his mother a few days later after she'd calmed down and would speak to him again that the man had hung himself in his basement. Committed suicide. With his hands tied behind his back, his mouth gagged, and the soles of his feet burned off with matches. Babe couldn't understand why someone would cause themselves so much pain and grief, or how he'd been able to tie his hands behind his back all by himself. It was only years later that he got his father's little joke.

That had been when they'd been living high, when he'd gone to school with more money in his pocket than most of the other kids' fathers made in a week. A pocketful of money and bruises all over his body and a cast on his arm, twice.

And now he was going to meet the man who'd left the bruises and who'd broken those bones. Those physical bruises that had healed he could live with, no problem. The others, though, they were the ones that always chased you, right there on your heels all the time and if you didn't watch your step they'd catch your ass and do you in.

He was going to meet the man who'd always made him feel inferior, always made him feel less than acceptable. No matter what he did, what he accomplished, this man would level him with a glance, and with a single cruel word would let him know that he didn't measure up, that he wasn't good enough. The physical pains always went away. The psychic pains never did.

When he was twelve and his father was in jail awaiting trial on the murder charge, Babe had performed his first B&E, had broken into a house in the Arizona section of Hegewisch that wasn't as nice as the area he was now driving through. Arizona had a lot of houses with fading siding that had begun life as roofing shingles. It was the other side of the tracks where Tone Nello and Panther Payne and the other really tough guys hung out. In the house he'd found a hidden money horde, fives and tens and twenties stuffed every which way into a large cookie jar in the basement, and he'd been smart, hadn't taken it all. It was obvious that the owner of the house hadn't counted the money, just stuffed it in there whenever he had a loose bill, maybe hiding it from his wife, maybe saving for a trip.

What Babe had done was, he'd taken a twenty, and the following week another, and then a five and then a ten and even though he never got to take as much as he would have if he'd robbed the entire jar that first night he never felt bad about it, because of the thrill.

There was one involved, of that there was no doubt. A large thrill in breaking into someone's house and being intimate with their belongings without their knowledge. There was also the chill of fear every time, and it never went away, in fact got worse every time out because you had to figure that eventually the odds would catch up with you and you'd get caught. But that fear wasn't greater than the attraction, than the kick of getting over on them. In fact, that fear enhanced the pleasure when you got away yet another time.

Later, when he was a teenager and a full-fledged thief, Babe would sometimes lie on the bed of the house he had broken into, would masturbate into the frilly woman's underwear he would find hidden in dresser drawers. He would take out any sexual devices he would come across and lay them across the bed, secret conspirators with the women, wondering about them, wanting to come back at night when they were home but somehow never doing it.

He had trouble with that now, with reconciling the person he was with the person that he had been. He could have been a rapist, had come that close. How had he escaped? Some of the journalists had written what they learned about him as if the town was to blame for his mental defects, and that had made some of the residents mad, had turned them against him, but he'd never said that it was Hegewisch's fault, had only stated that that was where he'd been raised. He knew these days what had made him come so close. He was going to meet the chef of that meal right now.

He passed St. Columba School, the site of some of his greatest humiliations. One of the boys he'd graduated with had gone on to become an anthropologist, another was a doctor. He knew that one was a judge and still another was in Washington, lobbying for funds for battered women. And he was sure that most of them had gone on to Catholic high schools, prep schools that would prepare them for a college education. He'd missed the boat and could he blame the town? Not anymore than those who had succeeded could give the area credit for their successes.

It was a town filled with neat bungalows and two-story houses with freshly washed siding. The sidewalks were sprayed down and the lawns were newly mown. Down the street was a public school that didn't have one spray-painted piece of gang graffiti on any of its walls. There were a lot of old cars on the street now that the mills had dried up, but they were clean, shining under the streetlights. Even the young people on the street corners weren't there to mug any old women, they were simply kids with nothing to do.

Except today, they didn't fight with baseball bats and bricks anymore. Guns were cheap and drugs were everywhere. Thank God that beer had been the forbidden fruit back then. He'd drunk it, as had many of the boys he'd known, and if crack had been freely available a lot more than a couple of dozen of them would have been dead, more than likely including himself. Most of the kids he drank that beer with had homes now, families, lives and dreams. Others had caught the bug from those first cold sips, and had descended into the insanity of chronic alcoholism. Some had died. Others were successful.

And what was he? What was James Hilliard?

He wondered about it, gave it serious thought as he drove down Avenue O toward the East Side for maybe the ten thousandth time of his life, the town different to him suddenly, Babe now a stranger. He wondered if anyone would throw a rock at him if they were to recognize him, wondered how many times he'd been cursed that day in bars throughout the town. Every block in Hegewisch had at least one bar, the ginmills catering to whatever frame of mind you might be in, from friendly, old-fashioned, family-run places like the South Shore Inn to wild joints with acid rock blaring through the doors, to joints that had Harleys parked on the sidewalk out front. Hegewisch was a town that catered to every taste, to every type.

And what type was he? He used to be a thief. Then he was a drunk, a bar brawler, and then a killer. Then a drunk again. And now he had taken his place among them, among the illustrious graduates of St. Columba School. He'd get a letter now and again from someone who claimed to know him in grade school, and he'd feel good inside. "Saw you in the Honda commercial, and you're as handsome as ever! (married yet)?!" Cutesy letters from the women, who remembered him as a little boy, and macho letters from the men, who tried to tell him that they'd once been playmates. Bullshit to that. When he wasn't with Slugger or Charlie back then he was alone, and that was the way it was.

It was all in your perceptions, in the way you saw things. A girl who'd gone to that school and been a cheerleader for the basketball team, a girl who'd gone on to college and medical school, would not remember Hegewisch the same way Babe did. She'd have been home in bed, her hair in curlers, her retainer in a glass beside the bed while Babe had been out stealing, getting his ass kicked by the cops and fighting in the park, drinking beer and gambling. She could get the *Hegewisch News* or the *Daily Calumet* delivered to her home and not even see the front page with the headline about the most recent senseless death, skip right past the Police Blotter section with the page of recent arrests in her haste to get to the news about the weekend's dance at Serbian Hall, in her speedy glance to find out what band was playing at the next Washington High School gathering.

But Babe saw those front pages, and more often than not he was acquainted with the guy who'd died.

It was all in the way you were raised.

And he was on his way to see the guy who'd raised him, who'd given him a lot of those painful memories.

He passed the LTV plant that used to be Republic Steel, with its huge smokestacks which years ago had belched smoke around the clock when the mills had been working three shifts a day and weekends. He would stand on the corner of 106th and Ewing in the late summer evenings and watch the pollution fall out of the sky like snow. Could the people who called the Heltz show deny that? Deny that in the mornings they had to wipe the stuff off their windshields in order to drive their cars?

There were tough, proud people here, in this neighborhood, people who saw community as what it really was, instead of as a catchword to describe the ghetto, the way a lot of the politicians did these days on the news. This was a true community, with spirit and heart and strength, and when the mills closed down they didn't turn to the government and demand welfare or a bailout, they picked themselves up, dusted themselves off, and went out and got two jobs to replace the one they had lost.

And the mayor wanted to turn this into an airport.

Babe could see it in his mind's eye, and he smiled even though he had made the turn off 112th and was now on Ewing, less than a mile from where he had to meet his father.

The day they broke ground, they better watch out, because if these people couldn't beat the airport through legal means, they'd bomb the goddamn equipment, and wouldn't that be something to see?

Babe passed the 7-Eleven and caught the red light at 106th, sat gawking at the changes that had occurred on the East Side since he had last been up here. The kids were still there, though, on the same corner where he'd once stood, a quart of beer hidden under his coat. He heard a car horn honk right next to him and turned to see a carful of teenage girls holding their hands in front of their mouths, gawking at him, giggling. He smiled and one of them screamed, pulled at her hair and began to cry and it made him feel good, seeing that. Not because she was crying, but because she had the ability to do so, had that much passion to waste on a man sitting in a car who happened to have been in a TV show she'd watched two nights before. He envied her, too, and powered down the window to blow her a kiss as the light changed and he jumped in front of their car, left them sitting there stunned at the light as car horns began honking behind them.

It was all in your perceptions, and these kids would go to school tomorrow and laugh together, tell their parents and friends about it and maybe even think about it before bed that night, imagining him there next to them. It was one of the reasons he did it, to seduce them, to make strangers fall in love with the character he became when the cameras rolled. He wanted to win their approval. They would have a story to tell their children one day when they were older, if Babe should hit it big and become a major star, and they'd be able to tell it without guilt. Unlike the guys who wrote him letters, talking about how close they had been to him in grade school.

It was all in your perceptions, and Babe's had all been negative. He had his, and they had theirs, and none of them would be reality.

He only knew that if they turned this area into an airport it would be a goddamn sin.

Babe passed under the viaduct at five-points, drove another block and made a left, saw the Tamburitza Tavern's name flashing in neon inside a filthy window and parked the car half a block away. He reached down to the car phone's keypad, punched out a number and sent out another call, got his brother's machine.

"Tim, it's Babe. I'm meeting my father right now in a joint called the Tamburitza Tavern at 99th and L, right off Ewing. It's across the street from a place called Mario's Meats. If all goes well with him I'm meeting with Spinelloid and the guys my father owes the money to at the Four Seasons Hotel in a little more than an hour." Babe squinted at the lit-up timepiece on the dashboard. "It's a little before eight now, and I'd appreciate it if you'd meet me at the track around midnight, if you can get away. If I'm not there, one of those two guys had me killed, and my money would be on the old man doing it." Babe paused, and in spite of his fear, he smiled.

"I took out an insurance policy, though. I'm taping both god-damned meetings, and if things work out we should be in pretty good shape."

Babe ended the call and patted the recording wire he'd glommed from the *Street Babe* set, which was now taped to the hair on his chest. Patted the battery pack taped to the small of his back, too. The wire felt like it was burning him, and the damn thing wasn't even turned on yet. Babe switched it on, made sure the cassette recorder on the front seat was spinning, then got out of the car and made his way to the tavern, to see his father for the first time in over ten years.

27

nthony walked into the tavern like he owned it, sat down at the bar next to Frank and pointed at his brother's glass, ordering a beer without having to open his mouth.

"You take care of things, babe?"

"Me that don't you call!"

"Calm down, shit, I didn't mean it that way." Frank leaned in a little and whispered, "You get the money or not?" and Anthony nodded.

"It got I."

"Relax, don't try and say anything, shit." Frank seemed embarrassed, ashamed of him maybe.

The bartender put the drink down in front of him and stood back, smiled, looking at the two of them, from one to the other without losing his grin.

"This your brother, Frank?" the bartender said. "Jeez, all you Hilliard boys look alike." He shook Anthony's hand and Anthony nodded, smiling back at him.

"I'm the"—He paused, concentrated—"best-looking!" Got it out and grinned widely at his ability to do so, a reaction the bartender couldn't understand. The man chuckled politely along with Frank and then moved down the bar, leaned his elbow on the backbar and looked up at the ball game on the television mounted on the wall high above his head in the corner.

He'd dressed the broad, after, made sure her clothes were back on. Maybe they wouldn't know about it, wouldn't think to check. He should have thought ahead, should have carried some rubbers with him. They could do things with that DNA testing, he'd read about it in the papers, that you wouldn't think would be real. James Bond shit they could do without half trying. Would probably be able to find out about his chemical imbalance if they checked his sperm, would know about his medication, too, and from there they would only have to run down all the doctors who prescribed such drugs and eventually they would have him.

He wasn't as worried about being caught as he was about what he'd done, the daydreams he'd had while he'd been doing her. Now he felt dirty, soiled. He hadn't shot her to death, like he should have, had instead beaten her to death with the same umbrella that she'd tried to brain him with. To teach her a lesson. But it had been more of an act of passion than the killing of her brother had been, and the cops wouldn't miss that fact, would jump on it and check her out and they'd find that she'd been raped.

Anthony fought his disgust, his self-hatred. He'd rather die at his own hand than face his father with the truth, than to be arrested for raping the sister of the man he'd been sent to kill. Shit, why did she have to come downstairs? It was the bitch's own fault.

Frank said, "I'm gonna call the old man, tell him you took care of business and see what he wants us to do. I hope we're through for the night, I got a date."

Anthony nodded his head, slapped his hand on the bar to signal the bartender, pointed at his beer. Slowly, with diligence, he said, "Let me have a shot too." Made it.

"What kind?"

"Walker Johnnie Red."

The bartender looked at him funny, puzzled.

"You mean a Johnnie Walker Red?"

"What I said, it ain't?"

He didn't like the look on the man's face as he poured the drink into a glass and put it next to his beer, but he didn't say anything. He wasn't feeling so tough all of a sudden.

Instead of worrying about facing his father, he knew he should worry about facing his mother. He wondered if he could. Doing what he'd done tonight was far different than lying in bed, day-dreaming about it. Jerking off was all in your head and nobody ever got hurt. And besides, he loved his mother, worshipped her. He didn't want to hurt her! Hell, for all Anthony knew the shots had been heard and someone might have walked right up to the house and in the front door, would have seen and heard him hitting the woman, driving it into her and calling his mother a bitch and a whore with every breath.

"My God," Anthony said, and his brother Frank said, "That's all right, you can just call me Frank," then sat back down on his stool and raised his beer glass.

"Come on," Frank said, smirking. "We got to go meet the old man, and guess who's gonna be with him in about five minutes?"

Anthony didn't know and didn't care. He took a pill out of his bottle and put it in his mouth, then thought about it and put another one in there. He washed it down with the whiskey, was drinking the last of the beer when Frank said, "*Babe's* with him, brother," and Anthony choked on the last of the beer, the golden liquid pouring out of his mouth and nose and onto the polished bar top.

The bartender waited until he was in the door then said loudly, "How you doin', Mr. Hilliard, welcome to the Tamburitza."

"My name's Hill," Babe said.

Christ, what a shithole. Smelled as bad as it looked, and it looked like hell. Filthy, cracked tile on the floor, mirrors faded and discolored from cigarette smoke. There were only three guys at the bar, older men and Babe could see from their slack-jawed stares that they had about eight teeth between them.

"You want a drink?" and Babe had to stop himself. Did he *ever* want a drink. But he wouldn't have one, would get through this without the crutch.

"Nothing," Babe said, and spotted his old man giving him a badeye from a booth in the back.

As he was walking toward him, the bartender yelled out, "Loved your show!" and Babe didn't reply.

His father was sitting with his chin down on his chest, looking up at Babe from under a wrinkled forehead, eyes burning. When was the last time he'd seen him? He'd visited him once in prison after he'd been married, but before Collin was born, so it had to have been eleven years ago.

The man looked terrible, overweight and mostly gray now, the wavy hair he'd been so proud of was these days flat and lifeless. Combed straight back like always. There were deep lines in his face, broken veins in his cheeks and across his pitted nose. This was his father? This was the man he'd feared for all these years?

"Sit down, Babe," his father said, and Babe slid into the booth, took a deep breath and went to work.

There were guys he'd worked with who'd told him that they had to dredge up their childhood memories of suffering to act, others who'd gone to acting school where they'd been instructed to sit in a circle and become a flower, a fruit, a cow.

Babe didn't play that shit.

He knew his characters, who he needed to be, and he slipped into their skin effortlessly, easily, and when the director yelled Cut he slipped back out, into himself, or whatever was left of himself after the job. There would always be a little of the character left within him, for a little while at least.

Now he played it cold, without a director or a crew or any lights to distract him.

"Long time, son."

"Gonna be longer till next time," Babe said. Then said, "I got news for you. You screwed some serious people out of a lot of money, and they're coming after you. They're gonna kill you . . ." Babe hesitated, then forced himself to say, "Pa." He gave his father his coldest stare, dug down deep. In his head, he was a hit man and this guy in front of him was a washed-up loser.

Johnny Hilliard said, "That's a two-way street," and Babe felt something hard touch his knee, looked down and saw the long barrel of a large pistol pointing at his belly.

"I'm not the guy they sent to do it."

"You're their fucking messenger." The pressure on his knee became greater, and he had to force his leg to remain where it was. He couldn't show this man weakness. When his father spoke again his voice was soft, filled with disgust and secret knowledge.

"So that's how you got the job, the movie. You sold your soul to them. I know all about Spinell, I been doing business with his brother for years. They don't want my ass or they'd own it, and they don't want it because they know that I'm a moneymaker. They just want me to *think* they want it and they send you down here to play the game after you ain't called me since I been out."

"They don't know I'm here."

"They don't?" His father pulled the pistol away and it disappeared down the front of his pants. He chuckled, malevolently. "Sure they don't. Tell them something for me, Babe. Tell them thanks for the warning." He lifted his drink and poured it down his throat, and Babe watched the flesh waddle under his neck, the neck that used to be filled with muscle, the neck Babe used to throw his arms around and hang off of thirty years ago and the old man had lifted him up as if he was a feather.

"They bought and sold you. They own you."

"I knew this was stupid, coming here."

"I'm glad you did. It let me see you for the punk you are." His father looked up, past Babe's shoulder at the same time that Babe heard the door slam shut behind him. Johnny smiled.

"You don't call your mother, you don't check and see how your brother's doing, with his sickness in the head. You sold your ass to the highest bidder and got in bed with guys who'd crawl over their father's grave to fuck their mother in the ass, and you look down on *me*? After all I've done for you? If it wasn't for me you'd be in the pen right now, taking it up the ass from niggers, and now you turn on me, forget who did what for you. You fucking punk."

If he didn't know that the man had a gun in his pants, Babe would have hit him. As it was he began to rise, staring hard at him, and noticed a shadow fall over him a second before his brother Frank slapped him on the back and pushed him back down into the booth.

"What's the haps, bro? Hey, nice TV show."

Frank slid into the booth next to his father and somehow Johnny seemed to grow three inches. Frank was smirking at Babe, his elbows on the table. Next to him, Anthony stood, looking about to cry.

"Babe," Anthony said. Babe looked at him and said nothing.

"You care so much about me, about *us*, about your family"— Johnny pointed his chin at his other sons—"why didn't you pay the bill when they told you about it? Why didn't you come across for me, you care so goddamn much?"

"Forget about it," Babe said, and began to rise again, and Frank stood, and Babe stepped past Anthony and hit Frank high on the left cheek, knocking him back into the booth.

Babe moved before his father had time to react. He stepped close and reached over Frank, pushed the gun down further into his father's pants and he grabbed at it, but by now the old man was reaching for it himself and Babe saw that he was going to lose. He jumped back and grabbed Anthony, turned him around so the kid was facing the old man and stood behind him, began walking to the door, his forearm around Anthony's neck.

"You come after me, you make one move out of that booth and I'll snap his goddamn neck."

Anthony was making whining noises, not of fear but of shame, like he'd done as a kid when the old lady had caught him jerking off and had announced it to the entire family.

"I mean it," Babe said, and was out the door, pushing Anthony into the street and running for the car.

"Babe!" It was Anthony, lying in the street and calling his name.

Babe got to the car and got in, started it and backed down the rest of the street, onto Ewing Avenue, pausing as he saw his father come out of the tavern, Babe watching Frank run to Anthony while his father pointed the big pistol his way. Babe swung out onto Ewing and never knew if his father had taken a shot at him or not.

Johnny hadn't; he couldn't get a clear shot. He stood on the sidewalk watching the big new Lincoln swerve down the street in reverse and he thought about it, leveled the gun at him, but you did time for shooting a pistol off within the city limits and he was a convicted felon and there were too many goddamn witnesses. He watched as Babe paused before swerving the car onto Ewing Avenue, and their eyes locked for one second. It took an act of willpower not to blast off a cap, but Johnny managed not to.

He put the gun away and looked over at his son, the killer, lying in the street sniveling.

"You all right, Anthony?"

"*Fine!*" It was a petulant whine. A spoiled child who was afraid not to answer but who resented having to do so. Christ, what a crew he'd raised.

"Come on, kid," he said, "I'll buy you a drink."

Which he did, after getting the ten grand from the kid. Anthony was fidgety, which was understandable after your first real hit, and Johnny didn't bother him by asking for the details. In the first place, you never knew when a regular hangout was wired, so it was best to do all your talking on the street or in a place neither of you had ever been before. And in the second place, he just didn't care. He had the money in his pocket and Parker was dead, which was a good thing. He would have hit for another eleven grand tonight with the bets he'd made on the early games alone.

The late game was just coming on the television in the corner and Johnny had been tracking the scores all night, adding figures in his mind, taking and making calls from and to the gooms, getting the amounts right in his notebook. They'd give him the cash in the morning, and if their slips came out right with what they'd told him he'd make a profit of three grand for tonight so far, not counting the two late games. Not enough to get him well, but enough to afford a trip to the doctor. The bartender, that dumb bastard, he was staring at the screen and ignoring everybody, terrified of getting himself killed by saying the wrong thing.

He looked at Anthony now, popping some kind of pill into his mouth and washing it down with the whiskey. Was this the same tough punk who'd told him just that morning that he'd make out all right in the joint? Didn't look like him, sitting there sniveling, with snot running down his nose. He would sit with his hand covering his mouth, as if he was trying to hold words in, knowing they'd come out all fucked up if he didn't hold them back.

He was nothing, a zero. Try as he might, Johnny could feel nothing for him. Frank now, he had his uses, but that little bastard there, he would be good for two, maybe three hits, and then he'd have to be retired. He was too much of a security risk.

Easy come, easy go.

Johnny didn't care about any of them anymore, about any of the punks to whom his wife had given birth. After tonight, after this thing with Babe, they were to be used and cast aside, like everyone else. He was tired of acting as if they were family. It had been a mistake from the very first, pretending there was more there than there really was. From now on, these punks were of no more use to him than the gooms were. Well, maybe a little more. These punks were dumb enough to love him, and that could be put to good use.

Johnny hid his anger, his disgust at them, and said, "You get rid of the thing?"

"What?"

"Anthony, the thing you used tonight, to do the job, you get rid of it?"

"No." The punk was finally wising up, spoke in one-word sentences so he couldn't screw them up. Johnny was surprised that the word hadn't come out "On."

"Do it tonight, as soon as you get out of here. Take it over to the lake and throw it out as far as you can, make sure you wipe it down good. This thing, it'll draw a lot of heat."

"Okay."

"What did Babe want?" Frank asked.

"Some bullshit, some wiseguys sent him over to try and scare me."

"Didn't work."

"Scared the shit out of Anthony, here," Johnny said, and turned to watch the game, ignoring the kid, knowing that Anthony had a gun in his possession but probably didn't have the balls to use it against him.

Without saying anything, Anthony got up and stormed from the tavern, and Johnny turned to watch him go, then turned back to Frank, a cruel expression on his face and a knowing look in his eyes.

"You want another drink, or you gonna go out and get *laid*?" he asked his son, and Frank stared at him for a moment, stunned, then told him no, he wasn't thirsty.

"See you later, Pa," Frank said, but Johnny only grunted and called for another drink.

The phone rang in the car and Babe let it. His hands were still shaking too badly to be able to punch the proper button to turn it on, and even if he could, he didn't trust his voice. It would have to be Kelly, and he wasn't anywhere near ready to talk to her just yet. She and Tim were the only two people who had the car phone number; the thing had been installed for his convenience, so his family could reach him if they needed him. He did not give that number to anyone else. Tim wouldn't be calling, he'd be sleeping right now.

It stopped ringing and he was relieved, the soft burring had been getting on his nerves.

Good God, what had he been thinking of? What had driven him to want to protect that man in the first place? His father was an animal, less than that. A subhuman whose only concern was for himself. And his brothers, what about them? Babe had never been close to Frank but Anthony, God, at one time he had been more of a father to Anthony than a brother. And now the kid looked like death with legs, skinny and sunken-eyed. The last time he'd seen Anthony had been at his mother's house, when he'd been forced to slap him around.

What had the old man done to that kid? Had he corrupted him, turned Anthony into an image of himself? Babe could understand how that could have happened, was terrified when he thought of what might have happened to him if the old man hadn't taken that last dope pinch. If he hadn't, Babe knew, there would have been three of Johnny's sons sitting there tonight, drinking with him, because Babe would have done anything back then, anything at all to have been accepted by that man, to be like him and to be loved by him. To be loved and respected by Johnny Hilliard.

His hands were steady on the wheel now, and Babe powered the window down an inch, lit a cigarette and took a deep drag. Let it out slowly through his nose. That was better.

There was thick fog forming above the expressway pavement and Babe cut through it, saw it swirl past his windshield and settle behind the car. There was little traffic heading north, and for that, Babe was grateful.

Sometimes it seemed as if he'd been in the devil's grasp his entire life, and the devil was so sure of his grip on Babe that he turned his back one time, and that was when Babe had escaped. He could feel that old familiar attraction, the desire to be one of them, right now, even after all that had happened. It was attractive to him, the thought of being an outsider, of drinking all night and sleeping all day and stealing whatever you wanted. It attracted him as it repulsed him, as he remembered the pain, the anguish that life had caused him all those years ago, before Kelly, before Mike was born.

He would sit sometimes in the barber chair at night, drunk, and spin himself around slowly, see his reflection in the mirror and be certain in the belief that there was all that truly was left of him. An unshaven, unwashed drunk. He was alone, with nowhere to go. He'd asked his mother, when he understood that he couldn't pay his rent, that he'd wind up on the street, if he could stay with her for a few weeks until he could get back on his feet, and she had turned him down. It would be too disruptive to Anthony, she'd told him. He knew that the reality was that he'd be in the way of her life, and he didn't hold it against her, he was a full-grown man and she didn't owe him anything but still and all, it hurt. That had been the moment when it had truly sunk in, that there was nobody left for him. And he'd sunken into the pit of homelessness and self-pity, had stared so longingly so many times at those always sharpened razors on the barber's back shelf.

And here he was thirteen years after the fact, desiring the lifestyle that had been the cause of that overwhelming loneliness in the first place.

He understood that he was a sick man, that he wasn't like

anyone else. But he had a hard time understanding just how sick he was. Didn't even want to face the fact that the desire to drink until he couldn't stand up, to eat until his stomach burst, that the desire to have instant sexual gratification and to live utterly without responsibility was so ingrained in him that he would covet it forever, that he would never be free from those urges.

But he had them under control. In spite of those insane urges he had a home, and a wife who loved him and kids that wanted to grow up and be like him and fans who wrote him letters. He was relatively wealthy and undoubtedly successful.

And he had a father who would have blown his head off tonight if he could have gotten a clean and clear shot.

Babe had trouble reconciling those two images, what he was with what he'd been, what he'd come from. As the Lincoln cut through the fog Babe thought about this, about his weakness, his lack of strength tonight.

He owed the man nothing. Should never have even made the effort to try and help him. His father was worse than the hungry cat Tim had compared him to, he was the starving tiger, and he'd feed where he found weakness, had a second sense that enabled him to smell that shortcoming in others. Instead of a saucer full of milk, his father would want a bowl full of blood to stave off his hunger. His father was a master manipulator, a man who twisted the minds and lives of everyone with whom he came in contact. Look at Frank, at Anthony.

And look at himself and John. Survivors who tried to appear normal and carefree in each other's presence but who saw themselves as inferior because they couldn't stack up to the legacy of their last name. They were men who Frank and Anthony looked down upon, saw as losers because they paid taxes and held down regular jobs. They were what they had allowed their father to make them.

Was he crazy, worrying about the man, trying to help him out? What was Babe's problem? Worse yet, why was he driving down the Dan Ryan right now, heading out to meet the people from whom his father had stolen a hundred thousand dollars?

Babe wasn't sure why he was still doing this. He wasn't even sure that he wanted to know the answer as to why he was doing it. All he was certain of was that it had to be done.

He took one hand off the wheel and turned on the small black tape machine, maneuvered the buttons until he was at the end of the parts he'd taped. Babe hit the Play button and heard Anthony's anguished shout, his call for him: "Babe!" Anthony pleading. He didn't want Tim to ever hear that part of the tape. He rewound it an inch, stopped it at the part where they were scuffling in the tavern, then stopped the machine. He'd tape Spinell behind that part, and no one would ever have to know about Anthony's loneliness, his confusion. The same confusion and loneliness that Babe had experienced years ago while sitting in that barber chair and staring into the mirror.

Somehow, though, he was sure that Anthony wouldn't be able to find his way out of the darkness.

Tim hated midnights. There was nothing that could be done about it, though. He owed the department his two months on the shift and he tried to make the best of it, and besides, when he was on that shift he could spend more time with the prisoners, trying to get into their minds.

The worst part about it, though, was trying to regulate his hours.

He'd worked all night and gone to school all day and then had met Babe for a workout, and by the time he'd gotten home he'd been utterly exhausted. But still, he couldn't sleep. There was unfinished business, and even though he'd had no problem telling Babe how to behave, talking and doing were two different things. He was off the next two nights but still, if he slept tonight, then got up early Wednesday morning, he'd be back on a normal pattern and that would screw him up when he went back to work. Better to stay up tonight, force himself to study or read, so he'd be able to sleep in the morning without screwing up his metabolism. And besides, he had someone to see.

He would take a shower and then go take care of business, maybe then go and get something to eat, maybe even give Babe a call and go running with him. If what Babe did could really be called running. Then he could come home and study until daybreak, then try to sleep again, get into the midnight swing of things.

Christ, how he hated this shift. It had to be affecting his good judgment. What other reason could there be for what he was doing? What logical explanation was there for what he found himself doing, Tim in his car, driving to the city, parking and entering the South Chicago Hospital?

The dying man lay on a bed that had steel railings drawn up on either side. Tim could hear him wheezing, gasping for each breath. He entered the room and let the door swing shut behind him, thinking for a minute that he was in the wrong room, that this couldn't possibly be his father, the huge, strong monster who had made his childhood so miserable. The man on the bed was skinny, emaciated, with tubes in his arm and nose. Outside the window, Tim heard an ambulance screaming. Further down the road, people would be packing the movie theater to view the latest action-adventure film; lovers would be gently kissing; tag artists would be spraying grafitti on a wall. Life was going on as usual, and people who had a highly over-developed sense of self-importance would be hurrying off to appointments, or home from work, thinking that they would live forever, or that the world would remember them after they were gone.

But what it came down to was this: The man in the bed, unaware of the life teeming outside his little square window, facing forever and suddenly terrified.

Tim had never seen his father afraid before. He could smell the terror in the room, hear it in the shuddering sigh that accompanied each exhalation of breath. His father fighting for life, the world ending for him and the man powerless to stop that from happening.

Tim looked within, at what he had inside. There before him was a man who had terrorized him for seventeen years of his life, made Tim's life hell. Broken Tim's bones and yanked out patches of his hair. This man had done all that, and how did Tim feel, looking at him drawing his last breaths?

Safe, for one thing. There was no way his father would ever be able to hurt him again. Strange thought for a sixth-degree black belt to have. Pity, too, that the man was going out and was aware of it. But there was no special bond, he felt no sense of loss. Not for what could have been, nor for what should have been. This was just a skeleton before him, dying slowly. Tim walked to the side of the bed and looked down upon his father. Tim's eyes were dry and his hands weren't trembling. This was a stranger to him; he'd seen death before.

"Tim?" The voice was feeble, unrecognizable. A gasp of weak wind that carried his name as it passed. Tim saw that his father's eyes were now open, staring up, burning into him. What did the man weigh, maybe ninety pounds? He'd lost a hundred and a quarter, a hundred and fifty pounds, easy. He was no longer in the least bit frightening to Tim. Their gazes locked, and Tim no longer felt any pity for the man. The old man expended a lot of effort, but was finally able to hold his hand out. Tim did not take it.

"Tim," that gasp again, a single syllable speaking volumes. Sadness and despair, disappointment, too. The hand dropped to the mattress and tears coursed down sunken cheeks. "I'm *dying*, Tim." Said as explanation. As if that made everything all right.

Tim looked down at the near corpse, his face blank. There were things he wanted to say, accusations he'd thought he'd make, statements thought up on the drive from Park Forest. He said none of them now, just nodded once. Then he turned and left, a feeble voice fading behind him as Tim walked down the corridor, moving neither quickly nor slowly, ignoring the voice that was calling his name, the voice anguished, cursing Tim for the last time on this earth.

The alarm went off at nine and Tim jumped out of the bed, in a fog, shaking and afraid, until he understood that it was only the alarm, nothing worse than that was after him.

Tim shut the thing off and sat on the edge of the bed, taking deep breaths. He wasn't one of the people who could remember any of his dreams but he was aware that all humans had them, and his inability to ever remember them was, he knew, a blessing.

He thought about that after his shower, while the coffee was brewing and he was sitting at the kitchen table, alert but tired.

What did he dream about? He was a man who lived in the very second of his present existence, who tried to never look forward or backward. The future was uncertain; the past, a ball of pain. Tim had to pull himself up short when he would catch himself daydreaming about a future, about maybe meeting a woman who loved him, settling down and having kids, but that would only bring the fact home more clearly that he had no one now, that he was alone. That sort of thinking could drive a man mad, especially when he was on the verge of forty and was again all alone. And to live in the past would be totally defeatist. Look at what had happened just a couple of hours ago. Seeing that man in the bed had brought it all back to Tim, brought back the past that he fought so hard to forget.

His childhood had been spent right here in Park Forest but his memories would be far different from those of Babe's kids, or anyone else who had a normal childhood.

So what did he dream about? What was going on in his subconscious that was so bad that the mere sound of his alarm could drive him from the bed in a cold sweat, staring?

His parents, he'd bet, would be in that dream. At the very least, his father, lying skeletal.

His father was always coming at him for any reason, taking all his resentments out on Tim and Tim taking the beatings, gladly, because if the old man was beating him then it meant that he wouldn't be hitting Tim's mother.

It had been a concentration camp more than a home, run by a dictator who thought that his house was his church and within its walls he was God. Babe had it worse because he had both parents beating on him and Tim had always had his mother to comfort him later, but she'd never step in to help him, not once, not ever.

It was only when he got into high school that he began to resent her for this. Before then he'd thought that the life he'd led at home was normal, that everyone's father beat them. He'd go to school and be amazed that no one else had marks on their faces, that no one else had teeth missing. It filled him with shame and he kept the family secret, even when the teachers would try to intercede. He'd tell them that he was clumsy and accident-prone, that he fell down a lot and walked into walls. His mother would tell him that his father brought home the paycheck and was under a lot of pressure, and back then Tim believed that the man had a right to do what he did to him. That he was stupid and bad and deserved what he had coming to him.

The shame and rage were right under the surface, but he found other ways to deal with it than Babe had.

Instead of hitting other boys and stealing things, Tim had gone into athletics, had run on the track team and played basketball and baseball and football and he excelled at them all, won letters and was courted by colleges in his senior year.

But he refused their offers, did not want the coaches in his house, speaking to his father about his talent. He knew what his father would tell them, knew too, that the coaches would use it against him, would treat him the way his father did, and that his stupidity would no longer be a secret.

The week after he graduated from high school Tim went into the Army, and it was during his enlistment that he found karate.

After the first few months of study, he knew his father would never lay a hand on him again.

The coffee machine stopped perking and Tim started, surprised that he'd been thinking back on those days. He took a check of himself, found that he wasn't emotional, that there were no tears behind his eyes and no weight in his chest. No lump in his throat. Good. He was well trained. As long as he kept his mind off that part of his life, he would be just fine. Even watching his father dying by inches hadn't moved him to sentiment.

He poured himself a cup of coffee and took it into the small living room of the two-bedroom house he owned on the city's South Side, sat down in his easy chair and saw the light blinking on his answering machine. He set the coffee down on the table and hit the button, curious, and when he heard Babe's voice, he knew from the tension in his friend's voice that it was going to be bad news.

Was this guy stupid, or what? Tim rewound the tape and forced himself to be calm. He sipped his coffee, put it back on the coaster, and took a deep breath, regulated his breathing and tried to relax.

Going to meet his father, wearing a wire. Was he insane? Didn't Babe know that men like his father assumed that everyone they met was wired? Did he have any idea what happened to guys who got caught wearing wires while in meetings with mobsters like Johnny Hilliard?

Tim picked up the phone then put it down again, had to look in his book to find Babe's car phone number. He dialed it and let it ring, and it rang four times before the recorded female voice told him that the customer he was trying to reach had left the vehicle or was out of range.

Tim hung up, the coffee forgotten, and sat back for a minute, thinking. He picked up the phone and dialed Babe's private line at home, and when Kelly answered he forced himself to speak calmly, to breathe normally and say hello the way he usually did.

But something was wrong and it was obvious in the way Kelly was speaking to him. So he had a right to ask her.

"We had a fight."

There it was. The asshole, he'd fought with his wife and had gone out to salvage his manhood by meeting with mobsters and killers.

"Got any idea what time he'll be home?"

"He didn't say."

"Kelly, is there anything I can do?"

She hesitated, reluctant to bring him into it. Kelly said, "You can talk to him, Tim. I know he talks to you, you're about the only male alive he *does* talk to about his problems."

What did she want him to say to Babe? He didn't want to ask. It would make him look dumb. But Kelly wasn't volunteering the information and he began to feel awkward.

"I'll talk to him tonight, if he runs."

"If you see him there, ask him to give me a call from the car, just so I know he's—all right."

"Kelly, you think he's drinking?"

"Last night, you'd have asked me that, I'd have thought you were crazy. Tonight, Tim, nothing would surprise me," Kelly said. "Goodbye, Tim," and hung up the phone.

That stupid bastard. Didn't he see what he was doing? How many men prayed to God every night that they would find a woman like Kelly? Tim himself had felt a few pangs of jealousy, just by seeing the way Kelly looked at her husband, by the way she was always touching him, by the love that shone from her eyes when they were together. And over some prideful hurt he may well have imagined he was jeopardizing that, threatening not only his own future but that of his wife and children.

Tim had to fight the urge to go to that place, what was it? The

Tamburitza Tavern, across from a meat shop on the East Side. Go there and if Babe was there snap a few front kicks into his shins, incapacitate him and then sit on his chest, explain a few things to him, tell him the facts of life.

But Babe's fight with his wife wasn't his business. What was his business was the fact that his best friend might be in trouble, might need his help.

It wouldn't do any good to go off half-cocked, racing around Chicago searching for Babe. He would wait by the phone for another hour, and if he didn't hear anything by then he would get into his shorts, throw on a windbreaker and the Nikes, and head for the track, run five fast miles and by then it would be midnight and Babe should be there if he was coming at all.

If he wasn't, then Tim would be forced to take some action, and he'd begin by looking up Johnny Hilliard.

Tim knew how to focus, how to concentrate with laser-like attention on an object until all else around him faded away. It was one of the first things he'd learned when he was studying karate, to focus his mind on what he was doing and to force all other thoughts aside. Now he forced his fear for Babe out of his mind, put it in a drawer and slammed it shut. There was nothing to worry about for another hour and a half. Babe was safe until then.

There was something he could study, while he waited, calmly. The Hilliard files. Which he kept in a drawer in his desk in the spare bedroom. The files that had the names and addresses and social security numbers of the entire Hilliard clan, even John, who had never gotten into trouble with the law in his life. Tim knew where all of them lived, knew what they looked like, even knew about the tattoos on Anthony's shoulder, on Frank's forearm and biceps. Knew the colors of them and what they represented. The thickest file of the bunch was the old man's, and if push came to shove he could make one phone call and have someone from the federal probation department go with him into Hilliard's house. When you were on parole, your officer didn't need a warrant to search your living quarters.

Tim got out of the chair and went into his bedroom, got his beeper and made sure it was on, then carried it into the spare bedroom and got the file out of the drawer. He went into the living room and placed the beeper on the table next to the cold coffee, put the file next to it then grabbed his cup, went into the kitchen and poured the coffee down the sink then got a fresh cup out of the brewer, added his cream and went back into the living room. He was in this minute, living in the now, and when you lived in the second that surrounded you you didn't have time to worry about what might be happening to a friend of yours who was too dumb to learn how to do certain things before going out and trying them for himself.

Tim picked up the file, opened it until he found the one on Johnny Hilliard, Sr., then slowly and deliberately began to read, his face determined, his eyes narrowed.

Gosh, but it was foggy tonight! Edna was afraid of it, of the white clouds that roamed the earth and surrounded the jogging track of the high school. From where she was sitting in the far bleachers she could barely see the fence that surrounded the track, couldn't see the track itself at all.

Although she had seen it, when she'd first found the place. Had walked around it a turn and was surprised at the softness of the track, wondered if it had rubber on top of it to make your feet feel better while you ran. It sure felt like it, soft and almost gooshy. There were lines separating the running lanes and numbers painted onto each lane, dividing them. Edna felt a twinge of self-pity as she walked, because there would be kids out here tomorrow, running and jogging, some fast-walking around the track, and she herself had never had the chance to get into any school athletics. Even when she'd been in school, she hadn't been allowed to take gym class. Daddy said that showing your legs to boys was sinful, and would have none of it. And didn't Daddy know best? Edna giggled. He surely did.

Thinking of him made the pity go right away. Other kids might have happy memories of gym class and high school and track and field games, but how many of them had a daddy like hers, one who loved her more than he loved his own wife? One who'd made so very sure that his little Edna was happy and always taken care of. That walk around the track had winded her, and she was afraid to get all sweaty. She didn't want to be stinky when she presented herself to Babe. Wanted to be fresh and beautiful and sexy. She knew just how she'd approach him, too. When she saw him running she would use the fog as cover and walk down to the far end of the track away from the lights of the school, at the farthest point away from the parking lot.

Edna played it over in her mind, what she'd do.

She'd stand in the dark until she heard his footfalls, then she'd slowly walk into his line of vision, her hands folded in front of her, smiling, coming out of the fog like his angel, in her white tights and her white shoes. All he would really be able to make out would be her clean dark hair, her smile.

Her confidence was strong. She knew that tonight, he would belong to her. Edna pulled the coat around her shoulders and shivered, deliciously. She wasn't hungry, even though she hadn't eaten since before leaving her house a good six or seven hours ago.

Well, she *was* hungry, but not for food. She'd eat well tonight, though. Later. She'd eat Babe alive, if he only could be made to understand.

And she knew that he would. There was no doubt in her mind. He would come away with her and they would live in her Daddy's house and sleep in her Daddy's bed and they'd make love every night and have sons, lots of sons! The daughters she would smother in the hospital, and tell him that it was crib death. There would be no daughters in her household. No little girls to turn their daddy's head. Edna had learned her lesson, as her own mother had learned hers.

She was a little nervous, though, there were butterflies in her stomach. It wasn't every day that you met the man of your dreams, the man God had created for you to love. She'd be a helpmate for him, as the Bible said. The rib from his side that had become Eve.

But what if he didn't love her right away, what if he still thought he loved his wife?

Edna nodded and reached into her purse, took out the little pistol and held it in her hand. The pocket of her coat had a little tear in it, but she thought the gun was light enough where it wouldn't rip through and fall into the lining. She put the gun in there, squeezed the handle for a second then let it go, put her hands together on her lap, primly. She pressed her lips together and wished that she had a watch. The papers said that he ran here every night, between eleven and midnight. She'd gotten off the bus at the Centre in the middle of town, and had asked directions to the school from there, and that had been at ten P.M. So it had to be close to eleven by now, didn't it?

"Dear God," Edna Rose said, "let him come to me tonight." She spoke and felt an answering warmth, God speaking to her, telling her everything was going to be all right.

The first thing that Babe did that got the night off to the wrong start was that he wouldn't shake hands.

Jerome had spotted him first, from where he was sitting at the table in the hotel dining room with his brother Milo and the two hunks of beef who were eating everything in sight, saw Babe walk through the door and he jumped to his feet, excited.

He nearly ran over to the guy, a big grin on his face which Babe had ignored, as he'd ignored Jerome. Snubbed him. Walked right by him and past his outstretched hand and went to sit at the table with his hands stuck in the pockets of his suit coat.

"Little cold out there, tonight?" Milo had said, and Babe had ignored that, too, had turned his attention to Billy and Floyd.

"I won't talk in front of them."

"Hey," Billy said.

"Who the fuck are you?" Floyd said.

"Billy, Floyd, get lost," Milo said, and Jerome couldn't believe his ears.

This punk had walked in here like he was Mr. Four Seasons himself, come to survey his holding, and just like that he had Milo Spinell doing his bidding? What had happened to the wild maniac who had kicked in the television set this morning then ordered these two goons to throw his own brother out a window?

Jerome kept silent, though, watched as the two hulksters, heads hanging, picked up their beers and plates and walked over to a table clear on the other side of the room. This was Milo's play, he'd already told Jerome to do nothing but introduce them then shut his mouth, and Jerome was glad to oblige.

"My brother Milo," Jerome said, speaking to Babe and nodding toward Milo. "This is Babe."

Babe said, "You the man going to kill my father?" and Milo seemed taken aback.

"What? Who told you that?"

Babe got up to leave. "I saw *The Godfather.* Read the book, too. I don't have time to sit here and play Sicilian games, Mr. Spinell."

"Sit down, Babe." Said softly. But even then, Milo's voice carried command. Babe complied.

Milo took a sip of his martini, pushed his plates away from him and set the glass down where they'd been. He got a cigarette going, tapped it in the ashtray. All the time his eyes never left Babe's. Jerome's head swiveled back and forth, from one to the other, wondering if either of these guys ever blinked. Was this some kind of game, some sort of macho thing they were doing here?

Jerome said, "Fellas, come *on.* This ain't no TV show. We're all friends here," and Milo told him to shut the fuck up.

But it broke the ice. Babe smiled and Milo returned it and Babe turned to Jerome. "Every day, out on the *Street Babe* set? I wanted to say that to you. You'd be running around like you were Cecil B. DeMille, checking the lighting, the cameras, telling everyone how to do their job, yelling at people, and I'd want to say that to you."

"Go ahead," Milo said.

"Jerome, shut the fuck up."

"I wasn't *saying* anything." Jerome picked up his Grand Marnier and sipped it, then tossed it back. Jesus, what was going on here? Why were they picking on him? He signaled the waiter for another.

"My brother, he tells me you two are like brothers. Told me he paid you a little visit today."

"It wasn't social. He told me my father owes you a hundred thousand dollars."

Oh, shit. Milo wasn't ready for it and he got caught with his pants down, shot a scathing look Jerome's way then tried to cover it up.

"My brother talks too much. Like you say, he's always trying to tell someone else what to do." The waiter brought the drink and Milo asked Babe if he wanted anything and Jerome saw him hesitate, saw the longing on his face.

"Go ahead, have a drink," Jerome said. "What do you want, some Scotch, a cold beer? Go ahead, I'll sign it onto my room bill."

"Nothing, thanks."

"You sure?"

"Jerome," Milo said, "I'm gonna tell you one last time, shut the fuck up. You can shut up now and stay or keep it up and wind up with Billy and Floyd over at the other table, it makes no difference to me."

That son of a bitch! Who did he think he was talking to? Jerome had a mind to just walk away from the table, but he couldn't. His brother had to finesse this son of a bitch into signing on to do the series, and there was something for Jerome to learn here. If Milo could do it.

Milo looked at him for a second, to make sure that he wasn't going to respond—Mr. Fucking Big Shot—then turned back to Babe, smiling.

"You're a serious man, you come and pay your bills, you don't shake the hands of fools. It's hard for me to believe that you're not Italian."

"I'm not here to pay any of my bills."

"Ah, but *famiglia*, it's all the same, right? Father's debt; son's debt."

"A hundred grand's a lot of money."

"Let me show you how I show respect to a man who knows how to do the right thing. You come here tonight and you tell me that your father owes me a hundred thousand dollars. But it's not your bill. Still, you came, no? Out of respect for that, I'm going to forgive half that debt. Your father, he owes me only fifty thousand right now at this time."

Babe nodded. "Jerome said he paid you ten."

Milo didn't get upset this time, didn't give Jerome any dirty looks, but Jerome could tell, he was pissed.

"He did? So that makes it forty."

"We keep this up, the old man will be even in no time at all."

Milo laughed, politely.

"It's not that simple, Babe. Your father, I've taken good care of him because he's always made money and he always stood up. Never ratted anyone out. You can't trust anyone anymore, and let me tell you something, I admire what you did, not wanting to talk in front of those two kids. I trust them, but does that mean you can? That shows you got a head on your shoulders." Milo nodded, confirming his words to himself. He sipped his drink, then lit another cigarette off the butt of his last. Jerome watched Babe take out one of his own cigarettes and watched Milo take out his gold lighter and light it for the kid. Jesus, did this guy have class, or what?

"I forgave half the debt tonight out of respect for you. I can forgive the other half, and never miss it. But we got another problem here, a problem I been hearing about from LA, and now from here, all day since my brother been in town.

"I put up a couple million dollars into a production company, Babe, me and another guy, and we put my brother in charge of it because he knows the business, been out there twenty years and he knows how to work the sets. I figure they'll make a couple of TV shows, maybe get a shot at a cable special movie, and we can shoot the things for two mill, charge the networks five and steal the other three. It's the way it's done out there." Milo chuckled softly.

"So what happens? First time out of the box, *bang!*" Milo clapped his hands together and shook his head in disbelief. "Somebody comes up with this idea and people start talking, writing about it. There's excitement over this show, about the writers, the stars, and what started out as a goddamn ripoff cable thing turns into the hottest show of the year, maybe even the decade. How you figure things like that?

"But then the problems start, Babe. The star of this show, he don't want to meet people, he don't want to make no friends. That's okay with me, I ain't in the business to make friends, I'm in it to make money, and as long as the guy does his job I'm happy.

"But then the guy, his father gets into me for some heavy dough, and I find out he's causing problems about wanting to star in the series. The network, Babe, it's scrambling, and right now it's working out to our benefit. They think we're playing hard to get and our price, it's going up.

"But that ain't gonna last long. You'll talk to some reporter tomorrow or next week and the cat'll be out of the bag, and the network, they'll get scared. Think it's gonna be a big general fuckup like *Moonlighting* or *Roseanne*, and they'll back off, 'cause those

kinds of headaches, no network's gonna put up with ever again."
Milo tapped the ash off his cigarette, slowly stubbed it out in the
crystal ashtray. He looked back up at Babe, and now he wasn't
smiling.

"We got a chance here to make millions, Babe. More money
than you ever thought you'd have in this lifetime. All from a couple
years' work on a TV show. You, I can guarantee you, right here at
this table, no agents or lawyers with us, I can fucking personally
guarantee the largest contract ever paid to a TV star in the history of
television. What would you say to a quarter million a show? All you
got to do is say yes, right here, and I'll shake your hand and it's
yours, for two years."

"And if I say no? You kill my father, or what?"

"Your father? What's he got to do with this? You come in here
and we talk and I see you're a man with balls. Your father, he spent
his life behind bars and never made the kind of money for it altogether that you'll make before the first commercial airs on your
series. Forget about your father, I already have. He's a soldier, a
button." Milo smiled, intimately. "You and me, we're generals. We
ain't got time to worry about soldiers." He spread his hands in a
magnanimous gesture, giving Babe a present.

"Whatever you decide tonight, your father's off the hook, he
owes me nothing." Milo sat back and folded his arms, his face giving
away nothing. Jerome knew what he was doing. Sweettalking the
kid, and he'd stick to his word, too. He was giving him a glimpse of
heaven, of what could be, and now was waiting to see if the kid was
smart enough to grab it. Jerome would bet that he was.

Milo said, "You want to make a quarter million a week, Babe?"
and smiled, sat there with his arms folded and you could just tell,
the kid, he was going to say yes.

The first time they'd called Babe out to LA he had wound up staying less than eight full hours. Some producers had called him, wanted to do a movie and they were talking about starring him in it, Babe Hill whose biggest payday before then had been seventeen grand and residuals for two days' work in a truck commercial. A stretch limo that had to cost over a hundred thousand dollars had pulled into the driveway of his forty-thousand-dollar house, the driver had called him sir and had opened the door for him, had stopped for coffee at the 7-Eleven on the way to the airport and Babe had been impressed.

The airplane ride was the same thing, first class and even though he couldn't smoke it was hard to be mad about it, the flight was so smooth, so relaxing and elegant. He would walk through the coach cabin on purpose, head back to the toilet there so people could see him, know that he was somebody.

At the LA airport a Mexican guy in a tuxedo had been waiting for him, holding a cardboard sign up high above his head, Babe's name written on the sign in black Magic Marker. Babe had let the driver carry his bags while he smoked a cigarette and tried not to gawk.

It was wintertime but it was gorgeous out there, sixty degrees and no wind and Babe had shed his topcoat, carried it over his arm and before you knew it they were at the limo, and the Mexican guy was ushering him into a back seat that had two phones and a fax machine, mounted in the rear. As they drove into town, Babe could see the famed HOLLYWOOD sign, up high in the hills.

"Where they got me staying?"

"The Beverly Hills Hotel, sir."
Babe could live with that.

The place had a high thin pink wall sign with green lettering telling the world who they were: BEVERLY HILLS HOTEL done up proud for all to see. Babe had walked on a red carpet under the covered entrance, past flowered patio furniture in a foyer before the lobby, in front of which were wrought iron coffee tables with real crystal ashtrays. Ed McMahon was standing in the lobby, holding a tiny child in his arms. The guy was around six-six and the baby was swallowed up, nearly hidden by the size of the man's arms. McMahon was looking at the child, rapturously. It made Babe feel better about being here, touched him in a way he thought he might never feel in a town with the reputation of Los Angeles. He turned away from them, not wanting to feel touched, wanting, instead, to stay cold and hard inside.

Which wasn't easy. He was nervous. This was a big thing for him and he wasn't sure if he knew how to play it. They'd been respectful to him on the phone, but there were no guarantees that their attitude would carry over when he was sitting with them on their turf.

The bungalows were smaller than he imagined they would be, and he had to walk a ways to get to his, through a lot of jungle-type growth that was neatly trimmed and dripped from its daily watering, held back from the walk by chain link fences. The sounds of laughter came to him from somewhere.

And there were palm trees everywhere.

He noticed them again later, after dismissing the driver and deciding to take a walk in the three hours left before the first big meeting was to be held.

Down Sunset Strip with the large palm trees jumping out at him, a culture shock to a kid who'd never seen a tree in his life before he'd joined the Marines. They were everywhere, casually lounging, reaching up into the heavens and nobody seemed to notice them except him.

There were houses here that were bigger than some of the jails he'd spent time in, huge stone mansions with electric gates and guard houses.

He was in Beverly Hills, but there was still danger around him.

A couple of Hell's Angels with sluts on the back of their hogs raced their engines at him while they waited for a stoplight, Babe the only pedestrian on Sunset Boulevard. He ignored them, as he ignored the black guys who seemed to be at every stoplight, holding out signs that read WILL WORK FOR FOOD, waved them at the passing Rolls-Royces and Jaguars. Some of the cars stopped at the light and a window would power down, a hand would reach out with a bill extended and the guy with the sign would race over and grab it, bowing, groveling before the new slavemaster of choice.

He saw the ugly side of it, because that was where he lived. If there was anything anywhere that could hurt him, Babe would be aware of it. And be angered by the other things.

Such as the Mexicans, employees treated as property, who stood outside the mansions and washed down the sidewalks, even though the papers and TV were crying about the water shortage, the terrible drought. It didn't seem to be having much effect on the habits of the rich. Weren't these the same people who got into the trends? Who were on the "front lines" of the environmental movement? Owning Mexicans and wasting water. Would he be like that when he made it? He hoped not. He hated hypocrites.

But there was beauty there, too, which even he couldn't miss, charm and things that made his heart ache with jealousy.

He passed the driveway that William Holden had driven through in the movie *Sunset Boulevard,* and he had to do a double take before he was sure if it was indeed that place. Ahead of him, high up in the hills, there were houses built on stilts. For five bucks Babe bought a map from an Hispanic guy that showed him where the movie stars lived, and he walked for two hours, passing Lucy's house, James Caan's. Up in those hills he could see what he believed to be Marlon Brando's estate, and right next to it was Jack Nicholson's.

"I'll be there with you, you son of a bitches," Babe said aloud, and unconsciously crushed the map in his hands, staring up into the hills, his sunglasses up in his hair, and he wasn't sure if he believed it.

"I'm as good as you are." This, he did believe. There was no way on earth he could think differently. He had the talent, and all he needed was someone to give him the outlet for it, the vehicle to express it to the world. It was why he was here, to prove to some big shots that he was more than qualified.

He wanted it, too, then. Bad. To have the biggest house and to walk into Nicky Blair's and get recognized, to get asked for autographs and stopped on the street. Wanted it with all his heart and soul. It was a *need* within him, consuming him, nearly swallowing him in its intensity, its power.

He stood on that corner and watched the expensive cars pass him by, some of them with tinted windows, but most of them with clear glass so the people inside—the famous, the *stars*—could be recognized as they drove down the street. Be recognized and then ignore those who recognized them.

He saw them and he hated them, resented them. Especially the teenagers in cars their parents had bought for them. What had they ever done to deserve such expensive toys? What suffering had they ever undergone?

He'd show them, someday. Maybe soon, if this meeting went well tonight.

Babe stood on that corner for a long time, wanting what he saw around him, the opulence, the outward appearance of great and important wealth. Wanted to someday be able to stop at this corner and have those bastards in their fancy cars screech to a halt when they saw who it was standing there, leaning against the palm tree. He wanted the biggest house in those hills, the most servants. The biggest cars and the most goddamned maids. Wanted it so bad he could taste it in his mouth, the bitter taste of envy. Slowly, he reached into his shirt and got out a cigarette, lit it and tossed the match out onto Sunset Boulevard.

"I'll be back!" Babe whispered, and when he came back, they would all know who he was.

He sat in the Polo Lounge and it was hard for him not to gawk. There were a lot of players in there and people who thought that they were, their cellular phones on the tables in front of them, ringing from time to time. Babe had never seen such devices before but he acted casual, nervous in his suit and tie in a lounge where everyone else was dressed casually.

Mixed in with the players and the wannabes were some stars, sitting with lizard-tanned older bald guys whom Babe presumed to be their agents.

Tom Selleck was there, who had a top-ten TV show going at the time; Charles Bronson, whom Babe had read had just signed for his fourth *Death Wish* film, sitting two tables down from Sylvester Stallone, who was with the tallest blond woman Babe had ever seen. She spoke with an accent and was treating Stallone like shit.

The men he was meeting with were Jewish, and they told him right away that they wouldn't hold the fact that he wasn't against him. The guy who did most of the talking was short, nearly tiny, but he had a large gut and oversized hands. His name was Milt and he claimed to have given Paul Newman his start and then been fucked by Newman after the actor had hit it big. There were liver spots on his bald head. Babe had his first doubts of the evening. Did he want to do business with a guy who held forty-year grudges? Milt told him that he was a good personal friend of Sinatra's. Was Babe a fan? Say the word and he'd call Sinatra's manager—Milt's dear friend Sonny Golden—and get a personally autographed picture to Babe, absolutely free of charge, no problem. The other big shot was a lot younger, young enough to be Milt's son. Taller and lean, and he steadily rubbed at his nostrils. His name was Robert and as he ordered drinks he warned Babe not to call him Bob. Robert was wearing a white raw silk suit with a red shirt. A yellow silk handkerchief was tied around his neck. He crossed his legs at the knee and watched them with his sunglasses down on his chin, hanging from his ears by the earpieces. Mr. Cool and Mr. Clown.

"So, the flight all right? The cottage okay?" Milt asked.

"They're bungalows, Milt," Robert said.

"Yeah, everything's fine, thanks."

"That's good, because we want you to get used to this kind of living, get real used to it. It's gonna get even better for you, baby, believe me, you play your cards right. You see that guy over there, Tom Selleck? When was the last time you think he went anywhere on a plane first class, go on, take a guess."

"I imagine he goes *every*where first class."

Milt laughed shortly, then smiled. "*Ha*, see? Gotcha on that one." Milt leaned forward, his elbows on the table, and spoke with the voice of authority. "Tom Selleck hasn't had to take a regular fucking airplane since *Magnum, P.I.* hit the top twenty. Tom Selleck wants to fly somewhere, *any*where, he tells some flunky at Universal and

they warm up the corporate jet. Stallone, the same way. Carolco got a jet sitting gassed on the ground at LAX just in case the prick *thinks* about wanting to go somewhere. That's the way the *real* stars live."
Milt suddenly sat motionless and dropped his ingratiating smile.

"What we got to know, kid, is if you want to be a star bad enough."

"Oh, I want that. You can bet your ass on that."

"No, we bet our asses on enough guys and lost. Me with Newman, Robert and me here, since we been in business, there's three guys in this fucking *room* we bet our asses on, groomed and took care of, and as soon as they made it, where were Milt and Robert? On our asses, out in the cold, and don't let the palm trees and the humidity fool you, baby, there ain't no place on earth gets colder than it gets in LA."

"It's Babe, Milt."

"Babe, Baby, what's the difference? You sign with us, you're gonna change the moniker anyway. How many women you think are gonna drag their husbands to the show to see some heartthrob named Babe?"

Babe kept his mouth shut, and his face went blank. He controlled the pain in his heart, would not allow it to show on his face.

"We can do it for you, kid. I told Robert that when I saw that fucking truck commercial after the Super Bowl game, you had your shirt opened to the waist and those stomach muscles were rippling, that hairy chest tight and strong, I said, 'Robert, there's the next Harrison Ford,' didn't I, Robert?

" 'Ford, Stallone, this kid, he can be bigger,' I told Robert," Milt said.

"But you got to remember that these guys paid their dues, baby. Ford was a carpenter before he got *Star Wars*. Selleck was the Salem poster boy. Charlie over there, Bronson, he was in a TV show and Jack Nicholson, he did horror and biker movies.

"Stallone, he should catch a tumor, did porno and bit parts on *Kojak*. He used to come to me begging and I couldn't find a part in my pictures for a palooka talked out of the side of his mouth, looked like a side of beef, but I had mercy on him, threw him a twenty now and again, and *Rocky* comes out and I call him up and all of a sudden I can't get through to the guy. Can't even speak to him on the phone.

Couple days after the call, I get a certified check for five hundred, with a personal note, thanks me for the loan and here's some interest for you, Milt. Fuck you, Milt, was what he was saying." Milt looked around, at a single man sitting at a table by himself. He leaned farther forward, and when he spoke, it was in a whisper.

"And there's the other side of the coin. Don't turn around now, but there's a guy not two tables down, sitting by himself. He used to play a cop on *Baretta*, had a regular part. Ten, twenty years ago, you couldn't get near him, he had an entourage with him everywhere he went. Now, he's sitting there alone, sixty years old and ready to climb under this table and suck my dick for a bit part."

Babe stared through Milt, his heart sinking further with each word that came out of the man's mouth. He looked away for a second and rubbed his nose, scratched his cheek, then put the mask back on.

"So they paid their dues, is what I'm saying, no matter what kind of people they are. And no matter how high they go, they can fall, Babe. Like I was saying to my dear friend Sammy the other night, we were having a glass of wine at Chasen's, I tell him, 'Samelah, none of these kids today ever had to *work* for it anymore, like you and Frank and Dean did. They're all phony as three dollar bills,' and he flashes that Sammy grin and throws his arm around my shoulder, he musta had a half a mill on that arm in diamonds, and he says, 'Milt, baby, you are *so* right, dad.' "

"How'd they pay their dues if they never had to work for it?"

"A cute one." Milt looked at Robert, hurt. "Did we send a limo to his house, get him a first-class plane seat?"

"We did."

"Did we go for a room at the hotel here for him?"

"We did."

"So, I want to know, Robert, why did we do all that, so the cat can sit here and make fun of us?"

"Maybe we made a mistake."

Babe lit a cigarette and Robert wrinkled his nose. Babe was trying, desperately, to keep his disappointment in check, to not show his emotion. "Maybe you did," he said.

"You know we want to sign you up for a five-movie deal? We didn't tell you *that* over the phone, but that's why you're here. We want to do that for you, Babe." Milt looked at Robert again, slyly this time, then back to Babe.

"And it's all right, you get a little upset with us. We *want* open communication. We want to establish *dia*logue with you. The reason I had my troubles with Newman, with Stallone, and hundreds of others, too, Babe, is that I didn't get it in writing. So now, everything I do, I put in writing. Standard forms, spelling out how much you get, how much we make together." He paused and sipped his drink, nervously wiped at his mouth.

"We got a package from Paramount. They're giving us five mill to make five movies. You can be a part of that, Babe, starting with preproduction next week on *Return of the Faceless Man*. We go on from there. Now I know you got this third-rate French guy for your agent, and you'll notice he wasn't invited here today."

"He's upset about it, too," Babe said. "I haven't called him since I got here, and I wasn't sure I wanted him here, either, until I found out if you were serious."

"Oh, we're serious, all right. Look, Babe, forget this Frenchie. And I don't know if you got a lawyer out in Chicago, but believe me when I tell you, when it comes to the people around you, you can fire them all right now. We got the best entertainment lawyers in the country working for us, and we'll take care of you, all the way down the line." Milt nodded his head, trying to convince either Babe or himself of his sincerity.

"You ask anyone in this business, no matter what they think of me as a person, and they'll say one word, every one of them, when they're describing my character. They'll say '*honesty*,' they'll say '*integrity*.' Those are the things I've been known for for the past fifty years, and they're things money can't buy, things that all the fuckings from the young punks in this town can't take away.

"So the question we have to ask you, Babe, is: You willing to sign? Five pictures, five hundred grand. Maybe eighteen months', two years' work. After that, we go to the top together, to the million-dollar deals and the private Learjets."

"Starting with *The Return of the Faceless Man*? Where do we go from there? *The Faceless Man Goes Away Again*?"

"You don't have to give us an answer now, Babe. I know it might sound a little small-time to you." Milt turned to Robert for support, spread his hands out helplessly. "Didn't I say he might balk? The kid hasn't even read the *screen*play yet."

"I did some time when I was younger, did you guys know that?"

"No, we didn't know that. But good for you, all right?"

"Milt, I wasn't bragging, I was trying to find out how bad you were disrespecting me by calling me a kid. In jail, you call a guy a kid? He takes his shank and rams it in your back while you're walking to the shower."

"What'd I tell you?" Robert said. He was sneering, setting his sunglasses in place in the dimness of the bar. He was drinking something green that perfectly matched the tablecloth on the tiny round table. "We bring him out here—"

"You had a deal with Paramount. *They* picked up the bills, and you know it. All you guys invested was a telephone call and ten minutes tonight, and the phone call comes off your taxes."

"Go on, go back home to Chicago," Robert said. "You think you can get far in this town, treating people like shit, only want to help you?"

Babe rose, shook his head. "Does this mean I don't get the autographed picture of Sinatra?"

Milt was staring up at Babe, his mouth open, silently pleading. Robert's sneer had turned vicious, and he turned his head away in a show of disgust, waved a hand, dismissively. "Go on, get the fuck out of here."

"Hey, Bobby?" Babe said, and Robert took an even worse attitude, quickly jerked his head back toward Babe and began to rise as Babe flipped his Pepsi onto Robert's jacket. "Have a Coke and a smile, asshole," Babe said, and stood his ground. Robert quickly slid back into his seat, wiping at his coat, frantically. Behind him, Babe heard someone snort laughter out of his nose, then giggle in a high-pitched tone. When he was sure that Robert wasn't going to make a move he turned and Milt was right with him, walking past the gawking celebrities, as if they had arrived together.

Milt finally found his voice at the front desk, as Babe was asking for his key.

"So Robert's a hothead and so are you. You gonna let that wreck your career? Come *on*, Babe, don't let's get off on the wrong foot."

"I wouldn't want to take advantage of your hospitality now that

I won't be accepting your offer. I'll go pack, right now, and be on the next plane out."

"What's your hurry? You're on the Coast, stick around a little while, lay on the beach, go see Rodeo Drive, have lunch, get laid. Christ Almighty, where you going?"

"Home."

"Listen, let's go have a drink somewhere, calm down, talk this over. Or you want to leave, fine. You can come back, another time."

There was a faraway look in Babe's eyes when he said, "Oh, I'll be back," and in his mind he was standing on a street corner a mile or two from where they now stood, looking up into the hills and thinking that maybe, soon, he'd be living there, too.

"Spend the night, at least. Come on. I'll send up some champagne, a broad."

"I don't drink and I don't want a broad."

"So what do you want, *two* broads? You think I can't swing that?"

Babe just looked at him and Milt got a knowing look in his eye.

"Oh. I get it. All right. You want a boy, don't you?"

And that was when Babe walked away from him.

And thought about it on the plane, and throughout all the years since then. How the game was the same as the ones run on the streets and in the jails, only instead of offering you cigarettes to get you in their debt they waved five-picture contracts under your nose. The bottom line was still the same; in the end, all you got was fucked.

It was a lesson that served him well and he would think about it when he got the desire to go back out there and look at the big houses on the mountainside, think about how it was all an illusion. A game. Smoke and mirrors and all the money in the world couldn't make smoke solid, couldn't make a mirror a diamond.

In all the years since that day, Babe never forgot that moment on a street corner in Beverly Hills, leaning against a palm tree with his heart in his throat, staring up in anguish at the homes of the master magicians. And these days he ran whenever he heard someone bragging about their integrity and their honesty.

But he never lost the most important part of that day's dream, the desire to be somebody. As time passed it became less intense and he put it in perspective, in the place where it belonged. That wasn't for him. Maybe Eric Estrada had fallen for the bullshit but where had it gotten him? The money, yes, Babe never stopped wanting it. And the recognition. He never lost the desire to be somebody, ever.

Until the day he died he would never forget that time in Beverly Hills, and the older he got, the more ashamed he was at the emotions he had felt on that Beverly Hills street corner.

So when Milo said "You want to make a quarter million a week, Babe?" Babe didn't take long to make his decision.

He said, "I wouldn't do *Street Babe* with you"—he jutted his chin at Jerome—"or with *him*, for ten million a week." He pushed away from the table slowly, looked Milo Spinell in the eye.

"It's over. The show's dead because without me there is no *Street Babe*. You'll make *shit* for your investment, and there'll be no syndication and there'll be no top-ten series and let me tell you something else." He stood tall and straight, closed his jacket button and nodded his head.

"Your brother came to my home today. One mistake, anyone's entitled to. I see him again, I shoot him. He comes near my wife, I castrate him. You send any mob punks after me, Spinell, you better not send the second team. 'Cause I'll kill them then come hunting you, and guess who the cops will believe when that happens?"

"Who will they believe, Babe?" Milo said. "A punk ex-con, a killer, or a well-respected Chicago businessman? You think the TV show is all that's dead, Babe?" His voice was controlled and level, and he was looking up at Babe coolly, with a hint of amusement. The two oafs at the far table had risen, were leaning forward, waiting for a command.

"You threatening me?"

"No, not you, uh-uh."

"Your father, though," Milo said. "We're gonna cut him up and send him to you in *pieces*."

"You do that," Babe said.

31

A nthony left the bar and got into his car and was surprised to find that he was hyperventilating. He pounded on the steering wheel until the side of his fist was sore, and then he began to cry.

It always came easily to him, crying. His father would only have to look at him when he was young and Anthony would feel so useless, so hurt, that the tears would flow. His father would look at him with disgust but his mother would hug him to her and sometimes even laugh at how sensitive her little baby was.

Later, the ability served him well.

He would be standing in front of some judge, charged with burglary or assault, and he'd hunch his shoulders, make himself seem even smaller than he already was, and he'd turn on the waterworks, let those tears flow, and once the judge had even told him that he could see that he was a young man of sensitivity, had given him probation on a charge that even his own father's lawyer had told him he'd do time for.

Anthony didn't think that he was so damned sensitive. He believed that they all hated him, his mother and father, the judges and cops, everybody. He cried out of frustration, not sensitivity. Whenever it happened he would tell himself that someday they would pay, someday he would show them all.

He'd killed four people last night and how long did that last with the old man? Twelve hours? And tonight he'd killed two more. He was a killer. More than that, a hunted killer. The cops would be after him and his father wouldn't do a thing for him, wouldn't raise his hand to help, not after what had happened tonight.

Which was all Babe's fault. If it had been anyone else, Anthony would have pulled his pistol after about two seconds and let the guy have it, *pow*, right in the head. But he couldn't do that to Babe. In fact, he'd expected Babe to grab him in his arms and hug him, tell him that he loved him.

Had he ever been full of shit, expecting love from that son of a bitch.

Anthony started the car and got onto Ewing Avenue, heading away from the shitty little East Side neighborhood, away from the boardinghouse in which his father had rented him a room. The old man wanted more? He'd show him more. Anthony had read every single word written about Babe throughout his brother's entire career. Had read and reread every article this past weekend, when the papers were filled with stuff about him, plastering his picture all over their front pages. He couldn't find the guy's house, but he knew some things about him, knew about some of his habits.

He drove the car down Ewing Avenue, wondering if Babe would stick to his normal patterns, do what he usually did, even after tonight's trouble. He'd probably need to run more than usual in order to be able to sleep. It wasn't every day you got into fistfights in ginmills. He had a gun, and he had a car with a great big trunk. What could Babe have made from that TV show? Ma, she thought he'd be a millionaire from it, but Anthony was more realistic. He figured his brother had probably cleared half a million, after taxes. Would maybe be worth more if Anthony wanted to fuck around and call Hollywood, make a stink, but that would draw attention to the situation and attention would draw the heat, and what Anthony was going to do would be federal; he didn't need the FBI coming after his ass along with everyone else.

So he'd settle for a quarter million. Grab Babe and hold him overnight and in the morning make a phone call and have that high ass bitch Babe was married to get the money out of the bank.

With a quarter million he wouldn't need the old man anymore, wouldn't have to worry about him. Or the police, who were maybe even now hunting Anthony down. He wouldn't have to worry about Frank or the Placebo Lounge or anything, ever again, because in Mexico, a quarter million would last him forever.

The further south he drove, the foggier it got, and Anthony

began to think that maybe, for the first time in years, he was catching a break. It would be dark and foggy and with the gun in his hand he'd be able to pull it off, no problem.

All he had to do was find a place to stay all night with a guy he'd kidnapped, and if push came to shove he could leave Babe in the trunk of his car, get a six-pack and go see how Ma was doing. Check and see if the cops had been around. That wouldn't be a bad idea. Go in and talk about Babe, while the skullsucker was lying in the trunk of his car, bound and gagged, fifty feet away in the parking lot.

It was a good plan, if only Babe would go running tonight.

Was Babe going running tonight? Edna began to panic. There was a lot of fog out here now, and she could barely see her hand when she held it up in front of her face. He was an actor, and his body was important to him. He might not risk a twisted ankle, or worse, a broken leg. Which might occur if he tried jogging around in this soup.

"Gracious," Edna said, and sighed. She pulled the coat around her more tightly, then settled down again.

What would she do if Babe didn't come out tonight? She didn't know. There wouldn't be a bus leaving from the Centre back to Calumet City until the morning, and she might freeze out here before then, waiting. If she didn't starve to death, first.

It had certainly gotten cold in the last few hours. She'd gotten on the bus and she'd been carrying her coat, but after she'd gotten off she'd had to put it on until she warmed up from the walking.

Edna wasn't used to walking and now her thighs and her feet were in pain. She didn't think it was from her weight, thought it was from the lack of exercise. She walked to Fannie May's back home and to the cemetery, but not a whole lot of other places. Where was she supposed to go? She was alone and sometimes afraid to go out, because the kids were out there and they could be mean. It had been a lot easier for her to be tough and act strong when Mama had been alive. She even was afraid of the dark sometimes now that Mama was gone, would sleep with a nightlight on and would awaken at any little sound.

When Mama had been alive, it hadn't been like that. Edna would swagger through the house and let Mama know who was boss. Never take any shit from the woman on one of the rare occasions when Mama would be feeling her oats and would want to say something mean.

Well, those days would sure be over, and pretty darn quick. Babe would protect her, and she'd draw strength from him. She'd call him Daddy and he'd call her his little baby and they'd be oh so much in love that it would hurt when they were apart.

Edna picked at a pimple on her cheek, felt it pop, said Ouch then brought her hand close to her face, inspected the fingers she'd used to pop the pimple. No blood. Good. She had to look her best for her Babe. As she thought of the last time Mama had said anything mean to her, Edna absently stuck the two fingers in her mouth and sucked them clean.

Jerome sat staring at his brother, as the two musclebound idiots came strutting over from the other table. Milo was looking at him with the same half-amused expression he'd had when he'd been speaking to Babe, looking at him and shaking his head.

Without warning, Milo reached out and slapped Jerome, hard, right across the mouth.

"He's like your brother, right, Jerome?" Milo wasn't smiling now. He slapped Jerome again and Jerome ducked, pushed his chair back and cowered, covering his head with his hands.

"I ought to kill *you*! I ought to send *you* home to your wife in goddamned packages!"

The two punks Milo kept with him were smiling, sniggering at Jerome's cowardice. The waiter came running over and was shouting something and when Milo spoke, it was to his body-guards.

"Shut this faggot up and get him the fuck out of here before I kill him." Then he spoke to Jerome.

"You been a thorn in my side for forty-five years. I gave and gave and you took and took and the one time I need you, the one time you can do something to pay me back, what do you do. You fuck it up."

Jerome took his hands away from his head and he could feel his toupee hanging over on the right side, over way too far, but he couldn't bring himself to straighten it out. "I—"

"Shut up! You think I didn't understand what that farce was about just now? What'd you do, go over to his house and hit on his wife? Did you fuck her? You always think with your dick, you little asshole."

"Milo, I—"

"Did I tell you to talk? Did I give you permission? If it wasn't for Mama, I'd break every bone in your body right in this goddamn restaurant, I swear to Christ."

Jerome sat, chastised, filled with terror at his brother's rage. All he wanted was to get out of there, get back to his room and pack and get on the next flight to LA, back to his loving wife; she always knew how to make him feel better when things were going badly.

One thing was for sure, he would never come back home again. Mama could kiss his ass if she thought he was coming back here before this psycho brother of his died of a heart attack, which he would any day now, the way he acted.

He had to play it right, though, had to make sure he didn't let his pride get in the way. This maniac was capable of anything, Jerome had learned that that very morning. Just put the ego aside and take it, and the second he was gone, whoosh, out the door and on a flight.

Milo was calming down, Jesus, inch by inch. You could see it in his face, the blood was coming back into it, and he was sitting there looking at the wall, thinking.

"All right. Here's what you do. You fucked it up, and you can't make it right. Go back to your room and don't have another fucking drink, and if you take even one snort of a drug, you go out the window, believe me. I think I might be able to shake this guy up, get his attention. When it happens, he's gonna hate me, but he might listen to you, he'll be scared enough. If he don't got the ass for you too, after whatever happened at his house."

"Milo, I swear to Christ, on Mama's eyes, I took his wife *flowers*. I took her *candy*. I never said one word was out of line."

"Hey, asshole, Mr. Spinell tell you to talk?" It was one of the muscle boys and Jerome looked at his brother, expecting him to straighten the guy out, but Milo was just looking at him, thinking.

"Jerome, get up to your room." He turned to the muscle boys. "Billy, you call Landini, right now, get him on the phone and tell him to meet me at my house in a half an hour. Floyd, you take the ticket, go and get the car."

"You want me to come with you?" Jerome said, and Milo looked at him.

"You still here?" Milo said.

Tim took a break and looked at the clock and was surprised to see that over an hour had passed. He got up and stretched, went into his bedroom and got into his running shorts, his shoes.

He'd drive over to the track and get a good five miles in before Babe got there.

He had no doubt in his mind that Babe would indeed appear. He'd calmed himself down, made himself relax. Babe was a big star now, a hit. Even a crazed killer like Babe's father would understand that, would realize how much heat would come down on his head if he hurt the man. Johnny Hilliard might grunt and groan and scream and yell, but he was smart, he knew better than to draw too much attention to himself. He was a survivor.

As for Jerome Spinell, there would be no trouble from that front. Tim was fully aware of who Jerome's brother was, had told Babe about him, cautioned him to cover his ass, be careful who he got chummy with on the set. But the same rules that applied to Johnny would apply to Milo Spinell. Unless Babe did something stupid like spit in Milo's face, there would be no physical danger for him, probably even less than there would be with his father.

Johnny was a soldier. Brutal and mean, a psychopath without a conscience, whose only concern would be for himself, for his own safety and welfare. Tim had known his type before, had arrested more than a few. And they weren't all killers and thieves. They would profess to love their wives and children, would work hard and bring home the paycheck, but when times got tough, their minds started working and before you knew it one of the kids would die under suspicious circumstances, and an insurance company would lay out some money.

No, Johnny would protect himself at all times. He was a street soldier with an unerring compass in his head, and he'd never make a mistake that would cost him over something silly like emotion.

Milo, now, he was another story. Would see every move coming and know exactly how to counter it. If Babe angered Milo, Milo would never let him know. He might send somebody out to hurt Babe later, but it would be a long time from now and they could worry about that when the time came.

Babe would be safe. He'd told Tim to meet him at the track at midnight and Tim would be there, already worn down pretty good from his own run. He could cool down while he loped next to Babe, who would be thinking that he was running his ass off. Tim shook his head and smiled, found his keys and locked the house, got into his car and drove over to the track. He hadn't thought of his father even once since listening to Babe's message.

E dna saw the headlights, could barely make them out through the fog, and her heart leaped into her throat. She clasped her hands together and held them under her breasts.

Could that be Babe? It had to be. It was hard for her to move, her legs were sore from the long unaccustomed walk, and she was breathing heavily, excited and nervous. There was a look of pure panic on her face. "Oh my God," she said, several times, her voice rising higher with every repetition.

Edna hurried off the bleachers and moved into position, on the other side of the fence, the chain link separating her from the running track. She felt trapped. Behind her, only a few yards away, was a very tall fence. And even though there was a gate somewhere down there that entered onto a street, one she'd seen before it got too foggy, she couldn't have found the thing now if her life depended upon it.

Edna clenched her fists, looked straight ahead but could not even see the car over there in the parking lot now. She was looking into a heavy veil of white, hanging motionless around her.

Oh, how it would look! She would step into his line of vision and smile, and he'd melt, and she'd tell him who she was and that would be all that it would take.

It would have to be that way. Edna was scared to death of the thought of what might happen if it didn't go that way.

Edna strained to hear the sound of running footsteps, but she couldn't over the pounding of her heart. She clutched her hands together, held them just under her breasts. She bit her trembling lower lip. She was breathing very heavily and she began to fear a heart attack.

Then she heard them. Footsteps running rapidly, very rapidly, toward her.

Didn't the paper say he ran slowly? Didn't Babe make fun of himself in that article, telling the reporter that power walkers—whatever *they* were—could catch him and pass him? Edna unclasped her hands and grabbed the pistol in her pocket, suddenly terrified. Was this someone coming to get her? Babe's bodyguard or somebody else who ran in front of him and made sure no fans were out there to bother the star? It had to be. Nobody else ran at night, Babe made a point of telling the reporter that that was the reason he ran late at night in the first place, because the place was deserted and he could be alone with his thoughts.

The footsteps were just on the other side of the fence now and Edna let them pass, then ran to the fence and stood there, looking at the retreating runner's back.

It wasn't Babe.

This man was too well built, too muscular to be Babe. Her Babe was a muscleman, yes, big and strong, but he was lean, like her Daddy. This man running here was solid, with large, wide shoulders and weightlifter's arms. Babe was built like that handsome Scorpio on *General Hospital*. This runner was built like Rocky Balboa.

Edna could have died on the spot. She lifted her hands to her heart, and a tear began to fall from her left eye, zigzagging down her puffy cheek. She swiped at it. She *wouldn't* cry! He would show up!

"Darn it!" Edna said.

But what if she'd stepped into the runner's field of vision, what if he'd seen her? It could have goofed up everything! He would tell Babe about the woman floating around in the fog like a ghost and Babe might be afraid, thinking it was one of his many fans come to harm him, not knowing that it was Edna, who loved him.

Well, even when Babe *did* come tonight, he wouldn't see her on his first pass around the track. Because Edna was going to check out every single runner that came around that bend, if there were fifty of them or only one more.

There would have to be one more. There would have to be Babe.

Edna slowly stepped back into the fog, her lips set in a determined line, and when the hand fell on her shoulder she gave an involuntary jump and cried out a little in fright.

"Waiting for someone?" the skinny boy said, and Edna sighed, sagged, and almost fainted dead away.

Anthony washed his car every day when he felt an episode coming on and the weather was nice, and even though it was a rusted out piece of shit, it shined in the parts where there was no rust.

It was one of the ways he dealt with the disease. He would focus on the car, on making it *shine*, on getting every smidge of dirt off the chassis, every speck of dust off the windshield.

In the winter he had a hard time dealing with an episode. He could only run his car through the Spot-Not once a week, to get the dirt and salt off. He'd vacuum the inside out real good, and spray some of that smelly junk in there. He'd long for summer because that was the time when his car looked best and he could sit in the park and drink beer—which was another way he dealt with the episodes, which would come three or four times a year—and it didn't cost as much as it did in the winter to get drunk. But the summer, as much as he loved it, brought its own set of problems with it.

Asshole bicycle riders who'd ride on the wrong side of the street and not even give hand signals before they'd turn in front of you. Joggers you'd have to go over into the other lane to avoid. Water sprinklers placed on sidewalks, to get both the lawn in front of the house and the little patch of grass between the sidewalk and the street. The water would spray into the street and onto every passing vehicle, and if you'd just waxed your car, it was enough to make you want to kill somebody.

He settled these problems in his own special way. He never gave way to a cyclist or a jogger, would lay on the horn and bear down on them, and it worked, they always got out of the way, at least up until now. As for the sprinklers, they were easy. Anthony always carried a six-inch steak knife in his glove compartment for protection, and he'd just park the car a block away and stroll back and slice those damn hoses to ribbons, then kick the sprinklers onto the offender's yard. Nobody had ever come out of the house to complain, either.

The knife came in handy at other times, too. Like when some skullsucker would park too close to you at the mall, would smash their door into yours and think they could get away with that. Sometimes Anthony would just slice into a couple of the guy's tires.

But if the other car was new and shiny he would walk around it, the knife held at his side, cutting into the paint all around the car. He would use that method on the cars of the other type of people who really pissed him off, too. Those fools who parked sideways, taking up two spaces, like their cars were so important that they could get away with it. Well, not when Anthony was around.

He was proud of all the cars he'd owned, even though they weren't as nice as Ma's or the ones his father drove. He tuned them up and changed the oil regularly and he never had one yet that hadn't gone over a hundred thousand miles. Sometimes, they had that much mileage before Anthony became the owner of them. He didn't like to drive them on dates or when he was going to some-place like the Placebo Lounge, pussy hunting. A lot of girls didn't appreciate a good older car, made fun of them and then Anthony would get mad at them, tell them to get the fuck out of his car and make them walk home. So he'd rather use his ma's, or, on rare occasions, his old man's, when the old man was over and in a good mood. But still in all, he took care of his cars.

This Ford here was a good example. Fifteen years old and in great shape, and sparkling like it was still on the lot because the weather had been nice and he'd known for about a week that an episode was about to descend upon him, felt it coming that long ago.

They all thought he was crazy all the time, his parents and his brothers, but they were wrong. Usually the pills took care of things, kept him level, and he could sometimes feel those little pills calm-ing him down, coursing through his system when he took them, *whoosh*, relaxing him and leveling him out.

But not this week. Not, at least, until just this moment.

The weather had been crystal clear and warm for about a week, and he'd waxed and polished that car in the apartment house park-ing lot, shined it until he was covered with sweat and exhausted, but it still didn't make the episode go away.

This wasn't like most times. Sometimes the attack would sneak up on him, and he didn't know it was coming because they were subtle, would slip into his mind and he wouldn't be aware of it until the voices came, whispering to him through the wind. He wouldn't go out and wash the car, wouldn't obsess on women who he thought looked like his mother and follow them around, trying to find out where they lived. When those sneaky ones came to him, they could be the worst because without the advance warning, there was nothing he could do to fight them. He'd be aware that it was upon him only after it attacked, but by that time he just wouldn't give a shit. Hell, by then, he was usually enjoying them.

And they'd leave the same way. One day he'd be torturing kittens in the forest preserve behind his house, slobbering, and the next thing he'd know he'd be fine again, normal and ready to go back to his actor/model career. He'd remember what he'd done, but it would be a vague memory, less than a dream. His only concern would be getting caught for the things he'd done while the episode had ahold of him. He knew he was crazy, but he wasn't crazy enough to think that a judge would believe that a voice in his head was telling him to do bad things. There was a time when you could get away with that in court, but not anymore, not these days.

This episode had been the worst in his memory.

This time, he wasn't just transposing his words and hurting animals or women, this time he was even transposing his thoughts, thinking in patterns that made no sense to him, living his life by instinct. And he'd become a full-fledged hit man this time. A rapist and an arsonist and a murderer.

It was all Babe's fault. If it hadn't been for *Street Babe*, if it hadn't been for that goddamn fucking TV show, the episode wouldn't have come. They only came in times of great stress, and what greater stress could he have possibly suffered through than that which had occurred this week? Every time he looked around, there was his brother, the family traitor, staring out at him from the TV screen in a commercial for the show. Or in the paper, talking about what a miserable home life he'd had, how he didn't have anything to do with his family anymore. It got so that Anthony was glad that he didn't have any friends, because if he did, he would have been ashamed to show his face in front of them.

It was all Babe's fault, and he would have to pay.

As Anthony drove toward Park Forest he knew that if a cop stopped him he'd be dead. There would be absolutely no way he could talk his way out of a ticket, not in the frame of mind he was in. He'd taken—what—six, seven pills? On top of a bunch of drinks, and he could feel them, was beginning to relax and he could tell, he was coming down. But he wouldn't be sure until he spoke to somebody, and he didn't want that person to be a cop.

He wanted it to be Babe. Wanted to see the look on his face when he held a gun in Babe's face. Anthony bet that he'd be able to talk just fine when that moment came.

Anthony drove slowly around the Rich East high school property, out on the street and trying to get his bearings, to find a way in without having to drive onto the property. There was a tall fence around the entire property, and there was a long, paved driveway that led to the running track. He could see that in the bright burglar lights that were mounted on top of the school. He was grateful for the heavy fog, for the sudden unexpected cold. It would keep everyone else off the track. But not Babe. Babe would show.

Babe always would exercise when he was mad, when he was upset. Anthony could remember times when he'd toddle downstairs after the old man or the old lady had torn into Babe's hide and there he'd be, hanging from the I-beam by his hands, doing pullups and grunting in frustration and anger.

Though he'd never get angry at Anthony, no matter how hard he'd been beaten. He would see his kid brother and drop down and hug him and tell him that he loved him, would hold him close. "They'll never touch you," Babe would tell him, "I'll kill them if they try." Anthony would feel safe and warm yet strangely afraid and resentful. His brother was talking about killing his parents! What if Anthony was bad one day like Babe and John and Frank were all the time and Daddy decided to spank his head? Would Babe kill them? If he did, it would be all Anthony's fault.

Yet they never did, no matter what he pulled. The other kids would get their asses kicked all the time but not Anthony, not the baby. He was Mama's sensitive little boy, and that must have been what saved his ass.

So what had made Babe so cruel? Sure, Anthony might have drunk too much beer around Babe when he got older, sworn too much and too loudly, but he'd only done that to become closer to Babe, not to drive him away. All he wanted in life was to be loved by his father and by Babe, and he'd fallen short with both men.

Well, his father knew what he was capable of, was afraid of him,

Anthony was sure. Even though his father had played the fool and made fun of Anthony in the tavern. His dad had been drunk, and his feelings had been hurt by Babe's insulting him, or by whatever had really happened before Anthony and Frank got there. His father had learned what Anthony could do. And now Babe would.

There was a street with a walkway that headed toward the track, a street sign said that it was West Rocket Circle. Anthony parked his car at the curb close to the walkway and got out, left the keys under the mat and the car door unlocked. He pushed the front car seat forward, so he could easily access the back seat. He walked past the one-family houses, through the fog toward where his car headlights had picked out the walkway, and he found it, walked down it.

Past high privacy fences on either side, which the homeowners must have put up so that people taking shortcuts from the track wouldn't be able to see into their yards. The fences were covered with graffiti, devil worship shit that these small-time punks out this way must have written to make themselves feel dangerous and evil. There were strong lights on in a couple of backyards, that cut through the fog, but Anthony didn't hear any voices so assumed that they were just security lights. He smelled marijuana smoke and paused, grabbed the pistol butt under his shirt and stood stock-still. Nothing. Maybe it was wafting out of one of the windows, from the home of some hippy who was old now but who hadn't entirely given up everything from the sixties. Owned a house and two cars and had a job in the city to which he commuted, but smoked his shit at night, trying to be young again. Anthony smiled. Get high and feel young and maybe step out into the yard and draw devil shit on the privacy wall next door. He continued on, through the gate and onto wet grass that could use a cutting.

There were floodlights surrounding the track, mounted high on poles, illuminating the track and damn near nothing else. It glinted off the top of the bleachers, but that was about it. All around the track was darkness; he couldn't have seen someone sitting on the bleachers, even if they were at that second sighting in on him with a night scope . . .

Shit! Get your mind off that kind of thing! He was alone and Babe would be along and that was all there was to it. After that, everything would be all right.

He heard feet hitting the track surface, the sound of labored breathing, and the sound made him feel better. Let him get another circuit, one more time around. The longer Babe ran, the less strength he'd have to resist. It would give Anthony time to find his way around, to learn where everything was.

"Darn it!"

Anthony heard the woman's voice speak close to him and froze, his hand on the pistol, pulling it out now and bringing it out in front of him.

What had he run into? Young lovers? No, that hadn't been a teenager's voice, Anthony could tell that much. And there was no reply from a male. The voice came from less than ten feet away, to his right. If there were two people, he'd hear the other one breathing from that close.

He edged toward the sound of the voice, the gun in his hands, pointed at the grass. He breathed through his mouth and inched forward until he saw her.

Christ, a huge woman with the whitest legs he'd ever seen, wearing a big black coat that looked like one his grandmother used to own. As he got closer, he could see that she was one ugly bitch. Looked younger than she dressed. She held herself like an old woman, her mouth set in a disapproving pout, like some old maid librarian. Smelled good, though. She must have bathed in perfume.

He came up close to her and put the gun back in his waistband, trying not to laugh as he thought of how badly he'd scare her. Would that fat jiggle when he grabbed her!

But if he grabbed her she'd scream before he could stop her, and that would alert people. God knew how far a voice would travel in an open area like this.

He reached out a hand, tentatively, and slowly dropped it on her shoulder.

"Waiting for someone?" he asked, and she gasped, jumped, and her knees buckled. She almost fainted, then got herself under control. She turned and looked at him, obviously put out at his being there. She paused, staring at him, looking very upset that he'd intruded on her privacy.

Then said, "Wouldn't *you* like to know."

Edna was frightened but the boy was very skinny, and didn't look to be in very good physical shape. She knew that some men wore their shirts out because if they tucked them in their sunken little chests would stick out and everyone would know that they had no bodies. And besides, how scary could he be, when she had a gun in her pocket?

She put her hand on it now, squeezed it for strength. There was a tearing sound from inside the pocket and Edna pushed the gun down a little bit, testing. There was no resistance. Darn, she'd ripped the hole larger! She stood looking at this young man and she was very angry, because this was the only winter coat she owned and now she would have to pay someone to sew it up again.

But she had to control herself, because the last time she'd lost her temper, the last time she'd gotten this mad, Mama hadn't come out of the bathtub, had drowned . . .

The young man said, "No, really, I'm waiting for someone myself, and I thought we could wait together." He was looking at her oddly, a little funny, as if he thought she was a joke. Was he making fun of her? If he was, Edna was afraid of what she might do.

"So are you waiting for someone?"

She narrowed her eyes at him, disapprovingly. "That's for me to know and for you to find out."

He laughed at her.

"I haven't heard that one since I was a little kid."

"Oh yeah? Well, why don't you just go jump in the lake?"

"In the lake?" He was speaking softly, but laughing still, trying not to crack up.

"Go jump in the lake? What are you, a retard?"

Edna saw red. She was about to pull the pistol and shoot him and to hell with Babe, to hell with everyone else. *No one made fun of her!* But suddenly the young man was straight-faced, sober. He looked frightened for a second then got a faraway look in his eyes, those eyes all bright and happy. When he spoke, his voice was anxious.

"Lady, lady tell me, do my words sound all right to you? Are they coming out sounding okay?"

"Now who's the retard?" Edna said. She relaxed her grip on the gun, though, left her hand in her coat pocket.

"Jesus, I'm *talking.*"

"Don't take the name of the Lord in vain." She said it and looked at him, but he didn't say anything, just put his finger to his lips.

"Shh."

She heard it then, the running footsteps. Still coming on fast. It wasn't Babe. She put her hand up, signaled for the young man not to move. She held her breath and when the footsteps passed she let it out in a long sigh.

"That's not him, and don't you make a noise until he comes."

"*Who?* Who're you waiting for, lady?"

She couldn't help herself. She had to let someone know, even if it was only this young fool here who thought he talked funny. Besides, it would let him know that she was nobody to mess around with.

"Babe," Edna said. "I'm waiting for Babe Hill. My Babe's coming for me tonight."

"Babe? You're shitting me." He was grinning widely now, as if they were partners instead of enemies. He poked his thumb into his chest. "*I'm* waiting for Babe, too. Ain't that a coincidence?"

Uh-oh. This smelled like trouble.

"You wait for him some other time, buddy boy. Tonight Babe's coming for me."

"He's expecting you? He knows you're here?" The boy looked disappointed.

"He'll know me when he sees me."

Edna was frightened, but the gun made her feel less afraid. If she had to, she would shoot right through the coat, cut him down before he could make a move.

But he didn't seem dangerous, now. He wasn't making fun of her. Just smiling a lot, like an idiot. Edna didn't trust people who smiled too much.

And yet he said he was waiting for Babe, and he sure did look a lot like him.

Edna took a shot in the dark.

"Are you his brother?"

"See?" the man said. "I *knew* you were no dummy, the second I saw you. Sure I'm his brother. Only he ain't gonna be happy to see me. I'm gonna have to convince him to come away with me."

"He's coming with *me*." Edna saw no way out of it. She would have to shoot this young smarty-pants. It would be the only way out.

"Sure he is, sure he is. But let me ask you something. What if he don't want to come with you? How you gonna make him? You got a car? You got a gun?"

Edna didn't have a car, and she wasn't as dumb as this fella might think she was. She wasn't about to tell him she had a gun.

"Nooo," she said.

He reached under his shirt and pulled out a big pistol, nothing at all like hers. His was flat and black and looked like the ones the gangsters carried in the TV movies. The kinds that held about a zillion bullets. She knew that the cylinder in her gun only held six shots, and that her bullets were very small.

"Well I got both a car and a gun. I could help him go away with you. But you gotta help me, too, lady. You got a place to take him?"

"I live in Calumet City."

"Alone?"

"Wouldn't you like to know."

"That's for you to know and for me to find out, right?"

"That's right." Edna could feel herself pouting now. This man was messing everything up. He was making her want to pee, waving that pistol around, too. But he was Babe's brother, and he wouldn't hurt Babe, would he?

And if she played her cards right he could come in handy. In case she was wrong, in case Babe didn't really want to come with her. He could make Babe come with her and once she had him in her house, well, she could pull her own gun when nobody was looking, and make this skinny boy leave.

But he didn't have to know that. Edna hid a smile, looked at him, right in the eye.

"You going to help me make Babe love me?"

"Oh, I can do that, all right."

Edna nodded, her decision made. "Okay, then. I've got a great big white house and I live alone in it and you can help me get Babe over there. But *only* if he doesn't want to come with me all by himself."

"Lady," the kid said, "you can bet the farm that he won't want to go with you on his own," and smiled, and Edna was about to give him what for when they heard the sound of pounding feet again but only this time the feet were going much slower, and this time there was the sound of two sets of them, along with the sounds of voices softly speaking.

Tim ran fast, thinking about his buddy, lost in his thoughts.

Babe was a man who thought that he stood alone in the world, but he was shortsighted. It wasn't only his family who cared about him.

The police department was full of people who at one time had been in near awe of Tim, because he was friends with a TV actor. Babe would come to the station and they'd want autographs for their families, and some of the women officers would even sometimes put the make on him. He would visit and leave and they would tell Tim what a nice guy he was, how important he'd made them feel.

He had that way about him. He'd look you in the eye when he spoke to you and pay strict attention to what you said, intense yet gentle. Babe would smile and his lips would curl up but his eyes would reveal his amazement, Babe surprised that he could find anything funny. A lot of people in this town thought him to be shy and humble.

Even the crowd at the gym liked him, although you couldn't convince Babe that they did. He didn't socialize with them, hell, Babe didn't socialize with anyone, but they would ask for autographs and he would stop what he was doing to give them one, and Tim would hear him in the sauna sometimes, talking to people, just giving them little bits and pieces, anecdotes about the business, Babe speaking with a towel up high around his shoulders, holding it there with his hands. He'd wait, too, until the shower was empty before stepping in, as if he thought that someone would take a picture of his scar if they saw it there on his back.

How could Babe be so blind? Was he that insecure that he felt that he had no friends in town except Tim?

Try telling that to Bob, at the 7-Eleven. He'd slap Babe if he ever heard that garbage, take it as an insult and his Italian blood would boil. Bob would collect for Jerry's Kids twice a year, would have paper hearts that donors could put their names on at Labor Day, shamrocks at St. Patrick's Day, and Babe would always buy a couple of hundred each time. Bob would put his name on them for Babe. Tim would stop for coffee and there would be all those HILL shamrocks or hearts hanging from the walls, the ceilings. Babe would stay away from the store until the things were taken down but Tim wouldn't, would hear the remarks from the customers, knew how many of them were proud to have a star living right there among them. Who wasn't too proud to stay where he belonged, who didn't run to Hollywood now that he'd made a few bucks.

The guy was a hit, and he didn't even know it.

Speaking of which, there he came. Tim could tell those big Lincoln headlights anywhere. He slowed down, stopped. Waited for Babe to park and enter through the little access gate.

"Like Creature Features, isn't it?" Tim said. "I expect to see the Wolfman pop out from behind the trees."

"I just left him," Babe said. He dropped his cigarette on the other side of the gate, let it smolder. "Been here long?"

"Just two laps." He began to gently hop up and down. "Thought you'd be later than this."

"I got done early."

"Been home yet?"

"Not yet. Got my sweat clothes out of my locker at the gym."

"Kelly is worried."

"I don't blame her. Shit, I'm scared to go home."

"I don't blame you. She's gonna kick your ass. You ready?"

Slowly, they began to jog side by side.

"I talked to the old man, then to Spinell and his brother."

"Babe, ah, Christ."

"The first mile always kills me. Slow down, will you?"

"You don't want a high profile, yet you hang out with guys like that. What if Kathy O'Malley or some other journalist got ahold of it? What if someone saw you with those scumbags? You're a *star*, for

Christ's sake. You want to see your name linked with the mob in the INC. column?"

"I wasn't breaking bread with them."

"What were you doing with them?"

Babe panted and smiled. "I was taping them."

Tim said, "Jesus Christ."

"The old man didn't do anything but show me how smart he was, how he got my number."

"And the Spinells?"

"It got a little better with them."

"They threaten you?"

"Not me. My father. Said if I didn't do the series, they'd cut him up into little pieces and mail them to me one at a time."

Tim had to fight a strong urge to punch him, just one time. Instead, he said, "That's extortion, Babe. We give that tape to the FBI and they go down."

"That can't happen."

"Are you nuts?"

Babe was laboring, pushing himself along with an effort. It had been a long day and he'd worked out hard many hours ago.

He said, "Nobody can know about this, Tim. If they do it'll all come out—who they are, what my relationship is with them. I got kids in the school system, my wife goes to college in the area. I won't have people looking at them, thinking that their father and husband is some mobster got caught with his hand in the cookie jar then decided to wear a wire for the feds to get himself out of trouble. I've worked too hard for that to happen."

"Why would they think that?"

"You know how people are."

"That's not what you're worried about, and you know it."

"Yeah? You sound like my old man." Babe was sweating in spite of the cold, was breathing unevenly and harshly. "I'm only gonna do a mile tonight, I'm dead." Tim was hardly walking fast, wasn't even pumping his arms.

Babe said, "What *am* I worried about, Tim?"

"You're only worried about your career, how this would impact on it."

"Fuck you."

"Don't you say that to me. I'm not Milo Spinell or your father, Babe. I'm your fucking friend."

Babe, silent, ran on, a little faster.

Tim said, "You're gonna do the *Street Babe* thing for them because they threatened your father? That's no excuse, Babe. Not when you have a tape that will put them away."

"I'm not doing the show, Tim."

"All the more reason to use the tape. How'll you feel when they carry out their threat?"

"Safe," Babe said, and began to sprint.

It wasn't hard for Tim to catch up to him, ease into the flow of the run.

"You have knowledge of a murder in advance and you don't turn it over to the proper authorities, you're an accessory."

They were coming around the last turn, their first lap finished. Tim was breathing normally.

Babe said, "The tape's in my car, on the front seat, Tim. Listen to it. Then take it, it's yours. You're the proper authority, as far as I'm concerned. Do what you have to do."

Tim stopped at the parking lot gate, leaned against it and stretched his legs while Babe ran on. Tim called out, "The keys in the usual place?" and Babe said Yeah.

Then said, "I'm sorry I said that to you, Tim, earlier," then said something else that Tim couldn't hear because he'd run beyond the line of Tim's sight and hearing.

Tim walked to the car and got Babe's key out from the top of the front tire, shut off the alarm and opened the door, got into the car and sat in the driver's seat, looking at the little tape recorder there on the seat beside him. In his anxiety, maybe his fear, Babe hadn't rewound it. Tim did that now, got it back to the beginning of the tape then hit Play, began to listen to it as Babe ran on, out there in the fog.

They'd had their first argument, and it was hard for Anthony not to laugh. He'd wanted to go out there and blast the bigger guy and kidnap Babe, but the fat chick, this Edna Rose, she'd told him that she would have none of that, that it was against God's law to commit the act of murder. This was fun, took the edge off his excitement, his fear.

Kidnapping wasn't against God's law? She'd told him that they weren't kidnapping Babe, they were only borrowing him. In an hour, maybe two, he'd be glad they'd borrowed him, once he found out who it was that had done the borrowing.

Was this bitch living in a fantasy world, or what? Anthony didn't care. He was so happy to be talking straight, to be thinking right, that she could have said anything she wanted and it would have been all right with him.

What had happened to him? Was this some strange rite of passage? Was he now a man? He didn't know. All that he was sure of was that he felt better than he had in years, better than he had in his life. There had been no *whoosh* from the drug, so maybe it wasn't even the Thorazine that was leveling him off. It was what he was now, a confident, strong man who had no mental confusion.

He thought that this must be how his father felt, in control and powerful. He'd had a glimpse of it back in Parker's house when he was getting it on with the sister, but even then, he knew that it was all a dream, that it wasn't real.

This time, it was real. It was in him, the strength.

He stood there smiling, the gun in his hand, shaking his head because this chick, she had no idea how close she was.

Anthony was going to give them a few more laps, wait until they were done running. If they were any kind of runners, they would walk a lap or two to keep their legs from cramping. If the other guy was with Babe, if he was Babe's friend, then Anthony would kill him and drag Babe out of there. If Babe walked the laps alone, he'd take him and the broad would do what she was told, as long as she had her Babe in the car with her.

Either way, it was all right with him.

But he'd rather not kill the guy, not with all those houses so close. Someone would hear it and call the cops, and he might have trouble getting away, fog or no fog.

He'd play it by ear, and not wait for any rushing wind noises or for any voices to come for him. Anthony would have staked his life at that moment that the voices would never be coming to him again. He was cured, that was a certainty.

This broad, though, she made his mental problems look tame. He'd told her his name was Anthony and she'd said that he was named for a gentle and loving saint. He'd told her that he'd been named for a saloon singer from the Bronx and she hadn't known what he was talking about.

Which made him feel pretty good. He'd be in trouble the second someone like this started figuring him out.

He'd heard about them, these types. Like that Ralph Nau guy who'd killed his little baby brother and then beaten the plea because some lawyer had convinced a judge that the guy was nuts. The cops hadn't taken that into consideration when they'd beaten his confession out of him. The guy had been put into a mental institution and from there had written a couple of hundred letters to Cher, to Olivia Newton-John, acting like he was married to them, that they'd had his kids and shit.

This was that guy, with tits.

She'd whispered it to Anthony, her ideas, as they waited. Trusting him suddenly, two old pals talking about their dreams. She'd stare into the night with a faraway look on her face and speak in a whisper about her feelings and a bunch of other crazy shit, like it was true, like she believed it with all her heart. About how his brother worshipped her and how they'd had a kid who'd died, but he didn't remember it. How she'd have to remind him of it. After he fell in love with her.

That was the craziest part. It was easy for Anthony to laugh inside and nod his head at her, say, "No shit," from time to time, acting in awe of her genius. But when she said that Babe was in love with her, it was hard for him to keep a straight face. Christ, she looked like a refugee from *Deliverance*, like her twin brother sat on the porch and twanged away at a banjo. Frank might fuck her, if she'd beat him up, but Babe wouldn't give her the time of day.

It was a good thing for her that Anthony had shown up. Without him, and his gun, Babe would have laughed at her. Now that Anthony was here, though, and this chick was going to let him take Babe to her house, maybe he'd return the favor by pointing his pistol at Babe and making him fuck her. Telling him that his choice was put it in her or put it up the barrel of the pistol, see how badly he wanted to keep it. If she had a camera Anthony could snap off a few Polaroids, so she could keep them for old times' sake, after Kelly paid the ransom.

"Here they come," Edna whispered, anxiously, but it wasn't any *them*, it was only one, and from the sound of it, it was a slowpoke, his brother the turtle, Babe.

Babe apologized to Tim as he ran, saying it over his shoulder. Apologized then told Tim that he'd been right, that Babe *had* been worried about his career, but not in the way that Tim figured.

He was worried because he'd spent all these years building, busting his ass with no help from anybody, and if Tim gave that tape to the FBI it would be in all the papers, who his father was.

And they'd all think that the old man had done it for him, had made him what he was.

Babe would rather be dead than to have anyone believe that.

He was coming to the first bend in the track and he saw sudden movement at the gate, through the fog. Heard the sound of someone jumping the fence and he stopped, squinting, his hands on his hips. Expecting to see some kid taking a shortcut through the school property, but if that was the case, why was he jumping the short fence? Why wasn't he just walking around it, or behind it, outside the tall fence too?

Babe found out real quick, when his brother Anthony came walking into sight with an automatic pistol pointed right at Babe's stomach.

Edna watched Anthony leap the fence easily and she ran to it, let go of the gun and felt it fall through the hole in the pocket and bounce off her leg, get caught up at the bottom, in the lining of the coat.

"Damnit!"

What would she do now? She was wondering if she should reach down there and inch it up, but Anthony had the gun on her Babe and Babe was squinting, looking this way. She couldn't let him see her doing something so unladylike, so unfeminine.

She tried to float over to the fence, tried to move with as much ease as she was capable of, and she smiled, forced it for him, but now he wasn't looking her way anymore. Now he was looking at his brother.

Babe said, "Anthony, put the gun down. Nobody's been hurt yet, you can just hop back over the fence and I'll forget all about this."

"And have the cops on my ass in a minute. Put those fucking hands up!"

Babe did as he was told.

"You got to understand something, Babe. I've already killed two people tonight, and I'll kill you if I have to."

"You're talking crazy."

"*Don't you say that!*" Anthony half-shouted the words and Babe raised his hands higher, in fear.

"That's the way, Babe, over to the fence. Easy now, climb it nice and easy. You try and run, and I swear to Christ, I'll put one right between your shoulder blades."

Babe was climbing the fence, hesitantly. He was looking up at the fat woman standing there in front of him, sweating heavily, her chest heaving. She smoothed her hair with hands that were shaking something terrible. Anthony laughed.

"Now move back, face me. Lie on the ground." Anthony negotiated the fence using only his free hand. "Get up."

Babe stood and faced them, his hands high again.

"This your girlfriend?" he said, and Anthony smiled.

"Say hello to a fan of yours, Babe. Her name is Edna Rose."

"Oh, my God." Babe's face went white and his mouth fell open. "Oh, dear God," he said.

Anthony said, "We're going to be staying with her for a while, big brother."

Tim listened to the tape and watched for Babe through the fog, figuring it to take about three minutes for Babe to make a complete circuit. Quarter mile track, Babe ran twelve-minute miles. Even if Babe was dogging it, he'd be around in three and a half.

Yet he wasn't. That much time had to have passed when Tim began to worry.

About what, though? Hell, Babe had gone through a meet with his father and brothers tonight, and a sitdown with one of the most vicious killers the outfit had ever known. How much danger would he be in on a jogging track in his own neighborhood?

Unless they'd somehow followed him.

Tim shut off the recorder and got out of Babe's car, stood leaning against it, staring into the fog and trying to tell himself that he was overreacting.

"Babe?" He called it gently, then a little louder. "Hey, Babe!"

Nothing.

Tim didn't go toward the gate. He merely ran to the fence and hopped it, cleared it with a foot to spare and began to run as fast as he could into the fog, calling Babe's name.

The smell of marijuana was very strong in the walkway, and Babe knew that kids sometimes hid there, hopped the privacy fences at night and smoked their dope. He hoped that someone was watching them, someone who would call the cops, have the presence of mind to get this kid's license plate.

Edna Rose. Good sweet Jesus. How had Anthony gotten hooked up with her? He didn't know. But he'd bet that he'd find out, and soon. The thing he didn't understand was, she wrote him letters saying how much she loved him, how she wanted him in bed with her. Explicit letters expressing her sexual fantasies toward him.

What was she doing with Anthony, who was threatening to kill him? Why had she thrown in with him?

He knew that his face had fallen, that he hadn't covered it up when Anthony had said her name. The woman had watched him and had looked as if he'd slapped her, then looked at the ground, and Babe thought that she might break down and cry. He had hurt her, and under other circumstances that would have been a good thing, might have sent her a jolt of reality, let her know that all her ideas were crazy. That Babe wasn't about to take her seriously.

But now her sadness was disturbing news. He needed someone on his side. If they got into a car, he'd have to have her as an ally, if he was going to escape. What he really needed, more than anything else, was to get away from these two just long enough to call Tim's name. Fade into the fog and call for help.

"Babe?" He heard his name being called faintly, from back at the track. Anthony was behind him, but how close? Could he make a move? Would the kid really shoot him? And where was the woman? No, he couldn't take the chance. Couldn't scream back for Tim to be careful.

"Who is that!" Anthony was at his side, the gun held tight into Babe's right rib cage. Babe could smell the woman's perfume, she was nearby, right behind them.

"My partner. He's a cop, Anthony. A sixth-degree black belt. He'll catch up."

"I'll kill him."

"You can't kill us both."

"Want to bet?"

"Anthony, somebody's coming!" It was the woman, and Anthony half-turned, and Babe made his move.

There was a beat-up old Ford about ten feet in front of him and Babe pushed back, hard, struck out with his elbow and felt it connect with Anthony's arm, the gun pointing toward the sky now as Babe ran, took two steps, three, then jumped over the car as Anthony got to his feet, ran toward him.

"Tim!" Babe shouted, and Anthony fired a shot at him, which missed but caromed off the hood of the car. Babe dropped flat, trying to crawl under the car but it was too low, his shoulders would not fit underneath.

Then Anthony was there, eyes blazing, the gun pointing down at him. Babe closed his eyes, thought that he was about to die.

"Get up." Hissed at Babe, Anthony angry.

Babe got up and was shoved through the open door and past the front seat and into the back, and the woman was getting in behind him even as Anthony was starting the car, putting it in gear and fishtailing out of there.

Tim heard Babe frantically call his name and he had to turn around, he was already three quarters of the way back to the parking lot.

The call had come from somewhere near the gate off West Rocket Circle.

Tim ran toward it, sprinting, leaped the fence and was heading toward the gate just as the night exploded with a gunshot.

Instinctively, he fell to the ground, thinking that the bullet had been fired at him. He crawled forward rapidly, using only his arms and feet, lowcrawling, making progress, but by the time he figured out that whoever it was had the gun wasn't shooting at him, he could hear the sound of the car, squealing into the night.

Tim got to his feet and raced to the curb, frantically looked around but couldn't even see the sight of retreating taillights in either direction.

He heard movement behind him and he spun, saw clothing and skin moving away from him in the shadows behind him and was on it in a second, his forearm in a throat.

He released the form when he saw that it was a young girl, terrified. Her eyes were red and it was obvious that she was stoned. He knew her, recognized her from the security shift that he worked at the school every now and then when he wanted the extra money.

"Did you see the car!"

"They were shooting!" The girl began to cry.

"Goddamnit, did you see the fucking car!"

"Are my parents going to find out about this?"

Tim grabbed her arm, shook her hard. "The next words out of your mouth better be an answer, or you're under arrest." There were lights coming on in houses up and down the street, and Tim instinctively pulled her down the walkway, into the shadows.

"No. Me and Michael were only having a few doobies . . ."

"Where's Michael?"

"He split when the trouble began."

She was frightened and Tim used it against her, did not feel the need to be gentle, or to tell the truth.

"I've got you for curfew, and for drugs. I can come up with a few more things in about thirty seconds. You want to go to jail? You want the diesel dykes at the County to have their shot at your fine young white ass?" She was shaking her head, crying.

"No, no, no, no, *no!*" She pulled her arm away and covered her head with her arms. "Leave me alone!"

"What did he look like? The guy with the gun? Tell me, and you walk right now."

"He, he was skinny, with long hair. The car was an old one, I don't know what kind. It was big and yellow. He had a big fat ugly woman with him." She was getting hysterical, her voice rising with each word. "She called him Anthony." She began to sob, long, drawn-out cries.

Anthony.

"One more question, that's all." He shook her again and she tried to pull away but Tim held her, got up close into her face.

"When Anthony pulled the trigger, did he hit anybody?"

"He—he hit the *car*, I think he only hit the *car.*"

Tim let her go. "Go ahead, get the hell out of here, right now."

"You aren't going to arrest me?"

"You tell anyone about this, and I will."

She was backing off now, her hands up in a gesture of sincerity. Her face was tear-streaked. Tim wasn't feeling a lot of sympathy for her. "Man, I won't even tell *Michael* about this shit."

He watched her go, wondering what the hell he was doing. He was a cop. He had a job to do. He could get fired for not reporting this, for not calling the kidnapping in.

But Babe had told him just that afternoon that he'd honestly rather die than to make the front pages in any way other than through his talent.

Babe's kidnapping would definitely be front-page news. Now Tim had to decide where to draw the line.

Tim saw that he'd have to make up his mind about it, and right now, because there were flashing lights coming down Sauk Trail, fast. Someone had called the cops. He'd let the girl go and that had been his first mistake, his first unprofessional act. He could smooth that one over if nobody had looked out the window and seen them.

So what was he going to do? He was a cop, and his fellow officers were on their way right now. He could give them what he knew, say that he himself had heard the name Anthony shouted out in a woman's voice. Could tell them that Anthony was Babe's little brother. They would call in the FBI and the feds would take over, probably find Babe before daylight.

But would they care if Babe was found dead or alive? And either way, it would make the papers, front page. It would be out of Tim's hands, and if Tim was any kind of friend, he couldn't let that happen.

Tim turned and ran, as fast as he could, toward the parking lot and his car. He'd sort it all out later. But first, he needed time to think.

erome Spinell sat in the room, withdrawing. He had gone through a detox center before, so he was aware of the symptoms, knew how they would affect him. The flu-like characteristics of the process were easy enough to handle, once you knew what they were, and you knew that they wouldn't kill you.

The craving, though, that was enough to kill you. Drive you nuts, at least.

There'd been a time when he'd thought that he could handle it. He'd learned better at the Betty Ford clinic. He'd lasted two days. He'd walked right out of the place, had ordered a limo and been out of there, and had found a Rancho Mirage pusher to help him satisfy his needs. He'd gone back home and told everyone that the place was for pussies, for weaklings, and that he'd handle his problem alone, without a bunch of faggots hugging you all the time and asking you to share and care.

But he'd known, right then, that he was hooked.

Most of the time that fact didn't bother him very much. He had pushers that he trusted back home; in his business, there were designated people at the studios, whose jobs were to find it, the good stuff, and hand it out to the important clients. Even though it was no longer the hip thing to do in LA, now that everybody was into saving the planet, there was still a brotherhood among them, between those who needed the fine white powder. Jerome would snort it and thought that it wasn't *too* bad a monkey, because he'd never shot the stuff up and never intended to start. Once you were on the needles, you were beyond all hope.

But there were other times when he'd be home, his family asleep, and he'd be staring at the stuff, his hands shaking, his nose full. He'd look down at the pile of shit and hate himself, hate what he'd become. At those times he would do as he'd done just this morning in the presence of his brother and the two big toughs. He'd flush the stuff down the toilet and make internal vows to quit.

It would make him feel good for a couple of days. Even though he knew that his friends were laughing behind their hands at him, waiting for him to relapse again. Their snide comments about his cleaning up would give him strength, was another reason to stay off the cocaine.

Until some pressure came his way. Then his bloodstream would get an itch that only cocaine could scratch. At those times, he couldn't think, couldn't function without a snort to carry him through. Every time, every single time that he'd tried to quit, he'd been forced back into it by the pressures of his life.

Were there some pressures on his ass now, or what?

His face was puffy, and he could feel his lips pulse with his heartbeat. He'd seen himself in the mirror when he'd gone into the bathroom to straighten his wig; there were marks on his cheeks, cuts on his lips.

This morning those two brain-dead creeps, Billy and Floyd, had almost thrown him out the window at his brother's order, and he wondered now what would have happened if the woman hadn't come crying through the door.

They would have done it. He knew that. Milo was his brother but first and foremost he was a businessman, and in his business, as in all businesses, the assholes at the top had to have somebody to blame when everything started going bad. The difference being, in Milo's line of work, you didn't fire the scapegoat or blackball him from the club. You killed him, because if you didn't, the people you worked for would come hunting your ass.

There were millions tied up in the Hollywood operation, and Milo hadn't put all of that money up himself. After Sunday's show, after *Street Babe* was a big success, the other bosses would have begun counting their money, and now it looked as if there wouldn't be any at all for them to spend.

Somebody's head would have to roll, and Jerome was sure that it would be his.

Fuck it. He couldn't live like this, with this terror in his mind.

Jerome picked up the phone and dialed the operator, told her to transfer his calls to the steam room. That would cover him for the ten or fifteen minutes that he would need. He left the room, his mind made up, the two hundred-dollar bills already folded into the left pocket, away from his other dough, and waited impatiently for the elevator, drumming his fingers on the elevator door. He was smoking, staring morosely into the sand of the standup ashtray, the cigarette stuck into the corner of his mouth. It was Jerome's equivalent of Frank Sinatra staring into a shot glass, alone in a saloon at closing time, his hat shoved to the back of his head, captured for all time on an album cover.

When the doors opened he saw that there were two young people in the elevator, dressed in jogging suits. The guy was a wimp, with thick glasses and thinning hair. No shoulders. The sweatshirt hung off him as if he were a small child. The woman, though, she had a rack on her. She was wearing one of those spandex deals that showed almost everything. There was a small black bag clasped around her waist. She probably had her personal computer in the thing. There was a neon headband around her head.

Their eyes opened wide when they saw him and he took his time getting in, held the door open with one hand while he stubbed the cigarette into the ashtray with the other. He got in, turned his back on them and hit the button for the lobby.

The man spoke to the woman in a whiny, high-pitched voice, and Jerome soon understood that he'd walked into the middle of an argument.

"Well, I wasn't about to wear my running shoes to play tennis."

"You wrecked the entire evening. Fucked up the mixed doubles because you forgot to pack the extra shoes."

"You found someone to take my place soon enough."

"He was a stranger." Jerome heard her blow air out her nose. "Maybe I should have let him take your place in other areas of my life, too. He wasn't bad-looking."

"Hillary . . ." The guy didn't say it in a warning way, more like in a begging tone. Jerome wanted to slap him.

"You should have packed your tennis shoes." What an icy bitch.

There was a tap on his shoulder and he turned, saw that the woman was smiling at him, openly. The man was looking at her, disbelieving.

"Excuse me, but aren't you Jerome Spinell." She knew who he was, didn't ask a question.

"Yeah," Jerome said. "And I don't play tennis or jog or golf or take any backtalk from my goddamn woman." He looked at the man and grunted his disapproval. He said, "I'm in forty-five-seventeen, sweetheart, you decide to lose the wimp."

There, that made him feel better. She was looking at him, in shock, but he thought he saw a hint of fascination in her eyes. She was intrigued by him, Jerome could tell. He looked her up and down without hiding what he was doing. The elevator stopped and a bell rang and as soon as the door opened the man stomped out.

"Damned TV celebrities. All ego and arrogance." Jerome smiled at the woman, who took her time walking out of the elevator. Once she passed him, she didn't look back, but she was swinging it.

"Hillary, would you stop that disgusting display? Can't you see he's wearing a *wig*?" The door closed before Jerome could comment on the punk's own baldness, and took him down to the lobby level. He would have to go to another elevator altogether to get to the ground floor.

He stepped out of the second elevator and onto the marble floor, thinking that this just might be his lucky night. Hillary had sure seemed impressed, and now there was his man, standing there outside the door, looking in at him with a big, eager grin.

"Mr. Spinell, how you doing tonight, sir."

"OK, my man." Jerome motioned for him to come aside, away from the other doormen. They stood together in the shadows of the building, Jerome shivering now because the night had turned cold and he hadn't put on his jacket.

"Can you get me some more of that shit from last night? Same kind? It was from primo stock."

"Happen to have some right here with me."

"Hundred a gram?"

"For you, yeah. Anyone else, it's a dollar and a quarter."

Anyone else, it was probably seventy-five. But Jerome was

in no position to argue. He said, "Give me two grams," and the doorman told him no problem. They made the switch and Jerome thanked him and he walked quickly back into the hotel, not giving the doorman another thought. There were other things on his mind.

Like Hillary, for one, somewhere in the back of his mind, swaying to and fro as the little wimp had stared at her bald display of sexuality, in shock. Jerome would bet that she'd been smiling.

But more importantly, another thought was beginning to form there. Something that terrified him just to think about, but there and real all the same.

He could pick up the phone and drop a dime, call the feds and in minutes he'd be safe. He knew enough about the Hollywood operation to be of value to them, and they would take care of him.

And he'd get a million dollars worth of publicity out of it. Get *Street Babe* back, too. Tell Babe a sob story about how his conscience wouldn't allow him to carry on with his brother, with Ackerman. Get Babe on his side and the two of them could do the show together, with an entire platoon of Chicago coppers guarding his ass day and night, his own private bodyguard crew who couldn't afford to let anything happen to him.

It was something to think about, and he'd have to dwell on it a little bit upstairs, after he relieved his tension.

Jerome was so lost in thought that he didn't see the doorman watch him and wait until Jerome was on the elevator, then enter the building himself, walk over to the security desk and speak to the man in a whisper.

The guard looked up at the doorman, nodded, and as soon as the kid walked away he reached for the phone.

Tim took Babe's car for several reasons, but mainly because when the cops got around to searching the parking lot they'd see his car and let it pass, would think nothing of it. They'd think that Tim had just left it there and was jogging around Park Forest, had maybe got bored with running around in circles.

He wondered if he was losing his mind, why he was doing this. It was the most unprofessional act he'd performed in all the years he'd been a policeman. He'd lose his job over this if it came out. When it came out. Because it sure as hell would.

Even if he got Babe back safely, he didn't think he could do it without somebody getting hurt. He couldn't shoot Johnny Hilliard or anyone else and just forget about it, go home and pretend that nothing had happened. Babe wouldn't talk, would probably be grateful. But Tim would have to live with it, and he wasn't certain that he could.

All right, take it one step at a time. Worry about the job, about going to jail, later.

At the moment, his brother was in danger, and Tim wasn't about to let the wheels of justice grind forward as long as that was the case. When it was all cleared up he'd come forward, and worry about the consequences of his acts at that time.

He felt good, now that the decision was made. Felt his coldness slip back over him. There would be no more emotional judgments. He'd just made one, and it would more than likely cost him his job, and maybe even his freedom. From here on out, he'd be a pro. He'd let the cold come into him, as he used to years ago, when his father had come toward him, hands balled into fists . . .

His first stop was at his own house. Tim didn't shower, just threw on a pair of pants over his sweaty underwear, a clean shirt over his bare chest. He put on fresh black socks and highly polished rubber-soled leather shoes. A sport coat covered his pistol. Less than three minutes after he entered his home, he was back in the car, heading toward Babe's house.

Milo was talking calmly, discussing death with Landini in low, even tones. They were sitting in the den of Milo's Highland Park home. The dark wood paneling and the heavy leather furniture gave the impression that the room was in a good men's club. Floyd and Billy were lounging around, looking tired and yawning. It had been a long day.

"We can't lose the operation. It's a bone to *you*, yeah, Milo, but you got to remember, it's a good fifth of my income." Landini was being reasonable and in a position to speak so frankly. He was a moneymaker.

"Johnny can go, yeah, no problem, and the spics, too, if you say so. But we got to have someone there right away to cover the market. We lose those Polacks out there, I'm fucked."

"You got someone in mind? Can anyone handle it on a couple of days' notice?"

Landini nodded. "Plenty of guys. The question is, would they want it after the last guy had it got whacked, him and his entire crew. That's something they'd have to think about."

"Then let them. Come on, Lenny, what are you worried about? None of them guys ever think they're gonna get hit themselves."

The phone rang and Milo looked up, quickly. "Grab that, Floyd, right away. I don't want it to wake up Sally." He turned back to Landini.

"So call the spics. Set a meet, tonight, right now. Tell them their boss grabbed the till and killed their goombah to cover it up, then cut them loose on him. They get caught, they'll do ninety years before they rat. They're more reliable than most of the Italians are these days. They get caught and go to the joint, we call in some favors and they catch it in the County. If they don't get caught, after they do the job on Johnny, you whack them out yourself. Billy and Floyd can help you."

"Why kill them at all? We can keep them collecting, I can meet with them myself two, three times a week. They work for nearly nothing and they steal less than anyone ever been on any of my crews."

Floyd was standing over by the phone stand with the receiver in his hand, shaking his head and speaking excitedly. He hung up and said, "Boss?"

"Can they handle the whole thing by themselves, without a boss right there to ride herd on them every day?"

"You got to see those guys in action, Milo. They get behind the wheel of an eighty-one Riviera and they get it in their heads that they're real high rollers. I think we should keep them."

Milo shrugged. "It's up to you, Lenny. Long as you know, they're your responsibility."

"Boss?" Floyd said. Loudly.

"I'll handle them, don't you worry about that." Milo could see the dollar signs in Landini's eyes. He could rob the half-a-niggers blind and they'd love him for it and beg for more.

Floyd said, "Hey, Milo!" and Milo turned to him.

"What the hell is it."

"That was one of your cop buddies, moonlights security over to the hotel, the guys you told me to have keep an eye on Jerome? It's about your brother, Jerome. He just scored two grams from the doorman at the Four Seasons."

Milo said, "That little son of a bitch," and slapped the table, hard.

36

She'd been waiting for him all night and it was close to midnight now, and Kelly was suddenly hoping that he wouldn't bother to come home. If he came home drunk, she decided, she'd throw him out.

She loved him, desperately. Even after all these years. But there were two sons to raise and they couldn't be burdened with the stress of their father's disease. Or with the shame associated with it.

Who did he think he was? What was the man's problem? There were times when it was difficult for her to understand him, his motivations. He had everything; they'd struggled for so long, and now it was right there in front of them to grab and he was pulling back his hand, letting the brass ring go by.

Which was his decision. She'd stood by him for almost half her life and she could do it again if he didn't want to shoot this TV series. What she wouldn't do was sit home every night, worrying like this, wondering if he were in jail or the hospital. Or if he was dead.

Her mind was made up. If he was drinking tonight, it would be all over.

She'd watched too many of her friends suffer, waiting for the man they loved to straighten out a drinking problem. Hoping that each day would be the one that he'd decide to change his life, futilely clinging to the slender thread of hope, making fools of themselves, was mostly what they did.

"You selfish bastard," Kelly said, with feeling.

The children were in bed and she should be, too. They'd want to know where dad was when they got up, if he wasn't back yet. And she'd have to sit them down and tell them that dad wasn't coming back. That dad was a drunk again.

It wasn't something she was looking forward to doing.

But it wasn't something she would shy away from, either.

There had been too many hopeless nights in her life. Cold and lonely nights without him, when he'd been drinking before. If he wanted to wind up back in the barber shop, sleeping on the floor in the toilet, then that was his choice to make and she wouldn't try to change his mind. But she wouldn't let him drag her down with him this time. And he wouldn't even come close to touching the kids, to dragging them through the mud. If he wanted to let his tribal secrets be the end of him, she could live with that. But the children, they would have to be looked out for.

So all he had to do was wander in with just one whiff of beer on his breath, and by God, she'd be calling a lawyer tomorrow.

She heard his car come into the driveway, pull into the circle, but she didn't hear the garage door opening. Maybe he was too damn drunk to get it into the garage without scratching it up. He liked that car more than he liked her, lately.

Who did he think she was, his mother? Did he really believe he could disappear every time something happened in the house that he didn't enjoy, and that she would sit back and take it?

Kelly was working herself up, getting angrier with every passing second, imagining him out there, fumbling with his keys. She forced herself to regain her control. She would *not* awaken her children with some shouting, ugly scene.

The doorbell rang and she muttered under her breath. She'd been right.

All right. She'd let him in before he woke everyone up, and she'd walk immediately away from him. Not talk with him at all tonight because she was upset and it would degenerate quickly. Besides, there was no arguing with a drunk.

Kelly walked down the stairs to the entrance hall, fighting for control. She pulled the door open with her mouth set determinedly, then felt her face fall when she saw who was standing there.

"Tim?" Kelly said. Then she saw Babe's car in the driveway. *"Tim?* What's wrong! What's happened to Babe!"

"So it's your call," Tim said, sitting on the hassock, his back straight. He'd told her what he knew, and what he wanted to do. If she told him to call the police, then that's what he would do.

"My dear God." Kelly was fighting not to cry. She didn't seem to want to make the decision. Tim hoped that she wouldn't get weepy, wouldn't blame him for not making the decision for her. He was staring at her with his cop's face on, giving her nothing.

Kelly surprised him. She literally shook herself, and, like a dog throwing off water, she cast aside all weakness. When she spoke her voice was strong and confident.

"They'll never leave him alone, not as long as he's living."

"They won't kill him, Kelly. I don't believe that. They want money from him, and they're banking on his not wanting to publicize the kidnapping. They're gambling on his feel for his public image."

"They're banking on his shame, Tim. That's all they're banking on. Anthony's nothing but his father's pawn in this, and Johnny knows goddamn well how ashamed of that entire family Babe is. They know he'll pay up and walk away. But I think you're wrong about their killing him. I think they would in a minute." Kelly was thinking fast, shaking her head.

"But you were right, we can't go to the police." She brought her eyes up to meet his, her gaze level, unflinching. "Whatever happens, we keep this in the family."

"For as long as we can. Once somebody gets hurt, all bets are off."

"You can get to Anthony's?"

"I've got all of their names and addresses. Anthony's still at home, but the mother wouldn't have anything to do with this."

"No. Marge thinks she's a martyr, and that image wouldn't make it if she was kidnapping people. Besides, she couldn't get her Manhattans at lunchtime in a prison cell. She's got more imagination than this, she'd see where it would put her."

"He'll take him somewhere else. Babe'll be in someplace

where they feel safe for a few hours. The father lives above a meat shop, they might have him in a meat cooler."

"I'll go talk to his mother."

"You have to wait here for the call."

"What call?"

"The ransom call, Kelly. They didn't do this just because they resent Babe. If there wasn't a profit in it for them, they wouldn't have done it at all."

"What should I say?"

"Act scared, as if you didn't know anything was wrong. Be terrified. Let them think they're in control. Agree to whatever they say, and buy us time. Whatever you do, make sure you tape that call."

"But what if they want more than we have in the bank?"

"Kelly, we'll worry about that after the call. If I don't find Babe tonight, we give them whatever they want, and we get it from somewhere. Let's take it one step at a time, and the sooner I get out of here, the sooner I find him."

"Tim, do you think you can?"

"Their options are limited. They have to hide a well-known person in a place where no one will find him. They'll be under a strain because even though they think they know what Babe will do, they don't know you. You're an unknown factor. If you go to the FBI, they're in prison for thirty years, and for Johnny it's a life sentence. In that case, they'd kill Babe. So you have to assure them that you'll do whatever they want."

"And if they come here?"

"They won't. They'll have you meet them somewhere, or make the drop at a place they can stake out well in advance."

"But if they *do*?"

"If they come here, kill them. Now there's two things we have to figure out. Where they're keeping him, and who the woman is."

"The girl told you the woman was fat and ugly. Babe's mother's gorgeous."

"I never thought it was her. Maybe it was one of Anthony's girlfriends. We find the woman, we find Babe. She was part of it and Anthony won't let her out of his sight until the ransom's paid."

"Get out there, Tim. Find my husband."

"Load a gun, Kelly, keep the safety off and if you think of anything or when they call you, call me on Babe's car phone."

"If you find them, Tim, if they've hurt Babe? Kill them. I'll spend everything we have to help you, to get you out of it. But you have to kill them."

"I'll keep in touch," Tim said.

There was a time maybe seven years ago when Anthony had been diagnosed by the state shrink, court-ordered and resentful about being with the guy. The shrink, though, he didn't see things that way, thought that they were friends.

He was a tall guy with almost no hair on top, young, probably just out of shrink school. He'd explained schizophrenic behavior to Anthony, calmly, told Anthony that there was nothing to be ashamed of. That it was the same as having diabetes or alcoholism. That it was a disease, and a treatable one at that.

He'd said, "Look on the bright side, if you have to have a disease, this is a pretty good one to have, all things considered. You could have had cancer. You could have had AIDS. There're a million things worse for you than this. We can control this."

"Do you got it? Is it a fun part of your life?" Anthony had wanted to know.

"No, I don't. But neither did the people who diagnosed it in the first place, or the folks who came up with the treatment." The shrink smiled warmly. "You know who else doesn't have it? The people in the state institution, where you'll be going if I decide that you're a menace to yourself or to society."

That had caught Anthony up short. Had taught him something about the uses of power.

The problem was, you had to get it first.

Well, he had it now. And it was fun.

Babe was in the backseat, with the woman, and Anthony figured that at any minute he'd make his move. Anthony was driving slowly, going the speed limit, out of Chicago Heights and maybe ten minutes away from Cal City, from the bitch's house. All he had to do was keep Babe in line that long. He wielded a little of his power, the same way the shrink had done.

"I wouldn't do it if I were you," Anthony said. "In the first place, the car's a two-door. You grab me from behind and I hit the gas, off we go, into a tree. I duck and you go through the windshield, fuck up that million-dollar face of yours." That sounded pretty good. Now that the episode was over, he would be able to come up with some pretty good lines without jumbling his words all up.

Although he always had to be careful. The shrink had told him about that, about the illogical thought processes of a person with his disease.

"A stitch in time saves nine," the shrink had said. "What does that mean to you?"

"I have my ma sew nine buttons on my shirt. Saves it from getting ripped."

"See?" The shrink felt that he'd scored. "You have your own logic. Which is all right, so do all great thinkers!"

"A stitch in time saves nine," Anthony said now, and the woman, back there with Babe, said, "Spare the rod and spoil the child."

Anthony loved that girl. Talk about a stitch? He said, "In the second place, I've got a gun in my right hand. You make one move, and I shoot through the seat. Shoot you, or your girlfriend back there." Edna swooned. Anthony heard the little happy noise she made with her mouth, sucking in breath. "We don't want that to happen, do we?"

"Anthony, so far all you've done is shoot off that piece within a village boundary. It's still no big shakes, even if they should catch you, which they won't. Stop the car and let me go right now, and I'll walk home. By then you and Edna can be wherever you want to go, and you'll never hear from me again. For Christ's sake, Anthony, I'm your brother!"

"Why weren't you my brother when you beat me up three years ago?" Anthony had to concentrate on the road so he wouldn't wreck the car. This phony bastard had him seeing red. "Why weren't you my brother two hours ago, in that fucking tavern!" He began to sniffle, and he shouted out his rage. "You pushed me into the gutter like I was a dog! How come you weren't my brother then!

"And Ma, what about her?" Anthony paused, breathing hard. "You got any idea what you've done to her?"

"Anthony, listen to me. When she was pregnant, when the old man went away?"

"That wasn't me, that was the other one, the one she aborted, yeah, I know about that, you ain't telling me no secrets. It should have been you!"

"No, this was when she was pregnant with you."

"What about it?"

"She blew out the pilot lights and turned on the gas jets in the stove, Anthony, made us all lie down in the living room and was gonna kill us all, you along with us, in her belly—"

"She didn't!"

"She did. If it wasn't for John standing up to her for once, none of us would be here.

"I always loved you, Anthony, it was the old—"

"Shut up, just shut the fuck up!"

"All right, Anthony, I'm sorry."

"Sit back here, Babe," Edna said. "Come on, move over a little." Anthony looked in the rearview mirror and saw that she had her arm around him, was comforting him.

"Jesus Christ," Anthony said.

It took them a while to find the house. The woman didn't know exactly where she was unless he could find Pulaski Road for her, which seemed to be the center of her universe. He was losing his temper with both of them, was starting to think about shooting them both, after he got the money. One shot for each of them, *pow*, right through the head.

She was staring through the windshield, leaning into the seat, and she looked pretty scared, which was a good thing. Anthony didn't want to have to worry about the both of them. As long as she had Babe, she'd be happy.

"There it is, there it is!" She was like a little kid spotting Disney World. Goddamn retard.

"Which way do I go?"

"Two blocks down, go left. It's a one-way street, so you have to go down two blocks then make a right, come up on it from behind. You'll see it, it's a big white house, the biggest house on the block."

Ugliest, too. The house was filthy, with rotting shingles hanging down over the roof lip which hung over a porch that was made with now near-black wood. There was a rusted swing on the porch, and a small table that had a filthy glass top. The steps were uneven, and the walls seemed swayed. A couple of years, and the place would collapse, if it wasn't condemned before then. Which was fine with Anthony. He'd only need it for tonight, and after that he didn't care if a tornado came along and demolished the town.

There was a driveway next to the house, with a carport that had a door leading right into the house. Last year's leaves, blackened and smelling, covered the driveway's surface.

Anthony got out of the car first and held the gun down at his side, stepped far back into the shadows of the carport and ordered them out of the vehicle. Babe came first, then Edna. She waddled up to Babe and clung to him, protectively, her hand around his waist.

"Get in there, fast."

Through the back door and into the kitchen, where Anthony made sure the door was locked, then turned and saw his own breath. Which maybe was a good thing. The place stunk something terrible, and if it was warmer, it might be too nasty to stay around in for long.

There was crusted brown stuff all over the top of the two-burner stove. The linoleum on the floor was greasy, slippery. The walls looked as if they had once been white. They now had streaks running down them, as did the ceiling, as if brown rain had fallen in the room. The wooden kitchen table was covered with cut-up newspapers, yellow and molding.

Anthony sniffed and said, "How many cats you got?"

Edna said, "None."

"It's freezing in here."

"Waste not, want not," Edna said. "I turn everything off when I leave the house. Besides, it's been warm."

He found the door that led down into the basement, as good a place for them to stay as anywhere else, he didn't want them upstairs with him. He made Babe go down first and Babe had to push the broad away from him to get down there. She looked hurt.

"You, too," Anthony said, and she looked at him.

"This is my house, Anthony."

"I'm borrowing it for tonight. Like you're borrowing Babe."

"I'm not going to be locked down there!"

Anthony shoved her, hard, and she barely moved, and it was a good thing that she'd been standing right on the edge of the steps or nothing would have happened. As it was, her left foot moved about three inches and as she tried to set it down again it slipped over the edge of the steps. He shoved her again and then it was easy, her own fat ass took care of the rest.

He followed her down the stairs, watched her roll and tumble, her screams in his ears, and he stepped over her, saw Babe looking at him, paying no attention to Edna.

The walls were well under ground, with small windows set up high, made of thick block glass. You couldn't break them out with a sledgehammer. Perfect.

Anthony thought it had smelled bad upstairs, but down here, even with the cold, it was brutal. Musty and pissy. There were water marks about six inches above the concrete floor, and all the way around the basement wall the area under the marks was blackened and mossy. The place, it was a cobweb heaven.

"Anthony . . ."

"Don't say another fucking word unless I tell you to." He looked around. "Sit in that wheelchair and don't move an inch."

"I think the woman's hurt."

"Fuck her. Sit your ass down."

"I'm in my jogging clothes, Anthony. It's freezing in here."

"Waste not, want not," Anthony said. "I get upstairs I'll turn up the heat, maybe even get you something to eat, you don't give me a hard time." There was a work bench against the far wall and Anthony fought his way through the cobwebs to inspect it, found no tools. Not a screwdriver, not a wrench, nothing that could be used against him. The only working tool to be found was a rusted standup dolly against the wall, with two straps that clamped to secure whatever it was you were moving. The gun was getting heavy in Anthony's hand, yet he searched the basement thoroughly. This was his one shot at freedom, and he could afford to take no chances. He found nothing that could even remotely be used as a weapon against him.

When he looked over, Babe was sitting in the chair, but what was different about him? It was hard to tell, Anthony was distracted. The Rose woman was in a heap at the bottom of the stairs, holding her legs to her chest and crying like a baby. Curled up like one, too. "Shut up."

"But it's my *house!*"

"Not anymore, Edna," Anthony said, then realized what was different about Babe.

The chair was about a yard closer to the stairs than it had been.

"You're a cute one, aren't you?" Anthony said it but wasn't amused. He walked toward Babe casually, nodding his head. "Gonna make a break for it, with me right in the room?"

"This is wrong, Anthony. I live, I die, either way you're going down."

"Think so?" Anthony said. He was standing in front of Babe now, looking down on him. Far enough away from him so the skullsucker couldn't kick him. "I'm in the room with you, and you're trying to run. What're you gonna do when I go upstairs?"

"Maybe you better just stay down here with me."

"I've got a better idea."

Anthony stepped in close, holding the pistol in both hands, then smacked the gun as hard as he could along the right side of Babe's head, stepped back and watched his brother go through some sort of convulsion and then lie still in the chair. The Rose woman gave a startled shriek, then began caterwauling again. She was waving her hands around her head, then stopped, threw them over her head and curled up protectively, howling. He considered shooting her, pointing the gun and pulling the trigger. Through her lungs, to shut her up. Babe had blood pouring down the side of his face. Had he killed him? Jesus, it wasn't like in the movies. The side of Babe's head had immediately ballooned, swelled up huge. Blood was flowing, so he had to be alive. Yes, there, he was moving again.

"Think that'll hold you?" Anthony said, but Babe wasn't paying any attention. He was sprawled back in the chair, his eyes closed, his mouth now working without sound. It was strange, the right side of his head looked like it belonged to somebody else. Like a Halloween mask. Babe's hands came slowly up to touch that side of his head. His legs twitched, convulsively. Anthony watched, fascinated, wondering how the guy could just sit there like that without saying a word, without screaming. Was he that tough? Could he somehow be a threat? Babe went limp again, passed out from the pain. He slithered forward a little bit, but didn't fall out of the chair. Poor baby. Anthony went to the dolly and removed the two straps, went over to Babe and pushed him out of the chair, onto the concrete floor. It took some effort, but he was able to secure the straps around Babe's chest, tightly. He clamped them shut from behind, the clamps in the middle of Babe's scarred back. He stepped back, sweating, breathing hard. That should hold the son of a bitch.

He thought about shooting him, in the kneecap or in the elbow, where the pain would be enough that Babe could think of nothing else. But he didn't. Kelly might not be willing to pay for damaged goods. If Ma was right, and the broad was with Babe because of his ability to earn money, then he didn't want to hurt Babe too much. Kelly had to go to the bank.

Anthony walked quickly over to the woman and kicked her hard in the ribs. She tried to roll away from him and he dropped down to his knees, put the gun right in her face.

"Shut *up*! You shut up or I'll kill you." She tried, he had to give her credit. She clamped her lips shut and she put her hand over her mouth, and most of the noise now was coming out of her nose, along with gobs of snot. Kee-rist. Her eyes were squeezed shut and she was nodding her head up and down, trying to tell him that she was doing as she was told.

Anthony felt himself stiffening up. What was wrong with him? This woman was nothing like his ma, didn't look, act or smell like her. She was two Mas, for God's sake. Still, the sense of power was incredible. Delicious.

"You got no phone down here?" She kept her hand over her mouth, still making the scared sounds through her nose. She shook her head no. The great mound that was her belly was jiggling all around; he could see it through the open coat, the cheap fabric of the dress not hiding a whole lot. He looked away. He had other things to do.

"You gonna try anything stupid? I got to smack you, too?"

She took her hand away from her mouth long enough to say, "No, sir." He liked the way her voice quivered when she spoke. He remembered the shrink again, how he had tried so hard to make Anthony see the bright side of mental illness.

He said, "Look on the bright side. You got what you wanted. Babe's here with you."

"Sir?"

"What?"

"Are you—" She bawled a loud one, got herself back where she could talk again. "Are you gonna *kill* us?"

"Kill you? Are you nuts? I won't kill nobody don't make me do it. In the morning I make some money and I'm gone. Now pull yourself together, you got a phone call to make in a couple of hours." Anthony got to his feet, let his eyes roam down her body once again. What a pig. "And while you're waiting, you can do anything you want to him."

It didn't cheer her up, but she wasn't screaming now, either. It took her about thirty seconds to say, between sobs, "There's a first aid kit in the upstairs bathroom. Could you bring it down for him, please, sir? I want to clean him up. And there's a pad of paper in the drawer next to the kitchen phone, if you could bring that down, I'd appreciate it."

"Gonna write out a will?"

"A list." Her eyes looked off, and for a second she seemed about to smile. "Things he'll need after you leave. What I'll have to have to keep him happy."

"You love him, don't you, Edna."

"With all my heart."

"You unclamp those straps, lady, and I'm gonna shoot him dead."

37

elly was filled with anger, directed at the Hilliards, and at herself. How could she have been so insensitive? How could she have sat there throughout the night and cursed him, convicted him of drinking and sentenced him to divorce? He might right now be suffering, maybe even dead.

She wouldn't even let herself think such thoughts. If Babe was anything, he was a survivor.

She sat in the chair in his office, certain that the call would come in over his private line. She had a cup of tea in front of her, steaming. She took one of Babe's packs of cigarettes out of the carton on his desk, opened it and took out a smoke. Non-filter. Ugh. How many years had it been? She lit it, took in a soft, short drag, and choked. She stabbed the cigarette out in the ashtray. She'd get through this without a crutch, she'd be like Tim, strong and tough. Like Babe, too.

There was a core of toughness in her that ran deep and solid, and she knew it, never doubted that it was there. The problem was, she'd chosen a life wherein she'd rarely had to use it.

She'd work when they needed the money although there was never any doubt that they would eat. She'd call the phone and the electric company, the apartment managers and the mortgage people, convince them to extend the payment for another week, a month, but how much courage did that take?

She had to go back to the way she'd once been, or she wouldn't be able to do what had to be done. And if Babe died due to her weakness, she'd never be able to live with herself. She couldn't fold now, couldn't start smoking again or search the house for some tranquilizers. God knew Babe might have had some around, as manic as he could get. She wouldn't run down to the 7-Eleven and buy a pint of booze, either, to relax her, although the thought had crossed her mind.

She had to get back to the state of mind she'd been in years ago, single, a teenager, and ready to raise a child by herself. She'd had it then, and the years hadn't done anything to take that away, had only made her life easier. What was it Babe had said to her just last night, after they'd made love? "You're my strength, you know it?" he'd said.

She'd been his strength for thirteen years. Had pulled him out of the gutter and forced him to make something of himself. He was aware of this but it was something she'd somehow forgotten over the years, as she'd watched his star rise and she began to get older, less secure in her sexuality, in his desire for her. Well, fuck some foolish phone call from a girl he'd gone to grade school with. And fuck her jealousy over fans who hadn't yet tried to seduce him. She'd been his strength, had given him what he'd needed to get off that barbershop floor and into a good and decent and normal life.

And she'd be goddamned if she'd let him down now.

First, she had to get organized.

She would call John, who had a right to know. Tell him what she knew and swear him to secrecy. He stayed in touch with them all, wanting to be their friend, part of the family. He might even know of a special place their father had, some building rented or bought, where Babe might right now be. Then she'd search this house upside down, find every financial statement they possessed, find out to the penny how much she could get in the morning if they called. *When* they called. They would call. They'd have to. Because if they didn't it would mean that they'd only kidnapped Babe in order to kill him.

Stop! She sat back and closed her eyes, took a deep breath and let it out slowly. This wasn't fun and games time. This wasn't school. This was the real world, the world Babe had lived in and had introduced her into. For years she'd tried to pretend that it hadn't existed, but it was here all right. A violent world full of deception and death. She'd had the indoctrination and now would have to play the game if she were to keep her husband alive.

Babe had files with all their legal papers and bank documents over there in his closet. A safe with the insurance papers and the wills, the life insurance policies that might be worth something if she cashed them in. She'd have it all together and be ready to tell Babe's father their exact net worth when that telephone rang.

Kelly held out her hand, and it was steady. She picked up the phone and dialed John's number.

Tim had his badge in his hand when he walked in the door of the Tamburitza Tavern and he spotted Johnny Hilliard right away, sitting in a back booth with papers spread all around him. Johnny's head was down and he was writing something, and he looked half-pleased until he looked up to see who had come through the door.

When he spotted Tim he began to gather his papers together and Tim shouted for the bartender to freeze, for nobody to move, and he walked quickly to Johnny, ran the last few steps and let his badge drop to the table, grabbed him by his lapels and lifted him out of the booth.

He swung Johnny around, got some momentum going then threw him against the wall. Johnny's eyes were wide and frightened, and he didn't know what to do. There was a pistol sticking out of his waistband, and that gave Tim all the probable cause anyone would ever need. He drew his pistol and aimed at Johnny's chest, the .38 held in both hands.

"Don't move!"

Johnny obeyed. Tim moved in on him, pistol extended. He put the gun under Johnny's chin and pushed his head up, grabbed Johnny's pistol with his other hand, took it out and shoved it into his own waistband.

"Violation of parole, right there, asshole. You go back for the rest of your fucking life."

"What's the beef?"

Tim shoved the pistol into Johnny's throat, and Johnny's head hit the paneled back wall. "The beef? The *beef*? You punk! You drug-pushing piece of shit! Where's he at? Tell me where he's at and you might come out of this alive."

"You ain't no cop!" Johnny said it and his eyes filled with terror.

"Where is he!"

"Who, Jesus, tell me who you want!"

The coward. He was looking death in the eye and playing it cute.

Or was he? This was a man who'd turn in his kids, his wife, his parents, anyone, in order to stay free and above ground. Anyone who couldn't hurt him would go down in a second. He had the rep for being a standup guy, but that came to people smart enough to know better than to rat out the outfit, guys who were willing to do their time and get their reward when they got out.

The look in his eye was genuine. He thought that he was getting whacked out and he honestly had no idea what Tim was talking about.

Tim leaned into Johnny, spoke the words softly, with force.

"Babe, you cocksucker. Tell me where Anthony took Babe."

"Anthony? *Anthony?* What are you talking about? He ain't taken Babe nowhere!"

Tim pushed him away, stepped back. He looked over at the bartender, then quickly pointed the pistol at him. "Get your fucking hands above the *bar*, asshole!" The bartender did, in a hurry. Set them flat on the bar and closed his eyes. He swallowed, hard.

Tim grabbed Johnny by the collar and shoved him toward the door, stopped to pick his badge up off the tabletop, then came walking toward Johnny, fast. "Outside. We're gonna take a little walk."

The first snort was heaven, got Jerome's head in a maintenance condition. Back to normal, and the next one would get him high. He took it, snorted hard, both lines. He threw his head back as the dope hit his system, his mouth open, his eyes closed, a look of rapture on his face. He let his head down slowly, stared at the cocaine he'd cut into ten lines on the coffee table the way a missionary might stare at a vision of Christ, appearing shimmering on a jungle pond.

Jerome got up, stepped over to the bar, feeling the rush, the euphoria. This was some good shit. He got an airplane bottle of White Label out of the liquor cabinet and locked it back up, scooped some ice out of the bucket, and dropped it into a glass.

The TV was smashed and the carpet had a cigarette burn in it, and the maid had done up the room and nobody had said shit to him about the damage. They would put it on the bill and everything would be fixed thirty minutes after he checked out. It was good to be treated like a star.

Jerome poured the Scotch and took a sip, walked with it back to the table and took two more deep hits of the cocaine.

What was he supposed to do? Sit there all night and suffer? Milo would like that, the idea of Jerome trembling in fear, unable to sleep in his terror at the big man.

Well, fuck him. Fuck those two jumbo goons of his, too. The doors in this place were made of heavy steel, and he had both locks on and the chain in its slot. If there was one sound at the door that he wasn't expecting, he'd run into the john and lock the bedroom and bathroom door behind him, call security and while the off-duty cops who worked there fought the two bozos, Jerome would be on the line to the government boys. It would serve Milo right. Teach him a lesson about pushing people around. There was only so far you could go with a person before they started pushing back.

The phone on the table rang and he started, then looked at it. Don't punk out now. He was Jerome Spinell and he had a hit TV show and nobody told him what to do. As it rang a second time Jerome half-wished that it was his brother. He would be tough with Milo, let him know that he wasn't some lightweight Chicago outfit punk that could be pushed around forever.

He grabbed the phone and barked into it.

"Yeah?"

"Mr. Spinell?" The soft female voice was hesitant, maybe scared. "It's Hillary? From the elevator? I tried to call earlier but they said you were down taking a steam." She giggled. "And when I called there they told me that the health club closed at eleven."

"I had some business to take care of."

When she spoke now it was as if the ice had been broken, as if they were old friends. She might have been discussing her portfolio with her broker, her voice all cool and professional, but with the underlying tone that insiders used when speaking to one another. "I was wondering, well, I'm just in town for a couple of days, and I thought maybe we could get together."

Jerome stuck his finger into one of the lines of coke, stuck it into his mouth and rubbed it on his top gum, felt that gum go dead.

"Come on up, doll," he said.

"We could have a drink."

"I got a full-stocked bar."

"Tonight? Well, I guess I could come up . . . "

"Where's your boyfriend?"

"He's in the bathroom." She chuckled again, throaty and mysterious. "He may be slashing his wrists."

"I'll be waiting." Jerome hung up the phone and took the playing card he'd taken out of the pack in the desk drawer, pushed the remainder of the drug around on the table and cut it up into four healthy lines.

"Hillary," he sang. "Hillary, Hillary, Hillary, ba-by." He put the card down and slugged his drink, feeling better by the second, wondering how he'd play it.

If she asked him about the bruises he'd tell her not to ask him about his business until they knew each other better. It wouldn't insult her, but would shut her up and give her the impression that the affair was going to last. Jerome knew how to play it. You didn't last for parts of three different decades in Hollywood without being smart, without picking up a few tricks.

There was a light tap at his door and he sang her name again, softly, to himself, as he rose from the couch. "Hill-a-ry." He danced over to the door and slipped the chain off, unbolted it and threw it open, smiling.

The smile dropping when he saw Billy and Floyd standing there, Billy leaning over, those huge shoulders filling the doorway, about to insert a passkey into the lock. He rose, slowly, smiling at the look of abject terror on Jerome's face.

"Hey, you *are* home. Well how about that?" Floyd said.

Billy said, "Jerome, you been a bad, bad boy," pushed Jerome into the room and slammed the door behind him. "Hope you grew some wings since this morning, little brother."

Babe's head was on fire. He moaned, tried to move his head, stopped. The pain was nearly unbearable.

Use it, he told himself. Remember it and store it away, register this pain on the screen one day and you'll win yourself an Academy Award. He kept it that way in his head for a second, convincing himself that it wasn't a waste of his life and time, that he wasn't crippled, merely wounded. He could tell without moving that the side of his head was swollen, badly. It throbbed with his heartbeat, bringing on waves of pain. Slowly, holding his head very still, Babe tried to bring his hands up, to feel the side of his head.

His arms wouldn't move.

Babe panicked, struggled, felt the canvas against his upper chest at the same time that a sheet of white pain descended upon his skull. He stopped fighting and lay still, nauseous, fighting the urge to vomit. He'd die if he retched, he was sure. And maybe that would be a blessing.

He wondered if his brain was bleeding, if blood was slowly seeping out of a broken blood vessel or vein. He needed help, and he needed it fast. Slowly, carefully, Babe opened his eyes and moaned again. He could see nothing through his right eye, it wouldn't open even a sliver.

Then she was there, shushing him.

"Baby, it's okay." Edna had been somewhere to his right, probably watching him. Or maybe doing more. He could see that her dress was up around her knees, and it was wrinkled. The white pantyhose she'd been wearing were nowhere in sight. Her left breast was completely out of the fabric, pulled out of the bra. It hung there on her chest like an obscene rotting melon, the nipple staring at him. Her voice was soft and husky, and she was breathing hard and fast.

"I bandaged you up, poured iodine on the wound." She was standing beside him now, bending over him, holding his head in one hand and stroking his hair with the other. The smell of stale sweat covered over with perfume gagged him. He was still in the chair, but either she or Anthony had tied him to it somehow.

"How bad is it?"

"You bled a lot, and the whole side of your face is real swollen. You're talking pretty good, so your jaw isn't busted, but from the hairline to past your nose is all purple and black and red. He tied you up and kicked you to the floor, but I put you back in Mama's wheelchair chair, so you wouldn't catch pneumonia." She was looking at him, expectantly.

"Thank you," Babe said.

"I was so scared, honey, I thought he was going to kill you."

"He won't, if we don't piss him off."

She pushed his head back a little way, and Babe grimaced in agony. When he could open his left eye again, he saw that she was looking at him with disapproval. "You shouldn't curse, Babe. I don't like it when you curse."

What was she telling him? She looked mean enough, ready to do anything. Her hand reached out and touched his head, on the right side, and pushed once then covered his mouth with her hand as he cried out.

"We don't want mean old Anthony to know that you're awake, now, do we?"

"That hurt."

"Well, I'm sorry, but how else are you going to learn?" The huskiness was deeper in her voice, she was whispering to him, like a lover.

"Come on." She slid him down out of the wheelchair, onto the floor. Babe writhed in agony, the pain in his head spreading down into his face, down into his chest, Christ, how bad was it? How much damage had been done? Babe tried desperately to clear his mind. He had to worry about getting out of this alive, first. Then he could worry about mundane things like maybe having a concussion or a stroke.

"Babe," Edna said. She was straddling him, the breast hanging down, in his face. There were veins in it, everywhere. She pushed it into his face, settled herself down on his groin. With her free hand, she began to push down his jogging pants. "I've waited so long for this moment."

"Don't, Edna, don't do this. I'll call Anthony and he'll shoot us both if I scream too loud."

"You'll still not love me? How about if I stand up and kick you in the head? Then will you do what you're told?" She snorted. "Besides, Anthony can't hear anything you say or do down here. We can hear him, sometimes, but he'll never hear us. This basement was built to take tornadoes." She was rubbing him again, playing with him.

He was trying to buck her off, but he was too weak. There was no strength in his legs, and he felt strong waves of nausea, the effort exhausting him. He lay back, breathing hard. He hadn't moved her an inch. "Lady, take an ax to my fucking head if you want, just get your fat ass off of me!"

Edna was kneading him hard, rubbing his penis with her left hand. She ignored the insult. "See? How can you say you don't want me?" She lowered her voice and mocked him. "I've got proof that you do."

"Anthony!" Babe shouted it and she slapped him, hard, across the mouth, covered his mouth with one hand and his nose with the other.

"Don't move, don't make a sound."

Babe tried to wriggle, frantically tried to escape from under her, but the agony in his head increased with every move. He tried to will himself to be still, but he couldn't breathe, she was all over him, holding his nose and his mouth and he—couldn't—fucking—*breathe!*

She took her hands away, and he gasped for air.

"There. Now isn't that better?" Edna smiled down at him, lovingly. "You can shout and scream and do whatever you want. Even if you got outside, Babe, nobody in this neighborhood cares. When people shoot their guns around here, the neighbors just close the blinds and go back to their TVs." She looked at him, spoke sincerely. "It's because they've all lost God, you know."

Then she said, "It's because of the baby dying, right? That's why you don't want to do it anymore?" Her smile was heartbreaking and terrifying, full of understanding and compassion. She took his head in both of her hands, held it still while she leaned down, softly kissed his lips. "We can have *more*, Babe. There's no law says we can't." Her breath was rancid, and he tried not to wince.

"And besides, I've got a plan." She fought her way off him and he took deep breaths, dry-swallowed several times and tried to get his wind back. He watched as she tiptoed over to her coat and picked it up, saw him watching and turned her back on him.

"No peeking, now!" She fiddled with it, her backside shaking as she played with the coat. She turned slightly so the light would fall upon her coat and he watched her in profile, Edna's tongue between her lips, concentrating on her work. Her breast swung back and forth and she ignored it. Beneath it, he could see the large bra pushed down.

Babe put his feet flat on the concrete floor and tried to push himself toward the steps, stopped when the pain in his head became so great that he was about to scream out.

Who was he kidding? Even if he got to the steps, then what would he do? Hop to his feet and climb them? Anthony had smacked him hard in the head with a .45 automatic. He was lucky that the shock hadn't killed him, that the head hadn't been torn clean off his shoulders. He had a concussion, at the very least, and his arms were secured at his sides. Babe could feel the cold steel clamps pinching into the flat of his back. There was no way he could move without help. He lay back, his shorts down around his ankles, his penis exposed, shriveled now, lying against his thigh. He took deep breaths, and was encouraged when, after a few minutes, the pain in his head began to subside.

The first order of business was to survive. He would do whatever he had to do in order to survive.

Edna finished what she was doing and turned to him, her hand behind her back, grinning secretively. She came toward him, stood close but away from his feet, as if she were worried that he would kick out at her and try to hurt her. She brought her hand out and showed him what was in it.

A small pistol, a .25 or a .32. A revolver, for Lord's sake. A Saturday night special, up against a .45. If they caught Anthony by surprise, it might work in their favor. If he could get her to untie him and the thing didn't blow up in his hand.

"Give it to me, Edna. You'll never get him to drop his guard. He never knew you, never trusted you. Take these straps off and give me the gun, and I can take care of him for us, get us out of this. You call him down and tell him I'm dying. After that, I'm all yours, anything you want."

"First. We do it first."

"Edna, there isn't time. He might be up there calling the rest of my family, and if they come here, how'll we get them all? They'll be armed, too. The only way out of this is to free me and give me the gun and call him down here."

"I'll give you the gun." She held it out to him, waved it a little in her palm. Pulled it back quickly, as if his arms weren't strapped to his sides. "After you make love to me!" Edna walked over and picked the coat up off the floor, as unselfconscious about her half-nakedness as a small child. She put the gun back in one of the coat pockets, dropped the coat to the floor.

"Give me a son, Babe. Someone for me to love." Edna got to her knees before him, wiped at his forehead with her palm. She reached out and picked him up again, began to masturbate him. "Love me, Babe," she whispered. A plaintive wail. Then, a whisper.

"Love me, Daddy, please love me," the words spoken and then she dove forward and took him in her mouth, and in spite of himself, Babe found himself beginning to respond.

nthony used the upstairs phone to call his father and he let it ring twenty times before he hung up the phone. He punched in the old man's beeper number, got the tone then punched in Edna's number and waited, but his father didn't bother to return his call. If the old man was going to return it, he'd do it in five minutes or not at all. He was either sleeping or had the beeper shut off. Either way, there was no way Anthony could reach him. The East Side was only about ten minutes away, but he wasn't about to take the chance, risk driving over there and leave those two down there alone.

He dialed his brother Frank's number, and let it ring. The machine didn't pick up, so that meant Frank was awake. Anthony had a good image in his mind as to what his brother might be doing.

A woman's voice answered the phone, regal and demanding. "What!"

"Put Frank on."

"Frank's not *Frank* right now." The woman laughed, viciously. "He's *Francine*, ace." In the background Anthony could hear Frank pleading.

"That's right, beg, you insect." The woman said, "He *likes* to be humiliated, he's nothing but an unworthy piece of slime." Then she was speaking to Frank. "How about it? Is *this* humiliating enough for you?"

"You bitch, stop it, untie me and give me the phone!" Frank's voice was distant, pleading. Anthony could tell that he was crying.

"He's tied to the bed," the woman told Anthony, and he could hear Frank screaming in the background, "No, no, don't say that!"

"And I'm whipping his ass with a belt and sticking Pepsi bottles into him." She was hissing it now, enjoying herself. "Shut up, slave," she said, and disconnected the line. Anthony hung up, shaken.

And they all said that *he* was the crazy one.

He had half a mind to go over there right this minute. Frank lived in Hegewisch, less than five minutes from here. Could the two down there be trusted alone together for that length of time? There had to be somebody he could tell, somebody in this entire rotten family he could brag about this to, maybe even get help from.

He could use that right now, some professional advice. As with everything else that he'd ever gotten involved in, there were details here that he hadn't planned on, things he didn't know how to handle. For instance, how would he know if the line at Babe's house was tapped when Edna made the call? Would there be little beeps on the line, clicking sounds? Or should he drag her off to a pay phone, just to be sure? But if he did that, who would watch over Babe? And what if his brother died? What if his wife demanded to speak to him before she paid, and the son of a bitch was dead?

It had seemed so easy, before. He should have planned it more, should have waited for the episode to run its course and then sat down and figured this whole thing out. If only Babe hadn't shoved him in the street, into the gutter . . .

Anthony knew that he had to calm down. If he got overexcited the episode could come back, and the last thing he needed was the mental confusion that went along with that. He was in control now, had his faculties mastered. He had to stay this way. By now there was probably one of those All Points Bulletins out on his ass, cops looking for him to charge him with murder, and he didn't have time to play games. He had to get some help, and soon, from a professional criminal who might not have kidnapped anyone before yet who would still know how things worked. And his family was full of those kind of people.

What had begun as an ego thing for him had now become a matter of necessity. He'd wanted them to know that he was capable, wanted Frank and his father to respect him and admire him. Which was why he'd tried to call them. Now, as the impact of what he'd actually done began to dawn on him, as the fear crept into him, Anthony saw that he might truly need them. Or at least one of them. He didn't want to blow his one chance at total freedom. But he couldn't make the call, or have Edna make it, if he wasn't sure how to do it, could he?

He tried his father's beeper again, left Edna's number on the thing, then hung up in disgust. He was sure that his father would not return the call.

Anthony walked over to the door and slowly pulled it open, listened for any sounds. Began to worry when he didn't hear any. Was there a way out of there that he hadn't seen? No, that wasn't possible. The door squeaked and so did the stairs, but he tried to be as quiet as he could, taking the steps slowly, placing one foot down on a stair and then easing the other after it. The gun was in his hand, pointed straight ahead. If they were sleeping, he'd let them be, they wouldn't be any trouble that way. If she'd untied them and they were lying in wait, trying to trap him, he'd kill them both and make the call himself. He didn't have time to play games with these two.

Although he'd miss the broad. That Edna, she cracked him up.

He heard them before he saw them, Edna's whines coming to him when he was about four steps down the stairway. Animal-like groans, grunts like a pig that was eating. Then Babe's voice, moaning, whimpering, crying in anguish.

He saw them and stood stock-still, shocked at the sight of the huge bare white ass humping on down, on top of Babe's stretched out body. His brother was a big man, muscular, but his body was dwarfed by the sight of that big white ass, those hairy legs.

Anthony wanted to throw up. It was the most disgusting thing he had ever seen. And didn't that prick brother of his have this coming?

He hoped that she could keep it up all night, that she'd give him a ride that he'd never forget. Babe might not appreciate it, but what Anthony was seeing had just saved his life. There was no way that Anthony would kill Babe now. He had to live. So he could relive this scene over and over again in his mind, forever, and suffer.

It was getting late but Margie knew that she'd never be able to sleep, not until Anthony came home, or at least called. He was, truly, the last one left, the only one of her sons that she could count on for support, for love. For understanding. Even as sick as he was, even with his mental illness, he was more of a man than the other three wrapped together. He was her baby.

They had their problems, sure, but any two adults living together would have them now and again. The thing of it was, she'd had four kids and three of them were weak, sickening. She believed that it was due to a lack of a male role model in their lives. She'd done her best, but how much could a single woman alone in the world be expected to do? They'd all turned out like shit, except for her baby.

Starting with John. He had no spine, no backbone or balls. He was married to a woman who pulled all his strings, who told him what to do all the time. There was a time there, at the beginning of John's marriage, when he would come over and sit with her, bring a bottle over that he and Marge would share, talking about his life, his work, his problems. That bitch John was married to would call and Marge would answer the phone and act all innocent, tell her No, she hadn't seen John. She'd put a laugh in her voice and tell the woman that she really had no idea where her husband might be. Then hang up and she and John would have a good laugh. Then John got involved with that cult, that AA mind control thing, and he'd turned his back on his own mother, told her that he was tired of living with her shame.

What kind of shit was that for a son to say to his mother? Marge knew that John resented her, was jealous of her strength. He hid behind her skirts for most of his life and she protected him, and as soon as he read some pop self-help book and joined that cult, he had abandoned her.

Babe had potential, ever since he was little. The cops would bring him home now and again and sometimes she'd have to go to court, take out loans to pay the lawyers who would defend him and who would then write letters to her ex-husband in jail and tell him that they'd gotten the kid off the hook out of respect for the great Johnny Hilliard. What bullshit artists. Some of them had accepted another form of payment, and didn't Marge enjoy telling Johnny about them, when he was free again, trying to woo her back? Babe was another weak one, though, got one piece of ass, one lousy roll in the hay, then forgot all about his mother. Quit drinking and became a servant to that bitch, Kelly, who was one step below a prostitute. Having children out of wedlock like that, bastards that carried the Hilliard blood in their veins. Thank God that Babe had changed the name, that it was no longer Hilliard. There had been enough dishonor brought upon the name without Babe pouring on more. He'd turned his back on his family, and wasn't Mother's Day just a few days away? Who knew how many of those Marge had left? Her heart might break at any time, burst in her chest from the load of grief her sons had laid upon it.

Though Babe sure had no problems using his family when it suited his purpose, when he was trying to wring sympathy from reporters. Telling them terrible things about his childhood. Like she was nothing, a child beater. That ingrate. Babe was a lost cause. John, Frank, if they ever got over feeling sorry for themselves, they might turn out okay. But Babe was dead to her, him and his whole rotten family.

As for Frank, he never was much of anything but trouble. She would have to take time off from work to go over and sweettalk the nuns into letting him stay in school, even when he was only ten years old. Always fighting, bullying everyone around. In high school, forget about it. They hadn't paid much attention to Marge's pleas, to her appeals to their compassion. They didn't want to hear about how that boy had been raised up by a working mother who had to juggle a full time job and child-rearing responsibilities all at the same time. Frank had been expelled on his fifteenth birthday and he'd had to go to special night classes until he was sixteen, that or he would have to go to reform school. Marge had never felt close to him, no matter how hard she tried to love him.

Anthony had always been the one she'd pinned her hopes on, had dreamed about and for. He would be something, would make his mother proud. Slight and frail, she'd fought for him in the schoolyard and the courtroom, had made sure that the dumb kid stuff he did when he was younger wouldn't be on any record that could harm his chances for success. She'd been relieved when they found out that Anthony had a mental problem, an imbalance. For a while, there, she'd thought that he'd just gone bad, as her other sons had. With the proper medication, he could be controlled, his illness would not affect his life.

Sure, they had their problems. Anthony would whine sometimes because she ran around the house in her bra and panties, making coffee and putting on her makeup, getting ready to go to work. He would shake his head and get all upset, ask her why she had to act like that or else he'd get mad when she said fuck in front of him, and she'd tell him that he was as perverted as the rest of them, did he think that she was trying to turn him on? She'd tell him that she hadn't raised him to be some sexist, and how much would it bother him if his father ran around the house in his underwear? It was the same with her boyfriends. When Anthony would get upset he'd yell at her, all outraged because someone was having sex with his mother, and she'd yell right back, tell him that his father screwed every damn hooker that came along, and did Anthony see that as wrong? What was good for the goose was good for the gander, she'd tell him. It was her life, and she'd live it as she damned well pleased. She'd tell him that anytime he didn't like the way she lived, he could move his ass out.

Didn't he know that she didn't really mean it?

She smiled now, sitting at her kitchen table, her chin in the palm of her right hand. The house was spotless, the way she liked it. On the rare occasions when people came over she would make them take their shoes off at the door. She could see the marks from the vacuum cleaner on her living room carpet, even in the dark. The house smelled of cigarette smoke and incense, mingling nicely. The taste of bourbon and cherry juice was in her mouth, lingering.

When Anthony was younger and would step out of line she would teach him a lesson, would pack his clothes and tell him that she was taking him to an orphanage. Her smile broadened as she remembered the look on his face, the tough guy he thought he was coming into line with the frightened little boy that he actually was. She'd never laid a hand on him, in anger or while trying to straighten him out. Wouldn't let Johnny hit him, either. She had learned from the mistakes made raising those other three, and she'd used that knowledge to raise her baby properly.

The smile faded and Marge looked at the wall clock hanging to one side of her. After one, and no word from her son.

She had called the hospitals and the local jails, had left her name and phone number with those people just in case, so they could call in the event that an Anthony Hilliard was brought in, the victim of a car wreck or a crime. She'd called that bastard ex-husband of hers a half-dozen times, had left her phone number on his beeper four times and had called two taverns that she knew he drank in, but they'd said that he wasn't there, and one had even been rude when she'd told them that she had to speak to Johnny right away. "Sure, lady, his wife, right, I got it," the bartender at the Tamburitza had said. Some five-dollar-an-hour-and-all-you-can-drink lush talking down to her, making fun of her. If it hadn't been for her fear for Anthony she would never have wasted her time speaking to such scum. She hadn't tried the Tamburitza since. That shitheel wouldn't get a chance to make fun of her again, not in this lifetime.

Where was Anthony? Marge wondered, praying that he was safe.

There was a knock on the apartment door and she jumped, grabbed her breast with her hand. She relaxed, slumped a little and took a deep breath, relieved. He'd lost his key.

Marge stood and walked quickly to the door, looked through the peephole and saw that it wasn't Anthony. It was her oldest son, John.

She threw the door open, Marge now terrified, knowing the worst had happened. She was shaking her head in disbelief, in denial.

"Where's Anthony," she hissed.

John just stood there staring at her, sad-eyed and whipped. She suddenly believed that her baby was dead.

She hit John, hard, across his cheek, grabbed him by the coat and pulled him back and forth, out in the hall and not caring one bit what the neighbors heard.

"*Where's my baby?*" Margie screamed, and John got himself together, held her close as she began to sob, then walked her into her apartment, closed the door and told her.

Johnny believed without doubt that this guy was a cop now, and that made him feel a lot better about the situation. He was mad, yeah, and he'd have this guy's job before he was done, but he could afford anger now, now that he was sure that he wasn't being hit.

He'd thought that at first, when this punk had barged into the ginmill. Had been afraid that he was about to get whacked out, and who would care, who were the witnesses? The bartender? The rummies drinking their small drafts? Like hell. Johnny had used the device more than once himself, knew how easy it was to pull off the act, to play cop until you had your mark disarmed and beaten. The witnesses never looked at your face; their eyes never saw anything but the phony detective shield.

But this guy was a cop, or he wouldn't have taken the trouble to grab his ID off the booth before dragging Johnny from the bar. He was using an official police department pistol, too. The final thing that made Johnny sure that he would live was the simple fact that he was still alive. If it had been a hit, the guy would have killed him the second he got him outside of the bar.

Which he hadn't done. Not then and not now, with Johnny sitting in a cheap wooden chair in his own apartment, his hands cuffed behind his back. If this was a hit, even if Landini had ordered him hurt then killed, the beating would have begun by now, they wouldn't be talking about any dumb kidnapping, if there really was one.

Although it did sound like the kind of stunt that Anthony would pull.

Johnny figured that he finally had the guy convinced that he didn't know anything about it, the guy now being reasonable. Johnny didn't ask him his name, didn't try to manipulate any information out of him. He was a friend of Babe's, that was obvious, and after he was gone all Johnny had to do was to call the law and tell them what happened, let them work for him for a change instead of against him. It would all work out, and once Johnny knew this punk's name, he could use some of his old contacts to make sure that the guy did time. That kept his temper in check, the thought of this big tough guy in a state joint, more than likely locked up with people who knew him, what he was.

His phone rang and Johnny was surprised that the cop ignored it, didn't rush over to answer it, try to pretend he was Johnny. It proved to him that this cop didn't care about any gambling action, about any of Johnny's business. Only about Babe.

"You think I'd do something to hurt one of my kids? You don't know me, nothing about me. Every time I been gone, that family got taken care of." He didn't care a whole lot about what this cop might know or learn; he was saying nothing that could work against him in a court of law. Johnny knew all about the exclusionary rule. Even if this cop had the backing of the entire Justice Department, nothing Johnny said to him now could be used against him. It would be the fruit of the poisoned tree.

"Loving father, yeah, I know what you think of yourself." The cop was pacing, deep in thought. A big guy, good-looking in an Irish way. Johnny got the impression of a caged tiger, prowling, seeking a way out.

"Look, Anthony got a sick mind. The kid been in institutions. I been taking care of him, supporting him. But he got mental trouble. You uncuff me here, and I'll make a few calls, see what I can do. If I can run down Anthony, I can find Babe, if Anthony really got him. This ain't got to go no further."

"You mean to an arrest?"

"Anthony needs help."

"You'll get that for him?"

"I didn't last this long without knowing a few people, making a few friends. I can get Anthony into a place where they can take care of him."

"Me, too," the cop said.

"Come on, take the cuffs off."

"Shut up, Johnny—" the cop said, and was cut off when Johnny's beeper went off. The cop looked at it, hanging there on Johnny's belt, looked off, thinking, then came over and took it off Johnny, pressed the button to cancel the beep.

Johnny watched as the cop hit the digital relay, watched the crystals float in front of his eyes. He took a notebook out of his coat pocket and began to write down the numbers. "This is your wife's. She called—what—four times? Or maybe Anthony's over there, with Babe."

"Forget it. She wouldn't let anything happen to Babe. That woman, no matter what she thinks of me, she took care of them kids."

"Babe's got the bullet mark on his back to prove it."

"That was a mis—"

"Whose numbers are these, the fifth and sixth one?"

"Those are clients of mine, a couple parties I know."

"What's their names?"

"I can't tell you that, come on, be reasonable."

"I'll reason your ass into a federal penitentiary."

"You want to take me in? Let's fucking go, right now. You Nazi son of a bitch."

Had he gone too far? Johnny began to think that maybe he had. But the guy, in the last few minutes he'd acted so much like a cop that Johnny had started to treat him like one. The difference was, right now, Johnny wasn't in a station house somewhere, with phone calls coming.

The cop hit him, hard, one fast punch to the mouth. The chair tipped back and Johnny thought he was going over, it teetered, then it straightened out, and he settled to the table, the chair legs hitting with a bang like a pistol shot.

"Take the cuffs off me, try that."

"Okay."

The cop came around the back of the chair and unlocked the cuffs, threw them on the table. "You're gonna do a minimum two years for the pistol, Hilliard." He stepped back, walked around the table and sat back down in his chair. Johnny slowly brought his hands out in front of him, rubbed his wrists where the cuffs had been pulled tight. His fingers were beginning to turn blue.

"Before the night's through, I'll bet I can get you for conspiracy to commit kidnapping. Turn you over to the FBI and you go down for the rest of your life. There's two numbers here I don't know, the fifth and sixth calls. They're all you got to give me and I'm out of here." The cop smiled at him. "You tell me to let you loose, and I do, and you're still sitting there. What's that tell us?" He leaned forward, crossed his arms on the table. Johnny put his forearms on the table and stared back at him.

"We both know what you are. What you're made of. If there was a witness in this room you'd have had to jump me after that, just to keep your manhood. But it's just you and me, so you sit there, thinking of a way out of this. I'm giving it to you. Tell me who these people are, and I leave."

"You leave alone? I stay here, that's what you're telling me?"

"That's what I'm saying."

Johnny looked at him, tried to weigh his honesty. All cops lied to you until they got what they wanted, but this wasn't a situation where you get anything in writing. Absently, Johnny flipped the beeper around until he could see it, ran down the list of numbers, squinting at the readout.

He said, "That first one's Marge, and the next three. The fifth call's from a guy named Eldimiro Mendez, but I just call him Decaf. He works for me. The last number, the sixth one, I ain't never seen before, but that don't mean nothing. Lots of guys call me from bars, from pay phones. That's a Cal City exchange. There's a lot of bars in Cal City."

As he was holding it the thing went off in his hand and quick as could be the cop had it, was holding it away from Johnny so he couldn't erase the numbers.

"The Cal City guy?" the cop said. "It must be an important call. He just called again."

"You gonna stand up? Or are you just another lying fucking cop?"

"I leave, you stay."

"That's the deal."

The cop stood and stretched, the man tall and muscular. There was a lot of hard strength under that suit jacket. Johnny was glad that he hadn't jumped, hadn't tried to take the guy. He'd thrown Johnny around like a rag doll down in the bar, Johnny didn't think he would have much of a chance unless he came up behind him with a baseball bat, or else was standing in front of him with a pistol.

One of those two things would happen, and soon. But first he had to get this cop out of his apartment.

The cop finished stretching and Johnny looked away from him, so didn't see him reach across the table, didn't know he was doing it until he felt the cop's hands on his jacket, felt himself being dragged across the table.

The cop dragged him across the room and threw him to the floor at the base of a radiator. The heat was on and the thing was hissing. The cop slipped his cuffs around the middle coil and grabbed one of Johnny's wrists, clamped it tight, then the other.

"You motherfucker." Johnny spat it out.

"I leave, you stay." The cop stood and looked down at him. Johnny tried to kill him with a glare.

"And when I come back I'll have Babe with me. If I find out you knew about this, Johnny, that you were in on it? I'll take your own gun and blow your brains all over that wall."

"I *don't* know nothing about it!" Johnny screamed, but the cop acted like he didn't hear him, simply walked through the apartment and out the door, leaving it open behind him.

He started Babe's Lincoln then picked up the phone, called the telephone company security number. Hung up and tried another route. Tim called Information and found out that both numbers were unlisted. Nothing about this was going to be easy. He called the security number again, told them it was an emergency and he didn't have a subpoena yet, but he would in the morning, and he needed the names off two unlisted numbers, with addresses, right away.

"Your name, department and badge number?" the woman asked, and Tim had to pause, debate on whether to use his own. For all he knew they had a computer right there with every policeman in the six-county area locked in and on file. If he gave them a false number, there was a slim chance that they would know that it wasn't a fact, or that they'd call and check the department on a different line before giving the numbers out to him.

Could he afford to risk it? If she hung up on him, he would lose valuable time. But then again, if he had to, he could call the Park Forest station, have the dispatcher get the addresses for him. If he gave her his name and badge number, there'd be a record that he'd called, and they'd be waiting for a subpoena, tomorrow.

Tim gave her a phony name, department and badge number, and he'd be damned if it didn't work, she put him on hold for a second then came right back on and in a cool, professional voice read out the two names and addresses that he'd requested. He was only interested in the second address and name, and when the woman read it to him he had to take a second to get over his shock before he could thank her and manage to hang up the phone.

Kelly had the information on their CDs, their Money Market Accounts, their checking account and their savings accounts in front of her, and she was surprised that they had that much cash at their disposal. It was an amazement to her, the kind of money he was capable of generating. They'd put half down on this house when they'd bought it last year, and he'd told her that money would be tight for a while, but there it was, in black and white, all that money. How tight could money have been?

There were monthly deposits that were never under five figures, sometimes in the high five figures. Residuals from all the commercials he'd done over the years, which the advertisers had been saturating TV with since news of the big new series, *Street Babe*, had hit the gossip columns. Trying to capitalize on Babe's new-found celebrity. The cars were paid for and the mortgage was small, and for once in their marriage a hell of a lot more came in than went out. Three hundred and seventy thousand dollars was at her disposal, every dime of it in her name.

For once, Babe's paranoia would pay off, grandly.

Were they hurting him, torturing him to get information from him? To find out how much money they had? Kelly wouldn't put it past them. If they'd kidnap him, they'd hurt him, and if they'd hurt him, they'd kill him. So she couldn't try and bargain with them, couldn't lie to them in the hope that they didn't know their net worth.

There might even be more, if she could cash in the insurance policies. Those, and the wills, were in his safe.

The combination was in the top drawer of his desk, taped to the bottom of the desk top. She pulled it out, fumbled with the combination and opened it, saw the cardboard accordion folders there, the leather packet which held their wills. She took all this out and saw something underneath it, a picture sticking out of a torn envelope, and a piece of lined stationery inside.

What the hell was it?

Kelly took the papers in her hand to the desk, dropped them there then went back to the safe and took out the picture and what turned out to be a short note, held the picture up to the light, stared at it for a second.

The woman in the picture was incredibly fat, her pimpled face grinning hideously into the camera. She was squatting down next to a wheelchair. Inside the chair was a grotesquely gnarled child, his hands twisted in front of his chest, his body all bent and broken. His hair was cut short and he was smiling bravely into the camera.

The letter read, "*Our angle now in Heaven with God, Love and Kisses, Ur Edna.*"

A shiver ran through Kelly, up her spine through her shoulders and into her brain, and for a second she was afraid that she might pass out. Her knees buckled and she reached out to the desk for support, shook herself and fought to regain her composure. She let the letter flutter to the floor, turned the picture over so she wouldn't have to look at it then placed it on the desk.

Tim had said there had been a fat ugly woman with Anthony.

Kelly ran out of the office and up the stairs, through the kitchen to the bulletin board, where both their car phone numbers were pinned to the cork, for emergency use only. She grabbed Babe's, frantically reached for the wall phone then thought better of it. Up here, the children might hear her, and that was something she wasn't about to let happen.

Kelly ran downstairs and sat down in Babe's leather chair, her Christmas gift to him. She grabbed the phone and fought to regain her breath as she dialed Babe's number.

Got a busy signal.

She hit redial, got a busy signal again. Three, four, five times she called, and she was about to call the cellular phone company and have them break into the line when the phone rang under her hand.

"Yes?" Kelly said, letting the fear creep into her voice. She was certain that this would be Anthony, and she wanted him to think that he was in control, for now.

"Kelly?"

It was Tim.

"Edna Rose!" Kelly shouted. "The ugly fat woman has to be Edna Rose, there's a picture in Babe's safe, I've got her address too, Tim."

There was a pause, and Kelly heard Tim draw his breath in, sharply. He said, "I know," then told her what it was that he wanted her to do.

Johnny was sitting on the floor, trying to keep his forearms away from the radiator. The thing was hot as hell, and he couldn't reach the shutoff valve with his foot to turn the damn thing down. His wrists were forming blisters, and he wondered if they were beginning to cook. The cuffs were taking most of the heat, conducting it to his wrists, and he thought about trying to pull them free, tear the one radiator coil away from the rest and roll away from the steam, but he didn't know if he had that kind of strength left these days. Years ago, it would have been a piece of cake, but he wasn't a young man anymore. Besides, the cuffs were on tight. He might pull his hands off his wrists before he pulled the coil away from the others.

He heard footsteps on the stairway outside his door, soft voices speaking rapidly.

"Hey!"

The steps and voices stopped, then he heard squeaks, as whoever was out there tried to steal their way silently upward.

"I hear you out there!" Should he call to them for help? No. He was the only person who lived up here, there were no other apartments. If these people were trying to be quiet, to sneak up on him, they wouldn't be friends, people who would help him.

He said, "I've got a gun," and heard an accented voice reply.

"We do too, Goom."

Decaf. Thank Christ.

"Come in here, Decaf, what the hell are you doing out there, skulking around?"

They came in, the five of them, Ginger, Brownie, Oak, Nestle and Decaf. Nestle was carrying an empty plastic two-liter bottle of Royal Crown Cola. They walked in quietly, looking around the room. The other four of them searched the apartment while Decaf stood in front of Johnny, then squatted down next to him, staring at him quizzically.

"What are you doing, Goom?" Decaf said. He cocked his head one way, then the other, bemused, playing it cute for the others, the bastard. "Is this some kind of game you are playing, some sort of a joke?"

"A cop left me here, for Christ's sake. Come on, turn the heat off, then get the others to help you get me out of this."

Decaf pursed his lips, thought about this. He made a face then reached over and turned the heat valve. The hissing stopped, but the pain didn't. It would take a while for the heat to stop passing through the steel cuffs.

"What are you doing here?"

Decaf smiled, shyly. "You are not happy to see us?" He half-stood. "We leave then, is that what you want?"

"Come on, stop kidding around, I'm in trouble here."

"Worse than you know."

The other four had come in the room and were standing around, staring at him, all with some form of a smile on their faces.

"Do any of you fellows have blood rushing to your privates? Are you hor-ny?" Decaf said, and the others laughed. Nestle walked to the door and closed it, firmly.

"He too old for me," Brownie said, and Oak said, "Roll him over and pull down his drawers, let us see what he has to offer."

But Decaf didn't touch Johnny, just squatted there, looking down at him.

"You do not return my call this night."

"It look like I can return a phone call?"

Decaf nodded, amiably. "That make sense to me." Then he wasn't so amiable. "Landini say you kill our friend, Moca."

"No, uh-uh, Landini's a fucking liar, trying to tear us apart, keep us working against each other."

"He do that okay," Decaf said. He reached into his waistband and took out a long-barrel pistol, a revolver. He turned to Nestle, who handed him the plastic RC bottle. Decaf stuck the bottle onto the barrel of the revolver then looked at Johnny.

"I didn't kill Moca!"

"It no matter," Decaf said, "Landini say he double our pay if we make certain that you die." He smiled at Johnny, cheerfully.

"You always tell us, Goom, you say, 'Watch for you op-por-*tun-ities*,' did you not? You say, 'You never know when they will come your way.' Well, Goom, this look like a pretty good opportunity to me." He nodded again, confirming his words, then raised the pistol and fired.

"I don't know how in the fuck you can let that happen to you, honest to Christ I don't." Anthony was sitting in one of the dirty chairs in Edna's kitchen, his coat still on. He hadn't turned on the heat. His brother Frank was sitting across from him, hanging his head in humiliation. He was wearing a leather bomber jacket, a brown one, with a hood. He had a red sweatshirt on underneath it, with the name of a college across the front.

"You can't tell the old man, Anthony, he finds out, he'll kill me."

"I been hearing about it for years, you think he ain't? I just never knew it was like this, that it was as bad as this."

When Anthony had finally called him back Frank had tried to lie his way out of it and Anthony had had to chew him out. Then had at last given him Edna's address, told him to get over there right away. He hadn't told Frank anything over the phone, and now that Frank knew that Anthony was aware of his perversions, he wasn't in a position to argue.

Anthony had taken him into the basement, the gun leveled, steady as they walked down the stairs. Babe had been lying on the floor, naked and silent, staring vacantly at the ceiling. There was a pool of blood around his head, blood was soaking through the bandage. The right side of his head was misshapen, the size of a medicine ball. Babe's hands were white from loss of circulation; there were red marks on his arms, just above the canvas straps.

Babe noticed them, turned a shaking head toward his brothers, had mouthed unspoken words at them, his eyes pleading. For just a second, Frank's face lost its mask of embarrassment and he lit up, looked around the room. At the gigantic woman sitting in the wheelchair, scribbling onto the notepad, her tongue between her teeth. She looked up at them and smiled, said brightly, "Oh, hi!" then went back to her writing.

Frank said, "Oh, this is beautiful, this is just beautiful."

"What are you writing, Edna?" Anthony asked.

"My list." She looked up. "Things Babe's gonna need to get better." She held it up for them to look at. "See? I put down some vodka, even, for him. I don't approve of drinking, but he's going to need something to help him sleep until the pain in his head goes away."

"You think of everything, don't you?"

"You want me to make that phone call now, Anthony? The sooner I make it and you leave, the sooner we can get upstairs." She feigned a shiver, great blobs of fat jiggling. "It's *coooold* down here."

"It's better for his head, the cold."

"It is?" she said, believing him. "You want me to make that call now?"

"Let's wait until the banks open, so his wife won't be tempted to call the cops. So she won't have time to think."

Edna wrinkled her nose. "His wife. He never loved her, you know."

"I bet you're right."

"Would you bring me some food, Anthony, could you do that? I'm starving."

"Sure." Anthony walked over to Babe and jerked his head up off the floor roughly, held his head up by the hair. "What's your phone number, bro?" He put his ear next to Babe's mouth, listened intently. "Okay. Where do you live?" Listened again, then nodded and let Babe's head drop, shook his head in disgust at his brother's moan of pain.

"On The Hill, can you believe it? Hill living on The Hill? Come on, Frank, let's go upstairs."

Frank said, "Is he sick? Is he gonna be okay?"

"Of course he's gonna be okay. Edna's gonna take good care of him."

Now, sitting at the kitchen table, Frank's humiliation had returned, was wrapped around him like a blanket without warmth. Anthony felt the power over him, the control, and it felt good. Was this the same man who'd threatened to kick his ass the other night before Anthony had torched the Placebo Lounge? The same guy who made fun of the way Anthony transposed words earlier this night, before the episode had ended? Frank didn't look so tough now, that's for sure.

Still, Anthony needed him. There were things that Anthony didn't know, things that Frank could help him with. Details that needed to be settled.

He decided to let him off the hook.

"Ma's screwing some guys from work, you know. Taking them on two at a time. It's why I moved out."

Frank looked up, grateful. "We're all of us fucked up, ain't we, Anthony?"

"We'd'a had a real dad, we'd'a been all right."

Frank didn't reply, just looked at him, his mouth open.

"I'm gonna need some help here, Frank, and if you do what I want you to do, I won't say nothing to the old man, to Ma, about you."

Anthony knew that it would work. Frank hadn't even registered surprise that Babe had been in the basement, strapped down, his head busted. Hadn't even asked what had happened. He was so hooked on his own degradation that nothing else in the world mattered.

"What do you want me to do?" Frank said.

Babe was in and out, sometimes aware of what was going on around him, other times in a dream state, a trance. He liked the dream-world better. When he was there, he felt no pain. Not in his head, not in his heart. When he was awake and alert, his brain felt like someone was holding it over an open flame, and his mind, good God what that was going through.

He remembered her getting off of him, rolling away and sighing, Edna having gotten hers, satisfied and happy. He remembered her telling him that she loved him.

Had he asked her about the gun? He thought that he had, but he wasn't sure. He did remember Anthony coming down, seeing him and his brother Frank looking at him, Frank grinning and saying something to him in slow motion while Anthony said something to Edna. Their voices had sounded very deep and slow, dragged out and frightening.

He was aware though now, knew that his brothers had seen him like this, and he was filled with disgrace, with a great sinking sense of the loss of his manhood. The tears welled up in the back of his eyes and he fought them off. There was still some honor left. If he had never been able to cry in front of the woman he loved, he'd be damned if he would in front of this animal, Edna. He would die first, welcomed the thought.

Behind him, the fat, miserable woman began to softly hum.

The concrete was like ice on his back, and he realized that he was shivering. His teeth began to chatter and he made some kind of shuddering sound. Edna stopped humming and Babe heard her say something sharp and concerned, then he saw her, upside down, looking down at him with concern.

"Baby, are you all right?" She got down next to him, knelt there, her face anxious and worried. There were bruises on it from her fall down the stairs, and her hair was in disarray. But at least she was fully dressed now.

"My goodness, you're freezing!"

The words made him feel even colder, and Babe managed to smile at her, weakly. She put her hands on him and rubbed him hard, biting her lower lip.

"I'll have Anthony send down some blankets."

"Hates me." It took him a few seconds to get out the two words, and he didn't know if they made any sense.

"He won't give them to us, you're right." She leaned forward, close, and whispered in his face. "He's a fibber. He was supposed to turn the heat up and bring me something to eat, and he never did either one." She rubbed him, her hands on his legs now. He felt them tingling, burning.

Was he in shock? Was he dying? He wished that it were so. He never wanted to see that face again, ever. She would be doing him a favor by killing him. Quickly.

"Babe? *Babe?!*" There was panic in her voice and he heard it from a long way off. He knew that his good eye was open, but he wasn't seeing anything. He heard her move, sensed that she'd left him and he lay there, shivering, hugging himself and welcoming death, praying for it. He felt himself being turned over, then felt tingling, burning in his lower arms and his hands, realized that Edna had taken off the straps. He felt something cover him, something heavy and coarse that smelled terribly of stale sweat. Her hands were outside of the material, rubbing him. It seemed like she rubbed him forever. Babe pulled his hands up to his arms and rubbed the numb spots where the restraints had held him.

The coat, that's what was over him. And the gun was in the coat.

He knew it and suddenly wanted to live.

Upstairs, vaguely, he could hear the faint jingle as the telephone rang, and Edna muttered something in a frightened, high-pitched voice, then was gone, and a second later he heard her feet thudding up the steps. He felt a little better, the spasms of shivering were still there, but less intense than they had been. He didn't trust himself to sit up. He felt too weak. But you didn't need a whole lot of strength to pull the trigger of a pistol. Slowly, his fingers began to search the fabric of the coat, patting it, searching for the pocket.

Frank hadn't fallen for Anthony's bullshit for one single second. His first instinct, upon seeing Babe in the basement, was to get the hell out of there, and fast. It looked to him as if Babe was about dead, and that wasn't a rap he would ever do time for. You didn't catch early parole behind a murder, especially if the murder victim was a celebrity like Babe. It didn't matter what Anthony knew, it didn't matter what he told the old man or the old lady. They could think what they wanted. Frank had gone over to the Cal City house just to try and reason with Anthony, and had fallen into more than he'd ever expected to get into in his lifetime. This psycho brother of his, he was finally over the edge. But Frank wasn't Johnny Hilliard's son for nothing. He knew how to play it when the going got tough, how to act. How to keep your face a stone blank and never let them know what you were thinking. You did it with the cops and you did it with the gooms, and you did it with everyone who might someday hurt you if you made a mistake in front of them just one fucking time. Frank had given Anthony exactly what Anthony had wanted, and Anthony had been so full of himself, so full of power, that he let Frank into the game. Had felt so dominant over his brother, so in control, that he figured he could manipulate Frank into doing whatever he wanted.

What Anthony would never know was something Frank learned years ago. The one who was being dominated was the one who truly held the power.

And when Anthony had told him what he wanted Frank to do, Frank hadn't been surprised. It was the way a new player in the game worked it. They believed that their power over you extended beyond a couple of minutes at a crack.

The kid, he was a dummy. Went on and on about the woman who had tied Frank up, had brutalized him. Didn't know that the second she had let Frank go he had beaten the shit out of her and kicked her out of his house, made her leave without paying her. Frank knew that she'd be back, on the phone begging him to forgive her. She'd gotten carried away, had acted like an amateur, the same way that Anthony had. Well, that was all right. She'd get over it, and so would Frank. As long as the old man hadn't called, as long as it hadn't been him on the phone, Frank could survive.

Besides, after tonight, who would the old man believe about anything, if it came down between him or Anthony?

Anthony's credibility would be a little weak, to say the least. Kidnapping Babe and holding him hostage, half-dead and in shock in a basement in Cal City with some crazy bitch there watching over him. Wanting Frank to go and sit at Babe's house, make sure that Kelly didn't call the cops. Well, Frank was on his way elsewhere, and it wasn't to Park Forest.

He was heading to the East Side, to get the old man and a couple of pistols. Then they could go back and take care of things, get out from under him before that madman Anthony buried them all.

abe was dying. Edna believed that because when she looked at him all she could see was the white of his one eye. It was open, wide open, but those famous black eyes were nowhere to be seen, replaced by swollen, red and bleeding closed flesh on one side and a single staring orb of white blankness on the other.

She got up and looked around the basement for something to cover him with, grabbed her coat and ran over to him, took off the straps and then covered him with the coat and began to rub him through the fabric. She was whispering to him, begging God to let him live. He had to live, or her entire life meant nothing. There, he was responding, lifting his fingers to his arms and rubbing them.

Just two weeks, God, just give us two weeks. In that amount of time she would either have him completely in love with her or, she vowed, she'd turn him loose, allow him to go back to his wife.

He hadn't wanted to make love to her, but he'd felt like a light pole inside her, so he must have wanted her, badly. His thing had worked without a problem. He was more than likely just a little embarrassed that she had to take care of him, that he couldn't have gotten stiff without her help. Men were like that, she knew.

She rubbed and watched him shiver, his entire body one big blanket of gooseflesh.

She would put him in the wheelchair and walk him down to the cemetery, show him their baby's grave. Spoon-feed him soup and mend his broken head, put a blanket over his lap and hold his hand while he watched the television. Just two weeks, was that too much to ask for?

Why wouldn't they leave? Anthony and his friend? They could make their phone call from anywhere, from any old phone, so why did they have to sit up there in her doggoned house?

If Babe was dead, would he still be any good to them? If they could call from a pay phone, what difference would it make?

Edna was beginning to panic. She had rubbed for several minutes now and there was still no reaction from Babe, he was still shivering like crazy, his teeth were still chattering. She began to cry, hysterically. She bit her bottom lip so Anthony wouldn't hear her.

Edna heard the phone ring and started. Who would call her at this hour? No, the call might not be for her. It could be someone returning Anthony's call. She had to know who it was. Had to find out if the call was for her or for Anthony, because Babe was dying and if it was for her then maybe Anthony and the other man would get scared and leave. Edna hadn't cared much about how long Anthony would stay until Babe began to shiver, began to die. Before that happened, she had been happy with her list, her notepad of things that she would need to make Babe happy. But now it was imperative that he be gone, that she be able to get Babe into a warm bed, somewhere where he could recover in peace.

She got up and ran to the stairs, mounted them as quickly as she could. Her legs were in agony, from all the walking she'd done in Park Forest. There was a large bruise on the outside of her leg, where she'd hit it on one of the stairs when Anthony had pushed her down the steps. That had caused her a lot of pain, that and the workout with her Babe and now she blushed, thinking about sex with Babe. It had been incredible, better than it had ever been with any man before.

She stood at the doorway and was filled with remorse. Had her loving him caused him to get so sick? She'd sweated him up enough. Edna put it out of her mind, she had enough things to worry about.

She heard Anthony saying, "What? Who the fuck is this! God-damnit, you better tell me!"

He sounded terrified. Well, good for him. Mr. Snot Nose. Sitting there in her house acting like he owned it. Edna having to be nice to him and pretend she liked him because he had the big gun. Well, she had one, too.

The gun. It was in the coat.

And she'd used the coat to cover Babe.

Edna turned and ran down the stairs, saw the gun in Babe's hand, just about clearing the coat pocket. She made it in time, turned it out of his fingers and he gave it up without a struggle, too weak to fight for it.

"You're a bad boy, Babe Hill!" He was staring up at her, pleadingly. He was so cute, it was impossible to stay mad at him.

Well, she had the gun now, and she would protect her Babe. Anthony had already proven that he was nothing but a big fibber, so how was Edna to believe that he would leave in the morning like he said he would? He might plan to stay there the rest of the week, or a month, or forever. Well, she'd call him down here and—

She wouldn't have to. She heard the bolt fly open and the door swung wide up there, and she backed against the basement wall at the same time that there was a mighty crash and all hell and damnation broke loose.

Kelly sat at Babe's desk for only a couple of minutes, thinking, determined, a cup of tea at her elbow. She'd sip from it compulsively, quick sips, the liquid burning her lips, her eyes never leaving the phone. She wanted to be with Tim, near him, and she could do this job from the car phone instead of from the safety of her husband's office. She wanted to be with him, there to help Babe, to kill all the people who had him captive and to hold him close to her, alive and well. Tim wanted her to wait until he was in position, then call Edna's house, distract Anthony while he himself stormed the door. The plan sounded vague, not truly thought out.

If Babe was dead, if they'd hurt him, she'd kill them all, no matter what Tim said or did. She'd take a gun out of one of Babe's hiding spots and go down to whatever jail they were in—the grieving widow who wouldn't be searched—and she'd ask for just one moment alone with them, to see the animals who had killed her husband. Maybe they'd even let Tim take her back to look at them. Then she'd take out the pistol and she'd—

Do nothing. That's what she'd do. To kill them would be to become one with them, and maybe she could live with that, but what about the boys? No, she wouldn't even think about it. Babe would be fine.

The phone rang and she got it before it finished its first ring.

Tim said, "There were two cars in the driveway, but one just left. It was Frank, alone, I saw him. So with any luck, Anthony's in there with the woman and Babe and nobody else."

"Why didn't you stop Frank?"

"And alert Anthony? Frank can wait. We can get him later, after everyone else is called in."

"How long do you want?"

"I'm parked a block down and a house over. Give me time to search the grounds, look things over, say, a half-hour from—" He paused, and Kelly looked at her watch. "Now!"

"Tim, call the police, right now, from the car phone. They'll get the SWAT team out and handle it, they've been trained for it."

"That what you want, Kelly? I can't do that. It's too late now."

She had to think about it. If the SWAT team were called, it would take hours before she would know if Babe was safe. They'd bargain, call and discuss options with Anthony, send him in pizza and beer and she wouldn't know about her husband's safety until God knew when.

Then, too, there would be the news people, swarming all over the place.

Kelly said, "I'm sorry. Go ahead, Tim, but you bring Babe back to me."

"Twenty-nine minutes," Tim said, and disconnected the call.

Kelly sat, stared at the phone, then stood and pulled the chair over to the air-conditioning vent in the far corner. She stood up on the chair and pushed the vent inward, reached around inside until her hand touched steel. She pulled out a revolver. Got off the chair holding the gun gingerly, and played with it a little, checking to see where the safety was, how it opened and closed, making sure that it was loaded. How could something so simple be an instrument of death?

Sure that she knew how to work the weapon, Kelly ran for the stairs. Babe was her husband. Not Tim's. He would need her, after the rescue. In a half-hour's time, at the time that she was supposed to call Anthony, she could be in Calumet City if she really hurried.

Anthony was pacing when the phone rang, wondering what he should have the bitch say to Kelly on the phone. He stared at the ringing phone, afraid. If he answered it and it was one of Edna's friends, what would he say to them? He knew. He'd tell them that he'd get her, and he'd do so, shove the gun in her back and tell her what to say, whisper it to her as she talked. Besides, it was probably the old man, just got home and decided to call the numbers on his beeper.

He shoved the gun down into his waistband and walked over to the phone, picked it up off the wall jack.

"Hello?" he said, and a female voice came back to him, all-knowing, laughing at him. Along with the voice he could hear rushing wind, somewhere in the background, as if the woman was calling from a pay phone.

"We know you've got Babe, Anthony, and we want you to know that you're dead. Look out the front window if you don't believe me." The line went dead in his hand and he held it away from his ear and stared at it, shook it in disbelief. "What? Who the fuck is this! You better tell me!" There was a click, then a dial tone.

Anthony hung up and heard the sound of heavy steps on the staircase leading to the basement. Edna had been listening.

Had she done it? Was there a downstairs line that she'd used to call him, try and scare him off? It had to be. It was either her or his brother had put one of his bitches up to it, they were the only two who knew that he was here, them and Babe. Would Frank do that to him, have some broad call him to try and scare him? He didn't think so.

One thing was for sure, there was no way on earth he was going to go and look out that front window. Over there, he was away from the hostages. If there was a sniper out there, a bunch of cops with guns, they would take him out unless he had one of the hostages in front of him.

Anthony began to panic. He ran to the basement door and threw the latch, was opening it wide and had his foot on the top step when the back door was kicked in and glass came flying in all over him.

Tim watched Anthony from the back porch window and he knew that he'd played it all wrong. He'd been certain that a mental case like Anthony would go straight to the front picture window, to see who was out there waving at him, and when he did that Tim could kick in the back door and give the kid a chance to drop the gun.

There had been other options. He could have shot him through the window, the man had a gun in his hands and Tim would be in the right if he had. But it wasn't something that he could do.

He watched as Anthony hung up the phone and pulled the piece, stood there indecisive, then he heard footsteps behind him and Tim turned in fear, the pistol at the ready, and he almost shot Kelly, who was running up the drive toward him.

"What are you doing here!" A frantic whisper escaped from Tim's chest, fear hanging off each word. He lowered his gun and looked back in the window, to make sure that Anthony hadn't heard him. The little idiot was still looking toward the front door, his pistol in his hand. When Kelly spoke her voice was in his ear, and there was not a trace of fear in her voice, only determination and an incredible level of strength.

"That's my husband in there," Kelly said.

Through the window Tim watched as Anthony made up his mind and went over to the basement door, and when Tim was certain that that was where he was heading he reared back and hit the door right at the lock with a front kick, and it smashed inward and slammed hard against the kitchen wall. Kelly was through the door and shouting before he put his foot back on the porch.

Anthony went down the stairs backwards, screaming, the pistol pointing at the basement doorway. "On come, motherfuckers you!" He was doing it again, the episode was back. He stood at the bottom of the stairs, angry because he hadn't pulled the door shut after himself. There was a lot of commotion up there, a woman's voice calling him dirty names, a man's telling her to get her ass back outside.

Was there only one man? One woman and one man? Anthony tried to focus his attention on the doorway, but it was hard. The wind was blowing in his mind, the tunnel wind coming on strong. What was it telling him, the voice? He fired a shot at the doorway, as much to clear his mind as to try and hit somebody, whoever was up there.

"Babe kill," he said. The voice was telling him to kill his brother.

Well shit yes, why not?

Anthony said, aloud, "Him I'll kill!" and turned, felt a bee sting his shoulder and heard a loud snap. He stepped back a little, stunned.

"No you won't!" Edna shouted at him. "I won't let you hurt my Babe anymore!"

"Fuck the what?" Anthony's mind was a mass of confusion, and he shook his head, tried to clear it. What had happened to his left shoulder? The gun was in his right hand, and he lifted it. That arm still worked. He couldn't raise his left, though. The wind was rushing around in his head madly, swirling as never before. It wasn't an unpleasant feeling. He faintly smelled the scent of freshly cut roses.

He saw Edna standing against the wall, holding her hand out toward him, as if in offering, wanting to help him. He saw fire come from her fingers and felt a hard blow to his stomach, as if someone had punched him one, hard. He staggered back, but didn't go down. Something hit him in the back, drove him forward, sapped his strength. He saw sparks fly off the wall beside Edna, and wondered where they had come from. He wasn't shooting at her.

The bitch, Edna, she had a gun. Was shooting at him. As was someone behind him, up there in the house. Oh, God. A shiver of fear raced through him, and then was instantly gone.

Anthony, weakening, suddenly wasn't afraid. In fact, he thought that was the funniest thing he ever saw in his life, fat Edna Rose with a piece in her hand, had to be a .25, at the most. Was he dying? He didn't know. What he did know was, he wasn't going to die alone.

He raised his right arm and it was very heavy, waving there in front of him. Something else slammed into his back, but he hardly felt it. In his head things were settling down, except for the wind, the voice. "Shoot," it told him, and he tried, but he was having trouble raising that damn hand.

He saw Edna come off the wall and walk toward him, quickly, like the nuns used to do in school when they were about to whip your ass, Edna racing toward him, her face stern and determined, walking rapidly. She held the gun straight out at eye level just as Anthony managed to get his own pistol raised. He heard footsteps running down the stairs but paid them no mind, every tiny bit of his strength was being used up, just holding the gun on the woman. He laughed at her, a small, unbelieving laugh.

Then he pulled the trigger, felt the gun jerk hard in his hand at the same time that he saw the bare beginning of flame racing out from the barrel of the tiny gun Edna Rose held pointing at his eye.

Tim had stood at the top of the stairs and had determined that there were two separate weapons down there. There were two people with guns down there, which was just fucking great. This maniac Kelly was breathing hard at his back, pushing at him, wanting to go back into the doorway and shoot some more, unaware that she had emptied the gun from the top step before Tim had been able to subdue her and push her behind him. She was yelling in his ear, trying to get to Babe. He had to forget about Kelly, had to think this through.

Anthony had a .45 or a 9-mm, that was for certain. Tim had seen it, from a distance of a few feet, staring through the back door window. They'd also had it fired at them, from down there in the basement, as they stood against the wall, preparing to head downstairs. The bullet had embedded itself in the plaster of the far kitchen wall, tearing through the air between himself and Kelly. It had taken a hell of a lot of the plaster out with it. So now what was he supposed to do?

Kelly was crying now, feebly hitting his back. Tim put it in the back of his mind, she couldn't hurt him, so she wasn't important. Those people down there, the ones with the guns, they were all that he could think about right now.

He waited a second, then spun into the doorway and raced down the stairs with his gun held out in front of him in both hands, doing the best imitation that he could of a combat stance while running down a stairway crouched down and terrified. He saw the woman who had to be Edna walking fast toward Anthony, saw that she had a pistol in her hand, much smaller than his. There was blood coming out of Anthony's back, spilling out of several holes in his shirt. Babe was a flesh-colored blur on the floor. Neither gun was pointed at him. Tim leaped down the last steps, landed in a crouch on the basement floor just as both guns fired, and both bodies fell.

He had Johnny's pistol out in front of him, somehow still thinking that they could get out of this without attracting attention to themselves, but there was no way that could happen now. Babe would have his face splashed across the front of both city newspapers, and Tim, well, he knew that he was going to lose his job. And might wind up in jail in the process. Behind him, Kelly was racing down the stairs, not paying any attention to the fallen bodies. She gasped and ran to her husband, held him up off the floor, crying.

Tim walked cautiously over to Anthony, kicked the gun out of his hand and it slammed against the wall. Not that he'd had to. The kid was dead, and he hadn't died easy. There were half a dozen little holes in his chest, exit wounds from Kelly's gun, entrance wounds from Edna's. Edna's gun was lying there at Tim's feet, and he turned to Babe, saw that the woman was crawling toward Babe, inching her way across the concrete. Kelly and Babe were ignoring her, hugging each other tightly. Tim stepped over Edna, and winced at the sight of Babe's face.

He crouched down next to Babe, pushed Kelly's hand away and gently touched the side of Babe's head. Babe's one eye was open, staring up at him, the coat pulled up to his neck. He was shivering and it was hard to make out what he was saying, Babe's teeth were chattering so bad.

"Thank God, oh, thank God you came."

"Did you doubt it?" Kelly said. There was anger in her voice, and her hand never stopped stroking Babe's forehead. Kelly was crying, shaking her head.

The woman, Edna, was moaning now, right there next to Babe, and Tim looked over at her with contempt. She was dying. He felt nothing but disgust for her.

"I'm gonna call an ambulance."

"No!" Babe said. "No doctors, no cops." Kelly looked up, spotted Edna Rose.

Edna was straining, using the last of her strength. Tim saw her raise her arm, let it drop on Babe's chest. He went to push it away but Babe lifted his hand, his face now set with a look of pure hatred. Kelly looked down at the hand with an expression on her face that Tim hoped he'd never see again. Hate was there, stamped on hard, pure, raw and ugly.

Kelly slapped at the arm, pushed it off her husband.

"Leave him alone, you bitch!"

Edna went completely limp and her arm flopped over, onto the floor, her hand and arm still rolling from the violence of Kelly's slap, rolling back and forth, back and forth on the floor. Then it was still. Babe closed his eye, bared tightly clenched teeth then opened the eye again, looked up at his wife and Tim.

"Help me up," he said.

"Just stay there," Tim said. "I'll get an ambulance, Babe, you could be bleeding up there."

"Bullshit you will." Kelly was no longer hysterical; that steel tone was back in her voice. "We've got to get him out of here."

"What about the door? I kicked it in. There'll be bullets in his brother from two different guns. We can't pretend we were never here."

Kelly said, "That's a problem for the Cal City cops, Tim. You wanted others in this, you should have brought them in when Babe got grabbed. Now help me get him the hell out of here."

Babe had pushed himself into a sitting position, and Tim and

Kelly helped him up, helped him settle into the wheelchair. Tim grabbed Babe's jogging shorts, and the two of them helped him into them. Tim looked over at Kelly, tried to see if she'd figured out what happened, but she was intent on her husband, on helping him. Her face showed nothing more than a little nervousness.

But Babe saw it, the look that Tim had on his face. Was staring at him hard with his one working eye. Then the eye closed, and Babe's face grimaced in anguish.

He knew that Tim knew.

"I haven't touched anything," Kelly said, "and your finger-prints wouldn't be on the door. Now put your arm around this man and help me get him the hell out of here." Tim didn't have time to think, just did as he was told. He lifted Babe out of the chair and steadied him with an arm around his waist while Kelly grabbed Babe's shoes and socks, shoved them into her coat pockets and ran up the steps ahead of them.

They stopped at the front door and Tim stepped out, looked both ways, didn't see any lights on in any of the houses. Hadn't anyone heard anything? Was the house that soundproof, or did the neighbors just not care?

Beside him, Babe was stiff, silent. Tim could feel the emotional coldness rolling off his friend.

"It's gonna be all right, Babe," Tim said, and did not get an answer. Tim looked over at him. Babe was looking straight ahead, his mouth set tightly.

"It's not the end of the world. No one will ever have to know."

"Know what?"

"Babe, I *smelled* it on you, for Christ's sake."

Kelly's car, without lights, pulled to the curb. Babe pulled away from Tim and walked unsteadily over to it, fell into the front seat while Tim got into the back.

"Around the corner, Kelly, I parked Babe's car there."

"He's got my Town Car?" Babe spoke to his wife. Tim hid his pain, tried to make light of the situation.

"Yeah, I know, Kelly doesn't even drive your Town Car."

"That's not what I meant. I left it at the track and that son of a bitch was shooting at me. I thought by now all three news stations might be announcing that I was kidnapped."

"Nobody knows, Babe," Tim said, as Kelly pulled the car over right next to Babe's Lincoln. When Babe spoke his voice was ice, dead sounds making sense, a computer program speaking.

"And that's the way it's got to stay, Tim, give me your word on that."

As if he had to ask.

Frank couldn't believe his eyes, could not believe what he was seeing. His father was handcuffed to a radiator, one bullet hole in the left pupil, the old man lying there dead. Staring up at Frank with wide round stuffed-animal eyes. There was blood coming out of his mouth, already dried on the floor. His tongue was out of his mouth, hanging out between his teeth, loosely.

Frank got out of there, racing down the stairs, whimpering. He was crying like a baby before he even hit the street.

The fog had lifted, and Frank drove slowly and carefully through the East Side streets, not wanting to attract any attention to himself. He didn't want the cops being able to put him in this neighborhood.

"Daddy," he said, and sniffled.

If it was Landini, if the mob had done this, they'd be after Frank next, because they knew that Frank worked with his father.

The old man had outdone himself, had gone crazy with the Parker thing, with killing Moca. Landini would know who else had been in those deals, who knew about them and maybe even helped the old man out.

There was nowhere he could go. No rock big enough to hide under. Landini would find him and he would be dead.

He didn't blow all his money on broads and drinking, like the old man did. Didn't pay for Anthony's way in life either. That had to be a big financial drain on the old man.

"Pa," Frank said, still crying.

He could get his hands on maybe eleven grand in the morning, and he could take off from the bank, drive off and never look back.

Thank God Anthony had called. In his heart, Frank was sure that Landini's men were even now at his apartment, waiting for him.

Where could he go? Where could he be safe? There was only one place. Ma's house. He would want to be the one to tell her about the old man's death, anyway. Seeing as he was the only one of the kids who was really close to their father.

Frank got his crying out of the way on the short drive to Homewood, pulled into the parking lot of his mother's apartment house and walked in a daze to her door. She was going to have a heart attack. It was almost four in the morning and she'd be getting up in an hour, having to get ready to go to work.

What would he say to her, what would he do?

He rang the buzzer and heard a chair scrape back, and was surprised. Was Ma already up? His brother John opened the door.

"John?" Frank was in shock. "John, what are you doing here?"

John was really lit up, drunk out of his mind. He staggered back and Frank entered the apartment, saw his mother sitting at her living room table, an empty booze bottle in front of her, a half-full replacement on a coaster next to it.

"C'mon in, join the party."

Hell. Frank saw her drunk more often than he saw her sober, but she was worse than he'd ever seen her since he'd moved out of her house. She was about to fall out of her chair. Maybe this was a good thing, maybe John had picked a good night to fall off the wagon and keep Ma up all night drinking. Frank could tell her what he had to tell her and then go to sleep in Anthony's room, and before she even got up in the morning he'd have cleared out of there, forever.

"You part of the deal?" his mother asked. Frank pulled a chair out and sat down, warily. "You part of the kidnap attempt?"

"Oh, Jesus."

"John's been here all night, waiting for the call from Kelly. We've called your father, we've called you, and he won't let me call the FBI." Ma was in her favorite role, the martyr. Frank sat back, took a deep breath as John came around and sat down next to him, picked up his drink and drained it. He was staring at Frank in a way that Frank didn't care for, and for the first time in years Frank realized that he was a pretty big mother. Mean looking. A Hilliard, all right.

"Pa's dead," Frank told him, wanting to wipe that tough look off his face, and it did the trick. John didn't even have to think about it. He immediately started crying.

Not Ma. She sucked in her breath and held her hand to her

right titty, her eyes opened wide. Her mouth was in a little O. Her eyes were so glazed that she looked dead and stuffed.

"No!"

"Yeah, Ma, he's dead. I just seen his body." Frank shrugged. "I thought I'd come over and tell you." He looked disapprovingly at the bottles on the tables. "I didn't think you'd be having a party on a worknight."

Ma got control of herself and Frank had to admire her. She always was one tough cookie. She stood, mustered as much dignity as a drunk could, and walked with barely a stagger down the hall and into her bedroom.

"Did you kill him, Frank?"

"What?" Her voice was faint, coming through the hallway. What was she doing in there? And what the hell was she asking him a question like that for?

Ma came out of the bedroom with her hand behind her back, her face set in that cocky look that Frank hated. The one she always got when she was drunk. Like she was a man, knew everything and could kick anybody's ass. She'd look at Frank's father that way and the old man would slap her one just on principle.

"Did you kill your father? None of you were any good. I should have aborted you all."

"Ma!" John spoke through his tears. He poured himself another drink and the bottle tapped against the glass several times. Shaky John the drunk. Frank looked at his mother, and began to feel fear.

"What's that in your hand, Ma?" His voice was rising, and he began to stand, frightened and sensing danger. "Ma?"

"I should have done this years ago. Taken care of you and then myself. Babe, too, he was never any good." She pulled the hand out from behind her back and there was a pistol in it, a big ugly one that was pointing at Frank's chest.

"Ma, don't, please," Frank said, crying, holding his hands out defensively, and that was the last thing he ever did say, and John would be the only one to ever know that his tough younger brother had gone out begging.

n another few minutes, Mother's Day would be over. Kelly sat at her kitchen table, thinking how much she'd changed in the past few days, about the things that had happened to her that would change her life forever, thought about these things on the worst Mother's Day she had ever known.

First off, she'd killed a man. Edna Rose might have shot the final bullet into Anthony's eye, but Kelly had killed him, had shot him several times. She would think about that and wince inside, but she didn't feel guilty; her man had been in danger and she'd had no other choice.

It hurt her worse that she'd lied to her children. For the first time in their lives, she'd looked into their young faces and told them a bald-faced lie. Told them their father had been mugged, and they weren't to discuss it with anyone, at any time, ever. She'd had to pull both children out of school last week after the headlines had blared about the massacre of Babe's family. She'd somehow gotten them off on Wednesday, but Thursday and Friday she'd kept them home, and they'd see about this week by the way things went tomorrow.

She'd lied to the police too, when they'd come looking for her husband. Told them he was in LA, and she would have him call them when he got home.

And she'd lied to Tim, trying to spare his feelings. Told her husband's only true brother that Babe had been sleeping when Tim came over Thursday morning. Babe had been in his office, poring over the newspapers. He'd told Kelly that he would not speak to

Tim, not under any circumstances. Had his office window been open? The shade up? She didn't know. What she did know was that Tim had known right away that she'd been lying. His face had gone hard as granite, and he'd nodded at her, his eyes slits. He'd turned and walked away with his head held high. And she hadn't seen or heard from him since.

Although they'd heard from everyone else.

Babe had simply unplugged his telephones, but Kelly's number had been somehow leaked to the press. Wednesday, Thursday and Friday, it hadn't stopped ringing, but there hadn't been a call all weekend, and Kelly knew even better than Babe how fleeting importance could be in this world. There were other things to occupy the minds of the public.

Such as Jerome Spinell, spilling his guts to the feds. A couple of security guards had been on their way to his suite to discuss some damages the room had somehow incurred, and they'd walked in on a couple of guys who were about to throw Jerome out of the window of his suite. Fortunately, the security men were off-duty Chicago cops, and they'd been armed and had been able to subdue the would-be killers. Jerome's brother had already been arrested and Jerome himself had been taken into protective custody at the MCC, and the feds had convened a special grand jury to probe the Hollywood corruption that Jerome was screaming about.

And that left Babe, who'd barely spoken since she'd brought him home.

He was taking it all personally, blaming himself for everything. Kelly and Tim and Edna Rose and Babe's brothers and mother had committed the true crimes Tuesday night, but it was Babe who was taking all the blame for their deaths.

Did he think that he was that goddamned important, or what? In a day when everyone was always acting as a victim, her husband forever saw himself as the guilty party. He hadn't kidnapped himself, she'd told him.

Which was about all that she'd been able to tell him, with the way he'd been acting since Wednesday morning.

He'd spent most of Wednesday in bed, sleeping. Kelly would sneak into their bedroom every fifteen minutes and listen to him breathing, making sure he hadn't died. His face looked absolutely terrible, but there obviously wasn't any internal damage. After a day and a night with an ice pack strapped to his head, the swelling had gone down a great deal.

When he was awake she'd try to talk to him, but he'd lock himself in his office and read everything about his family, coming out only to watch the news, to see what else had been learned. That or he'd go back to bed, sleep for another eight or ten hours.

If it weren't for her sons, she might well have gone mad.

But she was mad in another sense, and that anger had been growing since she'd stopped worrying about his maybe having a hemorrhage. It had been five days, and she had suffered silently too long.

Kelly got up from the table and walked over to the steps that led to the lower level.

Babe was sitting in his office, reading the clippings about the deaths of the people who had once been his family. The Cal City cops had no comment but several leads. The Chicago police who had found his father had no comment but several leads. The only agency who had anything other than bullshit to say was the Homewood police, who were satisfied that they had a murder–suicide on their hands. A witness to it, too, who had been questioned and released.

Babe could not reach John. His wife said that she'd last heard from him on Wednesday night, when he'd called, drunk, to tell her and the kids goodbye. Would they find him in a Dumpster, drunk, with his wrists slashed? Or over in the forest preserve, hanging from a tree branch? John's wife was strong, and she'd kept her voice level.

Had told him that John had left the house after getting a call from Kelly. Babe hadn't called her back.

Babe was not sure how he felt about that. Was Kelly responsible for what had happened after the call? How could she be, though? She didn't know how crazy they all were, he'd always kept that stuff from her, most of it anyhow, how hateful they could be.

If it was on anyone, it was on him. He should have told her about the scar, should have told her that his mother was a gun-crazy drunk. Saw herself as Scarlett O'Hara, standing on a hillside potato field, swearing before God that she would not be defeated.

And now the woman was dead. Along with Frank and Anthony and his father, Johnny. And John, being drunk, was maybe as good as dead.

If he'd moved to LA, none of this would have happened.

If he'd never gotten married, or fathered children, he would never have brought them grief.

His own selfishness was what was really at fault, his belief that he could ever be normal, like everyone else.

He was a freak, and that was a fact. Had felt that all his life, but he'd thought that success and financial security could somehow change all that. He'd justified and rationalized and look how he'd done his family. Keeping his tribal secrets away from the woman he'd loved, as if denying what he really was would somehow change reality. He didn't deserve that woman.

Kelly should have a chance at happiness with someone who did deserve her. Someone from a decent background, who had nothing to hide from the world. Someone who didn't have to worry about taking an AIDS test before he could sleep with his wife again. God only knew what someone like Edna Rose might carry.

And what about Tim. Jesus, what about him.

The best friend he had ever had, and he could never look into his eyes again. Not with him knowing what Tim knew, and Tim knew everything.

Babe searched through a drawer and found a legal pad, jotted out a few sentences, crossed out a few things and added a few words, wrote it all out on a fresh sheet and nodded when he thought he had it right.

Kelly walked in without knocking, and Babe shoved the pad into the top drawer of his desk. He could tell by the look on her face that this wasn't going to be pleasant.

"I love you, you're my husband," Kelly said, and Babe Hill looked at her blankly.

"I risked my life and my freedom for you, and that was my choice, that's all right." Babe said nothing still, just stared at the woman he loved.

"For the past five days, Babe, I've been holding this family together by the skin of my goddamned teeth, lying to our kids, comforting them over the loss of their grandparents and uncles. They try to tell you they're sorry, and you brush them off like flies. That's *not* my choice, Babe, that's yours. And it's *not* all right."

"They hardly knew any of those people. My father, not at all."

"How do you think they feel about that? Wondering why they can't grieve like other kids?"

"What do you want me to do, Kelly, tell them what those people really were? Tell them what *I* really am? All right, I'm sorry I married you. I'm sorry we had kids. I'm sorry I put you all through this, okay? I'm sorry I ever signed to do that fucking *Street Babe* TV show."

"And I'm not sorry about any of that, Babe."

Kelly's voice was soft and caring, and Babe's was cracking, he was on the verge of breaking down. She didn't yell and she didn't plead. What Kelly did was reason, and Babe had never been a reasonable man.

"Go ahead and cry, Babe, let it out for once." Kelly moved toward him, got on her knees before him. "Let it out and I'll hold you, I'll comfort you, I'll love you. Jesus Christ almighty, Babe, for once in your life, let someone love you."

"Men don't cry," Babe said, and his voice was suddenly strong. He got out of the chair and stepped around her, grabbed a windbreaker off a hook in the closet.

"Don't you leave, Babe, don't you run away again. I need to talk to you, Babe, I mean, I *need* to talk to you."

Babe walked back to the desk and grabbed a legal pad out of a drawer, hesitated, then put one hand on Kelly's shoulder, softly.

"And *I* need to be alone for a while."

"You've been alone for almost forty years, Babe." There was a melancholy note in her voice that made him wince.

"I'm just going running, I want to think things through."

Kelly waited until he'd pulled his car out of the garage before picking up the phone and dialing a number.

She'd put the chain across the driveway, and Babe had to get out of the car to unlock it. It gave him time to check out the street, to make sure that no one was surveilling the house. He got back in the car and drove over to Tim's, planning to put the letter in his mailbox, but Tim's car was there, in the driveway, and Babe left his car running while he ran over and threw the note on the seat of Tim's car. He ran on his toes and did not look up, so did not see the curtains part, did not see the weapon in Tim's hand, and did not see the curtains close after only a fraction of a second.

Babe shut off his engine and got out of the car, stretched while he smoked a cigarette and fought down his fear. He set the alarm and put his keys on the driver's side front wheel. He crushed his smoke underfoot, and walked slowly over to the track.

It wasn't so bad, at least there was no fog. The first time around the bend where he'd been kidnapped had been frightening, but he passed the spot and was gone, and no one came out of the darkness. As he made the curve heading back toward the lot he saw headlights coming toward the track, and almost stopped dead, but didn't. It wasn't his track. It belonged to the village. He wasn't the only person allowed to run out here at night. Babe jogged on, fighting the rising panic, and when he got close to the lot he was relieved when he saw that it was Tim.

"Got your letter," Tim said, running slowly alongside Babe. He wasn't playing around, running any games this time. Not walking backward to make fun of Babe's slow pace. His face was blank, letting things play out. The ball, Babe knew, was in his court.

"I thought you'd be working."

"They made me take a few days off. My father died."

"Mine, too."

They jogged in silence for a quarter lap, the only sound that of their gym shoes on the black, rubberized surface.

"Face looks good."

Babe said, "I'm healing."

"On the inside, too?"

"You never were one to fuck around, sugarcoat things, were you?"

"Your letter read like a goodbye note. I saw you put it in my car."

"Why didn't you invite me in?"

"I wanted to see what it said."

Babe swallowed hard. "I meant it, or I wouldn't have written it."

"And you still could never say it."

"No."

Tim said, "I didn't follow you over here. Kelly called me, crying."

"I'm going to have to leave her, Tim. I'm leaving and going somewhere, I don't know where."

"Why don't you try LA? Why don't you go out there and wear sunglasses everywhere and decline interviews and play the mystery man, the nineties Virginia Hill? I can see you now, 'No comment, sorry, leave me alone.' You'll be the hottest star out there, for about sixty days."

"I won't go out to Hollywood, that's one place I'm staying out of."

"Yeah? So where the hell you gonna go, Babe? Where you gonna go where *you're* not there to look at? You think there's a place that far away?"

"I'm leaving for the kids' sake, for Kelly's, so they don't turn out like me. It's in the blood, Tim, look at how things turned out, man." Babe's voice was rising, but Tim's was at a constant level, low and calm, simply stating his case.

"You're not stupid enough to believe that."

"I don't know what I believe anymore."

"Well believe this," Tim said. "That woman loves you, and if you're stupid enough to leave her, you don't deserve to have her. But if you divorce her, that's your business, and it won't touch me for a second. But those kids need you, pal. And if you walk away from them, we're finished. All you have in this entire world, Babe, is Kelly, those kids and me. You better get that genetic bullshit out of your head, and think about that. Those kids could *never* be like you. Never in a million years.

"But if you meant what you said in that letter, then I'm right here with you, like always. You can hide for a while behind public sympathy, but a lot of cops are gonna demand some statements from you, and soon. There're burials to be arranged, there're reporters to be talked to. There's an entire life that has to be put back in order. You've got me, you've got Kelly, and you've got those sons to help you. That's more than most people ever get, and you want to run away. I always knew you were a lot of things, Babe, but I never thought you were an asshole."

Tim wasn't even sweating, and Babe had, in his anger, unconsciously raised the pace. There was a slight throb at the top of his head, but other than that, he was feeling pretty good.

He didn't notice the glare of the second set of headlights coming toward their backs, he was absorbed in what Tim was saying, absorbed, too, in what Tim *wasn't* saying.

"And let me tell you something else. What happened wasn't shit, everyone that died had it fucking coming, and you made it through with just a couple of scratches. If you run it's only because you're ashamed of what happened in that basement. If you throw away everyone you love and who loves you back, then you're just a sniveling, self-pitying asshole."

"That's easy for you to say. It didn't happen to you."

They passed the parking lot but Babe didn't see the third car parked next to Tim's. He was angry, felt abused. Was hurt and ready to strike.

"It's not you might have syphilis, it's not you might have AIDS. You don't have to worry about what it feels like to have a woman hold you down and rape you, Tim."

"AIDS?" Tim was nearly laughing. "I don't mean to sound cold, but how many people you think fucked that woman these past ten years?"

"Oh, yeah, go ahead, make a joke out of it."

"I'm not joking," Tim said.

Kelly got out of her car and leaned against Tim's, watched Tim's and her husband's profiles then their backs as they quickly jogged past her. She caught snatches of words, of Babe's voice raised in anger, and Tim's coming back sounding half in jest. She hoped they wouldn't fight; Tim would kill him, and Babe's self-esteem was bad enough right now.

She would stay with Babe, no matter what. He wasn't capable of the sort of behavior that would drive her away.

At least not yet, he wasn't.

She'd give it some time, see how he bounced back. If this broke him, she could live with that. If it made him stronger, that would be ideal. She was here tonight to apologize to Tim, for lying to him, for hurting him. And she felt she had to do it with Babe right there to hear it. Maybe it would shock some sense into his head; God knew something had to.

She looked down at her shoes, thinking of how she would phrase it. It was important that she didn't put any of the blame on Babe. She idly looked over at Tim's car, saw the yellow sheet of legal paper right there on the seat. The window was open, the paper was right there . . .

Kelly picked it up and turned it to the light. It was written almost as a poem, in Babe's hand.

I've never been able to make any friends
But you were always my friend.
I've never trusted any man
But I always trusted you.
I've never loved a full grown man
But I've always loved you, Tim.
Thanks for hanging around longer than most, and I'm sorry
    I let you down.

It was signed, simply, Babe.

Kelly put the letter back in the car, ashamed that she'd read it at all. It was between Babe and Tim, not her business, but then again, maybe it was. It was a first step back, a move toward a change. She watched the two of them running, and when they passed her again, neither man looked up.

Babe said, "I'll talk to the cops, if you're there with me."

"And a lawyer."

"Screw the lawyer. What do you think, I didn't mean what I said when I wrote the letter?"

Tim sprinted a few yards ahead of Babe, turned and jogged backward, squinting at Babe's face. "It looks a lot better."

"Feels better, too."

"You were never Cary Grant to begin with."

"If I wasn't beat up, I'd kick your ass."

"It's gonna take time, Babe, but you got it, you know that. And you got me. And Kelly. And the kids. That's all you'll ever need." Tim hesitated, then added. "And I need you, too, Babe. You might not be able to say it, but I can. I love you, Babe. I never wanted to, always wanted to stay cold. But I love you. And if you were good enough to make that happen, then you must be one hell of a man."

For a second, Tim thought that Babe was going to cry. He watched, curiously, as Babe's bottom lip twitched, then he turned around and jogged next to his friend, the two of them at the curve that would take them back to the parking lot.

"You don't pay a lot of attention to what goes on around you, but there's someone over there who I think wants to talk to you."

Babe looked up quickly, terror in his eyes, and Tim felt for him, for the fear that he would carry around inside for a long time to come.

But the real strength in the Hill family was strong enough to carry them both until that fear passed, and here she came, onto the track, smiling shyly at them as they approached.

Tim stopped running, stood and watched as Babe ran to his wife.

"Oh, God, Kelly, I'm sorry, I'm so goddamn sorry."

She could feel his body shaking in her arms, her husband trembling from head to toe. In his voice, his eyes, there was pain, bottomless, profound. Love was there, too, and a need for understanding. Kelly shushed him, held him to her, and rubbed the back of his head, looked up at him without speaking. Her eyes could tell him what she needed to say; there was no need for her to speak.

What hadn't they been through since they'd been together? The anguish, the pain, but there'd been plenty of happiness there.

And now they had their own tribal secrets, a darkness they would carry within their souls for the entire rest of their lives.

But they also had each other, and she knew that they would heal.

See? It was already beginning. Kelly felt the joy fill her.

Because her husband had lowered his head to her shoulder, and she'd be damned if he wasn't crying.